PRAISE FOR NANCY CANE'S *MOONLIGHT RHAPSODY:*

"Nancy Cane creates a richly detailed futuristic world sure to stimulate the reader's imagination."

—Kathleen Morgan, Author Of *Heart's Surrender*

"Scintillating and heart stopping. Ms. Cane has definitely proven herself a master of this genre."

—*Rendezvous*

"*Moonlight Rhapsody* is an action-packed, fast-paced futuristic romance....Nancy Cane has a visionary gift of writing about the future in a manner that makes it seem like it's happening today."

—*Affaire de Coeur*

AND FOR *CIRCLE OF LIGHT:*

"An extraordinary reading adventure you cannot pass up."

—*Rendezvous*

"Nancy Cane sparks your imagination and melts your heart!"

—Marilyn Campbell, Author Of *Stardust Dreams*

Futuristic Romance

Love in another time, another place.

SIREN'S SONG

"You seem to relish the role of Dromo," Rolf accused Ilyssa.

"I hate it! The Satrap gives the orders and makes it appear as though I'm cruel and heartless. That way, no one will help me. It's part of Ruel's punishment."

"Why are you telling me this?"

"I have to free my parents from Ruel!" Ilyssa cried. "But I can't do it alone. I need you. You're a pilot. We'll need transportation to get off Souk. You can escape with us."

Rolf pretended to consider her offer. "How do we proceed?"

"You must have connections on Souk. We'll escape and—"

"What do you mean, I must have connections on Souk?"

"You're here on some sort of mission, aren't you?"

His eyes iced over. "Perhaps you should prove the truth of what you say."

"How?"

"Sing to me."

"I can't. You'd be mindwashed."

"Then sing to those guards outside your door."

"They're immune to the song."

"Hah!"

Ilyssa was enraged. "How dare you question me? You're supposed to be the one giving me answers!"

"So you did bring me here to interrogate me." Rolf challenged her with his steady glare. "I've told you all I can."

Other *Love Spell* Books by Nancy Cane:
CIRCLE OF LIGHT

MOONLIGHT RHAPSODY

NANCY CANE

Book Margins, Inc.

A BMI Edition

Published by special arrangement with Dorchester
Publishing Co., Inc.

Cover Art by John Ennis

Printed in the United States of America.

To my parents, Minnie and Harry Heller, whose love and support gave me the resources and strength of purpose to achieve my dreams.

With special thanks to:

Captain Al Hartman, TWA pilot, for sharing his knowledge of flight terminology and procedures.

Cantor Seymour Schwartzman, former leading baritone of the New York City Opera, for sharing his musical expertise.

Moonlight Rhapsody

Chapter One

Rolf had never been caught in such a violent storm. His spacecraft, buffeted in all directions, was like a plaything to the terrible ionic gale raging outside. Sweat beaded his brow as jagged streaks of blue lightning flashed in the darkness, but he was unable to see anything on the viewscreen except roiling clouds when the sky lit up.

Gripping the armrests of his seat, Rolf cursed his luck. His mission was dangerous enough without his ship being caught in a maelstrom. Unable to take a heavier vessel to Souk, he'd chosen a small, lightweight freighter meant for evading radar through swift maneuvering. But in this tempest, the ship was like a feather tossed by the wind. Updrafts and downdrafts battered at him, and his stomach wrenched with each thrashing.

Monitoring the computer readouts, Rolf prayed that the bursting ion streaks would avoid hitting his ship. He couldn't request emergency assistance from the Souks as his descent into their atmosphere was unauthorized, and he couldn't risk being detected as he neared the ground.

Nervously, he swiped at a strand of hair, pushing it off his face. Any minute now, the computer would initiate the landing sequence. Maybe then he could relax.

"By the stars!" he cried as a loud jolt rocked the ship, straining him against his safety harness. An ion bolt had hit home! The lights in the cockpit went out, then flickered red as the backup system kicked in. Sirens wailed as a series of warning lights flashed on his display panel.

"Systems overload!" warned the computer's impersonal female voice. "Switching off actuator valves one and two to reroute flow streams. Core fuel injectors remain operative."

The main power generator was out. Hopefully the secondary reactor conduits would hold. Moistening his lips, Rolf told himself he shouldn't worry about the blasted Souks picking up his approach. Concentrating on a safe landing was more important.

"Changing nose angle by point zero two five degrees," the computer intoned.

Sniffing, Rolf wondered at the pungent odor he smelled. It hadn't been noticeable before. His eyes watered and he blinked rapidly to clear his vision.

The helm didn't seem to be responding to the computer's command. According to the instrumentation, the ship was heading downward at an increasingly sharp angle. As a bolt of charged ion particles lit the sky, he caught a glimpse through a cloud break of the planet's surface below. Frowning, Rolf scanned the nav readouts for the altitude display. According to the readout, he was at fifteen kilometers. But from the view, he'd put his altitude around nine. The navigational sensors must be off. By the corona, that meant he could have strayed off course! He'd been warned against flying over—

A sudden lurch nearly tossed his stomach contents onto his lap. A loud claxon sounded in the cockpit as the red lights dimmed and then came back on.

The computer was down. Suppressing a momentary surge of panic, Rolf switched to manual override. Grabbing the control column, he yanked it back to raise the nose. The ship didn't respond, continuing its downward plunge toward the planet's surface.

Gods, the feed lines from the bimanthium crystal chamber must be inoperative! Perspiration ran in rivulets down the sides of his face. Maybe he could reroute some of the remaining fuel. Reacting automatically, he flipped shut several switches and toggled others open.

The helm responded sluggishly. He fought the bile rising in his throat and checked the overhead panel. Sure enough, a couple of drive circuits were popped. Instead of seeing six rows of black buttons, he saw four black and two white. He pushed the white buttons to reset them and the secondary generator came back on-line. Now he'd have short periods of thrust with which to maneuver the ship. If he could make differential power adjustments along the way, the ship wouldn't go down at such a steep angle.

Opening and closing the field relays, he managed to slow the rate of descent. But then a violent downdraft caught his ship and slammed it planetside.

Rolf coughed as the pungent odor in the cockpit grew stronger. White smoke stung his eyes. Burning filaments! Quickly, he programmed the sequence for fire control, then remembered the computer was down. There was no time for other measures now. Souk's surface was gaining, and he wasn't slowing nearly enough! As he broke out of the cloud cover, topographical features came into clear view, mountainous rises and rocky peaks, beyond which were the lights of civilization. Gods, he was going to crash into that cliff!

He activated the reverse levitators, forcing the screaming engines to break descent, but he was still coming in too fast. Using both hands, he yanked desperately on the control column. He had to exert all his strength just to get it to move back a notch. A small clearing was straight ahead if he could make it.

The impact came with the screeching sound of tearing metal and a bone-jarring series of thumps. Rolf was thrust forward in his seat, his body straining against the safety harness. An explosion roared in his ears. Billowing smoke choked his nostrils and clouded his vision. Finally, the vessel reached a shuddering halt.

Stunned, Rolf sat motionless until he realized the air was growing hot. Twisting his neck, he saw flames licking up from the rear of the ship. His hands trembling, he unshackled his restraint and attempted to rise. But his head swam dizzily, and the hazy smoke confused him.

Images of another time, another place, entered his mind. *We're under attack! Energize the laser cannon while I put out the fire. . . . Shields are down. . . . No, they've hit us again!*

His mind a disoriented fog of past and present, Rolf forced himself out of his seat. The cockpit was destroyed, and debris littered the floor. He stumbled through the smoke, coughing and choking while weaving a path toward the exit. Heat blasted his face from the raging fire. Blinded, he tripped across a fallen cable and toppled over, his arms flailing. His head cracked against a bulkhead in a white-hot explosion of pain.

The last thing he heard as he slid to the floor was a familiar female voice calling his name: *Rolf* . . .

The Souk officer's bluish skin quivered as he faced the smoking wreck. "Get the pilot out!" he screamed to his contingent of armed guards.

On patrol in the Beta sector, they'd heard the whine of engines before the spacecraft had become visible to the eye. The sleek vessel had broken through the cloud cover and plummeted toward the ground. At the last moment the nose raised, and the ship came in nearly level. But it was going too fast, and the crash had been inevitable.

O'mon's floppy ears lifted as his men popped the hatch. A cloud of black smoke billowed out from the interior.

"Fire!" Arg yelled, holding his snoutlike nose.

"Move quickly," O'mon barked to his point man. "Salvage what you can."

A few moments later, the troops emerged, two of them carrying a limp human form. Arg held a pilot's dispatch case.

"The ship's logs?" O'mon asked.

"Burned are the filaments. The logs are lost. The data cards in this case are all that's left."

"Cargo?"

"None, unless it was concealed. We'd be risking our lives to do a more thorough search. Too intense is the heat."

"Let us r-r-remove ourselves then," O'mon agreed.

The soldiers laid the pilot on the ground in a wooded area at a safe distance from the burning spacecraft. O'mon ordered one of his troops to take a holovid of the ship before it was totally destroyed, as it might be needed for evidence later.

Clasping his hands behind his back, O'mon sniffed gratefully at the cool air. The spicy scent of jell berries was a welcome relief from the pungent odor of smoke. Normally he enjoyed these night patrols. Nothing much happened, and he could listen to the howl of the rabba and relish the breeze from the Upper Drifts. But not tonight. Tonight the peacefulness of the night had been shattered.

O'mon turned his attention to the pilot on the ground. Even unconscious, the human exuded a certain presence. He was tall and muscular. Straight black hair reached his shoulders. He had thick eyebrows, an aquiline nose, and a jaw that showed determination even when slack.

The human's manner of dress gave no indication of his identity. He wore a blue shirt that sagged open, revealing a broad chest and flat abdomen. The shirt was tucked into tight navy pants, skimming his polished boots.

"Check him for weapons," O'mon ordered. He watched while one of his troops frisked the human.

"He'd make a good krecker," Arg growled, reflecting O'mon's thoughts.

"Aye. We'll see what Bolt says." The human had no weapons, nor did he possess any personal ornaments. "What could his business be in this sector?"

"Ask him yourself. Coming around is he."

Rolf returned to consciousness, gradually becoming aware that he was lying flat on his back on a lumpy surface. An unfamiliar spicy scent pervaded his nostrils. Voices murmured around him, harsh barks and growls but his mind was too foggy to pay attention. He put a hand up to his throbbing temple.

Remembering the crash, Rolf wondered if he was among friends or enemies. Should he use the chemical mind block provided for him now while he had the chance, or should he wait? The opportunity for this covert mission had come about unexpectedly. Rolf hadn't had time to learn more sophisticated techniques for resisting interrogation in the event he was caught. A memory molecule which only dissolved in saliva had been painted onto his fingernail. When he licked it off, it would provide up to 24 hauras protection against a Morgot mind probe, the favored technique used by the Souks to make prisoners talk. While under the influence of the chemical, Rolf would forget any important information that he possessed. But since he only had one molecule, Rolf decided to wait and assess the situation further before he used it.

Cautiously, he blinked. Dark shadows hovered, but his hazy vision couldn't quite make out who they were. Struggling into a sitting position, Rolf choked back a wave of nausea as his vision whirled. After a moment, he could focus. It was the dead of night and he was outdoors. The moving shadows shifted and solidified.

Four Souks surrounded him, pointing shooters aimed at his chest. The dogfaces wore gray uniforms with military insignia.

A frisson of alarm shot through him. The guards were alert and tense, as though they expected him to make a hostile move. His eyes darted about, looking for a possible avenue of escape. The twisted shapes of trees came into view. Overhead, clouds scudded by in the nighttime sky. Distant streaks of lightning lit the heavens in fiery blue bolts.

"Who are you?" a gruff voice demanded from beyond his line of vision.

Rolf decided to learn as much as he could. If it looked as though he would be tortured, he'd use the memory molecule.

"My name is Sean Breslow," he said, giving his false identity. "What is this place?"

An officer lumbered into the circle of guards. The Souk was large, his canine features fierce. "Your vessel crash-landed by the Rocks of Weir. What is your business on Souk?"

"I'm a trader from Arcturus. I have a client who wants me to arrange a deal involving rubellis gemstones." Hopefully his hastily created cover story would hold up under scrutiny.

"The r-r-rubellis quarries are on the other side of the Cobalt Wash," the Souk officer snarled. "What are you doing by the Rocks of Weir?"

"My navigational system malfunctioned in the storm."

"Liar! Too far off course are you."

"I speak the truth. Examine my ship for yourself. You'll see the nav sensor array was damaged."

"What is the name of your client?"

"That information is confidential."

"His location?"

"I can't tell you."

"Can't or won't? You try my patience, human. I do not believe your lies. A spy are you! We shoot spies," the Souk threatened. "Tell me the real r-r-reason why you are here!"

"I'm telling the truth," Rolf said, tasting fear in his mouth. It was an unfamiliar sensation. Shifting uncomfortably where he sat, he decided to try some inquiries of his own. "Where exactly are the Rocks of Weir?"

"It is I, O'mon, who will ask the questions, human."

"I need to know how far off course I've strayed!" His mission had a deadline, and he might miss it if he was detained. Even if he managed to escape, he had no idea how to get to his intended landing site from here. He needed specific information.

One of the guards gestured with his shooter. "The pilot's dispatch case might prove useful, Lieutenant."

"You are r-r-right, Arg. Bring it here!"

O'mon leafed through the data cards in the pilot's bag. Sticking one in his data link, he grunted with satisfaction after reading the display.

"What is it? Is there a problem?" Rolf asked anxiously, hoping they'd accept his falsified documents at face value.

"Sean Breslow is your name," O'mon conceded. "Records of r-r-recent transactions and credit transfers are these. They confirm that you are a trader originating from Arcturus." He looked up. "Why is there no evidence of your deal involving rubellis gemstones?"

Arg spoke up. "The r-r-rest of the data cards are damaged. It is possible he tells the truth, sir."

"Grrr," O'mon growled, looking skeptical. "Let's deliver him to Bolt. The satrap may be able to loosen his tongue."

"Who's Bolt?" Gingerly, Rolf touched the back of his head. A sticky substance clung to his fingers. Blood. No wonder he had a headache the size of a boulder.

"Find out soon enough will you. Get up. You go to the pens."

Two guards tugged him to his feet, and before he realized what was happening, they'd whipped his arms behind him and bound his wrists.

"What are you doing?" he cried, infuriated.

"You will speak only when spoken to, human. You're a sumi now," O'mon said. Rolf spoke their language, and he understood sumi was the Souk word for slave. "Disobey and you will be punished," the lieutenant warned.

"How dare you! I have rights. I'm not a—oof!" He grunted and doubled over as O'mon jolted him with an electrifier. "Damn you," he gritted, wincing at the pain in his gut.

"Wish you more, sumi? Come with us quietly will you." O'mon turned to his men and grinned. "A generous bounty will we get for this one. Let's go." He pointed the electrifier rod at Rolf. "Move, human."

Single file, they followed a winding trail through hilly territory dotted with twisted spirals of rock. Huge boulders lay haphazardly and jagged cliffs stretched toward the sky. Traveling through the eerie landscape, Rolf stumbled several times but was forced to keep going, his feet tripping over the rocky paths, and his arms bound at his back. Tree branches whipped at his face, and the night seemed to sing with empathy for him. A haunting whisper hung on the breeze, a melancholy note as the wind whistled through the leaves.

Passing through a short canyon, they approached a brightly lit enclave of buildings. Voices carried on the breeze, the wailing and crying of females, the shouts and curses of men. As they neared the dusty town, Rolf's eyes widened in shock. A group of poor wretches was confined inside a fenced area that was guarded by two sentry towers at opposite ends. An energy field protected the perimeter. The stockade was roofless and he could easily see the captives milling about inside.

"Join the others," O'mon said, chuckling. Grabbing Rolf by the arm, he thrust him forward as a sentry opened the gate.

Rolf fought and bucked against the large Souk. Suddenly a couple of bull-like Horthas bounded into view, swinging stun whips. One lash at his ankle and Rolf stumbled, crying out. With a final push, O'mon sent Rolf sprawling onto the dirt-packed ground inside the pen. The gate swung shut behind him with a loud clang, and a lock clicked into place.

Spitting the dirt from his mouth, he rose to a kneeling position, cursing.

"Save your breath," a weary voice said.

Rolf looked up into the soil-streaked face of a bearded man. "Who are you?"

"My name is Seth." Stooping over, the man undid the cord binding Rolf's wrists, then helped him to stand.

"Where are we? What is this place?" Rolf looked Seth over. He wore a loose tan tunic cinched at the waist by a leather belt and matching leggings. His form appeared solid. Judging from the streaks of gray in his dark hair, Rolf guessed his age was 40 annums, ten annums older than himself. He'd just celebrated his thirtieth birthday before leaving for Souk.

"We're situated in a remote mining district near the Rocks of Weir. It's part of Ruel's dominion." Seth gave him a keen look of assessment. "What's your name, friend?"

"Sean Breslow. My ship crashed in the hills, and O'mon's troops pulled me out of the wreckage." Rolf closed his eyes briefly to ease the throbbing in his head. "How did you get here?"

"We were captured in a raid. We're from the Alyte Garrison in the Omega sector." Seth waved at the cluster of men, women, and children huddled in a corner, bemoaning their fate, as the women clutched their offspring in terror. A few other species were evident in the pen as well, victims, Rolf assumed, of other raids or pirate attacks on civilian vessels.

Seeing the terrified captives brought a red-hot fury seething into Rolf's blood. His fists clenched. By the corona, he was enraged enough to throttle someone's throat! The rotten, liver-bellied Souks. All they brought was fear and misery to helpless victims. He'd come here to stop them, and now he was trapped, unable to carry out his directive. How he hated them!

The bearded man must have seen the anger in his eyes. "Go easy, friend. There's not much you can do. No one's ever escaped from Souk."

"Yes, they have." His friends, Sarina and Teir, had managed to escape the clutches of the notorious Souk slaver, Cerrus Bdan. Their adventures had been the catalyst for his current mission. Rolf struggled to get his temper under control, then asked, "How long have you been here?"

"Two days, but it seems like two annums." Seth looked at Rolf curiously. "You said you'd crash-landed. Why were you coming to Souk?"

"I'm a trader from Arcturus."

"So you have a legitimate reason for being here. Why have they put you in with us?" Seth's eyes narrowed suspiciously.

"O'mon thinks I'm lying," Rolf confessed.

"Are you?"

"No." He fell silent, lost in anguish. How was he going to accomplish his mission when he was penned like an animal and doomed to a life of captivity? It was all the Souks' fault, just like everything else in his life. Damn them! He had to escape! "What happens next? Do you know?" he asked Seth.

The older man nodded. "I spoke to a guard. Bolt is due to come on the morrow."

"Who in Zor is Bolt? I keep hearing his name."

"Bolt is the top military officer in the area. He holds the rank of satrap in Ruel's army."

Understanding lit Rolf's eyes, but he quickly hid it under veiled lids. It wouldn't be wise to show his intimate knowledge of Souk affairs. "I don't understand," he hedged.

"Ruel is pasha of this territory. Souk is controlled by various commercial cartels led by individual pashas," Seth explained patiently. "Together they form the Souk Alliance. Ruel is the most powerful pasha of all. He's the largest landholder, and his industrial interests extend into every corner of the planet. The Rocks of Weir, despite our desolate location, is very important to him. It holds valuable deposits of piragen ore which are the main source of Ruel's wealth."

He saw Rolf's questioning glance and added, "I'm a geologist. Piragen ore is not a common commodity. I've surveyed its distribution throughout this sector of the galaxy."

"What's its relevance to our situation?" Rolf asked.

"We could all end up as kreckers working the mines."

"Who makes that decision? Bolt?"

"No. A Dromo appointed by Ruel holds the position of authority here. Bolt merely carries out the Dromo's orders." Seth kicked at a rock on the ground. His face looked worn and weary. "The Dromo decrees who shall live and who shall die; who will labor in the mines or who will act as personal servers to the Souks. Bolt may choose women for his harem."

Rolf saw the direction of his pained glance. "Your wife?"

Seth nodded, not bothering to disguise the raw fear in his expression. "Aye. And my daughter yonder." He indicated a pretty girl of about fifteen annums sitting alone in a corner. She was combing her long blond hair with her fingers and staring vacantly at the night sky.

Rolf felt his gut clench. "You don't think Bolt would—"

"I've heard stories," Seth interrupted, his tone grim. "Human females don't last very long when they're taken by a Souk, and Bolt is said to prefer females with light coloring."

"By the stars, I'm sorry."

The night seemed to pass endlessly after that conversation, and when at last dawn came, Rolf stretched and yawned. He'd found a spare corner and lain on the ground, falling asleep instantly. He awoke cold and shivering as were most of his fellow captives. They looked wan and pale in the orange light seeping over the horizon. His stomach growled, and he wondered if they'd be fed.

Standing, he went over to a small enclosure to relieve himself in the hole in the ground intended for that purpose. The area stank and swarmed with flies. When he came out, he studied his surroundings.

The pen was at the very edge of the town which was situated in a narrow valley. The buildings were boxlike concrete structures, functional rather than aesthetic, painted in a uniform muddy brown color. A paved street ran down the center of the town, and already he could see it was bustling with activity. The Souks, dressed in flowing caftans of bright rainbow colors, moved about their morning business, totally oblivious to the cries from the captives at the far end. Other dwellings, residences perhaps, branched off from the main avenue.

Atop a nearby hill stood a completely incongruous palatial structure. White with silver specks, it glistened in the sunlight, isolated from the town's drabness and drudgery. No doubt that was where Bolt and his boss lived, Rolf thought, and wondered what the Dromo was like. Overseeing a work force of slaves in such a harsh environment was no easy task. The Dromo would have to be the most ferocious Souk around.

As he watched, a procession started down the hill. In the lead marched a large Souk wearing a gray military uniform devoid of any decoration. He had the meanest dogface Rolf had ever seen, a pudgy nose, ridged brows, and a perpetual snarl. He looked brawny, tough. He'd be a dangerous person to cross, Rolf figured, thinking the military man must be the Dromo. The Souk was obviously in a position of authority. Rolf could tell by his autocratic bearing, by the obsequious attitude of the slaves running beside him to obey his commands.

His gaze switched to the slender figure striding alongside the Souk. By the stars, was that a woman? Who in Zor was she? A human female with the Dromo . . . was she his willing consort or his slave?

As they neared, Rolf studied her further. Or rather, he couldn't tear his eyes away. Wavy auburn hair framed a face with such delicate features she could have been an artist's creation. Her brows were feathery arches the color of a fawn. He particularly liked the way her mouth was perfectly formed, with sensual pink lips.

His gaze trailed lower. From the fine bones of her face and her slender arms, Rolf would say she was slim, but she hid her figure under a shapeless rust-colored caftan. The way the garment fell over her body indicated that she possessed generous assets. Maybe that was why she dressed in such a drab fashion, so as not to attract undue attention. But who wouldn't be drawn to her startling beauty?

He realized the Hortha sentries were barking orders. Apparently the captives were to line up, single file, facing the gate. A long table was being set up outside the fence. The Souk and the young woman, who couldn't have been more than 20 annums, seated themselves in chairs behind the table. The Souk gave the signal for the gate to be opened.

"I am Bolt," he said in a loud voice. "You are to present yourselves in front of the Dromo. Keep your eyes lowered. You are not permitted to look upon her face. Anyone who disobeys will be punished."

Rolf nearly reeled in shock. Great suns! The woman was the Dromo! She was in charge of this enclave.

He became sick as he watched each captive, head bowed, stand in front of the Dromo as Bolt pronounced his or her fate. The Dromo nodded approval, her lips tightly pinched, her back straight. Her eyes were blank as she stared straight ahead. He wondered how she'd come to be in such an exalted position. Had she so pleased the pasha who ruled the territory that he'd honored her by putting her in command? Yet this settlement was far from any major city. Wouldn't it be more of a punishment than a reward to be isolated here?

Screams and wails resulted when husbands and wives were separated. Anguished cries rent the air when children were torn from their mother's arms. The ill or elderly were condemned to die. Horthas stood by with stun whips, making sure the pronouncements were followed. Groups began to form outside the gate. Whispering a question to the person in line behind him, Rolf learned what they represented.

The strong and able were being assigned as kreckers in the mines. Because of adverse environmental conditions, the piragen ore could only be extracted in this location by hand. It was exhausting work and slaves died in droves from the heavy toil. Those less fit individuals were assigned as servers in the Dromo's household. And for some, a fate worse than death was prescribed. Bolt took the youngest of the adult females to his harem. Supposedly it was a perk the Dromo allowed him for his loyalty.

"What about the children?" Rolf hissed.

"They're sent away to the capital city of Haakat where they're raised under strict supervision," said the sullen young man behind him. "When they're old enough, they receive their assignments."

"A life of slavery," Rolf stated, his face grim.

A woman screamed, and he glanced up. Seth's daughter had just been sentenced to join Bolt's harem, and it was her mother who'd cried out. Seth and his wife were being sent to the mines.

Rolf compressed his lips as his turn came. He stood in front of the table, his head raised proudly. He wasn't going to bow before anyone. He did, however, keep his gaze averted from the woman. Looking at her stirred something in him, even when he knew she was responsible for these people's anguish.

"Name?" Bolt barked, glaring at him.

Rolf stared back. "Sean Breslow."

Bolt wrote in a ledger with a computer stylus. "Profession?"

"I'm a trader from Arcturus."

Bolt's black eyes darkened. Against the blue of his skin, they appeared to be two opaque holes in his doglike visage. "You're the man whose ship crashed in the hills. I was not expecting a consignment. What were you doing in this sector?"

"My ship's navigational system malfunctioned during an ion storm and I strayed off course." A small sound escaped the woman's lips and he risked a glance in her direction. She was staring at him, undisguised interest in her expression. He returned the look, challenging her.

A stinging pain lashed at his back and brought him to his knees with a grunt. One of the Horthas had hit him with a stun whip.

"Do not look upon the Dromo!" Bolt snarled, leaping to his feet. "It is forbidden!"

Rolf slowly turned his gaze upon the Souk. A half-smile twisted his lips. "It will take more than your whips to subdue me, Bolt."

"You will address me as master!" Spittle formed in the corner of his mouth, and his face blotched with fury. "Punishment do you need, human. You are sumi here. Give him twenty lashes and then send him to the mines," he ordered the Hortha guards, sputtering in his rage.

"Wait!" the woman said. "Do you not want to find out more about his background? If he is beaten senseless, we will gain little information." Her voice had the honeyed sweetness of keela blossom nectar. Again, Rolf wondered how she came by such a position.

"He needs to be taught a lesson, Dromo." Bolt's eyes bored into hers. "Do you not agree?"

A flicker of uncertainty shone in her forest green eyes. It was quickly clouded over as her expression went blank again. "Of course. Carry out the sentence," she ordered in a flat, dead tone.

A couple of beefy Horthas grabbed Rolf under the arms.

"This will be a good example for the rest of you slaves," the woman shouted to the terrified captives still in line. She got up and walked around the edge of the table until she stood in front of Rolf. The top of her head reached the bridge of his nose. Defiantly, Rolf met her gaze. Looking down into her cool green eyes flecked with burnished gold, he smiled.

She slapped his face. "Strip off his shirt," she commanded the guards. "Let us see what manner of man he is when he feels the sting of the lash."

Rolf's shirt was ripped away. He was dragged a few meters toward a whipping post and his arms were yanked up. Facing the post, he winced when his wrists were tightly secured to the wood.

"Give me that," he heard the woman snarl behind him. He twisted his neck and saw her grabbing a stun whip from a startled Hortha. She circled Rolf slowly, studying him like a she-wolf about to devour its prey. Her eyes shone with a feral light. "I will beat you myself, sumi. You will bend your head in submission before I am through."

"I'll never bow to you or anyone!" Rolf spat out, enraged.

The lash whipped out, catching him on the upper back with its electrifying force. A stinging pain like a thousand needles pierced his flesh. He bit his lip and bore the subsequent shocks in silence. But after that first lash, the others were lighter, as though meant to do no real harm. The Dromo screamed out, cursing at him, calling invectives on his name as though she were beating him to Zor.

Rolf pretended to be defeated by the whipping. He didn't know what her game was, but he would play along. Maybe she was saving him for a worse punishment later.

The whipping left welts on his back, but the painful shocks to his system weren't bad enough to knock him unconscious. If one of those Horthas had delivered the beating, he would have passed out after the first few blows. In a way, he should be grateful that the Dromo had chosen to administer the punishment herself.

When it was done, and he hung half-limp from the post, his wrists were cut down. His knees buckled and he nearly fell. He'd been rendered weaker than he thought. A couple of Horthas caught him in their grasp.

"Take him to the mines with the other kreckers," Bolt ordered, sneering.

"Hold," said the Dromo, who walked over to stand directly in front of Rolf. "Not so proud now, are you, sumi?" she asked, reaching up to brush his cheek gently.

The tenderness of her touch sent a sensation through him stronger than the jolts from the stun whips. Rolf jerked back in surprise.

"Ilyssa, it is time to go," Bolt growled.

Immediately, she turned away. Her back was ramrod straight as she left, holding on to Bolt's arm.

Rolf watched her leave, curiously feeling they'd be seeing a lot more of each other.

Chapter Two

As Ilyssa walked away with Bolt, she experienced a tumult of emotions. By the heavens, that man Sean Breslow was the most impressive creature she'd ever seen! If he was a trader from Arcturus, then she was the cruel slave overseer everyone believed her to be.

In her mind's eye, she saw again the black hair that fell to his shoulders like a warrior brave, his shocking blue eyes as they insolently bore into her own, the determined lift of his jaw, the muscular physique of his bare back and chest. Just thinking of him brought a forbidden shiver to her spine. He didn't act or speak like a trader from Arcturus. The man had a noble mien as though he were used to giving orders, not receiving them. Who was he? Why had he come here?

"Gave a good demonstration did you," Bolt grunted, interrupting her thoughts. His dark beady eyes glanced at her with approval.

"I thought it would be effective," Ilyssa said. She'd only administered the whipping herself because she'd known the Horthas would have nearly killed the man. Besides, it helped to uphold her image as the nasty Dromo that Ruel wished to perpetuate. As pasha of this dominion, he had chosen this role for her and she was subject to his bidding. Each time she played along, Ilyssa knew her parents would be safe for a little while longer. Ruel held them hostage as insurance for her cooperation, and she didn't dare defy him.

The pasha lived in the capital city of Haakat which was further south by the Largess Lake, and was ruler over the whole of the southern continent. Ilyssa had lived in Haakat ever since the age of 12 annums when Ruel had captured her and her family, and had held a privileged position in his palace for nearly eight annums.

Then one fateful day, Ilyssa had committed a shameful indiscretion. In his fury, Ruel banished her to the Rocks of Weir, forbidding her the companionship of her own kind, and giving her the unpleasant role of Dromo. Ilyssa was terrified of incurring Ruel's wrath again because he'd warned her that if she did, her parents would suffer. So she did what she was told. Bolt was her warden, watching over her, making sure she didn't overstep Ruel's boundaries.

She'd been here nine months now and this miserable existence made it seem like nine annums. Her gaze swept along the dusty town and up to the Dromo's residence, her prison. Life here was bleak and harsh, unlike Haakat's pleasant climate, which was why Ruel had sent her here. She yearned for freedom, but she had to rescue her beloved parents before she could even think about saving herself.

She'd thought about escaping before, but now a sense of urgency gripped her. The last time she had seen her father he hadn't been well and she feared he was going into a decline. It was imperative she get him away from Ruel.

She'd been afraid to try anything after the incident in Haakat that had caused her banishment. But now an opportunity had arisen that could give her the break she needed. She'd gotten an edge on Bolt.

Working at Computer Central in the mining production center, Ilyssa had access to the data files, which were easily readable for her. She had her mother to thank for that. A computer expert, Moireen had developed Ilyssa's skills when Ilyssa had shown a superior aptitude for computers and all that training had served her well, especially now.

Looking for hidden files after noticing a deletion, Ilyssa had found a discrepancy between mine production and the profits. The records had been carefully concealed, but she'd been able to trace them. Someone was stealing shipments of ore on a regular basis. After searching the files more extensively, Ilyssa had determined that Bolt was the guilty party. Most likely, he was selling the ore for personal profit. She could even venture a guess as to the buyer's identity. All she lacked was proof, and it was time to work on that detail. With proof in her hands, she could trade her knowledge to Ruel in exchange for her and her parents' freedom. The piragen ore was the pasha's main source of income. He'd be eager to learn who was siphoning off his proceeds.

But why should Ruel agree to a trade? If she told him she possessed important news about the ore shipments, he'd merely force the information from her and she'd gain nothing. Bartering wouldn't work with him; he was simply too powerful. No, there had to be another way she could use the knowledge to her advantage.

What if she asked Bolt for a favor in return for her silence? Once she obtained proof of his treachery, she could threaten to show it to Ruel if Bolt didn't give her what she wanted. But what could she ask for that would serve her goals?

The slave Sean Breslow came to mind. He was a spaceship pilot, and Ilyssa needed a pilot to take her and her parents off Souk. There hadn't been many fliers among the sorry prisoners who had shown up at the camp. But more than that, Ilyssa felt something was special about that man. His bearing and boldness spoke of courage. His steady blue eyes possessed a magnetism that fascinated her. It was almost as though fate had dropped him out of the sky right at this time when she had the means to use him.

Ilyssa would offer him his freedom in return. If he helped rescue her parents from Ruel's palace in Haakat, she'd use her computer skills to purloin a ship at the spaceport. They could all leave Souk together. But would Breslow be interested, considering the high risks involved?

There was only one way to find out. She needed to question him, to learn what lurked beneath the surface of the man. The fastest path would be to get him into her household. Joie, her personal server, had been transferred and no one had taken her place. She could ask Bolt to assign Sean Breslow to the position. Her excitement grew as she considered a plan of action. She'd get proof of Bolt's guilt, threaten to show it to Ruel, and ask for the slave in return for her silence. Bolt would have to agree!

"When is my next scheduled inspection of the mines?" Ilyssa asked mildly. That would be the next time she got to see Breslow.

"Next week," was Bolt's terse reply.

They continued to walk together. As the sol rose higher in the sky, so did the dust and heat. Already a trickle of perspiration ran down her back.

Ilyssa kept her eyes lowered so the Souk wouldn't see the eagerness in her expression. Normally she hated to visit the mines, and he knew it. Bolt's job was to supervise the work force, but for it to appear that Ilyssa was the one giving orders, she was forced to go on inspection tours. Each time, a slave was picked out for punishment, and Bolt pretended to confer with her. Then he declared a horrible torture for the poor soul to suffer in front of everyone, including herself. It sickened her so much that she could barely eat for days afterward. Ruel had told Bolt he wanted the slaves to hate her. That way they wouldn't sympathize with her plight, which they would if they knew the truth. So Bolt helped maintain the illusion that she was the nasty Dromo. This next visit to the mines Ilyssa was looking forward to, but only because of Sean.

They veered off the wide paved street and headed for the Dromo's residence. The footpath followed a steep incline but Ilyssa was glad for the exercise. She walked outdoors whenever possible.

Glancing at Bolt, she let go of his arm. "What's the matter?" she asked. His ugly Souk face was furrowed in a frown.

"I don't trust that new sumi. Think he is lying do I."

"You mean the man who was whipped?"

"Krach," Bolt said in agreement.

"But O'mon said the data card from his pilot's case confirmed his identity."

"Too many details are left unexplained. Notify Ruel will I to get his advice."

Alarm shot through her. "Do you think that's wise? If the man is telling the truth, you'd be made to look the fool. Why not check him out yourself first?" Good heavens, Ruel must not be involved! That would ruin her chance to get to know the prisoner.

Bolt gave her a sly glance as though wondering why she was so interested. Quickly she changed the subject. "I wish to stop wearing these ugly caftans. They're uncomfortable and hot and make my skin itch."

He frowned. Why had she diverted his attention from the new slave to her wardrobe? Was she thinking about how she looked in front of the man? If so, that was a dangerous train of thought. "Wear them will you if I say so! Told to keep other males away from you, was I. It is necessary to hide your, grrr, generous assets beneath formless robes."

"I'm the Dromo. I should be able to choose whatever clothes I want!"

"You risk Ruel's wrath if you get in trouble. Remember what happened the last time you displeased him?" Not that he thought she'd draw attention from a slave, but there were other Souk males here besides himself who admired human women. He made quite a profit by selling some of his captives to them. Compared to the slave women, Ilyssa stood out like a flamebrush among a meadow of weeds. A Souk would risk a lot to possess her.

Ilyssa looked away. The incident Bolt referred to had left a hole in her heart that wouldn't go away. She could never forget the reason Ruel had exiled her. Flushing with shame and guilt, she snapped, "You don't need to remind me."

"Krach, I do. Aware of my duty am I. You are under my protection here."

Sure, she thought cynically. His brand of protection was to make everyone hate her so she felt isolated and alone. She was allowed freedom of movement around the mining camp but was always accompanied by armed guards. And everything she did, Bolt reported to Ruel. Some protection!

"I can't go to work yet," she said. "I need a break. May I go to the Waterdrop Cave?"

Bolt appeared to consider her request. Ilyssa was in charge of Computer Central. Her job was to supervise the input of orders received, percentages of orders filled, estimated and actual ore production, and shipping schedules.

It was a huge responsibility, and Ruel had recognized her skill with numbers and put her to use. But Bolt knew Ruel had another reason for assigning her the job. She was to keep an eye on him. The pasha didn't trust anyone, especially where his most important source of revenue was concerned. And she was due to report to Ruel within the next few weeks.

"All right," Bolt agreed, realizing it was important to give her a few concessions. "But do not be gone too long. New shipping orders are due in today and you've got to check the production charts." Snapping his fingers in the air, he summoned a couple of Souk bodyguards who'd been following at a discreet distance. "They will accompany you," he told Ilyssa.

A smile on her lips, she turned off the path and headed for a pile of craggy boulders jutting into the air. The only way she could escape her bleak existence was through her singing, and she had to do it where no one else could hear. The Waterdrop Cave was the perfect setting.

Her soft-soled shoes were not made for lengthy treks across the rocky slopes, nor was her burdensome caftan. But she found her way, eager to reach her sanctuary. At the foot of a steep mountainside, she paused, glancing upward. The cliff was barren of all vegetation, a dry bastion of shifting red soil, rocks, and giant boulders. But she was familiar with the terrain and her goal wasn't that far.

Eagerly, Ilyssa began the trek upward, grunting from the effort, digging her toes into whatever footholds she could find. The sun was hot on her back, and perspiration poured down her face. Her skin itched under the caftan. The guards waited below, situating themselves at strategic points. There was no other approach to the cave, so there was no chance of her meeting anyone. It was her hideout, her escape from reality.

Between two towering red rock spires was a wide, gaping hole. Ilyssa clambered inside, seeking comfort from the dark cave. Here no one would bother her. Here she was free.

Pushing a touch pad by the entrance flooded the cave with instant light. Bolt had grudgingly installed a few comforts for her, but she'd had to do favors for him in return. Using her computer skills, she'd manipulated a number of trade consignments through the central mainframe to get him certain items he enjoyed. Crates of Nadiran figs, cases of Mgorus rum, and soft werl sheets were some of the goods that had ended up at the Rocks of Weir instead of their original destinations. Nothing came freely in this society, as she'd learned early on. One had to barter.

Stepping further into the interior, Ilyssa squeezed past a narrow passage and made her way into the Waterdrop Cave beyond. A huge cavern, its flowstone walls glistened with water droplets which sparkled in the sconced flamelights like prized diamella gemstones. At the opposite end, a narrow stream of water gushed out of a hole in the wall, pooling at a dip in the floor. The runoff disappeared into a narrow outlet at the base of the pool.

Ilyssa made her way carefully past the different rock formations and crouched beside the pool. Letting her fingers trail in the cool water, she sighed. It was so peaceful here, so quiet. She sat down and closed her eyes, letting her ears pick up the sounds of the water, gushing, trickling. And she opened her mouth to sing, to join in communion with nature.

At first she sang of the ancient spirits, of how the Water God was at war with the Fire God, but the Goddess of Mother Terra interceded and they made peace. Deep within the interior regions, the three joined to carve out the land. And the land blossomed with growth, with life. Intelligent beings evolved who worshiped the gods and cared for their creations. And so a new day was born.

Ilyssa's eyes fluttered open. A feeling of sublime tranquillity had come over her as it always did when she sang.

Her mind floated, suspended in the air. She was at one with the cave, with the water trickling down the walls. Her heart filled with peace. If only her life could be this pleasant forever.

The tranquil feeling inspired thoughts of her past and her ambition. Ever since she was ten annums, Ilyssa had wanted to be an arbiter. Her homeworld, Circutia, was a cultural and artistic nexus known for its friendly people. The Circutians were pacifists, abhorring all forms of violence, and their arbiters, specially trained in using the arts as a medium for communication, were engaged to solve disputes. Their skills were so effective that their services were sought throughout the galaxy.

Ilyssa had been gifted with musical ability which she'd inherited from her father, Aran, a composer of popular music, who'd inspired her to use her beautiful voice to pursue a singing career. He taught her songs at an early age and found her a respected teacher who trained her for the operatic career Ilyssa craved. She loved singing and enjoyed learning all the appropriate vocal exercises and arias, but her practice sessions invariably ended with her singing her father's popular ballads.

Then an unexpected incident influenced her decision to change careers. One day during her lesson, her maestro, a renowned arbiter, was summoned to mediate a confrontation at the Trade Center between two foreign delegations. He invited Ilyssa along, and she was entranced by the calming effect his singing had on the hostile parties, inducing them to listen to reason. Ever since that day, Ilyssa then dreamed of being an arbiter and using her voice to promote peace like her teacher. It was a lofty goal, as only the best artists on Circutia passed the rigid application process to become trained arbiters, but her parents had encouraged her wholeheartedly.

But reaching 11 annums had put a crimp in her plans. At puberty, her singing range changed and she could sing high notes that weren't possible for her before. And then one day she hit a high C and asked her maestro how it sounded, but he just stared at her, unresponsive.

Frightened, she ran to a group of teachers in the music center for help, but their efforts were fruitless. It was her own screaming for him to wake up that snapped the maestro out of his trance.

When informed about the incident later, her mother had told Ilyssa that her broader vocal range must have triggered an inherited talent called siren song, a trait carried by Moireen's side of the family, which rarely appeared. In fact, Moireen couldn't even sing, but Great-aunt Agatha had possessed a lovely singing voice and, much to her family's dismay, had entertained travelers in dockside taverns. She hadn't possessed the siren song, but had passed on stories about it to Moireen before she died.

But Moireen had added that siren song was more myth than fact. According to tales that circulated throughout the galaxy, the bearer of the gift could mindwash males with her singing, giving her the power to command any male susceptible to the song. Supposedly, the ability crossed planetary boundaries, showing up in humanoid females every few decades or so, but remained elusive like the mystical planet Athos where siren song had reportedly originated.

Ilyssa had been devastated after further testing on men proved she truly possessed the siren song. She couldn't sing in front of an audience, as every man would be mesmerized by her voice. So, having a singing career or becoming an arbiter was out of the question.

Moireen, always a pillar of strength, had disagreed, telling Ilyssa that the siren song should be considered a gift, not a curse. It didn't have to deter her from her plans. Though she couldn't be a singer, she could be even more effective as an arbiter by ordering obstinate males to consider each other's viewpoint. There was only one danger, however. According to the myth, if Ilyssa lost her virginity, she'd lose her singing voice, a risk Ilyssa was unwilling to take. She had told Moireen she wanted to be an arbiter at all costs. But her mother also wanted her to have a full, satisfying life with a husband and children.

So at Moireen's instigation, Ilyssa, her parents, and her brother Devin set out on a voyage to Athos, hoping to learn more about the gift and to discover the truth about the myths. But they had to travel through a sector in space frequented by Souk pirates, and their vessel was attacked.

Knowing they were about to be boarded, Ilyssa had fashioned makeshift earplugs for her father and Devin. When the pirates came aboard, Ilyssa used her siren song to neutralize the Souks. Unfortunately, a few Horthas were among the pirate crew, and, unsusceptible to the song, they'd taken her and her family prisoners and reported to their master, Pasha Ruel.

Ruel had apparently heard of the myth of siren song. As a test, he forced Ilyssa to use the song on her father. Ilyssa had refused but Ruel threatened to harm her mother and Devin if she didn't cooperate. Terrified, Ilyssa had no choice, and Aran had been mindwashed. Following Ruel's orders, Ilyssa had instructed her father to obey Ruel. Ruel had commanded him to everlasting servitude, and to this day, Aran remained Ruel's mind slave.

In a similar manner, the pasha made Ilyssa use her voice against his enemies, bending them to his will after they were mesmerized by her spell. She was his secret weapon, and no one except Bolt and Moireen knew her sinister function. Everyone else thought she was Ruel's favored consort, but he'd never touched her, being careful to preserve her virginity so she wouldn't lose her valuable voice.

Ilyssa still dreamed of using her voice to promote peace, so she had practiced her vocalizations whenever possible, hoping that when she was free, she could still apply to become an arbiter. Her dream wasn't lost; it was just temporarily delayed.

Standing, Ilyssa thrust her shoulders back. She took a deep breath, filling her lungs with air. And then she began her exercises, starting slow and easy, running through the portamenti and sostenuto movements, then through the varied scales. She attacked repeated notes, triplets and arpeggios, and exercises for blending the registers. The whole gauntlet of vocal activities was hers. When she'd finished her turns, staccati, and trills, Ilyssa finished off with a song, this one a ballad of a young woman searching among the stars for her lost lover. It had been one of her father's most memorable compositions and singing it brought tears to her eyes. Since his mindwash, Aran hadn't been able to compose a single note.

Had he been in his right mind, Ilyssa knew Aran would encourage her to continue practicing. He'd taught her that each artistic endeavor included both technical and aesthetic components. An artist who could not master the first would never attain perfection in the second. By performing her exercises as often as Bolt allowed her to come to the care, Ilyssa had already achieved a great deal. Her maestro had given her the foundation upon which to advance. Over the annums, she'd managed to equalize her voice, neatly blend the registers, and master her vocal cords. Now she could sing well without fatigue or effort. That accomplishment allowed her to focus on learning the sentiment and expression of her favorite ballads. Her practice sessions were necessary if she ever hoped to achieve her dream of becoming an arbiter, a dream that was unattainable unless she first gained her freedom.

Her thoughts turned to Sean Breslow and she prayed he'd be able to help her and her family escape this dreadful place. The man was a pilot, but what else was he? His burned ship was reported to be a light freighter, one of the most common small trading vessels in the galaxy. Yet his cargo hold had been empty. Either he was here to make an illegal pickup, or he was telling the truth about striking a deal to buy rubellis gemstones. If so, with whom was he going to meet? Not that it really mattered, Ilyssa told herself. Trader or smuggler, at this point Sean would be interested mainly in obtaining his freedom. She could offer him that and riches as well. Ruel had given her jewels when she was in his favor. She could use them to pay Sean if necessary. And if she and her family returned to Circutia, she could pay him more. Her parents owned a large amount of property and were quite wealthy, or at least they had been before their fateful journey. Hopefully Uncle Meiras had taken over as guardian in their absence and they could regain their rights when they returned.

On the other hand, Sean might be more interested in information than wealth. Bolt had hinted that he might be a spy. If Sean was in the employ of another pasha, she could give him useful data. Having lived in Ruel's palace for so many annums, she'd been privy to numerous state secrets.

Or maybe Sean was a saboteur, hired by a rival pasha to damage Ruel's mining operations. If ore production was halted, even for a few days, it would seriously harm his business. Ruel's life would be endangered if his contracts to the Morgots weren't fulfilled. Look what had happened to his brother, Bdan. The Morgot leader K'darr had executed Bdan for not completing a contract of a different nature.

No matter who or what he was, Ilyssa felt Sean wouldn't harm her, although remembering how audaciously he'd looked at her made her shiver. By the stars, the man intrigued her! She drew a deep breath, savoring the sweet, earthy scent of the cave. Trickling water was the only other sound besides her breathing. Around the damp, glistening walls, shadows danced among the flamelights.

Outside, the bodyguards awaited her and back at the camp, Bolt expected her to go to work. Everything involved a trade-off, and the Souk was no exception. Tonight Ilyssa would work on getting the proof she needed to bend him to her will. If all went well, the slave Sean Breslow would be hers by the end of next week.

That night, Ilyssa sprang into action. Another piragen ore shipment was due for diversion, and she'd figured the best way to get the proof she needed was to holovid the transaction. It would be risky at best; life-threatening at worst. She'd probably be killed outright if discovered.

After everyone was asleep, Ilyssa rose from her bed and tiptoed to the fabricator in an alcove by the wall. There she conjured up a rubbery black hooded jumpsuit that would cover her from head to toe. Once dressed, she pulled the secreted holovid recorder from her wardrobe. It hadn't been difficult to obtain one. As Dromo, she had free access to all areas of the production center. She'd managed to slip into one of the equipment rooms during midday nourishment and pocket one of the pistol-shaped devices. Afterward, it had been easy to alter the inventory records on the computer.

Now as she tucked the holovid recorder into her belt, Ilyssa hoped she was doing the right thing. It was the only way she could get an edge on Bolt so he would agree to her demands.

Using the fabricator again, she requested a couple of chemicals that, when combined, would serve her purpose admirably. At least she hoped they would. Her idea was theoretical at best. Nevertheless, her fingers moved deftly, pouring the activating enzyme onto a thin round membrane and mixing it with a smooth powder. Her nose itched from the smell, but she resisted the urge to sneeze. Concentrating, she folded the membrane and sealed it. The finished product was a tiny pellet. Putting that one aside, she made another and tucked it into her pocket for later use. Then she picked up the first pellet and approached the door.

Outside in the corridor would be two Hortha sentries. Like others of their species, the bull-like creatures were highly sensitive to orange firepeppers. Smelling the spice induced an allergic fit of coughing, sneezing, hyperventilation, and, finally, loss of consciousness. The effect was temporary and lasted only until the aroma dissipated.

Her heart pounding, Ilyssa opened the door a crack. It would have been much simpler if she could have gone out the casement, but her window was set in a high wall and looked out onto a sheer drop. This was the only alternative. Holding her breath, she threw the small pellet. It exploded into a dark orange cloud. The Horthas sniffed the air, buzzing in puzzlement. Then the sneezing started. Within minutes, they collapsed onto the floor.

Ilyssa slipped out the door and rushed down the hall, exiting through the server's stairwell. Outside, she drew a deep breath of cool, dry air. The climate at the Rocks of Weir varied between harsh extremes: burning hot during the day and biting cold at night. The rubbery fabric of her jumpsuit insulated her from the low temperature, but she still felt the crisp, cold air on her face. It energized her while she gazed overhead at the two moons of Souk shining brightly in the clear night sky.

No one was about except for the usual Souk contingent of armed guards. It would be easy to slip past them since Ilyssa knew their precise patroling pattern. Standing in the shadows waiting for the troop to pass, she smiled. Her ability for keen observation had been one of the reasons Ruel had sent her here. Tonight it was serving her well.

At the moment when the patrol intercepted another unit coming from the opposite direction, she dashed out to take shelter among a clump of tall lippo trees. With their low outstretched branches, they made good cover. Once the path was clear, she started up the slope behind the house. Rounding the summit, she trotted across a wide meadow toward an overlook beyond. Time was of the essence: she had to be back before the Horthas, who might have awakened by now, performed their second nightly sensor sweep of her chamber. She'd gotten out of bed immediately after the first sweep. That meant she had a four haura interval before the next one, and 30 precious minutes had already passed.

Shivering in apprehension, Ilyssa surveyed the land from her high vantage point. On the right were the Rocks of Weir, the eerie red rock formations thrusting into the air. Behind them rose the Koodrash Mounts with the mining camp nestled in the foothills. To her left stretched a vast flat expanse.

The winding track of the cargo tram originated at the mine shaft which was situated among the Rocks of Weir. Twisting through the towering red rocks and dusty slopes, the track eventually flattened when it reached the plains. It ended at the processing plant in the factory town of Ma'ahmed, far in the distance. Each night, the loaded cars made this run.

From her review of the computer files, Ilyssa had discovered that on the first and third Fridays of every month, the production tallies for the plant didn't match those from the mines. They were lower, meaning the plant would expect to receive less ore than was actually produced. Someone had been altering the figures, and from the access code, Ilyssa had determined that it was Bolt and that he was diverting a car full of ore somewhere along the route. But what would he do with it? He'd have to sell it to make a profit.

Scanning the manifests, Ilyssa had noticed that Coak habitually showed up in town on those days. She'd met him once when Bolt invited him to dinner and insisted on showing her off. The slimy Amburian had given her the creeps. Today was the third Friday and she'd quickly checked the manifests and found Coak's name. He was in town again. He had to be the buyer! It was just too much of a coincidence that the Amburian arrived on the same days the ore shipments were hijacked. If she was right, she hoped to catch Coak in the act of transferring the ore to his sailbarge and paying off Bolt.

She had to reach the spot among the rocks where she suspected they met. It was the only place well concealed from the electronic sensors monitoring the track. She hoped the security system wouldn't pick up her approach but she hadn't dared tamper with it for fear of alerting Bolt.

Moving with quiet stealth, Ilyssa was alert, watchful for any unusual sounds or movements. She had to get to the Rocks of Weir from this high overlook, and her transport was hidden in the clump of bushes yonder. She'd brought the flyboard, another item she'd clipped from the inventory up here a long time ago, in case she needed it for instant flight. It paid to be prepared should Ruel decide he didn't need her anymore.

Crouching down by the prickly bushes, Ilyssa reached underneath and grasped the cold, hard edge. A few strong yanks and the flyboard was free. Quickly she checked the power source. Good, the display indicated the crystal chamber was still full and the system was operable. She'd been worried about the cold night temperatures affecting the feed lines.

The flyboard was basically just that: a narrow board in an oblong shape, curved at either end. It held just enough room for her to stand, two feet side by side. Attached in front were standing handlebars. On the right were fixed the controls for ignition and braking.

Ilyssa's heart caught in her throat. Where were the goggles she'd left here? She scrabbled on her hands and knees, scraping dirt away from the underside of the bushes. By the heavens, had someone else been here? She reached inside, wincing when the brambles pricked her skin. Her reward came when she touched a rounded object. Pulling it out, Ilyssa gave a sigh of relief. She donned the goggles, tightening the stretch band around the back of her head to keep them in place. Now she'd be able to see in the dark. The goggles enabled her to do one other thing, too. The infrared range allowed her to detect the energy waves monitoring the perimeter of the track. Now she'd be sure to avoid them. The only thing she'd have to watch out for would be the flying wingboxers that inhabited this area. They were nocturnal creatures, seeking food at night. With a wingspan of nine meters, they were not to be treated lightly.

Stepping onto the flyboard, she placed her feet on either side of the central bar, fastened on a safety strap, and grasped the handles. Her index finger jabbed the ignition button. The engine kicked on with a jarring rumble. Gritting her teeth against the rattling vibration, she keyed in the antigrav switch. Silently, the board lifted straight in the air. Manipulating the controls, Ilyssa angled the board toward the edge of the cliff and then pushed the throttle forward. She zoomed off into clear space, almost lost her balance, and regained control in time to steer toward the Rocks of Weir.

Wind blasted her face, a cold harsh wind. As the towering spirals of rock rapidly approached, Ilyssa heard flapping noises coming from behind. Twisting her neck, she gasped in alarm. Pursuing her were two giant wingboxers! Their glowing yellow eyes shone in anticipation of a tasty meal as they neared.

Turning forward, Ilyssa ducked her head, intent on reaching the lower regions of the wooded foothills. A shadow gained on her right. Out of the corner of her eye, Ilyssa saw one of the flying reptiles unfurl its huge claws in preparation for snatching her up. As the distance closed between them, the creature opened its immense pointed beak and gave a howl of exhilaration. Its partner answered the cry with one of its own. Climbing, the second wingboxer effectively blocked her path in an upward direction.

Desperate to escape, Ilyssa plunged her board down in a tight spiral. Her stomach rose and her grip slipped on the handlebars. Her heart was pounding so hard she thought she'd faint. Directly ahead were treacherous towers of rock, jutting into the air like hands reaching up to the heavens. Ilyssa dipped and swerved, zipping among them with screaming speed. Her hands clung tightly to the handles as she felt her feet sliding. The safety strap bit into her back as she strained against it. Please let me make it safely down! she thought, clenching her teeth.

Scanning the area for a landing site, she decided to come down at the Waterdrop Cave. The trek from there would be farther than she'd anticipated, but with the two wingboxers keeping pace, there wasn't much choice. They were skilled trackers, beside her now, snapping their beaks. One caught at her arm with its talon, nearly yanking her off the flyboard despite the safety strap holding her in place. She stifled a scream, going into a turning dive to get away. Both wingboxers dove with her, cackling at the sport.

Ilyssa saw her special mountain off to the side and veered in that direction, balancing sideways so she could fly the board directly into the gaping mouth of the cave. Inside, she immediately cut the power and glided to the ground. With trembling fingers, she undid the strap that had secured her and stepped off the board, shaking uncontrollably.

At least she was safe. Wingboxers were afraid of dark, enclosed spaces. They built their nests on clifftops, out in the open. They'd circle around for a while and then leave. But did she have the time to spare? Her throat constricted when she glanced at her chronometer. She had less than three hauras left. It would take too long to climb down the rocky slope in the dark, make her way to the foothills, and find the spot in the woods where she estimated Coak and Bolt met.

Her best bet was to wait until the wingboxers were out of sight, fire up her flyboard, and land close to the rendezvous point.

The minutes ticked by while she paced the cave, reviewing the possibility in her mind that she'd been wrong about all this. Nevertheless, she wasn't about to turn back now. A half haura later, Ilyssa decided she couldn't wait any longer. The wingboxers weren't visible, so she took her position on the flyboard and pushed the ignition. She zoomed out of the cave and flew toward the foothills, tracing the divergent track with her infrared beam. When she thought she'd found the spot where the two miscreants would meet, she landed and concealed the flyboard.

Crouching behind a cluster of thorntrees, she readied her camera and waited, her breath steaming in the cold.

Was she wrong? Was this divergent track from an old line that had long since gone unused? There was no sign of anyone having landed here previously, no telltale exhaust trails or flattened bushes.

Just as Ilyssa started biting her nails in anxiety, a faint whirring noise sounded overhead. Glancing at her chronometer, she noted that it was nearly time for the tram full of ore to pass across the main track just over the hill yonder. Could this be what she'd been waiting for?

Glancing around at her hiding place, she nodded in approval. Her flyboard was safely hidden; her holovid recorder was charged and ready; she had a clear view of the landing site. There was nothing else to do but wait.

Then Ilyssa heard the whirring increase in volume, and as it did, a hissing noise sounded from over the hill and then it grew louder. A section of bush across the clearing swung aside and a heavy tram car, bulging with ore and speeding above the ground, slid into view. Dust flew up in a cloud as the tram came to an abrupt halt. It leveled down until it rested flat on the ground.

From over the crest of another hill came a sailbarge, its single propeller whirring in a blur of speed. Ilyssa noticed that it was coming in so low by air that it wouldn't be detected by radar. The pilot probably avoided the protective energy beams surrounding the main track by using infrared detectors.

She watched as the sails deflated, and an obese man wearing baggy pants and boots stepped off the barge. Ilyssa recognized his fierce bearded face that was scarred into a permanent scowl. It was Coak all right! She shivered with dread. From the gossip she'd heard in Bolt's harem, the Amburians were pirates, but they took loot, not slaves. And they murdered anyone in their way. What would he do to her if she were caught? Coak wouldn't care that she was Ruel's special property. He'd probably share her with his men and then kill her.

Coak stalked to the tram car and grinned, his crooked teeth flashing in the moonlight. Ilyssa aimed the viewfinder of the recorder so she could see him clearly. She started the machine rolling, and turned it so the recorder could pick up Bolt zooming in on a flyboard.

The two exchanged salutes. Then Coak signaled to his men to bring Bolt a black case from the top deck of the sailbarge. Bolt had just opened the case and started counting the credits inside when Ilyssa felt something prickle the back of her neck. She looked up and nearly screamed. One of the wingboxers had found her! The flying reptile was swooping down, its toothed jaws open, its claws outstretched to snatch her. Clutching the holovid, Ilyssa dove under a tangle of liana vines just in time to avoid being swiped on the shoulder.

"What's that rustling?" Bolt barked.

Ilyssa's blood froze. Her fingers touched a long, thick branch and she grasped it, letting go of the holovid. Desperate now to get the wingboxer off her, she crept forward, exposing her top half to the creature. Giving a high shriek, it plunged after her. Ilyssa held out the branch. When the creature was nearly upon her, she thrust forward, jamming the stick between its open jaws.

The wingboxer's yellow eyes widened and it gave a muffled howl. Veering off, it soared into the air and away.

Ilyssa didn't have time to recover. She could hear Coak's men crashing through the undergrowth, searching for the source of the noise.

"It's just a wingboxer," Coak shouted from the clearing. "Get back in the barge," he told his men.

Ilyssa nearly sobbed with relief, but her mission wasn't over. Undaunted, she picked up the holovid recorder and began filming once again, trying to steady her shaking hands. Soon Bolt was on his way, case in hand. Coak's men loaded the ore onto the barge and took off. Ilyssa figured the empty ore car would rejoin the tram on its return trip.

Jamming the recorder into her belt, she was last to leave.

Bolt strode into her room as soon as it was daylight. Ilyssa had anticipated his visit, so she was up and dressed by the time he arrived.

"I received a report that the Hortha sentries outside your door reacted to the odor of orange firepeppers twice last night," Bolt said, his dark eyes blazing with anger. "Explain!"

"I couldn't sleep. I was hungry, so I obtained a dish of rami noodles."

"With orange firepeppers in the seasoning? You know the Horthas are allergic to the spice."

Ilyssa shrugged. "I didn't think it would bother them."

Bolt glared at her suspiciously. "I find it strange that the two incidents occurred between midnight and four o'clock, just after the first sensor sweep of your chamber and immediately before the second one."

"The time slipped past me. I fell back to sleep after my first snack, then awoke with a terrible craving for spicy food again. The only relief was to eat another plate of rami noodles. I had no idea the fragrance would drift into the hallway." She smiled sweetly, radiating an aura of innocence while inside her stomach churned with fear. She'd had to use the pellets twice, once when leaving her chamber and again when returning. Of course Bolt would be suspicious, but she was relying on the fact that her excursion had gone unnoticed.

"Grrr," Bolt growled, studying her. He was dissatisfied with her explanation. More than likely, she'd found a way to weaken his surveillance. Horthas were not susceptible to siren song. They didn't succumb to a hypnotic trance when they heard her singing, like males of other species did. That was why Bolt assigned Horthas to guard her at night instead of his elite Souk troops. During the day, it didn't matter. He could keep track of her movements.

His expression grew thoughtful. "Perhaps it is time to r-r-replace Joie," he said. "Obtain shall I another female attendant to wait on you."

Ilyssa pursed her lips to hide her smile of triumph. Bolt's offer of assigning her another attendant fell right in with her own plans, except she had the slave Sean Breslow in mind for the job, not another female watchdog.

"Yes, I could use another attendant," she replied, mentally reviewing her scheme. In a few days, she'd be ready to present her case, once she had written proof of Bolt's misdeeds to go along with the holovid recording. She'd obtain printouts of the bills of lading for the processing plant and the ore production figures from the mines. The printouts would show the discrepancies she'd detected and act as evidence that someone was hijacking shipments of ore. Her holovid recording would be irrefutable proof that Bolt was responsible. When she threatened to show it all to Ruel, Bolt would have no choice but to accept her bargain.

When Bolt left, Ilyssa felt excitement building inside her. At last, she was taking control of her life!

Chapter Three

The afternoon came for the inspection of the mines. Wrinkling her nose with distaste, Ilyssa entered the wardrobe room along with Bolt and a contingent of elite Souk troops. Hanging on hooks around the large room in the production center were utilitarian gray coveralls. Ilyssa snatched one and donned it over her sleeveless jumpsuit. At least she was able to access other clothing options from her fabricator besides those shapeless caftans Bolt favored, but her choices were restricted. The jumpsuit was a sickly olive color that made her fair complexion look sallow.

She wondered how the slave Sean Breslow would view her this time. Would he stare at her defiantly as he'd done before? Or would he bow his head like all the rest? New arrivals were quickly subdued by slave collars and stun whips. If those didn't work, the brutal punishments meted out on Visitation Day usually did. Bolt saw to that, and he also saw that she was blamed for them.

Her stomach clenched but Ilyssa refused to give in to the nausea she usually experienced on these inspections. Today would be different, she told herself, patting the objects in her pocket. Bolt would have to listen to her. She was ready to strike her deal regarding Sean Breslow.

When the inspection party was ready, all garbed in gray coveralls, they filed into the cage that would take them below. Ilyssa gritted her teeth as she was packed in among the guards, their weapons bristling, their blue dogfaces impassive. Bolt stood in front and keyed in the level. The gate shut, and the cage began its decent into the dark hole.

Down, down, into total blackness. The shaft wasn't lit, and Ilyssa squeezed her eyes shut as the drop increased. She hated this part. She hated the whole day. To calm her nerves, she thought of Sean and what would happen once she got him alone. Her first objective was to learn more about his character and identity. Asking the right questions would encourage him to talk. Then if his responses impressed her, Ilyssa planned to relate her story. Hopefully at that point, the man would agree to rescue her parents in exchange for his own freedom. *Sounds simple, doesn't it?* But Ilyssa had a feeling it wouldn't be so easy.

Still, the prospect excited her so much that her heart was pounding by the time the cage jolted to an abrupt halt 300 meters below ground. Light flooded the small space from the working level, and Ilyssa viewed it as the light of hope. From here on in, her fortune could change. It all depended upon her own ingenuity and the slave, Sean Breslow.

Rolf's chest glistened with sweat as he labored to remove a large solid chunk from the rock face. He'd been here over a week, and already he could see why slaves didn't last long. The hard physical labor and hazardous working conditions contributed to early deaths. His lungs burned and his eyes watered from the acidic gas in the air. The harsh environment was the reason robot drones couldn't be used. Machinery quickly deteriorated from the acidity, so the work had to be done by hand. It was a torturous process, made worse by the Hortha's stun whips and the horrendous slave collars. Rolf had balked when the overseer tried to snap one of the thick bands around his neck. As a result, his back bore more bruises.

Grimacing, he continued chiseling. Spiky particles of rock flew in all directions. Beside him other slaves, male and female, labored in silence. Their wheezing breaths resounded in the cool air.

"Fasten your coveralls, krecker," the overseer growled, striding over. He was a nasty-looking Souk, with hanging jowls and a bulbous nose. With a flick of his wrist, he activated Rolf's slave collar.

Rolf felt the choking sensation as a flood of red washed before his eyes. He lifted his hands to comply and the tightening hold was released. It wasn't in his nature to obey orders so readily, but he had yet to find a way out of this situation, and getting battered for disobedience wouldn't help.

He grasped a drill and attacked the rock face with renewed vigor. His fingernails were cracked, his knuckles roughened. He sniffed as the acidic air stung his nostrils. A vein of piragen ore glistened in the rock but he'd only made a dent in it. Using manual tools and his bare hands, he was nowhere near prying it loose.

The crackle of a stun whip sounded off to his left and a woman grunted. Swiveling his head, Rolf saw a slave fall under the onslaught of the whip. A Hortha buzzed over her, his bull-like body encased in a short armored tunic. The guard was exhorting her to rise in his untranslatable buzzing language and beating her when she didn't obey.

"The woman's caught her foot under that ledge, you fool," Rolf cried, throwing down his tools and leaping to the woman's aid. She was gray-haired, thin, with frightened eyes.

The Hortha's buzzing increased in volume and he turned his angry gaze on Rolf. Ignoring him, Rolf bent to help the woman. Her ankle was jammed under a narrow ledge and he could see where the skin was scraped raw from her trying to pull loose.

"Just a minute, I'll have you out of here." But then he felt the lash of the whip on his torso and the shock of it toppled him. Two other Horthas rushed to join the first. The three of them struck out at Rolf and the whimpering woman with the full force of their whips.

With a roar of rage, Rolf charged at the nearest Hortha. "She needs help, goddammit! You're killing her!" His head rammed into a solid stomach and he bounced back, his senses reeling.

"Grrr, you deserve punishment, sumi," snarled the Souk overseer who'd spotted the commotion and come over to watch.

With a flick of the overseer's wrist, Rolf's collar tightened. Choking, Rolf fell to his knees, clawing at his neck. His chest wall ached with the strain of his efforts to breathe. The pain grew too much to bear, and Rolf's vision dimmed. Through the haze he heard the woman's screams as the Horthas beat her senseless.

"Hold! What goes on here?"

Immediately the constriction around Rolf's neck loosened. He remained on his knees, trembling. His breaths were deep, shuddering gulps of air.

"I said, what goes on here?"

"This krecker attacked one of the Hortha guards, mistress," the Souk overseer said.

"Explain, sumi," the female demanded.

Rolf realized he was being addressed. Glancing up at the speaker, he narrowed his eyes. It was the Dromo. The last time he'd seen her, she'd taken a particular delight in beating him. How would she punish him now?

Quietly, he explained about the slave's foot being caught under the ledge. The slave woman lay in an unconscious heap behind him.

The Dromo's mouth tightened. He thought he saw a brief flicker of compassion in her eyes but then it was gone. Bolt, the slave master, was beside her. He nudged her and she spoke.

"The old woman is a sumi," the Dromo said in a flat tone. "If she cannot work, she'll be shot. Free her leg," she ordered a Hortha.

Her glance wandered in his direction. Rolf kept his head lowered as he felt the heat of her gaze. Was this what he'd come to, a slave bowing before his masters? Blast it, no!

His eyes raised, and he met her gaze head-on. He saw the shock register on her expression as his mouth curved into a grin.

"Insolent wretch! Seize him and take him to the block!" Bolt barked. "Choose the punishment, Dromo."

Ilyssa gasped. She couldn't let him be tortured in front of everyone. Yet every Visitation Day, she was expected to give this demonstration of her ruthlessness. If she refused, Ruel would know about it. She followed helplessly as the Horthas dragged the man over to a horizontal stone slab. Before she could protest, they'd stripped him down to his briefs, laid him out, and manacled his outstretched wrists and ankles to iron receptacles.

Mutely, he stared at her, his blue eyes furious.

"No!" she cried as Pten, the Souk torturer, approached with a set of sharp, gleaming instruments that would cut and mutilate.

"What is your pleasure?" Pten asked, his ugly dogface leering as he awaited orders.

The Horthas hustled all the slaves to where they would be forced to watch. A hush fell over the crowd.

Ilyssa looked at Bolt and wet her lips. "I must speak to you in private, Bolt."

Bolt grasped her arm and squeezed so hard he left marks on her skin. "Are you forgetting your place?" he hissed close to her ear. "Everyone awaits your word. You *must* issue an order."

"No, I can't."

"Very well, I'll issue it in your name, as usual."

"Not this time! I mean it. You have to let me show you something first."

Bolt scowled. "You'd risk my displeasure as well as Ruel's?"

"You'll risk a lot more if you don't listen to me," she warned.

Something in her eyes must have convinced him, because he followed her to a shadowed corner.

A few minutes later, they returned to the block.

"Release the sumi," Bolt ordered to Rolf's astonishment.

Rolf had lain there, thinking this was the end. He hadn't needed the memory molecule, because he wasn't being questioned about his mission. He was simply going to be punished. The Dromo was a sadistic bitch, enjoying the torture and beatings, and she'd obviously singled him out for more. But now he was being released and given back his clothes. But why? Not hesitating, he dressed himself and waited, glaring at her.

"Do not look upon the Dromo!" Bolt snapped, enraged. This sumi had been trouble ever since he'd arrived. Ilyssa seemed unduly interested in him, and Bolt wondered why. Sean Breslow was a robust physical specimen, but they'd captured many such human males in the nine months that she'd been here. So why would she be drawn to this one in particular?

Of course, the man Sean was the first sumi who'd dared to look boldly into her eyes. Perhaps his arrogance was a challenge to her womanhood. In that case, Sean could be dangerous to her.

Aware of his duty to protect the Dromo, Bolt cursed her intelligence. He'd never expected Ilyssa to be so clever, but she'd not only discovered his dealings with Coak but also obtained substantial evidence against him. Now he had no choice but to go along with her unusual request or she'd expose him to Ruel.

"You are to accompany us," he said to the sumi whose surprise was evident in his expression. "The Dromo has something else in mind for you today. As for the rest of you," he said to the other slaves, "the Dromo decrees that your rations will be withheld and you're each to work four more hauras without a stop! Anyone who falls will be given ten jolts." Ten jolts from the overseer's electrifier was strong enough to kill.

Beside him, Ilyssa gasped. "Isn't that rather harsh?"

"They are slaves, Dromo. Must I remind you that you are one of Ruel's?"

She lowered her head. "No, that won't be necessary."

"R-r-report to him of today's doings, shall I."

"No! If you say anything to him about Sean, I'll tell him about your little profit-making scheme."

"Grrr," Bolt growled. But she had him. He'd have to deal with the sumi on his own.

Later in the wardrobe room, when they were dressed in their own clothes and ready to depart, Bolt turned to the man Sean. He was standing nearby, quietly awaiting his fate. The two were close in height, the slave being just a notch taller but considerably leaner. Bolt tugged at his military uniform in a gesture of superiority.

"Listen carefully, sumi," Bolt growled, his brow furrowed with displeasure. "From here on in, you are under Ilyssa's direct command. She has control of your slave collar. You will obey her orders instantly or r-r-risk death for defiance."

"Yes, master," Rolf said, bowing. Despite the fact that he was grimy, garbed in a filthy tunic and leggings, and sweaty from the mines, it was an elegant gesture that wasn't lost on either Bolt or Ilyssa. Bolt's misgivings deepened, while Ilyssa's hopes for the future soared.

When they were outside breathing fresh, clean air, Rolf fell into place behind Ilyssa and Bolt. A contingent of Souk bodyguards surrounded them. They headed off for the Dromo's residence via a shortcut from the production center. The dirt path followed a winding trail through the hills before a steep incline to the gleaming white structure ahead.

As he walked, swinging his arms and feeling the warm sunshine on his back, Rolf wondered how Ilyssa had garnered her position as Dromo. When he'd studied Souk culture, he had learned it was a male-dominated society. Harems were the fashion, with no limit to the number of consorts a male could take. Souk females lived in seclusion in a separate section of the household. All of the important decisions affecting their lives were made by the males. In such a restrictive culture, it was unheard of for a Souk female to hold public office. Ilyssa's position was obviously an exception. He wondered what she meant to Ruel that the pasha had given her such an important and visible role.

On top of his list of questions was the obvious one. What did she want with him? She strode forward with a purposeful gait, her back rigid. Did she have in mind a private torture for him, perhaps? Rolf shuddered at the thought. Women persecutors could be much more sadistic than men, and the Dromo's reputation for meting out harsh punishments was well known. The sumis were terrified of her. He wasn't sure what game she was playing, but it behooved him to cooperate until he learned more. Once he understood the rules, he could twist them to his own use. In the meantime, he'd keep a low profile and pretend to be submissive while planning his escape. It was crucial he get out of here in time to accomplish his mission.

Up front, Ilyssa was aware of Sean's heavy tread behind her. Despite being dressed in filthy rags and subdued by a slave collar, the man still emanated a powerful presence. Ilyssa knew he must be worried about what was in store for him. Unfortunately, she couldn't relieve his mind on that score. While she was with the Souks, she had to maintain her image.

Beside her, Bolt cut a neat military figure. As satrap, he outranked all the other Souk troopers stationed here. Ignoring military protocol, Bolt set his own code for the mining camp, and it was strict. Everyone except Ilyssa cowered before him.

His dogface folded into a scowl as he glanced at her. "See to it will I that the sumi is assigned a bunk in the servers' quarters." He spoke in a low tone so no one else could hear.

Ilyssa shook her head, her tight braid swinging back and forth. "I don't think so. After he is properly cleansed, send him to me. He'll stay in my parlor."

"What!"

"As my personal server, Sean should be close at hand should I need anything in the night. Joie used to sleep there, remember?"

"Joie was a female."

"What difference does it make? Sean is a sumi. He's under my command." In the bright sunlight, she squinted.

"I will not allow it!" Bolt shouted. Aware of the guards' attention, he gave a quick apology. "Forgive me, Dromo. I am concerned for your safety." Then he lowered his voice and growled, "Sworn to protect you, am I. Too dangerous is this man."

"Oh?" Ilyssa arched an eyebrow. "How so?"

Bolt sputtered for a reply. "He is insolent. The sumi does not know how to obey orders. He needs to be broken before he can be of proper service."

"He appears to be quite docile right now. If you're worried about my being alone with him, I have control of his collar. Even without that, there's my special gift. I can always use my siren song to protect myself." She lifted a hand to shield her face from the sun. "The matter is settled. Send Sean to my suite once he is prepared."

Realizing the battle was lost, Bolt fell silent. He knew she was partially right. No man could take advantage of her while she wielded the power of her siren song. But what about the power of the human's masculine appeal? What if Ilyssa didn't want to stop him if he made advances? If Bolt was in the sumi's place, he'd use whatever weapons were available to better his position, including seduction. Ilyssa was inexperienced enough to fall for someone like him.

Ruel had told Bolt that he knew Ilyssa was vulnerable after the incident in his palace and had put a personal safeguard on her that would alert him if her virginity was breached. According to ancient folklore, Ruel had explained, if she lost her maidenhead, she'd lose her gift of siren song. No one knew for sure if it was true, but Ruel hadn't been willing to take the chance. Bolt knew that if she lost her gift, she'd be useless to Ruel and then who would he blame? He'd blame Bolt.

If it was up to him alone, he'd kill the slave and be done with it. But Ilyssa would probably get even by betraying him to Ruel. Yet there was another path that could prove more fruitful, and that was if Ruel himself ordered the slave's execution. Ilyssa wouldn't dare defy the pasha's decree.

The key was to be found in Sean's identity. Bolt had checked into the man's background earlier and hadn't found any Arcturian trader listed on the central manifest by the name of Sean Breslow. He'd let it go since the man was already under detention. But now with Ilyssa's interest in him, Breslow's background had become more important. If he could prove the man was a threat to the mining operation, Ruel would have him eliminated.

Bolt didn't waste any time in setting his plan into motion. As soon as he'd instructed his steward to supervise Sean's cleansing, he entered his chamber and tapped into his private comm unit to call Haakat, the capital city. In his mind, he pictured the creature who would answer. Pah was a gecko, an insectlike being with a hard red shell covering, two legs, two arms, and two antennae that served as olfactory sensors. Most of the time, he and his partner Orr worked for Ruel, but they often accepted profitable assignments on the side.

"Captured a new sumi, did we," Bolt explained when Pah responded with the proper code. "He's a human who crashed his ship in the foothills. The man claims to be a trader, but I think he might be a spy or a saboteur, working for one of the r-r-rival pashas or even the rebels."

"You want me to check him out?" the gecko said in his peculiar clicking tongue.

"Krach," Bolt acknowledged. "His name is Sean Breslow. He says he's from Arcturus but I checked the trade manifests and he's not listed."

"I know who can help, but it will be expensive."

Bolt was aware that the Souks had a paid informant in the Coalition government center located on Bimordus Two. A member of the General Assembly, Ruzbee, an elected representative from Arcturus, would be the best person to investigate the human's background.

"Make it worth your while, will I," Bolt crooned.

"How much?"

"Five thousand credits, and another five if you get evidence proving the human is a spy."

"Twenty thousand," Pah chittered greedily.

"Fifteen, and that's only if you get irrefutable proof that the human is conspiring against Ruel."

The gecko sighed. "Agreed. I'll get back to you."

Just as Bolt was powering down, another call came through. It was Ruel, desiring a report.

"How is Ilyssa? Is she behaving?"

"Aye, master," Bolt replied.

"You sound hesitant."

"There are not too many amusements here for a human female of her status. Grows r-r-restless does she."

"Too bad! I sent her there because she displeased me! Your job it is to keep her behavior within bounds."

"You give her a position of import but limit her freedom. She chafes at the r-r-restraint."

"For all her airs, she is a sumi, Bolt. If she becomes unruly, let me know."

"Krach, my master." He rang off, fearing Ruel's reaction if he learned of Ilyssa's interest in the krecker. The man needed to be removed as soon as possible.

Ilyssa had washed and changed and was brushing her hair in front of the reflector when the slave appeared at her door. She whirled to greet him, the dark green caftan she wore swishing at her feet.

"Well!" she exclaimed. "You certainly look . . . improved." Sean was dressed simply in a belted black tunic and leggings, but with his clean hair, shaven face, and piercing blue eyes, Ilyssa thought he looked magnificent. Her heart began a rapid staccato even as she disguised her feelings with a mask of icy disdain.

"You may enter," she said in a cool tone.

Rolf strode inside and halted in front of her, his hands clasped behind his back, his head bowed. The tight band of the slave collar around his neck reminded him that she was in control.

"Look at me," Ilyssa commanded. When he'd raised his face, she said in a purposefully loud voice, "I have brought you here to act as my personal server."

Rolf's jaw dropped in surprise. *Her what?* His gaze met hers questioningly.

"I'll expect you to assist me with my meals, keep my chamber clean, maintain my wardrobe, and satisfy any other needs of mine that may arise. Hopefully, in time, you will grow to anticipate my requirements."

Rolf was speechless. Was this her way of telling him that he was to be some sort of glorified lady's maid? Or did she have a different function in mind? What exactly did she mean by "other needs"?

"You'll sleep in the adjacent parlor," Ilyssa said, contributing to his growing suspicion. "That way, you'll be close at hand if I want you during the night. Now, shut the door and I'll show you where I keep everything."

Rolf complied, closing out the buzzing of the Hortha guards stationed outside the door.

"Pardon, mistress, but I'm not exactly clear on my duties. You wish me to maintain your suite and serve your meals, but what else am I to do?"

As Ilyssa rattled off a list of chores, Rolf listened carefully, but it was the unspoken duties that worried him. She'd said she might want him during the night. That meant only one thing as far as he was concerned. She expected him to service her personally. Rolf wondered if he would be able to perform under forced circumstances. Studying her physical attributes, he decided it shouldn't be too difficult. Soft waves of auburn hair cascaded over her shoulders. Tiny wisps framed a face with features so perfect they might have been chiseled from porcelain. Her eyes were a remarkable shade of green flecked with gold. Her mouth was full and sensual. She was lovely, he admitted, but with the beauty of an ice queen. It didn't extend to her heart.

Rolf let his gaze travel downward. She appeared slender, even though her figure was hidden under a loose caftan. He supposed he could get aroused by touching her body. With cool calculation, Rolf thrust aside any distaste he might have at the role and thought about how he might benefit. If he pleased her, she might reward him with useful information.

Ilyssa noticed that Sean had stopped paying attention to her recital of his duties and instead was looking her over as though she were a piece of cattle. Ungrateful wretch! Was he figuring a way to take advantage of her? He should be happy she got him away from the mines, from the torturer. She hoped he wasn't going to cause trouble.

"Let's go into the parlor," she said, gesturing somewhat brusquely. "It's more comfortable in there."

They passed through her dressing area and she stopped to point out the items in her wardrobe that needed repairs. Ilyssa was aware of the odd look Sean gave her. Her clothes were drab, and her dressing table lacked the usual female collection of cosmetics and perfumes. He was probably wondering why she didn't make herself more attractive. *Maybe that's why he's been examining me so clinically. He's been trying to assess my worth as a woman. Well, I don't need fancy clothes to be feminine.* Besides, why in Zor should she care what he thought about her?

"In here"—she abruptly strode next door—"is the parlor which will be your sleeping chamber."

They entered a spacious, bright room furnished with a lounger, a chest of drawers, a small round table, and several chairs. It had a single casement high up on the outside wall and very few embellishments.

With a shock of surprise, Rolf felt the slave collar loosen around his neck.

"You may remove the collar. I have released it," Ilyssa told him.

Slowly, Rolf took off the band and threw it on the floor. He stood watching her, waiting.

"Please take a seat," she said, pointing to the lounger.

When he'd complied, Ilyssa sat on an upholstered chair facing him. She sank back onto the cushions as though the weight of the world were pressing upon her.

"Now we can talk," she said wearily. "Who are you?"

Rolf's expression clouded. "I'm Sean Breslow, a trader from Arcturus. You know that already." He sat on the edge of his seat, coiled with tension.

"Come on, you can tell me the truth." She gave him an encouraging smile.

"I am telling the truth."

"Are you?" She studied him. His black hair fell straight to his shoulders in a blunt cut as though he'd been in a hurry and shorn it himself. She didn't care for the style herself. Somehow it didn't suit him. "If you're really here to arrange a deal regarding rubellis gemstones, who were you going to meet?"

"That information is confidential." Rolf's eyes narrowed with suspicion as he shifted uncomfortably on the lounger. Was this why she'd brought him here, for an interrogation? And if he gave the wrong answers, what then? Was she under orders from Ruel to seduce him into cooperation, or would she give him back to Pten, the torturer? He compressed his lips, waiting.

Ilyssa contemplated her next move. Obviously the man wasn't going to talk so easily. Either he was a trader who honored his confidentiality to his clients, or he was lying. From the wary look on his face, she'd bet it was the latter. Telling him her story might loosen his tongue.

Leaning forward, she looked him in the eye. "I don't know whether or not you're being honest with me," she stated, "but there's something I want you to know. I'm a prisoner on Souk just like you.

"My name is Ilyssa Barr and I'm from Circutia. My family and I were on a voyage to the planet Athos when we were captured by the Souks. I was twelve annums old at the time, my brother Devin nine. Ruel discovered that I possessed the gift of siren song and demanded a test. He ordered me to sing in front of my father. If I refused, he threatened to hurt my mother and younger brother Devin." Her anguished eyes bored into Rolf's. "Have you heard of siren song?"

He gave a curt nod. As a child growing up on Nadira, he'd become familiar with the folktales and fables that transcended planetary boundaries. "It's a myth about women who beguile men with their song. Supposedly siren song originated on the planet Athos, although the trait isn't restricted to that world. Rumors have abounded about females demonstrating the talent but as far as I know, neither Athos nor the siren song exists. You say you were on your way to Athos. Do you know the exact location of the planet?"

Ilyssa shook her head. "We had the general coordinates. No one has ever been able to verify its location. I'm sure we would have found it." She leaned forward, clasping her hands on her lap. "Let me finish my story. Ruel promised to give my parents jobs in the palace and their own separate apartment if I cooperated. So I sang, and my father fell under the spell. Now he follows every command from Ruel as though it were the word of God. I assure you that siren song is very real."

She gave a long sigh, and Rolf didn't interrupt. He was too fascinated by her tale even though he didn't believe a word of it. No doubt Ilyssa was telling him this sob story to gain his sympathy; then she'd question him about his own background. Well, he was too smart to fall for her clever ruse. Siren song was mythological bunk and so was the existence of the planet Athos. If she thought he'd fall for a story like this, she was badly mistaken.

"I was given my own bedchamber with a Souk caretaker to attend me," she continued. "She was a female named Henna who acted like a prison warden. Devin was allowed to remain with our parents. I felt so isolated. It was agony to be separated from my family!"

Tears filled her eyes as she thought of how much she still yearned for the comfort of her mother's presence. Being deprived of Moireen's company had left an ever-present emptiness inside her.

After a moment of struggling to regain her composure, she went on. "My parents were able to live in relative comfort as long as I cooperated with Ruel. He let me visit them once a week, and our partings were always sorrowful. Ruel constantly warned me that my family's fate depended upon my compliance with his demands. He turned me into his secret weapon, using my voice against his enemies so they became his mindless slaves."

"Why couldn't you use your siren song on Ruel?" Rolf asked, trying to knock holes in her story.

"Both Ruel and Bolt are immune. They've programmed their implanted translators to selectively block changes in pitch of the human female voice."

"Didn't you ever try to escape?"

Ilyssa swallowed a sudden lump in her throat. "Only once. I thought I'd found someone who could help me. Not all the Souks condone slavery, and one of Ruel's ministers was very sympathetic toward me. I was going to ask him for help. But as I pleaded my case one afternoon, he grasped me in his arms and said he was entranced by my beauty. He'd help me escape from Ruel . . . only if I entered his harem.

"Ruel found us locked in an embrace. I was struggling to free myself but Ruel couldn't see beyond his rage. He executed the minister on the spot. As my punishment, because he couldn't physically harm me, he ordered me to watch my brother Devin's torture." She choked on her last words. "I've never seen him since," she whispered. Guilt and shame overwhelmed her. She shouldn't have been so naive!

"So how did you end up here?" Rolf asked, affected by her words even though he suspected they were lies.

"Ruel thought I was too vulnerable to remain in Haakat. It is said that if a siren loses her virginity, she'll lose her singing voice. Ruel doesn't want to take the chance of this happening, so he sent me here to get me away from temptation."

"You seem to relish the role of Dromo," he accused her.

"I hate it! Bolt gives the orders and makes it appear as though I'm cruel and heartless. That way, no one will listen to me with a sympathetic ear . . . and my mistake will not be repeated. It's part of Ruel's punishment."

"Why are you telling me this?"

"I have to get my parents away from Ruel!" she cried, desperation in her eyes. "My father wasn't well the last time I saw him. I fear for his health. But I cannot do it alone. I need your help."

"Why me?"

"You're a pilot. We'll need transportation to get off Souk. You'll escape with us."

Rolf pretended to consider her offer while admiring her talent. No wonder Ilyssa was put in charge of his interrogation. With her sad eyes and tale of woe, she was a consummate actress. "How do we proceed?"

Her eyes fired with hope. "You must have connections on Souk. We'll escape the mining camp and—"

"Wait a minute. What do you mean, I must have connections on Souk?"

"You're here on some sort of mission, aren't you?" she said, meaning a trade mission.

His eyes iced over. "Perhaps you should prove the truth of what you say."

At first Ilyssa didn't comprehend. But when she saw the look of disbelief on his face, her jaw dropped. "You think I've been lying?"

"Offer me proof that your story is true."

"How?" She spread her hands. "I've just put myself at great risk by telling you all this. If Ruel knew, he'd kill us both instantly."

"Sing to me. I'll see for myself what happens."

"I can't. You'd be mindwashed, and if you're to help me, you need to be able to think independently."

"Then sing to those Horthas outside your door."

"They're immune to the song."

"Ha!"

Ilyssa couldn't believe her ears. She'd just spilled out her life story, and the man dared to doubt her! She leapt up, anger blazing inside her. "How dare you question the truth of what I say? You're supposed to be the one giving me answers!"

"So you did bring me here to interrogate me." He stood, towering over her, challenging her with his steady glare. "I've told you all I can."

Liar, she wanted to say. If he was a trader, why didn't he jump at the chance for freedom? "Is it wealth you want? I can offer you whatever riches you desire."

"Ruel has let you keep credits?" Her story was getting more and more incredible by the minute.

"No, but he's given me jewels I can sell. If that's not enough, when I return to my home planet, Circutia, I can pay you a bonus. My family is quite wealthy."

Rolf didn't hear past the part where Ruel had given her jewels. The woman was no helpless prisoner. She must be one of the pasha's favorites for him to reward her so generously. Making her Dromo had to be a promotion, not a punishment. As far as being a secret weapon was concerned, she damn well was a convincing liar. A less gullible man might actually believe her tale. What if he accepted her story? He'd escape with her and lead her to his friends. Then Bolt would show up and capture them all. It was a clever ploy.

Ilyssa saw the shifting emotions on his face and cursed him for not believing her. Damn the man, couldn't he see she was telling the truth? What would it take to convince him? Annoyed and frustrated, she stalked to the fabricator to get a warm beverage to calm her nerves.

"What are you doing?" he said, coming up behind her. "I thought I was supposed to wait on you."

"I detailed your duties for the benefit of the guards listening outside our door. When we're alone, we can be ourselves. You're not my server any more than I'm yours." She procured her drink and whirled around, facing him. Her breath caught in her throat at his nearness.

"Indeed." Rolf looked down into her startled gaze and his lips curled. Her answering blush almost erased his doubts. She wouldn't be reacting this way unless she was as inexperienced as she let on, would she? Yet how could he believe such an extraordinary tale?

"W-would you like something to eat?" she stuttered, feeling at a disadvantage. Her back was pressed to the wall. She'd have to slip around him to get away.

His stomach grumbled at the thought of food. "Now that you mention it, I am ravenous."

"It must be hauras since you've had a meal. You do know how to use a fabricator, don't you?"

"Of course." They were common on Bimordus Two, the Coalition capital city where he lived and worked. The device worked on the principles of molecular alteration, and it was quite efficient for obtaining whatever items one required. Standardized codes were built in by the manufacturer so that you could use the same directory no matter which world you were on, and the choices were as diverse as the Coalition constituency. The Souks didn't belong to the Coalition but they kept up with the technology.

Rolf stepped aside to allow Ilyssa to pass; then he approached the keypad beside the alcove on the wall and poked in the 001 prefix for a food order. A plate of spicy Therian noodles materialized on the grid. He took his plate and approached the table where Ilyssa was already seated.

"Is there something else I can get for you before I sit down?" he asked, deciding to be polite and attentive. After all, she'd saved him from the mines. It was the least he could do for her in return.

Ilyssa raised her eyebrow at his gentlemanly tone. "The smell of those spices is making me hungry. If you wouldn't mind, I'd like the same dish." She hadn't realized she'd skipped a meal, but she'd been engrossed in relating her story. Sean probably needed some time to think over her proposal. She'd let him sleep on it and then bring up the subject again tomorrow.

As they ate, Rolf was charmed by her hesitant smiles and graceful manner. She made small talk as though attempting to put him at ease, mostly on the subjects of music and art. Rolf was well versed in those topics and responded appropriately. While Ilyssa spoke, he noted how her golden-tinged green eyes radiated warmth without any trace of coyness. The sense of innocence that enveloped her was infinitely more appealing than the more practiced airs of the women he was used to meeting.

"Shall I prepare your bedchamber?" Rolf asked after they'd finished eating and cleared the table. If she was being truthful, he didn't need to act as her sumi, but the idea of getting her ready for bed was too stimulating to pass up.

"I told you that you don't need to wait on me," Ilyssa stated, but his words unsettled her. What would it be like to have him moving about her chamber while she readied for the night? It was a titillating thought, one she'd better put aside very quickly. His cultivated manner was disarming, and their conversation had only increased her conviction that Sean Breslow was someone more important than a trader. Yet she needed him because he was a pilot, and she'd better remember that fact. It was too dangerous for her to think of him in any other fashion.

"We'll talk more tomorrow, Sean. Please consider my request. Good night."

Rolf watched her leave, his mouth open in surprise. He certainly hadn't expected her to depart so abruptly. An odd feeling of disappointment washed over him.

Combing his fingers through his hair, he analyzed the sensation. He hadn't experienced genuine interest in a woman since Gayla who'd died over ten annums ago. It could be that Ilyssa reminded him of his lost love. Physically, they were similar in height and stature and both had oval-shaped faces. Gayla's eyes had been amber, her hair a glossy chestnut brown. Ilyssa's mane was a vibrant dark red that excited him. He liked the way her green eyes glowed when she described her precious music. Gayla had exhibited a similar enthusiasm for her favorite subject, writing poetry. At his home on Bimordus Two, Rolf kept an album with her love poems inside. He'd lost count of the numerous times he'd thumbed through those special pages, missing Gayla's sweet voice reading them aloud.

Not even Sarina, the legendary Great Healer, had captured his attention in the same fashion. That wasn't surprising when he'd merely been doing his duty by offering to wed Sarina to fulfill an ancient prophesy. Although he'd become fond of her during their betrothal, his feelings had never grown beyond a warm affection. When she married Teir Reylock, they'd settled for maintaining a close friendship. So why did Ilyssa stimulate his interest? Unable to answer satisfactorily, Rolf assumed it must be due to her vague resemblance to Gayla.

Gayla was the reason why he'd come to Souk. When he was 19, they'd fallen in love on his home planet, Nadira. Gayla was not yet of age, so they faced a lengthy betrothal period. Too impatient to wait, Rolf had insisted on an elopement. With the help of his friend Artemus, he obtained a spacecraft, and he and Gayla set off for a star system where they could be joined in peace. Since he was Lord Rolf Cam'brii, second son to the Imperator of Nadira, his actions were bound to have repercussions, but they weren't what he and Gayla had expected.

Their ship was intercepted by Souk pirates. In the ensuing battle, Rolf escaped but Gayla was killed. Overwhelmed with grief, he returned Gayla's body to her parents on Nadira. As was the custom, he submitted himself for their punishment. Realizing the Souks had caused their daughter's death, they made Rolf vow to dedicate his life to ending the slave trade. He entered the diplomat corps and made it his life's work. As a member of the High Council, he'd sponsored the First Amendment to the Articles of Coalition. The amendment passed, permanently banning the slave trade within Coalition boundaries. Before the vote, assassins were sent to try to stop him. He'd traced them to Souk but didn't know who'd given the order. After the amendment passed, another attack occurred. Someone on Souk wanted him dead, but Rolf didn't know who or why. Hopefully he'd learn the answers while here.

Sitting on the edge of his lounger, Rolf reviewed how this mission had gotten started. A message had been smuggled off Souk asking the High Council for help. It came from a resistance leader who'd met Sarina and Teir when they were prisoners of Cerrus Bdan. The liberation movement was asking for assistance in obtaining arms and opening a link of communication to the Coalition government.

Rolf had volunteered to come at once. He had his own agenda to accomplish in terms of avenging Gayla's death.

He hoped to find the Souk officer responsible for the attack that had killed her.

The resistance leader informed Rolf that a conference of the Souk Alliance was scheduled to take place on Lexin thirty-fourth. All forty pashas would be present to discuss Souk's economic crisis brought about by the Coalition's trade embargo. The Souks had a paid informant in the Coalition government, a high official who kept them alerted to Rolf's movements. The rebel contact said the mole would be present at the conference. As previously arranged, Rolf had planned to establish his link with the resistance, travel with his friends to the conference site in his guise as a trader, and then switch identities to become a server to Pasha Hyrn, a rebel sympathizer. In that role, Rolf could observe the conference proceedings without playing an active part. He realized the informant had to be someone close to him in government circles and assumed he'd be able to recognize the traitor on sight. Once he knew who it was, he'd inform Glotaj, the Supreme Regent.

Shifting his attention, Rolf surveyed the room, and his eye caught on the chronometer by the lounger. The date read as the first day of the month Lexin. He stared at it, aghast. Gods, had that much time passed already? How was he going to make the conference? Only 33 days remained!

Sweat beaded his brow as a sense of urgency overwhelmed him. He had to break out of this place. There'd barely be enough time for him to meet his contact and confirm the arrangements. Yet what could he do? Horthas guarded the residence. Souk troops patrolled outside. Unless he accepted Ilyssa's offer, he was trapped!

With a howl of frustration, Rolf snatched a pillow off the lounger and threw it across the room.

Chapter Four

"We're under attack!" Rolf screamed.

The girl seated beside him in the cockpit of the small spacecraft gasped in horror. "What'll we do?"

His fingers flew over the control console. "Initiating evasive maneuvers." But as the computer adjusted the ship's altitude, he gazed in horror out the viewscreen. "There's too many of them! They're coming after us. We've got two on our tail."

"We'll never escape!"

He turned to the lovely dark-haired, golden-eyed beauty beside him. At the age of 17, Gayla was in her full blossom of womanhood. Rolf hated to think what the Souks would do to her.

"I won't surrender," he promised, his eyes full of anguish.

She reached out and grasped his hand. "I'd rather die first."

Another volley of laser fire hit their ship. A flash bright-

ened the cockpit and the circuit panel exploded from behind.

"Fire!" Rolf yelled, seeing the flames licking forth. Unsnapping his safety harness, he jumped out of his seat and stumbled for the extinguisher on the wall.

"Get over to the turret," he ordered. "Use the laser cannon to hold them off while I put out the fire. We've still got fifty percent of our shields."

As Gayla followed his instructions, he popped the safety seal on the extinguisher can and aimed the nozzle at the growing flames. But his hands were shaking badly, and foam sprayed everywhere. Gayla ducked out of the way and climbed up a small ladder to the turret atop the ship.

"I don't know how to engage this thing!" she cried, her voice muffled.

Cursing, he rattled off instructions just as he got the last of the flames under control. Rolf knew she understood when he felt the shuddering vibrations of the cannon.

It was answered by a fierce volley from the Souk attack ships. Stumbling back to the pilot's chair, Rolf glanced at the readouts on his command console. "By the corona, our shields are down. Watch out, here comes an incoming missile." He put the extinguisher on the floor and braced himself. Another bright flash, this one exploding directly overhead. Black smoke poured into the cockpit. "No, they've nit us again!"

When Gayla didn't respond, Rolf called her name. "Gayla?" He couldn't see the turret. The gangway was obscured by smoke. "Gayla!" Coughing and choking, he stumbled blindly toward the direction of the ladder. When his outstretched hand felt the rungs, he pulled himself upward. "Gods, no!"

Gayla was slumped in her seat, her head forward. The remains of the laser cannon smoldered in front of her.

"Gayla, my love!" He pulled her bleeding body out of

the chair and slung her over his shoulder to carry her down into the cockpit. Carefully, he lowered her to the floor, ignoring the screaming shudders of the ship as the computer continued to carry out its programmed escape maneuvers.

Gayla's eyelids fluttered open. Her golden eyes had dulled to a limpid shade of sand. From the corner of her mouth, blood trickled. "Rolf," she murmured. "Rolf . . ."

Rolf's eyes snapped open as he thought he heard his name called. Where was he? His glance took in the comfortable furnishings, the casement high up on the wall, the chair where he had draped his clothes the night before. His skin was damp with sweat, and his heart raced as though he'd been involved in a fight to the death. As awareness flooded him, Rolf tried to hold on to the image of Gayla, but she was already gone. With an anguished feeling of loss, he sat up. Over ten annums had passed since her death, but he still had nightmares about the battle that killed her. The only way to find peace would be to get revenge.

"Sean!" Ilyssa called from the other side of the closed adjoining door.

From the faint light streaming in at the casement, he figured it must be dawn. He glanced at the chronometer on the table beside the lounger, wondering what Ilyssa could want at this early haura. Surprised, Rolf noted it was seven-thirty. He must have been exhausted to have slept this late!

His muscles ached as he stretched, stifling a groan. Although he had stayed fit through workouts in the physiolab back on Bimordus Two, nothing had prepared him for attacking solid rock walls with his bare hands as a krecker. For whatever Ilyssa's story was worth, at least she had relieved him of that torment!

"What is it?" he asked her.

"I just wanted to know if you were up. It's getting

late," Ilyssa chided him. "I'll be in for breakfast in a few minutes."

"All right." Rolf stood, grabbed his underwear, and pulled it on. Stumbling into his private sanitary, he glared at his image in the reflector. Gods, he looked a wreck. Dark shadows sunk under his eyes, and his hair was askew. A fuzzy growth of stubble covered his jaw. After washing, he ordered a shaver from the fabricator in his room. The first order of the day was to get rid of his beard.

Finished with that chore, Rolf combed his fingers through his hair and stared at himself with disquiet. He wasn't used to seeing himself this way. When Glotaj, the Supreme Regent, had given his approval for Rolf to go on this mission, he'd suggested Rolf surgically alter his face as a matter of precaution. Otherwise, because of his status, he'd be easily recognizable to the pashas at the conference and the Souk spy who would be attending. Just a slight change in the angles of his cheekbones and nose had proved effective. He'd taken a hair growth accelerator and a follicular color changer as well. Instead of his usual short curly blond style, he wore his dyed ebony hair straight to the shoulders in a blunt cut. The dark eyebrows and bodily hair were more difficult to get used to. Rolf would be glad when he could reverse the process and get back to normal.

Striding over to the chair in his room, he fingered the tunic and leggings he'd been given to wear the day before. These dull clothes didn't suit his taste at all, yet he had to dress appropriately for his current position. Passing through the corridors the day before, he'd noticed household servers wearing different styles of clothing. It should be acceptable if he chose something else as long as it was conservative.

Throwing the black garments in the disposer, Rolf obtained a tan leather jerkin and leggings from the fabricator. He'd just finished putting them on when a bold knock sounded on the adjoining door.

"Sean? May I come in?"

Rolf smiled, liking the musical lilt of her voice. "Yes, you may enter."

Ilyssa cruised inside, looking bright and fresh in a sleeveless teal jumpsuit. Her auburn hair was tightly braided and she wore no makeup, but her features were lovely enough without embellishment. Rolf found himself staring at her.

"How do you feel this morning?" she asked politely, heading for the fabricator.

"A little stiff, but I'll be all right. May I help you get your breakfast?"

"No, thanks, I'll manage."

He held out a chair for her at the table. As she sat, her arm brushed against his chest. The unintentional contact sent a charge of electricity through him. He hastened away to get his own meal.

Ilyssa watched him as he strode to the fabricator. She still felt the imprint of his solid chest on her arm, and the lingering warmth discomfited her. She couldn't afford to get close to any man, let alone this one whose looks were too handsome by far. Her own personal ambitions forbade it, as did Ruel's safeguard.

Yet there was no denying the effect he had on her when they were together. The man emitted a powerful presence. It couldn't hurt to admire him from a distance as long as he didn't notice. Moistening her lips, she let her gaze wander leisurely from the top of his head down to his booted toes, then back up again. His broad back stretched the fabric of the leather jerkin taut. A wide belt cinched the jerkin at his waist. Her gaze lowered, lingering where his leggings hugged his hips.

She averted her eyes as Sean approached with a bowl of cereal and a glass of fruit juice. He settled across from her, and they ate in awkward silence.

Finally Ilyssa spoke. "We'll be going to Computer Central this morning," she said in an informative tone. "No one will think it unusual that I bring along a personal server. Most Souks in high positions have one."

"I see." Rolf sipped his juice, wondering where the conversation was leading.

"Ruel assigned me to audit the production figures because he doesn't trust Bolt. I have to go to Haakat periodically to report to him, but I'm hoping to escape before being summoned again. Have you thought any more about my offer, Sean?"

"I'm considering it. How do you intend to implement your escape plan?" he asked, hoping to glean more detailed information.

"Tell me the truth about why you're here and I'll explain," Ilyssa countered.

"I have told you the truth." He looked away, not wanting her to see the lie in his eyes.

"I know you're not a trader. You're just confirming what I've felt all along."

"What are you talking about?"

"Your hair is wrong. The style doesn't suit you," she said. "Then there's the way you carry yourself. Your bearing is much too dignified for a mere trader. Your voice and mannerisms are cultured. You're even knowledgeable about the arts. If I had to guess, I'd say you'd be more at home in the palace at Haakat than in the bazaars of Souk."

"So? I'm an educated trader," he replied, keeping his expression impassive. She didn't need to know that she'd hit right on the mark.

"Sure, Sean." Ilyssa gave a long sigh. He wasn't making this easy. "I'll tell you what. This morning when we're at Computer Central, I'll tap into the main data link at Haakat. If you're really here to strike a deal regarding rubellis gemstones, there must be someone you were going to meet. You can contact your business associate and let him know you've been detained. Maybe he could work toward your release. Would that be helpful?"

Rolf responded by covering her hand with his. She was trying so damn hard to appease him. Why? Because he was a pilot and she needed him to fly her and her family off this lousy planet? Or because she wanted him to reveal the names of his contacts on Souk?

Ilyssa jerked her hand away as though his touch burned her. "Sean, I don't—"

He never found out what she was going to say because just then a loud chime sounded.

"Computer, open channel," Ilyssa called, absently rubbing her hand where he had touched it.

Bolt's voice thundered into the room. "Ilyssa, come to my quarters."

"Yes, Bolt," she dutifully replied, waiting until the comm link terminated before she rose.

Rolf stood and faced her, feeling anxious.

"I have to give a report on you," Ilyssa told him. "Bolt suspects you're a saboteur or a spy for a rival pasha. I'll tell him you're working out just fine as an obedient sumi, but you must be cautious where he's concerned."

Rolf watched her leave, his frustration mounting. Her words reminded him that he shouldn't trust her with any confidences. Even if she was telling him the truth, Bolt would have ways to get her to talk.

The morning was warm and bright when they started out for the production center. Sean strode behind her, his head bowed in an appropriately subservient attitude. Beside them marched a contingent of Souk bodyguards. Bolt had already left for the pens. A new cache of prisoners had arrived, courtesy of a raid on the *Luniss*, a civilian passenger liner carrying vacationing Coalition citizens to Pot's World. Ilyssa had been sick when Bolt told her about it in his quarters. Selection Day was tomorrow, and she dreaded her role in the process.

She'd reported on Sean, saying he was compliant and his work so far was satisfactory. Bolt had mumbled his dissatisfaction with the arrangement.

"No harm is coming from it, Bolt," she'd reassured him. But she hadn't liked the evil grin that lurked on his face when she left.

The sol was already high in the sky even though it was early morning, and a thin sheen of perspiration glistened on her skin despite the sleeveless jumpsuit she wore. They reached the squat rectangular structure that housed the production center. Ilyssa was grateful for the blast of cold air that hit her face when she entered the air-conditioned building.

Behind her, Rolf watched the sway of her hips. She moved with the grace of a dancer, and it was difficult to keep his head bowed when he wanted to observe her more closely. But he was aware of the Souks surrounding them and of their watchful stance as far as the Dromo's security was concerned.

His eyes widened when they entered Computer Central. Mounted on the walls around the huge room were giant maps, the deep blue of the Cobalt Wash separating the continents. Scattered about the land areas were glittering pinpoints of light, Ruel's industrial empire, Ilyssa proudly informed him. The guards left to take up their posts outside. Ilyssa strode to her station, nodding to the Souk controllers sitting at rows of computer consoles along the way. They acknowledged her greeting, casting brief glances in Rolf's direction. He felt uncomfortable surrounded by so many dogfaces, but Ilyssa seemed unfazed. Of course, they believed her to be their superior.

Ilyssa remembered her promise to tap into the main data link at Haakat to contact Sean's business associate, but first she wanted to make a few inquiries on her own. She didn't need Sean standing at her back while she did so.

"Sean, why don't you take a look at the maps on the walls and acquaint yourself with Ruel's territory? Our master is rich and powerful. It will benefit your position to understand just how vast his empire is." She said it loudly and in such a way that those listening would approve the suggestion.

As Ilyssa sat at her console, Rolf wandered about the room. He was stunned at the magnitude of Ruel's operations. Souk's geographical contours were familiar, since he'd already committed them to memory as part of his mission briefing, and it helped that he could read the written Souk language.

One map that held his interest detailed the mining camp, the track that the ore cars followed, and the surrounding districts. He stood before it for a long time, memorizing the topography. Assuming he could make his escape alone, how would he reach his rendezvous point?

The Rocks of Weir were located in the southern hemisphere. To the north rose the Koodrash Mounts. He had to cross the mountains to arrive at his intended destination. Having missed his initial connection at the Copper Dunes in the Nurash Desert, he'd have to establish communication with an emergency contact in a small fishing village by the Salts of Dorado. But what would be the best method of transport to get from here to there? He needed a route wherein his movements wouldn't be easily traced.

Ilyssa signaled to him and he hastened to her side. "Do you want to contact your business partner?" She asked. "I've got a line open to Haakat."

When he looked at her blankly, Ilyssa reminded him in

a clear tone, "You did say you were here to buy rubellis gemstones, didn't you?"

"Oh, yes, of course," he said, recovering quickly. "I don't think this is the best time to reach him."

She gave him a suspicious glance. Her quick check of the trade manifests at Data Central hadn't shown anyone from Arcturus by the name of Sean Breslow listed. Now she was more certain than ever that he wasn't a trader, and she had to assume that Bolt had done a background check as well. But if he probed deeper into Sean's history and turned up anything important, Bolt might blackmail her in return for his silence!

Restless, she shut down her unit and got up to stretch. Deciding she wanted a drink, she strolled toward the water dispenser, beckoning for Sean to follow.

"This place is fascinating," he commented, getting her a drink and handing it over.

"Are you familiar with Souk history, Sean?" She had no idea if he'd ever been to the planet before.

"Somewhat. The Souk worlds, located in the Capellan star system, are rich in minerals, but the valuable ores are difficult to mine due to adverse environmental conditions. The Souks have always depended upon slave labor as a work force. Their pirate raids have caused unaccountable grief and tragedy in terms of lost lives and captives."

She heard the bitterness in his tone and motioned to him. "Let's go to the fabricator. I'd like a snack, and it's more private in that corner. We can talk about this further." Video recorders were trained on all the stations, and guards were posted outside the doors, but no one would be able to overhear them in that location.

Ilyssa ordered a refreshment. As her sumi, Rolf wasn't allowed to join her. His stomach growled as he watched her suck on a lypis ice.

"I've learned a lot about Souk politics since I've been

here," she began. Ruel had educated her, allowing her access to news media and videos so she could converse intelligently with his ministers. Until she'd come to the Rocks of Weir, she'd been well informed.

"You've learned what the Souks taught you. Is it the truth?" Rolf asked. Leaning against a wall, he folded his arms. It could be useful to sound out her political views. "Allow me to review Coalition history for you. One hundred fifty annums ago, Arcturians and Vilarans made first contact. Shortly thereafter, relations were established with four other worlds. Sixty annums passed before these six founding members adopted the Articles of Coalition at a conference held on Bimordus Two. At that time, the Souk Alliance offered to join if they were paid a bonus of twenty billion credits. They claimed their valuable mineral resources were worth an incentive payment. Their request was denied."

"I know all that," Ilyssa said. "I also know the Coalition expanded to include more than five hundred members. A Defense League was formed to provide security. Then the ruling High Council, a twelve-member forum with a Supreme Regent at its apex, voted to impose an economic embargo against Souk companies, ports, and shipping interests that participated in the slave trade.

"Boycotting Souk ports was a controversial move that bankrupted a number of companies dependent on Souk trade. The Arcturians supported trade with the Souks because of a scarcity of minerals on their world, and they began a protest movement against Coalition policy. Nevertheless, Lord Cam'brii, a prominent member of the High Council, proposed a First Amendment to the Articles of Coalition to permanently ban the slave trade within Coalition territory. The amendment passed late last annum. After this date, no vessel operating within Coalition boundaries was allowed to carry slaves. Stiff criminal penalties for transgressors were established. The Souks were furious. They felt their livelihood was threatened. If you think about it from their viewpoint, Sean, it was unfair of the Coalition to rule over something that really is a Souk internal matter."

"Who told you that? Ruel?" he scoffed. "Is that why we're both sumi here? Blast it woman, you can't believe that slavery is acceptable?"

"I don't believe slavery is acceptable under any circumstances," Ilyssa countered. "But I don't see any quick solution to the issue on Souk. An underground resistance movement has formed, and if it becomes active, civil war could result. I hate to think violence is the only alternative."

"The Souks practice violence every day when they enslave innocent victims," Rolf said coldly.

"Yes, that's true, but I still feel fighting can be avoided." Throwing her empty container in a disposer, she signaled for him to follow her back to the workstation. "We can continue this discussion later," she hissed along the way. At her console, she pointed to a chair.

Rolf sat, periodically getting up at her command to perform a service. A chime signaled the break for afternoon nourishment, after which he resumed his post. As the afternoon passed, his muscles tensed from inactivity and he yearned for some real physical exercise. This is better than the mines, he reminded himself.

Restless, Rolf used the time to study Ilyssa's profile. Tiny tendrils of hair fanned her delicate face. Long silken eyelashes swept like half-moons to shade her eyes, and below, her nose jutted perfectly straight. Her lips curved up at the corners, tempting him to wonder how she tasted. Her mouth would be soft and pliant under his. For a moment, he fantasized what it would be like to kiss her.

Guilty thoughts of duty intruded and he blinked, remembering his mission. He couldn't allow himself to be sidetracked when he still had so many tasks to accomplish. His first allegiance was to Gayla's parents and the Coalition.

Straightening in his chair, he stretched his legs and tried to focus his mind on a plan of escape, but his gaze kept wandering in Ilyssa's direction.

Aware of his steady gaze, it was impossible for Ilyssa to get any work done with such a handsome hulk peering at her all afternoon. Having hardly accomplished anything, she turned off her unit, whirled in her chair, and looked into his sharp blue eyes.

"Why don't you return to the residence now? I'll be along shortly."

"Where are you going?" Rolf jumped up as she rose.

"Somewhere private. I need to be alone." She couldn't think straight with him so close. She'd go to the Waterdrop Cave and practice her singing.

Curious, Rolf watched her walk away once they were outside. A contingent of guards surrounded him to escort him back to the residence, while another group accompanied Ilyssa. Rolf wondered where she was heading. Could she be going to report to Bolt? He hadn't said anything revealing during their conversation earlier, had he?

As he marched along the path to the residence, Rolf reviewed his words and concluded he'd better be more careful. It bothered him that Ilyssa had mentioned the resistance. That she knew of it at all disturbed him, because she could only have heard about the underground movement from Bolt or Ruel. How much did they know?

Rolf plowed his fingers through his dyed black hair, wishing he didn't feel so alone. His goals seemed overwhelming for one man. How could he establish contact with the resistance, attend the conference to expose the Souk informant, and discover who was trying to assassinate him? It was too much! And on top of it all, he had to learn who was responsible for attacking his ship and killing Gayla.

An ally would help him move faster. His decision was easy; he didn't see any viable alternative.

He'd accept Ilyssa's offer of escape.

Chapter Five

Ilyssa entered the suite, her shoulders slumped. Tiredly she pushed back the loose strands from her braid. Somehow the day had been more fatiguing than usual. Or maybe it was that tomorrow was Selection Day and she dreaded having to go with Bolt to pronounce the fate of the pitiful captives. She'd had to pass the pens on the way to her residence and could still hear the prisoners' wails in her mind.

She went directly into the parlor, curious as to what Sean had been doing in her absence. Apparently he'd showered and changed because he wore a loose blue shirt tucked into a pair of tight navy pants. He stood before the reflector combing his hair. It was still damp; moist tendrils clung to his forehead. A few drops of water glistened on his freshly shaven jaw.

"I see you've been making yourself comfortable," she remarked, her pulse quickening at the sight of him. Casually, she strolled into the room.

Sean glanced at her and put his hairbrush down. "You look tired. May I get you a cold drink?"

"Yes, please." Touched by his thoughtfulness, she smiled.

He grinned back, showing a disarming flash of white teeth in his handsome face. Ilyssa thought how easily she could get used to having him around. Quickly, she dismissed the idea as too dangerous even to contemplate.

Sinking onto the lounger, she watched him get her beverage. As he handed her the tumbler, their fingers brushed momentarily. Ilyssa drew in a sharp breath and hoped he didn't notice. "What is it?" she asked, disconcerted when he remained standing in front of her.

He cleared his throat. "I have a favor to ask you. When I was confined to the pens, I met a man named Seth who was very kind to me, and I'd like to do something in return for his kindness. His daughter was taken by Bolt. Is there anything you can do to get her away from him?"

"You mean she was selected for Bolt's harem?" At his nod, Ilyssa lowered her eyes. "I have little contact with Bolt's females, although I am permitted free access to the harem facilities. I've spent time there weaving silk patimas. But as to Bolt's pleasures, it is overstepping my boundaries to protest." She shuddered, knowing Bolt had always wanted her to be a part of his harem. Like Ruel, he shared the perversion of taking humanoid females to satisfy his lust, although a Souk female was still his favored gima.

"Can't you do anything to get the girl reassigned?"

"I can find out how she is faring, that is all." Ilyssa could learn if the girl was still alive. Some of the frailer human females didn't survive Bolt's assault. It was horrifying but there was nothing she could do. "What is her name?"

"I don't know. She has long blond hair and appears to be quite young." He paused. "How old are you, if I may ask?"

Ilyssa smiled. "I'm twenty. And you?"

"Thirty."

No wonder he had such a worldly air. He was a full ten annums older than herself.

Sean gave her a brilliant smile. "I'd appreciate your efforts," he said.

Ilyssa rose and went to the comm unit. "Let me see if Bolt's in now. I can take care of it right away." But no one answered her signal. "I'll go to him later," she said, throwing her empty tumbler in the disposer. "In the meantime, I'd like a bath and then something to eat."

"Do you need help with your bath?" he offered, raising an eyebrow.

Ilyssa recognized the look in his eye. "Thank you, but I can manage," she replied stiffly.

Rushing to the privacy of her chamber, she let out a long breath. The man always seemed to set her nerves on edge. How on Souk was she ever going to survive being alone with him if they escaped? It was her own reactions she feared, not his. Ruel had been wise to banish her to this remote place, far from the path of temptation. But she was beginning to think nature had a way of evening things out.

It took a long soak in the hot jet tub before she felt in control again. After choosing a loose-fitting beige caftan to wear, she picked up a hairbrush and ran it quickly through her wavy auburn hair. Two barrettes held it back from her face. Satisfied with her image in the reflector, she turned toward the parlor. She couldn't wait to be with Sean again despite her earlier doubts.

He was standing by the fabricator sipping a cold drink, and Ilyssa's nervous system went into hyperdrive at the sight of him. She just couldn't help her response. His aristocratic bearing and brooding good looks set off a yearning inside her that was difficult to resist.

"Have you dined yet?" Ilyssa asked. He wasn't under any obligation to wait for her.

"No, I'll join you." He offered to get her food order and then helped her into a chair. She appreciated his courteous formality. It was almost as though the man wished to keep a proper distance between them and that suited her just fine.

"Have you thought any more about my offer?" she persisted while he was at the fabricator.

"Yes, but I'd rather wait to discuss it until you talk to Bolt about the girl. Do you mind?" He approached the table, tray in hand.

Ilyssa understood he felt obligated to help a fellow sumi. Besides, he sounded like he was going to agree to her plan. "Not at all," she said, suppressing her excitement.

Having served her meal, Rolf returned to get his own. Holding his tray, he took a seat across from Ilyssa and ate while studying her covertly. She looked lovely in the loose gown, her wavy hair cascading over her slim shoulders. He was very well aware of her desirability as a woman and from her responses, he knew she was attracted to him as well. Every time she looked at him, interest flared in her eyes, but it was just as quickly hidden. He understood that circumstances prohibited any closeness between them. Ilyssa believed that losing her virginity might lead to the loss of her singing voice. She wouldn't take the chance of finding out if it was true or risk Ruel's wrath by defying him.

Figuring they could both use an activity that would provide an absorbing distraction, Rolf posed a question.

"What do you usually do in the evenings?" he asked, wondering how she spent her leisure time. He hadn't noticed an entertainment center in her suite.

"I read a lot. Luckily, Bolt allows me an extensive library. The books are in a concealed shelf in my room."

Somehow Rolf couldn't picture them reading quietly together. Tension crackled imperceptibly in the air, and he sensed she was as aware of it as he. "Have you ever played kather sticks?" he queried.

"No, what's that?"

"It's a game of strategy. I can teach you if you like. I'm sure we can conjure up the supplies on the fabricator."

"It sounds like fun!" Grateful for the distraction, Ilyssa hastened through her meal so they could play.

The first game took over two hauras, and she liked it so much that they had a rematch. Ilyssa grew quite adept at flicking the colorful twisted sticks with the pointed ends and blocking her partner's moves.

After they'd stored the long sticks and dice, Ilyssa left to seek out Bolt to inquire about Seth's daughter. A few moments later, she returned. "He wasn't in. I'll try again tomorrow," she told Sean and then retired for the night.

The following morning was Selection Day, and Ilyssa had to go to the pens. Too many guards were in attendance for her to get a private moment with Bolt. Sickened by the proceedings, she pleaded a headache afterward and slinked away to the Waterdrop Cave. When she returned to her quarters, Bolt insisted she put in her hours at work so no one would suspect her of being weak, so she was forced to spend the rest of the afternoon in the production center.

It was late when she got back to the residence, but she headed for Bolt's apartment. Striding down the corridor, she passed by her suite where the Hortha sentries were posted at her door. Souk patrols marched past and she ignored them. The residence was arranged around a central courtyard. Public rooms faced the front, with hers and Bolt's suites at opposite sides. To the rear was the harem.

She crossed outside, moving past the enormous fountain, spraying cooling water into the air, and the single bangus tree which attracted mingka birds from the nearby hills. A couple of the brilliant red creatures sat in the branches, twittering as darkness stretched across the sky.

Ilyssa approached the pair of Souk soldiers guarding the entrance to Bolt's chambers. "I wish to see the satrap," she said in her most commanding tone of voice.

One of them nodded and barked into a comm unit. Bolt's voice boomed back and the door slid open.

Ilyssa took a deep breath and entered, stopping just inside the portal. Bolt had company.

The ugly dogface was lying on a lounger half atop a scantily clad Souk female, rubbing her nose. He looked up when Ilyssa entered. "R-R-Remove yourself," he barked at his gima. She scurried away, and Bolt beckoned for Ilyssa to approach.

Ilyssa cleared her throat, intimidated by the fact that Bolt seemed loath to rise. "I have a request for you," she began hesitantly.

Bolt's dark eyes studied her. His moist snoutlike nose sniffed the air to catch her scent. "What is it?" he growled in an irritated tone of voice.

"I'm concerned about a girl in your harem," Ilyssa said, discomfited by the way Bolt was glaring at her. "She's young and has long blond hair. You acquired her during the previous Selection Day."

"Krach, I know the one. Her name is Mila."

"Is she . . . have you . . . ?" Ilyssa couldn't say the words.

"I haven't gotten to her yet. The girl's mind seems vacant. Spends her time staring out the casement, does she. What about her?" Bolt's nostrils enlarged and his ears peaked.

"I'd be grateful if you would release her from your harem. Can you get her reassigned to a merchant in town, someone who would treat her kindly?" Her afternoon at Computer Central had proved productive. Now Ilyssa could offer Bolt a trade.

"What's she to you?" He sat up, adjusting his uniform top.

"I've taken to her, that's all. I don't want to see her harmed."

"You've never made a r-r-request like this before. Why now?" Bolt grumbled ominously.

"Humor me," she hedged. "By the way, I noticed a new shipment of reeka pears coming into port. Would you like me to procure a crate for you?"

"Reeka pears! They're my favorite fruit!"

"It's easy for me to manipulate the consignment. I'm just asking for a small favor in return."

He glowered at her, finally muttering, "Oh, all right. The girl no longer appeals to me. Assign her to the baker lady, shall I. But you must get me a good supply of fruit. Be certain it has been treated with antispoilage lime."

"Agreed." Straightening her shoulders, she turned away.

"Going back to your slave?" Bolt sounded resentful.

"No, I . . . uh . . . have to get cleansed. It's been a tiring day."

"Be waiting for the pears, will I, Ilyssa. Make sure I'm not disappointed."

She grimaced and left. Hurrying back to her chamber, she entered, eager to share her results with Sean.

When she walked in, he was doing sit-ups on the parlor floor, having finished the palace chores he'd been assigned for the day. Ilyssa stopped short, blushing. He was wearing nothing more than a pair of loose activity shorts. Her gaze trailed over his bulging muscles and tall, fit form.

"Ilyssa!" He jumped up, grabbed a cloth, and wiped his brow.

"I've just come from Bolt. I asked him about the harem girl. Mila is her name. Bolt said he'll reassign her to the baker lady. Luckily, he hadn't touched her yet."

"Thank you!" Rolf felt overjoyed that he could do something useful for Seth's daughter. Taking two long strides forward, he grasped Ilyssa by the shoulders. "I'm really grateful, Ilyssa. You've done a lot for me, and now I'll help you in return. Let's talk about our escape."

"At last!"

Her eyes shining with hope and excitement, she tilted her face and stared up at him, and before he knew what he was doing, Rolf lowered his head and kissed her.

"No!" She jumped back.

"Forgive me. I didn't mean to offend you," he said.

"You didn't. I . . . I'm sorry if I gave you the wrong impression." Flushing, she looked at him miserably. "That's what got me into trouble the first time."

"What do you mean?"

"Remember I told you I was banished here because of the incident with Ruel's minister?" At his nod, she turned away and began pacing the room. "Well, I'd better explain what happened to me when Ruel found us in the palace garden. Perhaps what I have to say will help you understand how I feel."

Rolf sat on the lounger, listening intently. He remembered she'd said her brother Devin had been punished and she'd been banished here as a result, but what else had occurred? From the way her face was pinched with horror, he considered it likely that Ruel had done something more to traumatize her.

"The pasha used his electrifier, killing the minister instantly. Then he called for his guards. I was taken into custody." Ilyssa's voice faltered and she couldn't go on. The intimate details were too embarrassing to relate even though she wanted to share them. Instead, her mind, stuck in a groove like an old recording, continued to replay the terror as part of her own private torment. Her brother's screams echoed in her ears as she had been led away, a sobbing, wilting wreck. It was the last she had seen of Devin.

"I must get away from here!" she cried, terrified of incurring Ruel's wrath again.

Rolf saw the fear on her lovely face and felt an uncontrollable urge to console her. Clearly she'd been deeply hurt, so much so that she couldn't even tell him the rest of her story. He felt certain that Ruel had done something to her that had been terrifying. She'd said before he couldn't physically harm her, so what could he have done? Some sort of torture that didn't leave marks?

It was obvious she blamed herself for the incident. Now she was afraid to repeat her mistake, although their situation was totally different. Rolf wasn't going to take advantage of her innocence like the minister, and besides, no one would walk in on them in their private suite. No matter what he said, though, Rolf didn't think Ilyssa would accept any words of comfort. Her fear of Ruel's punishment was too intense.

He rose and walked over to her. He didn't know what horrible things Ruel had done to her, but he wouldn't let her be hurt again. Gently, he touched her cheek. "We'll get your parents safely away from Ruel so you can escape this *maug* planet. I'll get dressed and then we can talk about our plans." Her cruel treatment at the hands of the pasha just intensified his hatred of the Souks. He couldn't wait to get out of there to resume his mission.

Ilyssa's knees felt wobbly. She took a seat while he pulled on his shirt and pants and brought her a soothing warm beverage. She was glad he was so understanding, but the incident in Haakat wasn't the whole of it. Even if she weren't afraid of incurring Ruel's anger again, she had another good reason for not wanting to get involved with a man.

But as she watched Sean move, her resolve wavered. He'd only half-fastened his shirt so that it sagged open at the chest, revealing dark swirls of hair. If that weren't distracting enough, his pants fit his form so snugly that every part of his lower body was sharply delineated. It wasn't as disconcerting as when he'd had on the activity shorts, but her attention was hard-pressed to remain on the business at hand when he still looked so virile.

He took a seat opposite her and she began. "I'll tell you what I had in mind for our escape. At the end of each shift, the mined piragen ore is weighed and graded. A loaded hovertram leaves the production center every night, making its run along a heavily monitored track to a processing plant kilometers away. There the ore is melted down and combined with liquid nutrium to form Pirium, a plastel used in shipbuilding.

"The plastel sheets are flown by cargo skimmer to a distribution center by the Como River. From there, shipments either go by skimmer to the spaceport at Haakat for off-planet sale, or they go by sailbarge across the Cobalt Wash for sale to other pashas. Some shipments go to Ruel's own shipyard on the coast. Now, this is what I propose."

She folded her hands and leaned forward. "The nearest city is by the processing plant. It would be too far for us to walk, and anyway we'd never make it through the Rocks of Weir on our own. Passenger flights come in to the mining camp twice a week, but we can't board. So our only option is to take the tram. We'll pick it up outside the production center. I can disable the security system monitoring the track, but it'll be nighttime—when the wingboxers are out—and we'll have to be extremely careful."

"I've heard of them. Nasty creatures, aren't they?"

She twisted in her seat, imagining the dangers involved. Detection was only one of them. "We can use my flyboard to get further down the track, but then you'll have to manually lower one of the emergency gates to stop the tram. I'll make sure the lapse doesn't show on the time log."

Sean nodded. "So we hop the tram to the processing plant. Then what?"

"We have to reach the capital city of Haakat. I'm hoping Bolt will try to find us before notifying Ruel. That would allow us more time. If we can reach the Como River, we'll be able to catch fast transport to Haakat from there. Once we're in the capital, the actual rescue of my parents will be up to you. I'd be too easily recognized, so I'll give you the palace layout and then I'll keep out of sight."

Rolf considered her scheme. Thirty-one days remained until the 40 pashas congregated. He needed time to cross the Koodrash Mounts, establish contact with the resistance, and pass over the great sea, the Cobalt Wash, in order to reach Drobrok where the Souk Alliance conference would take place. But his plan left precious little time for a detour to Haakat in what promised to be a dangerous excursion. And what would he do with Ilyssa and her parents? He couldn't take them with him to Drobrok. He'd have to leave them with his friends in the resistance until he completed his mission.

"What do we have to do first?" he asked, stroking his chin thoughtfully. Ilyssa wouldn't be happy about the delay in leaving Souk but there wasn't much choice. If she wanted his help, she'd have to accept the constraints. He wouldn't reveal his mission until they were safely away from the Rocks of Weir.

Excited, Ilyssa jumped up and began pacing. "We'll need supplies. I'll start working on that tomorrow. And I have to check the schedules. It may be a few days before we can make our move." She didn't want to leave on a night when Coak was coming for his shipment of illicit ore.

They discussed the supplies they would need and then Sean said, "I need a shower. Would you like to freshen up first? I'll conjure us up a meal after I've showered."

"All right." She smiled at him gratefully.

"Want to play kather sticks later? You beat me in the last match and I have to catch up."

Ilyssa eagerly agreed, then left to wash and change.

Rolf watched her go, his feelings mixed. Seeing the fear in her eyes tonight had aroused his male protectiveness. Now he felt himself drawn to her more strongly than before. Again he asked himself why she should appeal to him so forcefully when no one else since Gayla had done so.

He'd certainly had the opportunity with Sarina. She'd even moved into his apartment on Bimordus Two during their betrothal. By agreeing to wed her, he'd hoped to unify the Coalition and aid the passage of the First Amendment. But his dutiful approach hadn't impressed Sarina, and she ended up marrying Teir.

Rolf had thought at the time that he was still in love with Gayla, but now he knew that wasn't true. When he saw the happiness Sarina and Teir shared, he'd yearned to feel a similar closeness with a woman again. Was this why he felt so attracted to Ilyssa? Was his subconscious telling him that Ilyssa might be the one to capture his lonely heart?

Rolf shook his head in bewilderment. He didn't know the answer, but he did understand that if he was going to explore his feelings for Ilyssa, he'd have to tread carefully. She had valid reasons for being fearful of intimacy, and he didn't want to offend her.

Chapter Six

"Tomorrow night," Ilyssa said. "I've got everything ready. Our supplies are in a knapsack by the storage shed at the edge of town." They'd just returned from the production center and were alone in their suite. She'd waited excitedly all day to tell Sean the preparations were complete.

He looked at her, his eyes glowing. "Tomorrow! I thought the day would never come."

Ilyssa obtained a fruit beverage from the fabricator and drank greedily. "I've got the food rations, water, medic kit, and tools. Today I was able to get a data link. We'll need that to override the sensors monitoring the track. I've already encoded the computer to open the necessary pathway at my command."

Sitting on the lounger, Ilyssa considered if there was anything else they needed to do. Two days had passed since Sean had agreed to escape with her. She'd been busy checking the ore production schedules, manipulating the security files, and secreting supplies. During their free time together, they'd discussed the different risks involved. Both of them were anxious to make the break.

Sean went to get a drink, and Ilyssa studied his muscular physique as he moved in his tan tunic and leggings. The impending escape wasn't the only source of tension between them. She was very much aware of his manly presence, and she knew his eyes were often on her as well. She could feel his gaze caressing her everywhere she went. It wouldn't be easy being alone with him when they were on the run. Even though Sean had made no further move to touch her, she didn't trust her own inclinations in that regard.

His kiss had been an awakening. Ilyssa had never thought the desire for physical closeness with a man could be so compelling. She could still remember the touch of his mouth on hers, his hands on her skin. She craved to experience the same sensations again and more. Sighing, she warned herself of the dangers involved and tightened her resolve not to weaken.

Of course, Sean could have his own reasons for not wanting to get involved with her. He seemed to be purposefully keeping his distance, displaying an attitude of polite formality at best. For the umpteenth time, she wondered about his identity and his purpose in coming to Souk. Maybe he'd confide in her once they were free of the mining camp.

Facing the fabricator, Rolf felt her eyes on his back. Much as he yearned to sweep her into his arms to share his excitement, he couldn't risk upsetting her. She'd made it clear that any physical intimacy was prohibited between them. And even if that weren't an issue, he had his own mission to complete. His pledge to Gayla's parents took precedence over everything else. Since his crash on Souk, Gayla's image kept haunting him with increasing frequency in the form of nightmares. It was almost as though she knew his attention was straying from his duty and she was warning him.

Yet despite his wish to remain aloof, he couldn't help the way his glance followed Ilyssa as she performed her daily tasks, or the way he longed to smooth his fingers over her soft flesh. Her quick intakes of breath whenever they made accidental contact told him she was affected by him as well. It just made him ache for her more.

"Ilyssa, I've got to ask you something," he said, pushing aside his turbulent feelings and addressing a subject that concerned him. "Where do you go in the afternoons when you say you want to be alone?" Each afternoon for the past two days, she'd disappeared without telling him where she was going. It bothered him that she hadn't explained when they were so near to sharing a dangerous adventure together.

Illyssa looked away, focusing on a spot on the far wall. "I go to the Waterdrop Cave. It's my private sanctuary, one of the few luxuries Bolt allows me. I practice my singing."

"Why can't I go with you?"

"I told you about my siren song. You'd be affected if you heard me sing."

He compressed his lips, accepting her explanation but not liking it. He still only half believed the myth.

A loud knock sounded on her bedchamber door. Rolf hastened to open it for her, then stepped back as the captain of the guard saluted the Dromo.

"Master Bolt has informed me that you've been summoned to Haakat. I have a troop ready to escort you to the airfield. Be prepared to depart in ten minutes."

"What?" Ilyssa felt the color drain from her face.

"Ten minutes," the officer repeated.

She noted the contingent of guards lined up behind him and shut the door in his face. Whirling around, she stared at Sean. As though in silent agreement, they sped into the parlor to talk.

"Is there any way you can delay this trip?" he asked,

his voice tight with emotion.

"I'm afraid not. We'll have to postpone our . . . journey. Maybe I'll get to see my parents while I'm in Haakat."

"Why is Ruel summoning you now?"

"He requires a report on the production figures, and . . . and he might want to check on a few other things." She shivered in dreadful anticipation. "He could have someone targeted for my siren song while I'm there as well. I'm so sorry." From the look on his face, she could see he was terribly disappointed. So was she, but it couldn't be helped. Hopefully Ruel wouldn't keep her long.

Sean helped her to prepare for her trip. Ilyssa was quiet, her shoulders sagging as she gathered a few items. She didn't need much, as Ruel kept a chamber in readiness for her visits, stocked with all the necessities. Via scramjet traveling at supersonic speed, the trip to Haakat would take less than 15 minutes.

When Ilyssa said she was ready, Sean opened the door and as she exited, she heard the captain of the guard reassign Sean to other duties during her absence. She only hoped he would be all right while she was gone.

Allowing for travel time between airfields, it was an haura later when Ilyssa settled into her room at the palace. Bleakly, she gazed at the familiar surroundings. If nothing else, she was grateful for the plush comfort of the ceiling drapes and the colorful tapestries which brightened her bedchamber. A huge four-poster bed, a loveseat, two chairs, and a dressing table replete with cosmetics and perfumes made up the furnishings. Since Ruel liked to show her off as his prized possession, Ilyssa was expected to adorn herself while in Haakat. In her wardrobe were caftans made of diaphanous silks. Pushed back behind them were the harem outfits for Ruel's private viewing, but Ilyssa hid them so she wouldn't be reminded of her status. Unfortunately, Ruel never let her forget she was a sumi.

A female caretaker was sent to serve her, Ruel's precaution against her using her siren song to get away. He'd also posted his private bodyguards, the Hazars, an elite troop of Souks, along the corridors and at all the arched portals.

After the female attendant left to take up a post outside her door, Ilyssa paced the chamber in dread. Would Ruel summon her now? What did he want her for besides the report on Bolt? Did he need to use her siren song again?

About an haura later, as she lay on her bed, wondering if her parents were well and plotting how Sean could get them safely away, she heard the special chime. She jumped up and ran to the north wall of her chamber. Her fingers fumbled nervously for the concealed latch. A hidden lock clicked open, and Ilyssa hastened through a secret interior passage illuminated by flamelights. The route dipped down, grew colder, passing underneath the lushly manicured gardens outside the palace walls. She shivered as she hurried along the tunnel path. An incline made her breath quicken and then she entered the Shell Grotto, a structure at the far end of the formal garden. Moving silently, Ilyssa left her secret entrance and took her place behind a curtained partition.

Ruel brought his special guests here. They were enemies he needed tamed or allies he didn't trust. With the excuse of showing them the wondrous structure built entirely from seashells, he lured them into his lair.

Once inside and with the outer door closed, Ruel signaled for her to begin. Ilyssa sang, her music reverberating off the shell walls. Concealed behind the curtained divider, she always heard the exclamations of joy from Ruel's victims and then the silence which quickly overwhelmed them as her siren song worked its magic. She always gave the same directive, commanding the enthralled guest to everlasting servitude to Ruel.

As she left the Shell Grotto, Ilyssa wondered who the unlucky victim was this time. If Ruel invited her to attend a state banquet, she might find out. The dinners were a splendid source of information since many of the conversations centered around politics and social gossip. Ilyssa was curious to see who else was visiting the palace.

Early the next morning, after she'd breakfasted alone in her room, she sent a message to Ruel asking permission to visit her parents in their private apartment. The permission was granted with the stipulation that she present herself to Ruel, properly prepared, at 1400 hauras. Ilyssa swallowed her dread and agreed.

Her mother was overjoyed to see her. Moireen jumped up from the chair in her parlor and rushed to embrace her.

"Ilyssa! When did you return?" Moireen knew the reason for her banishment.

"I'm just visiting, Mama. Ruel sent for me."

Moireen's face showed sympathy. "I'm sorry, angel sweet. Have you seen him yet?"

"No, I have to present myself this afternoon."

"Then we have all morning! I have a light work load today."

Working for Ruel's Ministry of Finance, Moireen performed her job via a comm link hookup to the central office and rarely left her suite. Ilyssa knew her mother looked forward to Ilyssa's brief and infrequent visits and she now studied Moireen with tender affection. She looked well, despite eight annums of imprisonment. Her auburn hair, clipped short yet full, added a roundness to her oval face and accentuated her large green eyes. Ilyssa knew her mother swam daily in the palace pool and her trim figure belied her 45 annums. Though still attractive, she'd never appealed to Ruel. It was Ilyssa who had always intrigued the pasha.

"How's Papa?" Ilyssa asked, glancing toward the closed bedchamber door.

Moireen sighed. "Aran is losing weight and becoming forgetful. I do not like it, angel sweet. I fear your father is beginning the downward spiral of senilis disease."

Ilyssa gasped. Senilis was a form of dementia, supposedly the end result of a mindwash. She'd known he hadn't looked well on her last visit, but this? "He's only forty-nine annums!" she cried to her mother. "According to the stories we've heard, senilis occurs much later in life."

"Aran has been a mind slave to Ruel for eight annums now, my child. Possibly for a man of his sensitive nature, insanity is a way to terminate the rape of his conscious will."

Ilyssa sank onto a lounger and put her hands over her face. She shuddered to think of her father, a renowned musician, succumbing to such a terrible end. She'd always thought it was fortunate Ruel hadn't murdered her parents or condemned them to a life of hard labor, but this was a longer, crueler path to death as far as her sensitive, artistic father was concerned.

Moireen paced the room, wringing her hands in despair. "I don't know what I'll do if your father dies. He's the whole reason for my existence. If it weren't for his needing me, I'd lose my mind."

Rising, Ilyssa hastened to her mother and grasped her shoulders. "Mama, do not give up hope. I met someone who is willing to help us."

Panic washed over Moireen's features. "Not again! You know what happened the last time—"

Ilyssa put her finger on her mother's lips. "Hush, this isn't like the last time. I can't explain the details, but have faith in me."

Moireen's wide green eyes gazed at her in terror. "Whatever you're planning to do, please be careful!"

The bedroom door crashed open and her father entered, weaving across the room in their direction. Instantly, they halted their conversation. Aran would report anything he overheard to Ruel, his master.

"Papa!" Ilyssa exclaimed, embracing him. She was shocked by how much thinner he felt in her arms. Standing back and surveying him, she noticed his face had narrowed, making his aquiline nose more prominent. The gray in his hair had extended from his temples and subjugated the rest of his black hair like weeds taking over a lawn. His hazel eyes regarded her with a blank expression as he stood motionless, his arms hanging by his side.

"Well? Aren't you glad to see me?" she asked, dismayed by his listlessness. Even though he'd become Ruel's minion, there had always been a gleam in his eye for her or Moireen. This empty response frightened her. Was he so far gone to senilis already? It was said the symptoms worsened for an annum before death relieved the sufferer. How much time did Aran have left?

"My daughter," Aran mumbled.

Her face softened with relief. "How do you feel, Papa?"

"I am being summoned," was his answer. He turned his back and headed for the door.

"Wait! I came to see you. I won't have another opportunity." From previous experience, she knew Ruel would allow her only one visit during her stay.

"My master calls." The portal hissed open and he exited, accompanied down the corridor by two uniformed Hazars who'd been waiting outside the door.

Overwhelmed with sadness, Ilyssa stood beside her mother watching after him. She knew her escape must proceed at the next possible moment or her father would be lost forever.

* * *

For her presentation to Ruel, the female caretaker had made certain Ilyssa was properly bathed and attired. Her jade caftan of the finest silk had woven glistening silver threads. Covering her hair was a pale green veil of the lightest gauze. Her face was highlighted with cosmetics, and perfume scented her skin. But although her outward appearance was pleasing, her stomach churned in nervous anticipation. Underneath the loose-fitting garment, Ilyssa wore the harem bra and girdle that Ruel demanded of her. The attendant had produced it from her wardrobe with a meaningful smirk.

At the sound of a chime, the Souk female announced it was time for Ilyssa to go. Ilyssa followed her into the corridor, feeling like a prisoner with a warden dictating her every move. They wound along a familiar mazelike path through the palace corridors. At last they crossed a courtyard and arrived at the pasha's private apartments. Four uniformed Hazars stood guard in front of the massive oak door.

Inside, two more Hazars frisked her with an electronic scanner before she was allowed to approach the closed door to Ruel's inner chamber. The female caretaker hung back, waiting to accompany her when she exited. Trembling, Ilyssa poked a finger at the comm channel and identified herself.

"Enter!" Ruel barked.

The door hissed open, then shut immediately behind her after she stepped inside. Rainbow-colored ceiling drapes hung everywhere, and a massive gold lamé curtain decorated the enormous round bed against a far wall. Ruel awaited her at its foot. His tall, brawny frame looked more imposing and frightening than she remembered.

"Come closer, little bird," he said, using his term of endearment for her. They were quite alone, but Ilyssa was aware of the sentries just outside the door. She did as she was told, cringing as she neared him. His ugliness never failed to disgust her.

Ruel had a long, oval face with erect, small ears placed close to his head of brown hair. His triangular-shaped, deep-set onyx eyes slanted up at the outer corners, and were piercing. His underjaw was well developed, giving a mean-looking thrust to his face.

He walked slowly around her, inspecting her from head to toe. His brown nostrils enlarged as he sniffed her. Finally, he licked his thick lips as he nodded approvingly. "Disrobe, Ilyssa," he commanded.

Ilyssa's trembling increased until she thought she'd sink to the ground. Ruel's particular perversion was that he liked her to undress in front of him, although he'd never touched her. Afraid to defy him, she protested nevertheless. "Please, Master Ruel, I have followed your commands. My maidenhood remains intact."

"I wish to see for myself. Do as I say, or I'll have you r-r-removed to the clinic for a more complete examination."

Knowing the threat those words implied, Ilyssa felt a rush of fear. Defeated, she loosened her caftan and let it slide to the floor. Bowing her veiled head, she couldn't help feeling exposed in the gilded bra and girdle. The air felt cool on her bare skin. Ruel's breathing quickened and his heavy wheezes seemed to fill the room.

"Off with everything!" he shouted.

Biting her lip to suppress a cry of anguish, Ilyssa unfastened the harem garments and threw them to the floor. She shook with fear and shame at her nakedness. No matter how many times she endured these sessions, she never got used to them.

"This show of r-r-resistance does not please me. Cooperate, or you'll be severely punished! Now turn around, slowly." He examined her, drooling, as she rotated before his lecherous gaze.

Apparently satisfied that she remained unblemished, he strode to a bedside table and obtained a mediscan from a drawer. Walking back, Ruel ran the device up and down her length. Tiny beeps emanated from the unit as the sensors analyzed the findings.

"Good, the safeguard is still lodged firmly in place. No one can violate you without my being aware of it." He lowered his hand and gave her a probing stare. "Bolt seems to think you're getting r-r-restless. Need you satisfaction, woman? Be happy to oblige, would I." His gaze lowered to her breasts and he snorted in anticipation.

"No! You once said you'd never touch me!"

"Only because of your gift, little bird. I'd be afraid that if I started with you, I wouldn't be able to stop. See what happens to me when I gaze at your luscious body?" Ruel fondled himself where a huge bulge tented his caftan.

"I can't help it if you prefer human females to Souk ones," she said disdainfully.

"Bitch!" Growling with rage, Ruel slapped her across the cheek. "If you ever let anyone touch you but me, your parents are dead. Remember that! Now give me your report."

Ilyssa related the mining production figures before being allowed to dress, but it wasn't until she reached the privacy of her chambers that she gave in to her horror. Sinking into a hot bath, she scrubbed at her skin, trying to wash away the memory of Ruel's touch. Her body still burned from humiliation. How she hated him! He'd stolen annums from her life and had caused her pain and suffering.

As the scented water soothed her body, her thoughts jumbled and twisted in her mind. Resentment turned into rage as she thought about all that had been lost. Somehow she'd make Ruel pay. She owed it to herself, to her parents, and to her dear departed brother Devin. But then just as quickly, she disavowed the promise. Violence should not avenge violence, Ilyssa reminded herself, espousing the pacifist ideology of the Circutians. But in her heart, the doctrine battled with her furious need for revenge.

Her caretaker brought her a sedit beverage for its calming effect. The warm drink slid down her throat, eventually bringing her a feeling of tranquillity. She closed her eyes, allowing her thoughts to drift in a more pleasant direction. Sean's handsome face floated before her mind. She pictured his heavy arched brows, flowing black hair, and mesmerizing blue eyes. Her imagination traced the noble line of his nose, caressed his determined jaw, and kissed his sensual mouth. Thinking of him made her yearn to feel his touch. For a man so strong and virile, she sensed he could be supremely gentle. Was it any wonder she felt he was the answer to her dreams?

Rolf awakened, lying on the carpet in Ilyssa's parlor, having apparently fallen off the lounger in the throes of his nightmare. Not again, he thought, running a trembling hand across his dampened brow. Would these horrifying remembrances of Gayla's death never cease? The dreams seemed to be afflicting him more often. Either his recent crash had revived the memory, or else his guilty conscience was telling him to focus his mind on his mission and not on Ilyssa. Yet he couldn't help it if his waking thoughts were of her. He was worried about her safety and the precariousness of his own situation.

Bolt had given him an evil grin yesterday, making him aware of all sorts of mishaps that could happen to him while Ilyssa was gone. Anxiously, he tugged at the slave collar around his neck. Bolt had put it on him as soon as Ilyssa had left. His sense of danger had increased, but there was nothing he could do. He needed Ilyssa to make his escape. Only she could disable the security system monitoring the ore track.

Rising, Rolf went to the fabricator and ordered himself a cup of fragrant citron tea. A glance at the chronometer told him it was five-thirty in the morning. Soon Bolt's men would come for him. He'd been reassigned to the bricklayer during Ilyssa's absence, but the satrap hadn't wanted to risk her wrath by having him stay in the slave quarters. Rolf wanted to tell Seth his daughter had been given to the baker lady, but he hadn't been able to get to the barracks on his own.

He wished he could tell Ilyssa that Bolt had followed through on her request. When was she coming back? Ruel might decide to keep her for weeks. Was she being interrogated about him? Was she in trouble? He missed her pretty face and sharp wit and prayed for her swift return.

Ilyssa was anxious to leave Haakat, not only to get away from Ruel, but because she missed Sean. She felt lonely without his strong comforting presence and hadn't realized until now how much she'd come to rely on him.

But her visit had been extended as Ruel wanted to show her off at a couple of lavish banquets, decked out in jewels, looking the part of his favored gima. She took no delight in outfitting herself so lavishly but it was the image Ruel ordered her to project.

And as she sat at tonight's sumptuous evening meal prepared with real food by talented chefs, she noticed a change in Hern, the minister of agriculture. Whenever Ruel spoke to him, the Souk nodded his head in vigorous agreement. Ilyssa watched them with narrowed eyes. Last month when she was here, they'd discussed various means to improve seed yields. Hern had hinted they'd do better if they could use the Coalition's scientists' newer techniques. She'd bet by his behavior now that he had been the guest in the Grotto, since his views had clashed with Ruel's more than once.

Beside her at the long table laden with delicious delicacies, including a few dishes with live bugs, the controller for the division of economy leaned closer.

"How are you, my dear?" the Souk rasped, the garlic on his breath wafting in her face. "Missed your lovely presence, have I. Are you back to stay?"

She shook her head. "I fear not. This is but a temporary reprieve." The ministers knew she had displeased Ruel but the true reason was unknown to them.

"I'm so sorry. Hoping was I that the pasha would extend his forgiveness and invite you to r-r-remain."

Ilyssa took a sip from her goblet of wine. "Not this time."

"Ivex, did you get the figures tabulated for this month yet?" asked the foreign minister, Spic, from across the table.

"Aye," replied the Souk at her side.

"And?"

"I told you, they'd be better if it weren't for the trade embargo enforced by the Coalition."

"What are you talking about?" Ruel barked from the other end of the table.

"Our treasury coffers would be bolstered if we were granted free trade r-r-rights," Ivex said bravely.

"Discussed this before, have we," Ruel said. "The Coalition intends to ruin us."

"Only because of the sumi issue. You know my views on that subject."

"Grr, I'm afraid the time is coming when we must do something about your deviant ideas," Ruel warned.

"Your secret weapon doesn't frighten me. Used it on Hern, did you? I see how he grovels at your feet. The sumi issue is a more important topic." Ivex jabbed his finger in the air. "Isn't that the reason for the Alliance conference on Lexin thirty-fourth? Some of the other pashas feel slavery should be abolished. There's enough cheap labor available for us to staff the mines and other workplaces. Then we'd be eligible to join the Coalition. Souk would benefit in the long run. You can't escape progress, Ruel."

"Have no need for the Coalition do we!" Ruel screamed, rising.

"I disagree. The Morgots buy our exports but they can't be trusted. Wasn't K'darr r-r-responsible for the execution of your brother, Cerrus Bdan?"

"Grrr," Ruel growled, his ugly face turning purple with rage. "I hold someone else r-r-responsible for my brother's death."

"Who? Sarina, the Great Healer, and her mate, Captain Teir Reylock? They were only trying to escape from Bdan's entrapment. Bdan was under orders from K'darr to capture them."

"No, I hold responsible the man who revived the legend of the Great Healer. He's the same man who's been against us from the start, sponsoring the trade embargo and writing the First Amendment to the Articles of Coalition. We have a personal matter to settle as well. Lord Cam'brii shall not continue to elude me. I want him, and I'll pay generously whoever captures the councillor and delivers him to me. My previous attempts to assassinate him failed. This time, want him alive do I!"

"Is there still no word from your Coalition spy?" gruffed a sympathetic deputy at his side.

"He says the councillor is not on Bimordus Two, and we've checked his home planet Nadira. Lord Cam'brii isn't there either. Our agent suspects he's on a secret mission, but details are unavailable. He can't stay in hiding forever. Find him, will I. And when I do, he'll pay for my losses. Lord Cam'brii will beg for death but it will not be an escape I'll allow him!"

Bolt was getting impatient that his efforts to incriminate Sean Breslow hadn't shown results. Anxious to dispose of the human, he put in a call to Haakat, and Pah came on the line at once.

"Well? Have you the proof I r-r-requested that the slave Breslow is conspiring against the pasha?" Bolt demanded.

"I'm working on it," Pah answered.

"What have you got so far?"

"Pay me ten thousand credits and I'll tell you."

"Agreed." Cursing the wily gecko, Bolt stuck his data card in the connector and arranged for the transfer.

"My source on Arcturus was unable to find any reference to a trader by the name of Sean Breslow. He couldn't get any further leads on him." Pah made a nervous clicking noise. "It is my opinion the man is using a false identity."

"How long before your so-called proof is r-r-ready?" Bolt was aware the gecko planned to create his own incriminating evidence.

"Another week, if you want it to look good."

"Make it sooner, you chattering insect, or the ten thousand will be all you get." He closed the comm link, disgusted. The gecko wasn't acting quickly enough to suit him. If it were up to him, he'd get rid of the sumi and be done with it. But then Ilyssa would report his ore thefts to Ruel. Grrr, she wasn't here now. What was to prevent him from staging an unfortunate accident? If Breslow was killed in her absence, she wouldn't be able to prove he had anything to do with it.

Grinning, Bolt summoned two of his most trusted aides.

Finally, Rolf got the opportunity to visit Seth. The bricklayer had ordered him to fetch four stalwart slaves to help move a heavy load of construction materials to a new section of town as levitators weren't available in this location.

Rolf handed his orders to the Hortha captain guarding the male slave barracks. The bull-like creature read it over and nodded for him to enter. Rolf went directly inside toward his former berth. He saw the older man asleep in his dirty tunic and leggings on the next bunk.

"What do you want here?" a voice said, unmistakably hostile in tone.

Rolf whirled to face a group of slaves who didn't look friendly and were blocking his exit to the door. "I need four men," he said calmly.

"You work for the Dromo," a bearded fellow accused him.

"I'm a sumi, like you," Rolf replied, pointing to his slave collar. "While the Dromo is absent, I've been assigned to the bricklayer. He needs four men to help move a heavy load. Anyone want to volunteer? It'll keep you out of the mines today," he added as an incentive.

Angry grumbling erupted. For a moment, Rolf was afraid he'd have a major fight on his hands, but then one or two arms shot up.

"Hey, mate," Seth greeted him, sitting up and rubbing his eyes. "What's going on? Why are you here?"

Rolf explained, then added, "I'd like you to come. I need to talk to you."

Seth nodded and joined three others in accompanying Rolf outside. On the way into the village, they strode ahead so they could talk in private.

"Ilyssa got your daughter reassigned to the baker lady," Rolf told Seth right away. "Her living situation is vastly improved."

Seth grasped his arm. "My heartfelt thanks, friend. However did you manage to accomplish it?"

"The Dromo's situation is not what everyone thinks. She's a prisoner like us, forced to do Ruel's bidding. Bolt is the one who gives the real orders here. You'd like her, Seth. Ilyssa is intelligent and kind. She radiates a sweet innocence that's utterly charming. She really cares a great deal about the slaves but is helpless to do anything."

The older man shot him a suspicious glance. "Sounds like she's got you under her spell."

Rolf shook his head. "It's not like that. I'm telling you, she's not what she seems."

"Can she get my wife out of the mines? Karan won't last long in that harsh environment."

"Have you been able to see her?"

"No, they don't let us visit the women."

"It might be risky for Ilyssa to make a second request to Bolt. Have you thought of finding a way out for yourself?"

Seth wiped the sweat from his brow. It was midafternoon and the sol was high in the sky. The air was hot and dry. A few straggly trees shaded their path but they were few and far between.

"You're familiar with the tunnel system in the mines," Seth said. "There's no route to the surface other than through the production center. We can't explore with our slave collars on and electronic sensors monitoring the levels, and with the solid rock face, digging would be impossible anyway. It's hopeless, friend. You're lucky you got out of there."

Rolf had nothing to say. He wished he could offer Seth prospects for a brighter future but he couldn't. If he and Ilyssa escaped, they couldn't take anyone else with them.

The bricklayer was waiting at the workshed for Rolf when the chore of moving the construction materials was finished.

"Got another job for you have I, sumi." He ordered Rolf to retrieve a wheelbarrow full of red clay that had been left at the opposite end of the encampment. With his slave collar on, Rolf wouldn't need an escort.

Dust clogged Rolf's nostrils as he stomped over the dirt trail bordering the town. The path wound around the hills, narrowing considerably as it twisted among tall, rocky spires. Ahead of him, towers of solid granite bordered the path, making any detour impossible.

Rolf lowered his head, trying to avoid the bright sunlight shining directly onto his face. Perspiration trickled down his back and his tan tunic felt itchy and warm. He yearned for the cool comfort of the Dromo's residence, which made him think of Ilyssa again.

Suddenly he heard a sound and a giant boulder came crashing from above, landing directly in front of him. Scudding to a halt in a cloud of dust, Rolf glanced up as two uniformed Souks jumped out from behind the rocks, shooters pointed at his chest.

"How unfortunate that you are going to have an accident, sumi," snarled one with a droopy bloodhound face.

"What are you talking about?" Rolf said as the other officer ran behind Rolf, blocking a retreat.

"That large boulder tumbled down just as you were passing by. It grazed your head, knocking you to the ground." Bloodhound produced a sharp-edged rock from a pocket and raised it in his left hand. With a growl, he leapt forward, swinging his arm.

"Wait!" Rolf blocked the attack by swiveling sideways and lifting his elbow. The blow was barely deflected by his quick action.

As he was recovering, a stunning shock hit him in the back, throwing him to his knees. The Souk at his rear had used his shooter on a light stun setting. At once, Bloodhound charged him, crashing a rock against his brow. Rolf cried out as a white-hot sensation of pain seared his brain.

"Use my shooter again will I if necessary," the second Souk said, hovering over Rolf as he moaned on the ground. "We were ordered to make your death appear as an accident. Shift yourself further back toward that r-r-rock."

Dizzily, Rolf gazed up at him. Obviously the bricklayer had set him up by sending him off alone on this errand, but who'd told the bricklayer what to do? "Who's behind this?" he croaked.

The two Souks bent over and tugged him by the arms until he was stretched out beside the biggest boulder. At eye level, he noticed a dark crevice at the bottom of the rock.

"The Dromo has no further use for you," Bloodhound said.

The Dromo? Ilyssa had ordered an ambush? No, that couldn't be true! "You're lying. Bolt must have sent you."

"The satrap wouldn't kill you. He'd assign you to the mines. The Dromo is the one who wants you dead. She gets rid of all her personal servers in this manner when she tires of them," the Souk sneered.

"I don't believe you!" Rolf tried to sit up, but Bloodhound put a boot on his chest and shoved him down. "Why would my death have to appear as an accident if she ordered it? She's in charge."

"Because if Bolt knew she was wasting valuable human flesh in this manner, he'd report her to Ruel. She's coming back this afternoon and wants you gone. Now be silent while we wait."

"Wait for what?"

The Souks laughed and didn't answer. Rolf rolled sideways, tackling the second Souk's legs. He'd grappled the large male to the ground before Bloodhound could stop him. Their arms and legs entwined in a struggle for the shooter in the Souk's hand. Rolf nudged the dogface toward the rock so he could bang his head against the solid surface. Suddenly the Souk screamed. His eyes rolled up in his head and his body convulsed. Within seconds, he was dead. Rolf crouched and stared. Coils of slimy black snivets slithered over the Souk's neck and then slid back into the crevice.

"Snivets!" Rolf yelled. "You intended for me to get bitten!"

"Son of a liver-bellied nargot, Vagus wasn't supposed to die!" Bloodhound lifted his shooter and fired. Rolf felt an agonizing pain as he was hit in the leg. "That'll keep you from moving until they get curious and come out again."

"I thought this was supposed to be an accident," Rolf croaked, grasping his leg above the wound.

The Souk grinned. "I'll just say I saw the snivets crawling over you and fired to chase them away. I missed and hit your leg instead." He glanced at the crevice. "Poking its head out now is one. Maybe it'll come for a closer look."

Rolf felt the sweat trickling down his face as he stared into the snivet's reptilian eyes. For a long moment Rolf and the creature appraised each other. Then the snivet slithered back into its hole.

Desperate to move out of range before another slimy creature became braver, Rolf shifted slightly on the hard ground. Vagus's body was right beside him, and suddenly his fingers contacted a cold metallic object. Tracing the outline, Rolf realized that the shooter lay half under the dead Souk's limp form, out of sight from Bloodhound, who must have forgotten about it. His heart thrummed with excitement. Maybe, just maybe, he could still effect an escape. Inching his hand forward, he grappled for the handle.

Making contact, Rolf screamed as though bitten by a snivet. At Bloodhound's startled look, Rolf yanked the shooter out, aimed, and fired. Bloodhound's finger twitched on the trigger but his shot went wild, and he fell.

Alone with two dead bodies and a few centimeters from the crevice, Rolf scraped his fingers in the dirt to drag himself away. Finally at a safe distance, he collapsed and let the pain and trembling wash over him. The bricklayer would be wondering what happened to him, unless he was in on the plot to kill him. But Rolf didn't think so. Bolt wouldn't want anyone else to know what was afoot in case his plot failed.

Rolf didn't for one minute believe that Ilyssa had had a hand in the ambush. She planned to escape with him. She wouldn't order his death. But obviously Bolt was willing to take risks while she was gone, and that made Rolf's remaining here dangerous. The satrap could arrive at any moment to see if his assassination attempt was successful. In any event, he'd be curious as to why his henchmen hadn't returned.

Rolf supposed he could return to the bricklayer after he tended his wound and continue as though nothing unusual had happened. No one could point the finger at him if the two bodies were discovered. He'd arrange their weapons so it would appear they'd fired on each other.

That task done with painful slowness, he headed for the storage shed where Ilyssa had said she'd hidden a knapsack full of supplies. A medic kit should fix him up until she returned. He hobbled along the path, looking over his shoulder every few meters. At the far edge of town, he reached the shed. Peering carefully inside, he spotted a dull bundle on the packed dirt ground in a corner. He felt a surge of gratitude that no one else was around as he limped inside and grabbed the sack. Quickly he rifled through the contents: food rations and water, tools, medic kit, data link, and—Great suns!—a set of kather sticks and dice! What had she been thinking? With a shrug, Rolf pulled out the medic kit and opened it.

After eyeing the provisions, he ripped off the bottoms of his leggings, but not so short as to show the burn mark from the shooter. Now that his wound was accessible, he used the tissue regenerator to heal his injury. Exhausted, he needed a stimulant to regain his energy, for there was no time to rest. A vibration along his neck told him someone was using the locator on his slave collar. If it was the satrap, Bolt would know Rolf had escaped his snare. Rolf hoped it was only the bricklayer.

Packing up, he moved out, hiding the sack at a spot closer to the Dromo's residence. His tunic was drenched with sweat so he removed it, feeling better as the air hit his naked chest. The slight breeze provided some relief from the stifling heat. Readied, he made haste to return to his current master.

"Where in Zor have you been, sumi?" the brawny Souk roared, grabbing a stun whip and flogging Rolf's bare back.

Already weakened from his ordeal, Rolf fell to his knees with the first shocking blow. "Forgive me, master," he groveled, forcing a show of humility. "I could not find the wheelbarrow, and the heat and lack of nourishment made me weak. I will work twice as hard to make up the lost time."

"Aye, so will you." The bricklayer ordered him to mix a pool of thick cement.

Two hauras later, Rolf's exposed chest and legs were covered with scraps of clay and his body glistened with sweat. The sun was descending and he was beginning to despair of Ilyssa's arrival. Fearing what would happen if he returned to the Dromo's residence and Bolt was waiting for him, Rolf slowed his pace so as not to finish his task too soon.

"Heavens above, but you're filthy!" a sweetly feminine voice proclaimed from a spot behind him.

Rolf threw down his trowel and spun around. "Ilyssa!" Gods, she was a sight for sore eyes. Framed in the archway to the work hall, she looked as fresh and clean as a spring dewdrop. His gaze roamed hungrily over her lovely features, then trailed downward to take in her flowing amber caftan and slippered feet. She wore her hair loose, and the fading sun backlighting her cast her in an ethereal glow. He felt an incredible urge to run and grasp her in his arms. From the yearning in her eyes, she looked like she would approve.

"How have you been?" she asked, obviously restraining herself from a more demonstrative greeting.

"I've survived," he said dryly. "Thank the stars you're back! Did Ruel . . . was he . . . are you all right?"

Ilyssa nodded. "I've released you from the bricklayer's service. Perhaps you should wash before we go back to the residence. There's a faucet out in the yard." She moved aside so he could pass.

Rolf didn't miss the quick step back she took as he strode by. Resisting his need to touch her, he headed for the outdoor spigot that was connected to a long pipe. He turned it on and splayed his fingers under the running water, warmed by the sun. Bending his head, he washed his face and scrubbed his long hair until it felt shiny and clean. He was aware of Ilyssa's eyes on his back and wondered what she was thinking.

"I don't have a towel," he said, shaking his head.

"You won't get chilled. It's as hot as Zor today."

The way she was appraising his body made him feel hotter. He needed a cold shower, not a lukewarm sprinkle. "Did a guard troop accompany you here?"

She nodded. "They're waiting in the outer courtyard. We'll talk when we're back in our suite at the residence."

"What about my collar? Can it come off?"

"Later. Let's go."

She hadn't said a word about their impending escape. Had their plans changed because of her visit to Ruel? What had transpired during her time in Haakat? A worried frown creased his brow, and he trudged behind her, wondering how he was going to escape if she'd changed her mind.

He'd just have to make sure she came with him, one way or another. Tonight would be the night. By the time the two moons of Souk faded into the brightening sky the next morning, Rolf Cam'brii planned to be far away from the Rocks of Weir.

Chapter Seven

"I'm so glad to be back!" Once they reached the haven of her parlor, Ilyssa whirled to face him, her green, gold-specked eyes sparkling.

"I missed you," Rolf answered, remaining a safe distance from her. He was afraid to come any closer or he'd end up embracing her, and he wouldn't be able to stop with a mere hug. It was becoming increasingly difficult to be near her and not touch her.

She stepped forward and took his hands in hers. Rolf knew that for her it was a meaningful gesture, but he wondered if she knew how it affected him.

"I missed you, too," Ilyssa said quietly, then stepped back and dropped her arms to her sides. "Ruel wanted to show me off at a couple of state banquets, and he had me use my siren song on one of his ministers. I got to see my parents, Sean. Papa is ill with senilis disease."

"What's that?" he asked, puzzled.

"It's the outcome of a mindwash. One's consciousness will reject the constant strain of being controlled, and insanity results. He has less than an annum before . . . before . . ." Her voice broke on a sob.

"We'll escape tonight, Ilyssa. Agreed?"

She looked into his eyes and nodded slowly.

"Can you remove this accursed collar?"

"Of course, forgive me for not doing it sooner." Ilyssa hastened to use the control she'd obtained from the bricklayer to free him of the restraint. "Did anything unusual happen in my absence?"

Rubbing his neck where it chafed from irritation, Rolf nodded. "Bolt sent a couple of goons after me." He told her about the ambush.

"By the corona, he'll pay for this!" she exclaimed, her eyes flashing.

"No, you're not to see him. It's best if we make a clean break without any fuss."

"I suppose you're right. Let's review our plans and make certain everything's ready."

They spent the remainder of the evening rehearsing their moves.

Slightly past midnight, her hair tightly braided, her black jumpsuit hidden under a coarse robe, Ilyssa flung open her door and marched out into the corridor. She spoke brusquely to the Hortha sentries who came quickly to attention.

"I'm going to Master Bolt's quarters. We have a lot to discuss since my return from Haakat. My sumi will escort me. You may remain at your posts."

Aware that the elite Souk troops patrolled the corridors, the Horthas grunted their acknowledgment and appeared to look forward to a break. Trying to hide a grin, Ilyssa crooked her finger to signal Sean to follow. He hurried out of the suite after her, a shadowy figure in a hooded robe.

"Are you sure Bolt isn't in tonight?" he whispered when they were out of earshot.

"I told you he met me at the airfield. He's with a business associate in town," she rasped back.

Snapping her head forward as a patrol of four Souks stomped past, she slowed her pace so as not to appear in a hurry. Ilyssa led Sean outside to the courtyard around the trickling fountain and headed for the rear entrance. Before going farther, she nodded to him.

Rolf reached up, inserting the wax earplugs Ilyssa had supplied. Then he followed her inside to another long corridor. Directly across from them was an ornately carved set of double doors which would be the entrance to the harem, according to what Ilyssa had told him earlier. Two mean-looking Souks stood guard in front of the doors, and they bristled to attention at his and Ilyssa's approach. A flash of panic raced through Rolf's mind. They'd never let a man in there! How was Ilyssa going to get him past them?

As she'd instructed, he kept his head bowed, his face in shadows. Unable to hear anything, he jumped when Ilyssa tapped him on the shoulder. Silently, she signaled for him to follow. Rolf risked a glance at the enraptured look on the Souks' faces and hastened after her. Touching a panel by the portal, Ilyssa waited until the doors slid open and then she strode inside, Rolf following at her heels. At once, the doors snapped shut, locking automatically behind them.

They turned to face a roomful of astonished harem females. Most were Souks but a few young girls were present. Gasps and shrieks accompanied his presence, or so he gathered by the widened eyes and open mouths. He still couldn't hear a thing.

This apparently was some sort of sitting room, with colorful cushions strewn about. The ladies who were lounging on them were dressed in gilded bras and girdles that left little to the imagination. Their faces were elaborately made up. He wondered if they were waiting for their master to make his appearance and felt a sudden urge for haste. If Bolt was expected tonight, he might arrive at any time.

He saw Ilyssa talking but had no idea what explanation she gave. While he was waiting, a couple of plump Souk females lumbered in his direction, eyeing him curiously. One of them said something and grinned, her jagged teeth yellowed and uneven. Reaching out, she made a grab for his groin.

Rolf leapt back. His horrified expression must have provided a source of hilarity, as the Souk females roared with laughter. Four more of them got up and joined the pair circling him. Lust played on their ugly dogfaces.

Ilyssa glanced at him and, seeing his plight, rapidly drew her explanations to a conclusion. At her request, one of the girls obtained a folded green cloth and a pair of matching slippers and handed them over. Ilyssa gave a grateful nod, stuffing the items into the small satchel of belongings tied at her waist and hidden under her robe. Smiling broadly, she strolled in Sean's direction. The poor man was being pawed by the Souks. In another moment, they'd be all over him.

A few sharp words from her and the aggressors backed off. Raising her eyebrow to signal him, she turned and marched toward a back door, and Sean followed.

At the rear exit, Ilyssa spoke into a comm unit and appeared nonplussed when the portal swung open and a contingent of Souk soldiers faced them. Ilyssa waited until Sean was beside her. Then she opened her mouth to sing. After she'd commanded the Souks to forget ever seeing her and her companion, she gave Sean the signal to run.

A moment later they were charging up the hillside into the darkness, leaving the entranced troops far behind.

Clumps of trees and rocks studded the path but they continued to climb.

At the summit, Rolf caught up with Ilyssa and shouted, "Can I remove these now?" He pointed to his ears. She nodded, and he glimpsed a flash of white teeth in the moonlight. Relieved, he drew out the earplugs.

"Your siren song really worked!" he said. He'd been astonished by the looks on the Souk males' faces. It was incredible, but the myth was true! He'd have to think about the implications later. Now there wasn't time.

"I wish I could have gotten an adjustor to alter your implanted linguist patch. It would have been much simpler," Ilyssa said, brushing a stray wisp of hair off her face. The moonlight cast a halo around her, wrapping her in its embrace. Even though her dark clothes hid her figure, Rolf could see her porcelainlike face framed by the luminescent glow.

Stuffing the earplugs into his pocket, he replied, "If it's been so easy for you to escape this place, why haven't you left before now?"

"And abandon my parents? Bolt knew I wouldn't go far with Mama and Papa still under Ruel's domination." She gave him a sly glance. "If you're going to question me, maybe I should have let you be devoured by those Souk females in the harem."

"Not funny," he muttered, a shudder running through his body.

"I kind of think you're cute in that robe, too." She smiled.

"Ease off, Ilyssa."

He was right. She'd better not tease him, or she'd pay the consequences. Yet the thought of what he would do to silence her was so tantalizing that she couldn't shut herself up. "I don't know about their taste, though," she persisted. "Compared to you, Bolt is so much more . . . animalistic." She had had to think a moment for a word that would describe the disgusting brute.

"Ilyssa," Sean warned, a dangerous glimmer in his eyes.

"We should move on. If the guards catch us, they might throw you back in the harem as your punishment."

Sean gave a low growl and stepped forward, grasping her by the shoulders. "This is your punishment, woman," he said, and he drew her close and kissed her.

Ilyssa felt the urgent press of his lips on hers and gave in to his kiss. She wasn't going to break it off in terror this time. Feeling the first taste of freedom, she wanted to experience what it was like to be a real woman for a change. Seeing those females lust after Sean had just increased her own desire. Wrapping her arms around him, she told herself she'd stop after just a moment, after a sampling of what she'd been missing all these annums.

Rolf felt her arms encircle his neck and he groaned and pulled her closer, fusing his mouth with hers, making no attempt to be gentle. He couldn't help it. He'd waited too long for this to go slowly now. Her sweetness drove him wild with need and he traced the outline of her lips with his tongue, urging her to part them. When she did, his tongue thrust inside, hotly exploring her depths.

Rolf felt her soft body sway in his arms and he grasped her tighter, aware that time was running out and they should part. But he could no more stop kissing her than he could stop breathing. He put a hand behind her head for support and moaned. "Gayla . . ."

"What did you say?" Ilyssa jerked free of his embrace.

Rolf looked at her, puzzled by the angry frown on her face. "I just called you—"

"Gayla."

"No, I couldn't have said that!"

Ilyssa studied his face as he paled visibly. "Who is she, Sean?" Suddenly realizing how little she knew about him, she felt her heart sink. "Do you have someone back home, is that it? Are you married, perhaps?"

He lowered his head. "No, I'm not married. Gayla and I were . . . affianced . . . a long time ago. She died."

"Oh." Ilyssa swallowed hard.

"Forgive me. Her memory still comes back to haunt me. She won't let me rest until I finish what I came here to do." He smiled wanly in the dim light. "It was you I was kissing, not her. I meant to say your name."

Feeling hurt despite his explanation, Ilyssa turned away. She'd been wrong to let him kiss her, to give in to her desire for him, and this was her retribution.

"We'd better move on," she mumbled, stumbling over the rise of the hill. The Hortha guards outside her chamber would put out an alert if they weren't back by the next sensor sweep. They had three and a half more hauras to go, and Ilyssa hoped to be long gone by then.

"Wait. I've got to get the knapsack. It's not far from here."

Sean loped off, and Ilyssa stared after him. Upset, she'd forgotten about their hidden stash of supplies. The minutes seemed to tick by while she waited, and she became aware of the nighttime sounds: tree branches rustling in the wind that whistled down from the Upper Drifts, the incessant droning chorus of ceeka insects, the occasional bloodcurdling howl of a creature from the wild. She shivered, realizing the temperature was dropping, and she drew her robe tighter around her body. The spicy scent of jell berries tickled her nose and made her sneeze.

"May the Light of the Aura bless you," Sean said from behind her.

Ilyssa jumped with fright. "You scared me!" He moved into her line of vision, grinning, the knapsack slung over one shoulder.

Rolf was aware he'd offended her tonight by letting Gayla's name slip. He should tell Ilyssa the truth, who he was and why he'd come to Souk. Maybe she'd understand why he felt responsible for Gayla's death and was compelled to exact his vengeance on the Souks. Yet he wasn't sure it would be wise to confide in her now. They still had a long journey ahead of them. If they were caught, would Ilyssa inadvertently blurt out his real name? Would she be forced, painfully perhaps, to reveal his identity? No, it was better to wait. He shouldn't burden her with his mission until later when they were safely away from here.

Ilyssa strode ahead to the flat meadow, beyond which was the overlook where she'd hidden the flyboard after she'd last used it. Glancing back, she was reassured that Sean followed close behind. Once at the right spot, she knelt down. Scrabbling on her knees in the semidarkness, she yanked the vehicle from under the bushes and brushed off the sticks and debris. The crystal chamber showed a 50 percent charge. She hoped it was enough to get them down the line.

"The goggles," she said to Sean. He swung the knapsack around and retrieved their night glasses, but before she put hers on, she asked for the data link. "I've got to disable the sensors along the track where we'll be heading or they'll pick up our approach. I've programmed the main computer to ignore the lapse. The security system will continue to show normal readings."

She activated the hand-held device and set up the comm link to Computer Central. A few seconds later, she was done. After stuffing the data link back into the sack, she donned her goggles. "We only have a window of fifteen minutes. Then the system reverts to full alert. Hurry!"

Rolf eyed the narrow, oblong-shaped board which was curved at either end. Attached in front were standing handlebars. On the right side were controls for ignition and braking.

"I can't ride that thing in this cumbersome robe." He threw it off, stuffing it into his sack for later use.

"It's going to be cold," she warned, watching as he straightened his forest green tunic and leggings.

When he didn't respond, she instructed him in the instrumentation. Then she placed her feet on the narrow board, grasping the handlebars in front. Rolf took a position directly behind her and fastened the safety strap around them both. His strong arms encircled her as he reached for the controls. Feeling her stiffen, he winced.

"Look, Ilyssa, I'm sorry about what happened, okay?"

Ilyssa considered his words. Obviously he still felt something for his precious Gayla if her name hovered on his tongue, but he seemed earnest in his apology. She should at least try to trust him. Yet how could she, when he'd told her so little about himself? Resolving to get answers later, she turned her attention to the task at hand.

"Let's move out," she ordered curtly.

Rolf sighed. Their escape was going to be more difficult if she distrusted him. Saddened, he reminded himself that personal concerns like these could interfere with his mission if he let them occupy his mind. It would be better for them both if he kept his distance. But with her body pressed against his, it wasn't easy. He felt his own body's response even though he willed himself to resist.

"Watch out for wingboxers," Ilyssa warned just before Sean fired up the ignition. The full moons provided plenty of light and the flying reptiles could easily detect loose prey.

The engine kicked on with a shuddering vibration. Rolf's teeth rattled as he keyed in the antigrav switch. The board rose in the air and hovered. Veering in the direction Ilyssa indicated, Rolf pushed the throttle forward. They zoomed off the cliff and soared into free space.

Wind whipped at them, fluttering Ilyssa's robe and tossing Rolf's hair about his head. Feeling his eyes water, he was grateful for the goggles. Cold air lashed at his bared arms. He made a few spiraling turns, bringing them closer to their target. Even from their vantage point, he could trace the line of the track. It originated at the mining camp, snaked through the Rocks of Weir, and straightened out in a direct line toward the factory town of Ma'ahmed beyond the horizon. He didn't feel comfortable about bringing them down where Ilyssa had said. They'd be totally exposed in that open territory until the tram car made its run.

A few moments later, they were there. Breathing a sigh of relief that no wingboxers had shown, Ilyssa waited while Sean shut off the ignition and secured the safety strap. Wishing to see more clearly, she removed her goggles and stuffed them into her bag.

"What do we do with the flyboard?" Sean asked, holding the craft upright by its handlebars.

Ilyssa's eyes widened in surprise. "I don't know! I didn't think of that. We can't just leave it here."

"Will there be space on the tram?"

"We'll have to make space. We'll be getting off just before the tram reaches the processing plant, so I'm sure we can find someplace to hide it there."

"We could use it to reach Ma'ahmed. How far from the factory is the town?"

"About ten kilometers."

"Were you planning to walk?" he asked wryly.

"That detail escaped my notice," she said somewhat sheepishly. It was good Sean was with her. The details of their escape plan had consumed her attention, but apparently she hadn't been able to think of everything. Ilyssa pointed to a huge cranelike device beside the track. "You've got to use that to lower the gate. When the tram comes, it will stop here for exactly three minutes."

Sean rested the flyboard on its side. Putting his hands on his hips, he glared up at the huge structure. "You've got to be kidding. How do I move that metal arm?" He took off his goggles to get a clearer view. Ilyssa retrieved them and added them to her bag.

"There's a pneumatic actuator to provide leverage," she mentioned.

"Ah, yes." He eyed it gingerly. Climbing up posts was not his usual leisure activity, but there wasn't much choice. Throwing his knapsack to the ground, he strode over and grasped the lower climbing hooks. He ascended the crane with a series of grunts. By the time Rolf reached the actuator release, he was sweating profusely and his muscles ached from the strain.

It took a few tries before the release switch unlocked, but then it was easy to swing around the huge overhead arm. With a loud hiss, the pneumatic drive lowered the gate across the track.

Rolf jumped to the ground after he'd descended to an easy level. "How do we get it back up?" he rasped, panting from exertion.

"There should be a reset switch somewhere around here." Ilyssa circled the lower part of the metal structure. "Here's something."

Rolf hastened over. "I guess that'll do it. We'll stash the flyboard in one of the trams. You'll get in another. I'll push the reset switch and hop in after you."

"Right." A low rumbling alerted her. "Here comes the hovertram now!"

From behind the rise of a hill burst the snakelike tram, shooting toward them on a cushion of air. They leapt back as the cars approached, slowing and then finally coming to an abrupt halt just before the lowered gate. With a loud hiss, the tram sank onto the track.

"Now!" Rolf yelled, grabbing one end of the flyboard while Ilyssa grabbed the other. Together they thrust it into one of the open tram cars. The cars were all loaded with ore, the black rocks piled high. Rolf dug around the edges of the flyboard to make a bed for it. He didn't want to lose the vessel over the edge of the tram.

That job done, Ilyssa jumped into the next car, then signaled for Rolf to raise the gate. He pushed the reset button and hopped in after her with the knapsack, wincing when a jagged rock edge caught him in the side. "Gods, how are we supposed to sit in this thing?"

She didn't have time to answer, because the tram lurched into action, rising onto its renewed cushion of air and then speeding forward. Rolf toppled onto Ilyssa, who was crouched beside him, knocking her over. She lay beneath him, her eyes wide, her body stretched out under his.

Ignoring the wild rocking motion, Sean grinned down at her. In the moonlight, it was easy to read his features. Ilyssa didn't like the look on his face.

"Sean," she warned. "Get off."

"I can't. I'm stuck here." In truth, the motion of the tram was making it hard for him to adjust his position. All around them, the ore rocks rattled violently. He was afraid to move or he'd dislodge them and they'd be bombarded.

"My back is being cut into by the rocks. Please move."

In answer, he snaked his arms around her, trying to shield her from the sharp bed underneath. She gazed up at him, trying to will him to move. His face was so close to hers she could feel his warm breath on her cheek. In the moonlight, his eyes glowed with intense brightness. Her lips parted, and she felt her breath laboring. She could feel every part of his hard muscular form against hers. And one part of it was becoming even harder.

"Is this so uncomfortable now?" he said huskily, putting one hand under her head to cradle it and one under her back.

"No," she whispered, ignoring the cold wind rushing above them. He was keeping her warm . . . hot, in fact.

She was feeling very hot. "Oh, God, Sean, kiss me," she pleaded. She couldn't resist the longing anymore.

His eyes fired, and he slanted his mouth over hers. The kiss was gentle, just a feathery brush, a light touch that promised more. Teasingly, his tongue traced the outline of her mouth. He continued to taunt her with light kisses, nibbling gently at her, until Ilyssa arched toward him. Unable to move her arms, she flicked her tongue out instead to let him know she was ready for more.

She closed her eyes and gave in to the marvelous sensations. She'd never felt so weak and yet so empowered with energy that she thought she'd explode. When his mouth crushed down onto hers, she met his kiss with her own fervent hunger. Their lips ground together in a passionate symphony.

Ilyssa lost all awareness of her surroundings. All that mattered was Sean's nearness, the movements of his mouth on hers, the gyrations of his hips atop her. Feeling his weight pressing onto her soft body made a coil of tension spring into her groin. She squirmed, moving her legs further apart to ease the feeling. It only intensified, making her shift uncomfortably, seeking relief.

Ilyssa wished he would touch her breasts. Her nipples ached with a sensation she'd never experienced before and somehow she knew that only his touch could ease the strain. But he was as helplessly pinned into position as was she. Bringing her knee up in an attempt to free an arm, she inadvertently thrust her leg between his thighs. The rocking of the train made her rub against him. Suddenly his body shuddered violently and he cried out. Then he collapsed, panting, his weight crushing her.

"What's the matter?" she asked, alarmed.

"Don't you know?" He lifted his face to gaze at her, his lip curled in amusement.

"Why, no, I—" Her voice ended in a shriek.

Something sharp stabbed at the back of his head. Rolf glanced up and froze. Two wingboxers were circling overhead, preparing for another dive.

"Dig in," Rolf said, scooping ore rocks out of the way. When that didn't work, he grabbed some and threw them at the giant flying reptiles when they swept in for their next approach. He hit one on its leg and it veered off with a screeching howl. But the other one kept coming, its talons unfurled, its pointed beak open, its yellow eyes glowing mad. Rolf had no protection. He felt it scrabbling for a hold on his back, his tunic tearing open at the fierce attack. Stinging pain assaulted him and he shifted sideways, thrusting an arm up so as not to be stabbed in the eye.

Ilyssa shrieked as one of the talons encircled him and started pulling. Desperately, Rolf nodded at the knapsack. "Get the sticks," he rasped. He couldn't keep his balance with the rocking of the car. The wingboxer's grip tightened around his waist, squeezing him in a vise. He felt himself being lifted.

Ilyssa dragged the sack over and rummaged in the contents for the kather sticks. Removing one, she thrust it at him. Rolf grasped it and jabbed at the creature's underside. With a cry of rage, it knocked the stick out of his grasp and jerked him upward. He grabbed on to the side of the ore car and held on with all his might.

By now the other wingboxer had descended and was aiming to grab Ilyssa by the hair. Screaming, she warded off its blows with another one of the sticks. Its sharp claws swiped at her, catching her on the forehead. She felt the blood well up as she fell over, stunned. Something tight encircled her stomach and squeezed, chasing the breath from her.

It's over, she thought dazedly. From somewhere far away, she heard Sean shouting. And then something exploded in her head. No, it wasn't coming from her.

A loud crack of thunder shook the air.

With a piercing squawk, the wingboxer released her. And suddenly they were gone, vanished into the sky as quickly as they had arrived.

For a long moment, Ilyssa couldn't move. She gazed upward, wondering where the stars had gone. Heaving clouds scudded overhead, heavy and laden with moisture. Blue lightning lit up the heavens and another volley of thunder erupted.

"Ilyssa." It was Sean's voice, but it sounded more like a whisper on the wind. Lifting her head with difficulty, she saw him on the other side of the car, stretched across the top of the rocks.

"I'm coming," she said, reaching into the sack for the medic kit. But another bolt of lightning opened the clouds, and rain pounded down upon them. Time passed endlessly until she was able to get closer. The rocks shifted beneath her with each movement and the rain was so intense she couldn't see. But finally she got to him.

His back was a mess. Open gashes were being cleansed by the rain, but they had to be causing him considerable pain. He was still awake, fighting unconsciousness, his face white with agony. Ignoring the throbbing in her own temple, she used the tissue regenerator and healed him. Then she took care of her own wound. With another instrument, she melded the fabric of his tunic back together.

The storm was over as quickly as it had started, but she was grateful for it. It had chased the wingboxers away. And now that they were nearing the end of the run, the creatures wouldn't be a danger any longer. But would Sean be able to continue on to Haakat in his weakened condition? She gave him a hyperspray of stimulant, which appeared to help.

"Are you all right?" he asked, lifting his head to glance at her. He lay on his stomach, and Ilyssa crouched beside him, trying to keep her balance as the tram sped forward above the trackbed.

"I'll be fine. I'm more worried about you. That wingboxer nearly got you."

"I know." He slid his hand out and put it on her knee. "Thanks for your help."

She smiled and shifted forward so that his head rested in her lap. Gently, she caressed the side of his face. His jaw was roughened with a light growth of stubble but she liked the feel of it. Noting the coolness of his skin, Ilyssa wished they had a blanket. The best she could do was to pull her robe across him to shield his body from the wind.

"What's going to happen after we free my parents, Sean? Will you fly us directly off Souk?" She feared he might have his own tasks to accomplish that would interfere with her interests. He'd told her precious little about himself and it was time the man remedied that situation.

"Let's take things one step at a time, shall we?"

She didn't care for that response. It sounded like a dodge. "Who are you?"

"I can't answer that yet."

"Why not? After what we've just been through, don't you think I'm entitled to some explanations? Or do you still not trust me?"

He shifted his position, wincing with discomfort as the ore rocks cut into him. He managed a half-crouch beside her. "It's not a matter of trust," he said, his eyes gleaming darkly in the moonlight. "It's for your own safety that I'm not telling you everything."

"Why? In case we're caught? I won't reveal what I know."

"I'd rather not take that chance."

All he cared about was preserving his precious secrets, she thought, overlooking his mention about her safety. Anger and resentment flowed through her at his closemouthed attitude. "If I didn't need you as my pilot, I wouldn't have brought you with me!" she retorted.

"Don't you think I know that?"

His quiet tone of accusation made moisture spring into her eyes. She turned away, not wanting him to notice. "We'll continue this discussion later. It's two-fifteen now. In a quarter haura, the tram will decrease speed for the approach into the processing plant. We have to prepare to detrain."

"Tell me what to do."

The relief in his voice was unmistakable. Ilyssa gritted her teeth, resolving to force the truth from his lips at the earliest convenience. Otherwise, she just might have to go off to save her parents on her own!

Chapter Eight

"We have to get the flyboard," Ilyssa said. She sat up, striving to keep her balance as the hovertram raced forward. "What do you suggest? It was your idea to bring it along."

Sean glanced over his shoulder at the tram car behind them. "How much will this thing slow when we approach the terminal?"

"The tram decelerates considerably. I don't have the codes for the security system at this end, so we'll have to move fast or we might trip the sensors."

"I was under the impression that you'd planned our escape in detail."

"I did the best I could," she snapped.

Rolf's eyes were beginning to tear from the wind. He requested his goggles and put them on after Ilyssa retrieved both pairs of night glasses from her bag. Squinting at the tram cars thundering along behind them, he came to a conclusion. "I'll have to jump it."

"What?"

"When the tram slows, I'll hop over to the car with the flyboard."

"You'll have to watch your footing," she warned him.

Rolf gritted his teeth. "I'll manage."

About ten minutes later, he had his chance. The speed decreased, and the wind stopped whipping against his face so violently. Gingerly, he edged himself over the jagged corners of the rocks to the end of their car. Peering over, he looked down. The cars were held together by some sort of coupling device. Was it possible to gain a foothold on it with all this rocking? He studied the distance between cars and realized there was no other way. He couldn't leap the distance required.

When the tram slowed sufficiently, Ilyssa urged him to make haste. She was afraid the processing plant's security sensors would pick up their life-form readings. They had to detrain now.

Holding on to the knapsack and her own bag after putting her goggles on, she watched anxiously as Sean precariously made his way to the next car. Breathing a sigh of relief after he made it, she waited while he balanced himself on the flyboard and jabbed on the ignition. In a tumble of ore rocks, the flyboard rose straight in the air.

"We're off!" he yelled exuberantly, heading for Ilyssa's car.

She was barely able to crouch upright as he approached, his arm extended to grasp her by the waist. Another instant and she was being lifted into the air and thrown in front of him. She caught onto the handlebars, nearly sliding off the other end.

"Take it easy!" she cried, but they were in a careening spin to get free of the tram. There wasn't time to fasten the safety strap. Luckily they didn't need it; Sean landed the craft a short distance away.

"Are you all right?" he asked, dismounting after shutting off the ignition.

"I think so." She was trembling but unhurt. "We don't have any time to waste. Ma'ahmed is in that direction." She pointed to the southwest. At two-thirty in the morning, the sky was still punctured by a myriad of stars, but the bright moonlight made it easy to distinguish landmarks.

"Let's get back aboard."

Sean took his position behind her, centering his feet on the board and securing the strap around them both. When he reached his arms around her to grasp the controls, his chest pressed against her back. He pushed the start button, and with a shudder, the flyboard lifted into the air.

The fuel gave out about 20 minutes later. Stranded in a desolate area of tall grasses, Ilyssa peered around. Like Sean, she'd removed her goggles, being able to see clearly enough without them. "At least we can leave the flyboard here and it won't be readily spotted," she remarked.

"Yes, but this is more lost time. Now we have to walk."

She heard the accusatory note in his voice. "Sorry," she commented.

"You should have checked the crystal chamber ahead of time."

Putting her hands on her hips, Ilyssa glared at him. Leaning against the flyboard handlebar, he was eating a food ration and appeared as though he wasn't in any particular hurry. "I had a lot on my mind," she told him. "It would help if you didn't keep blaming me when things go wrong."

"If you'd have let me in on all the details, I might have had some ideas."

"Look, I got us this far, didn't I? Be grateful you're not in the mining camp any longer . . . sumi."

"That's it." He rose to his full height. Throwing away the empty ration wrapper, he approached, a dangerous gleam in his eye.

Ilyssa backed away, aware of how very alone they were . . . and of how little she knew about him. What if he really was a spy or a saboteur? He could murder her now and then complete his own mission in freedom.

"I d-did my best," she stuttered, edging away. At least she'd taken off her bulky robe. She could fight him better in her jumpsuit and heeled boots.

"Do you admit that you need me?" he growled, coming closer. His long black hair was askew, and with his angry eyes and stubble-darkened jaw, he looked quite menacing. His arm muscles tensed as though he was getting ready to grab her.

"What does that have to do with anything?" she croaked. She should be trying to convince him that she was more valuable alive than dead, but her throat seemed unusually dry.

"It has to do with everything," he said, catching her by the hand before she could increase the distance between them. "I need you, too." And he turned her hand palm up, bowing as he kissed her soft flesh inside.

Ilyssa gasped. "What are you doing?"

"Showing you how much I appreciate your efforts." He began kissing her finger tips, one by one.

"No, Sean." He was trying to charm her, but it wouldn't work. He didn't trust her enough to confide in her, and now he'd accused her of being incompetent on top of that! Well, she was still in charge of this escape, not him.

Withdrawing her hand, she said coolly, "It's nearly three o'clock. We only have an haura to pick up transport in Ma'ahmed and get away before Bolt sends out an alert." Her fingers tingled where he'd stroked them, and she clasped them behind her back.

"You're right." Stooping over, he rummaged through the sack, then threw her a ration. "Here, eat this. We might not have the chance later."

After they'd taken a drink and repacked the sack, he slung it over his shoulder and started forward. Ilyssa scampered to catch up. Why, the arrogant lout! Taking the lead already, was he? With her chin held high, she stalked past him.

Rolf watched the proud tilt of her head and smiled. She was so brave and yet so vulnerable. The stubborn woman wouldn't admit that she needed him in any capacity other than a pilot, but he knew differently. Although she had her own opinions and was used to fending for herself, Ilyssa had no one with whom to share her experiences. Her loneliness and longing shone in her eyes. He found himself wanting to make her feel happy and secure, but with physical intimacy between them being prohibited, he felt limited by how far they could go. Having that one sample of her in the ore car had increased his desire tenfold. Yet he knew that even with the fear of Ruel's wrath out of the way, Ilyssa still might not wish to sacrifice her virginity. He'd seen the power of her siren song. Would she be willing to give that up for a man?

Striding ahead, Rolf caught up with her. "What time is it?" he asked more curtly than he'd intended. Soon Bolt would know about their break. They couldn't have gone far without some type of aircraft, and with a little thought, Bolt would figure out they'd hopped the tram. What he would do after that brought a shiver to Rolf's spine. He didn't want to find out.

"It's three-thirty," Ilyssa said, glancing at her chronometer. "We have to find quick transport to Kantina, our destination on the Como River. It's not as close as Svenski because Bolt will probably look for us there, but it's not much farther to the east."

"Ma'ahmed isn't any small hole in the wall," Rolf said, pleasantly surprised as they reached the outskirts of the town. Tall buildings, paved streets, and orderly landscaping made the arid setting more attractive than he would have expected, even though the structures all possessed a uniform squareness. But the town appeared dead. Flamelights on posts illuminated the streets, and shadows flickered along empty walkways. A vibrating rumble from the nearby factory was the only sound that broke the stillness.

"What's that smell?" Rolf wrinkled his nose at a putrid odor.

"The breeze must be picking up emanations from the processing plant. The factory is open around the clock. We'd better be out of here before the shift changes."

"So where to?" Rolf stood beside her and surveyed the wide avenue facing them.

"There are several ways out of this town," she said, wiping her forehead. Despite the coolness of the night, Ilyssa was sweating. Now that they were in a populated location, the chance of discovery had increased and so had her nervousness. "We can go by air, train, common carrier, or speeder. I would say the first three are out because Bolt will be checking all the public transportation schedules. Our best chance is to borrow a speeder."

"Borrow?" He raised an eyebrow.

"Our pictures might be broadcast if Bolt puts out a full-scale alert, so we can't rent one. I hate to use the word steal, but that's the general idea."

"All right," he agreed.

Loping off down the street, Rolf signaled for Ilyssa to follow. The speeders weren't all that different from the ones on Bimordus Two. Glancing up and down the street, his eye picked out a two-seater white vehicle parked along the curb about a block ahead.

"Check for security alarms," he told Ilyssa when they reached the speeder. "Your data link can do that, can't it?"

"Sure." She whipped the device from the bag tied around her waist and did a few quick manipulations. "There isn't any alarm system," she said, relieved. Another touch on her keypad and the electronic lock on the door unlatched.

"We're in." He yanked open the passenger door, and Ilyssa slid inside. So far their movements had gone undetected, but that could change at any time. Eager to leave town, she waited anxiously while Sean dropped into the driver's seat and flung his knapsack into the rear. He faced forward and studied the dashboard, frowning.

"How do we start this thing without a key code?"

"I almost forgot!" Ilyssa reached into her bag and retrieved a data card. "Here, I brought this universal decoder. Stick it in the connector and we'll see if it works." He complied and the ignition charged on. They rose onto a cushion of air as Ilyssa programmed the computer for their destination. The vehicle picked up speed gradually as they veered around a corner and headed straight down a wide avenue for the southwest end of town.

"I'm going to sleep," she said, barely able to keep her eyes open. The soft interior of the vehicle molded to her form. Her limbs relaxed and the tension flowed from her body.

"How long is this run?" Rolf asked.

"We're twelve hauras from Kantina."

"Twelve hauras? We'll be picked up easily along the way!"

"It may help if we switch speeders at one of the fuel stations en route. That will confuse whoever is tracking us. I'll program the computer to make a stop." That done, Ilyssa closed her eyes.

Leaning back in his seat, Rolf calculated how much time remained before the owner of their vehicle woke up and noticed it was gone. They had a good two, maybe three haura head start. But Bolt would be alerted to their absence anytime now. And then what?

"What do you mean, they're missing?" Bolt's thundering bellow could be heard all the way down the corridor from his suite. He faced Commandant Mrek, who was in charge of his Souk troops. The thin-faced soldier quaked visibly as he elaborated on his report.

"The Horthas outside the Dromo's apartment said she did not return for the four o'clock sensor sweep, master. The Dromo and her slave were last seen marching off to your quarters. Ilyssa claimed she needed to talk to you about her visit to Haakat."

"You idiot, I didn't see them! I was in town with a business associate. Search the complex. Make sure you check the production center and surrounding areas. I'll look for clues myself at her terminal in Computer Central."

Once Mrek had left, Bolt wiped a sweaty hand over his face. If Ruel found out she was missing . . . No, he had to find her! But what if she and that sumi of hers had escaped the mining camp and were even now at Ma'ahmed, the closest town? Thinking hard, Bolt decided not to issue a full-scale alert or the pasha's agents would pick up on it and notify Ruel. He'd do better to pretend that everything was routine. Meanwhile, he'd send his best hunter team after the pair. The special sniffers should have no trouble following their scent.

He switched on the comm unit and put in a call for Kraus and Lork. Using the jet flyer in his private hangar, they could be at Ma'ahmed within 20 minutes.

Ilyssa and Rolf reached Kantina without incident. They'd changed speeders at a fuel station along the way and blended in with the traffic going to and from the river cities. Rolf was glad they'd both had the chance for a rest. He'd been thoroughly exhausted, especially after the adrenaline charge that had been keeping him going had dissipated. After getting a few hauras' sleep, he felt refreshed.

Ilyssa was stretching awake beside him. Putting a hand on her knee, he asked, "How do you feel?"

"Better, thanks."

His hand began making small circling motions on her leg, but she brushed it off.

"We have to get air transport in Kantina," she stated in a firm tone that warned him to stick to business. "I don't think we'll have any problems unless Bolt's put out an alert."

"Don't you think he has already?" It was nearing 1600 hauras in the afternoon, and Rolf couldn't understand why they hadn't encountered any roadblocks. Surely Bolt had notified the local authorities?

"We can't check to see if there's a bulletin out for us or we'll run the danger of being located."

"Right." Rolf scanned the roadway. Other speeders and a few cargo transports sped past. He had kept a moderate speed, afraid of attracting attention if they went too fast. Their direction was still southwest, toward the Como River. Already he could see lush vegetation marking the irrigated lands. And he needed to be north, across the Koodrash Mounts, on the other side of the hemisphere.

"It won't take us long to get to Haakat, depending on the flight schedules." Suddenly she pointed. "Put in there. We can hop on the commuter tram to Kantina."

A car park was off to one side, allowing visitors to the city to save fuel and take public transportation.

"Won't the speeder be conspicuous if we leave it there?" When they changed vehicles at the fuel station, they'd selected a sleek black one. Since they hadn't run into any search teams, it was likely the owner hadn't shown up yet. As soon as he put in an alert, whoever investigated would know exactly where they'd gone if the speeder was found in the car park.

"What do you suggest?" Ilyssa asked.

"Bury it somewhere."

"Fine," she said dryly. "You find a place."

Rolf drove into the city, winding around a confusing maze of tree-lined streets during the bustle of afternoon activity. In a quiet residential area, he spotted a canal, one of many that belonged to a city-wide drainage system.

"Let's follow the waterway," Rolf suggested. "We should leave the speeder in a remote area where no one will notice it for several hauras. That'll give us a head start." He kept on driving until they came to a section of town that was sparsely inhabited. "Here's a good place." He pulled off the road onto a sandy shoulder and shut down. Grabbing his knapsack, he joined Ilyssa by the roadside.

"Okay, now what?" she asked. Her bag bulged at her waist and Rolf wondered what she had stuffed in there besides her robe and that green cloth the harem girl had given her.

"It's your call," he said casually, letting his eyes roam over her. Her red hair, loosened from the braid, tumbled about her head in glorious disarray. Its brilliant color contrasted sharply with her snug black jumpsuit. His gaze lingered on her curves, and he remembered how soft she'd felt pressed against his chest on the flyboard. His imagination soared into erotic foreplay.

"You're going to have to do the talking." Her curt tone disrupted his fantasy. "Women don't usually go about town alone unless they're in business, which is rare. I've got to pretend I'm a member of your harem." She pulled out the mysterious package of folded green material from her bag. Shaking it out, Ilyssa held it up, revealing a caftan and matching veil. She had soft-soled shoes to match as well.

A wide grin lit Rolf's face. "Sounds good to me."

"Don't get any ideas. Now turn around. I've got to take my jumpsuit off." She started to undo the fastening strip at her side, but as he continued to stare, she stomped her foot. "Turn around!"

"As you wish," he said politely. Spinning around, he stared at the murky water of the canal and tried to close his ears to the sounds of her disrobing. Despite his best efforts, blood rushed to the more attentive parts of his body, and the sexual fantasy he'd begun before blossomed into full-color display in his mind.

"Okay, I'm finished," she said.

He spun around and nodded in satisfaction. The green caftan with its characteristic yoke designating it as a harem outfit was appropriately shapeless.

"Protocol prohibits any other Souk male from looking at me," she remarked. Demurely lowering her gaze, she fixed the veil atop her head. The green gauze lightly shielded her face. As she bent to retrieve her jumpsuit and pair of short black boots, her hand brushed his when he rushed to help her.

"Sorry," he said, jerking back. The contact sent a rush of heat through him.

Ilyssa stuffed the items into her bag. "Would you mind carrying this for me?" she asked, holding out the sack to him. "It's not appropriate for me to wear at my waist, and it'll show if I hide it under the caftan."

"Where are we going?"

"We need to head for an air ticketing center, but I'm not sure where to find one. We'll have to check at an information kiosk."

For the first time since their arrival in the city, she appraised his appearance. They'd washed up at the fuel station where they'd exchanged speeders, brushing the ore dust from their outfits as best they could. Sean's forest green tunic and leggings were smudged but should pass muster. She supposed he could claim to be a maintenance worker. With his bulging muscles, unruly long hair, and chipped fingernails, he looked the part. Except as soon as he opened his mouth, his cultivated voice gave him away.

Aware of her scrutiny, Rolf took her elbow, steering her toward the business section of town and forestalling the questions that were hovering on her lips.

"Assuming we're able to obtain tickets, what then?" he asked, glancing at her out of the corner of his eye. She wore a frown on her pretty face.

"We go to the airport, check in, and board the flight."

"Won't airport security be alerted to look for us? Surely Bolt will guess you're headed for Haakat."

"Not necessarily. He won't know we're going after my parents. Haakat may be the last place he expects us to go. In any event, our fake ident cards should get us through, but it might be advisable to go down to the bazaar and get some new clothes."

They found an information kiosk at a crowded street corner in the center of town. Souks bustled by, jostling each other in their rush. Although it was getting late, it was summer season, and everyone worked until dark. The temperature was mild with a pleasant breeze blowing off the river.

"How do you work this thing?" Rolf asked, standing before the kiosk. A flat screen display at eye level showed a menu listing several choices including news, transportation, hotels, sights, current financial quotes, and communications.

"It's touch activated." Ilyssa was careful to maintain a demure posture beside him.

Rolf selected transportation and a new list of choices appeared: type of conveyance, schedules, reservations, and Department of Transportation advisories. "Now what?" Rolf hissed as a Souk family passed by.

"Pick flight schedules."

Using that board, Rolf indicated Haakat for the destination. A big red alert sign flashed on the screen.

"What's that?" he said in alarm.

"I don't know." Ilyssa felt her heart thump rapidly in her chest. Could Bolt have notified Ruel about their escape after all? If so, their pictures might be displayed and a reward for their capture posted.

A moment later, a travel advisory flashed across the screen. *Attention all travelers: Haakat is currently closed for incoming transport. A radiation leak at the Foque Power Plant has necessitated evacuation of the city. All residents have left. Attention travelers: Haakat is currently closed to all traffic. . . .*

"No! No, that can't be!"

"Do you know where Ruel might have gone?" Rolf asked quietly.

Numbly, she turned to him. "He has a winter palace at Zeyna." Ignoring protocol, she stepped forward and escaped back to the main menu, then touched the pad for communications. When the screen activated, she requested Zeyna Palace. Access was denied. "The palace is unoccupied!" she said, reading the display. "Where could Ruel be if not there?"

Frantically, Ilyssa contacted various members of the government, oblivious to the risk involved. Ruel had gone north, she learned, but no one knew exactly where or with whom.

Rolf was afraid their location would be pinpointed, so he shut off the display. Taking her elbow, he steered her away. He was as shaken as she but for a different reason. If she couldn't locate her parents, he didn't have the extra time to spend searching for them. He should carry on with his own mission instead. This was already Lexin thirteenth. That left 21 days before the Souk Alliance conference.

Feeling Ilyssa's body tremble beneath his hand, he glanced at her and noticed her fearful expression. "What's the matter?" he asked, concerned. Of course, she must be worried about her parents' safety.

She gave a long sigh and met his gaze. "It's clear what I have to do, Sean. I'm going back to Bolt."

Chapter Nine

"What do you mean, you're going back to Bolt?" Rolf thundered.

"Let's find a better place to talk about this," Ilyssa suggested, glancing at the Souk businessmen scurrying about with their brightly colored caftans swishing at their feet. "The bazaar is just a few streets over."

Fuming, Rolf waited until they reached the crowded marketplace. Strolling along the riverfront stalls, he hoped they were inconspicuous among the shoppers, food vendors, and hawkers of wares. Colorful banners waved in the wind, and all around them, people chattered. Souks and their gimas, puppy-faced children playing tag and munching on treats, and harem females out for an excursion with their masters were only a few who made up the late afternoon throng.

"We should stock up on supplies while we're here," Rolf remarked.

"What for?" She turned to him. "I told you, I'm going back to Bolt."

He set his mouth in a firm line. "We need to talk about that."

"There's nothing to say. You're free to go, Sean. I have to do what I have to do. I don't want my parents to suffer because of me."

"You're trying to rescue them, remember?"

"That's over now. I don't know if I could locate them even if I tried. I'll have to wait for another opportunity."

"Bolt won't let you have one."

She lowered her veiled head. "I'll take my chances." She could accept any punishment Bolt meted out as long as he didn't betray her to Ruel. He couldn't physically harm her or the pasha would find out. Knowing Bolt, he'd probably find other means to satisfy his perversions. Imagining them brought a shiver to her spine. But Ilyssa didn't see any alternative. She had to get back to Bolt before Ruel found out she was missing or her parents would be killed.

What she suggested was not even an option as far as Rolf was concerned. Throwing herself at Bolt's mercy was ridiculous. Even her fast wits and bravery wouldn't save her from what he would do to her.

She had to come with him. It was the only way he'd be sure she was safe. His friends in the resistance might be able to locate her parents and help with a plan to rescue them. But how could he convince her without revealing too much? He wrestled with his conscience, feeling he should tell her who he was but afraid to burden her with the knowledge of his identity.

"Let's get a table at that cafe," he said, pointing to an outdoor eatery located on a patio overlooking the river. "We can continue this discussion while we're eating."

They were seated and placed an order. Ilyssa was surprised to hear him speak fluent Soukese.

"Where did you learn the language?" she inquired.

"I picked it up when I was younger. I always had a gift for dialect. It's been very helpful in my line of work. The written Souk language was more difficult to master."

Glancing around, Sean then leaned forward. "Let's get something straight. You're not going back to Bolt. You'll come with me for now. I have friends who might be able to help with a plan to free your parents."

"Friends? What friends?" Ilyssa frowned, puzzled.

"I can't give you any details."

"Like you can't tell me who you really are or why you're on Souk?" She shook her head, saddened. "When are you going to trust me, Sean?" Not that it mattered what he did; once she went back to Bolt, she'd never see him again. Besides, if he wouldn't tell her the truth about himself, why should she believe he'd keep his word?

Pain flickered behind his expression. "Believe me when I say it's for your own security that I don't tell you more. Isn't it enough that I'm promising to help you?"

"Not really, but let's say we did rescue my parents. What then?"

"Then there would be some more decisions to make. Don't worry; I'd make certain that you reached safety."

He hadn't actually said he would fly her off Souk. The liar! He was using her. Now that they'd escaped the Rocks of Weir, he must have some other purpose in mind for her. Go with him to his friends? Who was he kidding? They could only be a bunch of spies or saboteurs like himself.

"If you really cared about me, you'd tell me who you are. I won't expose your identity to Bolt. You might even convince me to go along with you."

She waited, but when he tightened his mouth and didn't respond, she was enraged. "I've told you everything about myself. I trusted you, but now doubts are clouding my mind. Unless I learn more, I can't go on with you. Ensuring my parents' safety is too important. My only option is to return to Bolt." She didn't know why it was so crucial for him to understand, but it was. However, where she sought compassion there was none. His eyes chilled, and he remained silent.

Frustrated that he couldn't sway her to his viewpoint without revealing more, Rolf glanced away from the hurt look on her face. He'd have to think of another way to convince her. But when he considered how obstinate she was being, he could only envision one path. Later he'd tell her, when they were safely out of Ruel's territory and he was secure in the knowledge that the pasha or Bolt couldn't get to her.

Ilyssa wasn't going to like what he was about to do. Neither did he, for that matter, but he was going to do it anyway.

"I have to use the sanitary, but do you want to go first?" he asked, nodding at the public facilities a short distance away. It wasn't so far that he couldn't catch up to her if she decided to make a run for it.

Ilyssa narrowed her eyes. "Yes, I think I will." Rising, she glanced at her sack laying at his feet. "I'll just take that along with me, if you don't mind." Reaching down, she made a grab for it, but Rolf kicked it between his feet.

"I'd better keep it here," he said in a casual tone. "Harem females don't usually carry large bags like that. I'll be waiting here for you."

Turning on her heel, she strode away.

As soon as she was out of sight, Rolf yanked the knapsack onto his lap and rummaged inside for the medic kit. Opening the small case, he reached for the small packet of fine white powder he'd remembered seeing before. Tearing the plastic package apart, he emptied the entire contents into Ilyssa's fruit drink. Then he signaled for the server. It was time to put into action the rest of his distasteful plan.

Ilyssa looked into the mirrored reflector with troubled eyes. The nerve of the man, not even allowing her to keep her bag. Did he believe that would stop her from carrying out her plan? By the sneaky look on his face, she'd guessed he had something up his sleeve. Well, she didn't have time to play games. Papa was getting sicker by the day, and each haura she was gone was another one in which Ruel might discover her absence. Her return to the mining camp was imperative, regardless of how ill she felt about the consequences. There wasn't any other choice.

Setting her mouth in a determined line, Ilyssa marched toward the exit. With a short lead, she might be able to get away from Sean. Ducking outside, she rounded the corner without even looking in his direction, then felt a hand clamp onto her shoulder.

"Going somewhere?" Sean's voice drawled.

She whirled around. Their two sacks were slung across his back, and in one hand he carried a paper bag. He gripped her with his other free hand. "Let me go," she said, twisting in his grasp.

"I'll release you if you agree to discuss this rationally," he said mildly. The fury in his eyes belied his casual tone.

"All right." She had no wish to make a scene.

He dropped his hand. "It's getting late. I suggest we rent a room and then decide what to do."

"I can't waste the time. I need to get back to Bolt."

"Very well," he said, much to her surprise. "If you're insisting on that course of action, you should think up an excuse for your absence so Bolt won't punish you."

It was a good idea, Ilyssa conceded. She dreaded facing the militant Souk again and snatched at the excuse for a delay. Either way she'd still have to go back, but at least if she gave Bolt a good reason for her absence, the satrap might be more lenient with her. Nodding, she fell into step alongside her handsome escort. A lock of black hair had fallen across his forehead, giving him a rakishly appealing look. His brow was furrowed in concentration as he focused his attention on weaving a path for them through the noisy throng.

"I brought our food. I'm sure you're hungry," he said, catching her eyes on him. He withdrew her covered drink from the paper bag and handed it to her with a smile. "I know I'm famished."

"Thank you," she murmured, accepting the plastic cup. His warm gaze made her heart flutter, and she distracted herself by lifting the lid and taking a sip. Her throat was uncommonly dry. Tilting the container, she drained the contents.

"We'll find a place with a fabricator, so you can get another beverage later."

Sean watched her lick off a droplet of fruit drink from the side of her mouth and Ilyssa flushed. Although her course of action was set, she had to admit she was reluctant to leave him. Even without knowing who the man was or why he was on Souk, she felt drawn to him by a compelling magnetism she couldn't explain.

They headed for the section of town by the train station. It was a deteriorated area, with a lack of maintenance evident in structures with peeling paint and broken casements. Sean suggested they look for a place to stay where their ident cards wouldn't be requested. They found a run-down building on a quiet side street. A sign offered rooms for hire.

Reminding Ilyssa to act her role as a demure gima, Rolf reflected upon the irony of it as they ascended a short flight of steps to the warped door at the top of the rise. It hadn't been so long ago that she'd been cautioning him to act his part as an obedient sumi.

Standing beside him, Ilyssa bowed her veiled head as he haggled with the proprietor in fluent Soukese. His delivery was smooth and practiced as though he were a skilled negotiator. Although she admired the easy way he took charge, Ilyssa resented her own acquiescence. It seemed to be the story of her life so far. First it was Ruel, then Bolt, and now Sean telling her what to do. If she didn't feel so tired, she'd give him her advice on how to deal with the Souk. But by the time he'd pushed open the door to their room, she could barely stagger to the round bed in the center.

"Sleepy?" he asked solicitously, shutting the door behind them and dropping the sacks. In two quick strides, Sean was at her side, assisting her into a reclining position.

She couldn't even protest. Her eyelids were too heavy. "I jus' need a little resh," she slurred, closing her eyes.

"Sleep tight," he murmured, pulling a light blanket over her. Those were the last words she heard.

When Ilyssa awoke, the first thing she felt was a rocking sensation similar to the motion of the ore tram, but without the jarring rattle of the rocks beneath her. It was a soothing movement, and she was loath to open her eyes. Aware that she was stretched out on a soft bed with a comfortable head cushion, she listened to the sounds around her. The soft hiss of an air-filtering unit and a low vibrating engine hum came to her ears.

An engine hum?

Her eyes flew open. She was lying on a lounger bed, and directly across from her, a narrow aisle separating them, was Sean seated on another. He was reading something off her data link, a frown on his face. Her glance perused his refined features, clean square jaw, and hunched shoulders. Even a short distance away, she could feel the heat his hulking presence radiated.

Peering around, Ilyssa saw a curtained casement, a door leading to a sanitary, and another closed door, presumably an exit from this small compartment.

By the moons of Agus Six! Her eyes widening in shock, she recognized where they were and bolted upright. The motion made her head reel dizzily. "This is a train!" she croaked. "How did I get here?"

Flushing, Rolf deactivated the data link and stuffed it back inside the knapsack. "So you're awake," he murmured, glancing at her from under his thick, dark brows. "How do you feel?"

"Terrible. I'm dizzy, and there's a funny metallic taste in my mouth. Where are we going and how did we get here? I don't remember anything."

He cleared his throat, obviously uncomfortable. "We're on a hovertrain."

"I realize that. Why is my mind such a blank?"

He gave her a sheepish grin. "I put a sedative in your fruit drink. It was only a mild dose. I didn't know you'd sleep all night."

"All night?" She brushed a hand over her face as though to clear the cobwebs from her mind.

He strode over, sitting beside her and putting his arm around her. "The means I used may have been despicable, Ilyssa, but my intentions were honorable. I won't allow you to return to Bolt. If you're with me, I can keep you safe."

He'd tricked her, and she didn't care what rationale he used. "Get your hands off me. You've taken me against my will, putting my parents at risk. Every minute I'm gone from the mining camp increases the chances of Ruel finding out. He'll kill my parents the instant he learns I've fled."

"We'll find another way to rescue your parents once we locate them. Please forgive me. I couldn't bear the thought of Bolt having you at his mercy." He bent his head and nuzzled her behind the ear.

"Stop that!" His nibbling sent tingling sensations along her nerves. "How long is this train trip going to take? Where are we heading?"

"Across the Koodrash Mounts." He led a trail of kisses down her long neck.

"What?" It would take days for them to cross the high range of mountains to the north of the equator.

"I have business on the other side."

"I'll bet you do." Furious at his deception, and even angrier at the way he was attempting to distract her, she twisted out of his arms and jumped up. "How in Zor did you manage to pay for our tickets?"

"I had plenty of credits," he said.

"From where?" Her eyes narrowed suspiciously. "You didn't!" she cried, snatching up her small bag and flipping it open. "You stole my jewels!"

"I didn't steal them. I just exchanged them for credits. Now we have enough for whatever we need."

"How dare you?" It didn't matter that she'd brought along the jewelry Ruel had given her for just that purpose. Sean was a thief and a liar. She swung her sack at him and missed. "I'm leaving!" She rushed out of the compartment.

"Wait! I need to talk to you!" he called after her.

Ilyssa ignored him. Infuriated, she dashed from one car to another. Covered metal grids surrounded the swaying platforms and she had to grip onto handrails as she stepped across each one. Outside, gray skies released a driving rain. The dismal weather reflected her mood. They must have already reached the foothills of the Koodrash Mounts. Through the casements in the cars, she saw a broad lake and evergreen forests and rolling terrain. Soon the train would begin a long, snaking ascent. Her mother had briefed her on Souk geography, so she knew rock slides were a danger at higher altitudes. As they crossed through the Upper Drifts, avalanches would pose a threat.

Across the Koodrash Mounts? Sean must be crazy! That was thousands of kilometers from Haakat. What about the additional hazards of border guards and attacks by roving carnivore tribes, primitives who lived in the remote reaches of the mountains and occasionally descended to storm the train? She'd heard horrifying stories about what happened on some of the runs. If Sean had to go in this direction, why hadn't he chosen to go by air?

She left the private compartment section and entered tourist class where rows of seats faced forward. It wasn't until she'd passed through a few cars that Ilyssa realized the threat she was posing to herself. People were staring at her. She was dressed for the harem and her master was nowhere in sight. Slowing, she altered her pace to a more suitable saunter. Her veil was back in the compartment. Sean must have taken it off while she slept. Her auburn hair would stand out in this crowd of brown-haired Souks like a bonfire on a snowy peak. If Bolt had sent someone after her, she'd easily be detected.

For a moment, she considered the option of letting herself get caught. But the orders issued for her capture might not specify alive or dead. Bolt could be so infuriated that he wouldn't care.

"Here you are!" Sean's angry voice snarled, and gripping her arm, he yanked her backward.

"Let go of me!"

His furious blue eyes bored into hers. "You don't go anywhere without my permission, understand? Come with me. We're going back to the compartment."

"You arrogant son of a belleek." But Ilyssa didn't protest as he led her back toward the private compartment section.

"I said I wanted to talk to you," he remarked once they were inside their compartment and the door was closed.

She thrust her chin in the air. "What about? If you're going to offer excuses for your behavior, I won't accept them."

"I'm ready to tell you who I am."

Her jaw dropped as she saw from his expression that he was serious.

"My real name is Lord Rolf Cam'brii," he began.

"Lord Cam'brii!" she shrieked. "Of the Coalition High Council?"

"Aye, mistress." He gave her a sweeping bow.

Seeing the elegance of his gesture reminded her of the other times she'd observed him. His courtly mannerisms, his cultured voice, his familiarity with the arts and politics—it all made sense. But Lord Cam'brii . . . !

Ilyssa staggered to her lounger and sank down, sitting on the edge. "I don't believe it. Yes, I do. I always thought you were more than a trader." Her eyes locked with his. "But why didn't you tell me sooner?"

He paced, his hands clasped behind his back. "At first I wasn't sure of your loyalties. Remember that conversation we had in Computer Central? I had to consider the possibility that you disapproved of my actions against the Souks."

She didn't comment on that. "You must have decided to trust me to some extent, because you agreed to escape with me."

"Yes, but then I hesitated telling you anything in case we were caught."

"You were afraid I'd expose you? Don't you know me better than that?"

"There are ways to get people to talk, Ilyssa. Unpleasant ways."

"That's ridiculous. I would never—" Wait a minute, what had she heard the last time she was in Ruel's palace? Lord Cam'brii was being sought after by the pasha's agents. "Sean . . . I mean, Lord Cam'brii . . . Ruel wants to capture you!"

"What?" He halted in his tracks, staring at her.

"Ruel has agents searching all over for you. He has some sort of personal vendetta against you."

"Personal vendetta? What for? We've never even met."

Ilyssa closed her eyes, trying to remember what she'd heard at the state banquet. "He holds you responsible for the First Amendment abolishing the slave trade within Coalition territory."

"I'm proud of that accomplishment."

"He also blames you for the death of his brother, Cerrus Bdan, at the hands of the Morgots."

"But I had nothing to do with that!"

"Apparently you were in league with the Great Healer, Sarina, and her mate Captain Reylock."

"But that's preposterous to blame me!" He paused, stroking his chin. "Maybe Ruel's the one responsible for the assassins," he remarked. Explaining to Ilyssa, he said, "I was attacked by a band of Twyggs when I was showing Sarina a replica of the Rainbow Glen last annum. We were in the Rain Forest Biome on Bimordus Two and it was during our betrothal period."

"Yes, I'm aware of the legend. Sarina had to fall in love with a member of the ruling House of Raimorrda for her healing power to become activated. The plague called the Farg and the Morgot invaders were destroying the Coalition and the High Council had pinned their hopes for salvation on the Great Healer."

"Captain Reylock turned out to be the Raimorrdan in the legend," Rolf went on. He and Teir were both descendants of the noble lineage that crossed planetary boundaries. But Teir's heritage had been hidden until his love for Sarina prompted him to seek his birthright. "Once Sarina became the Great Healer, she eradicated the Farg," he said. "The Morgots were forced to retreat after a decisive battle in the Tendraan system. And the First Amendment passed the vote in both houses of government."

"Much to the dismay of the Souks."

"As the amendment's sponsor, I was a target for their assassins before the vote, but I've been puzzled as to why someone still wants me dead even after the measure has been enacted into law. You're saying Ruel is after me?"

"He did say he'd sent assassins to kill you," Ilyssa said, her concern showing in her eyes. "Right now he has orders out for you to be captured alive, but his agents haven't been able to locate you." She gave a small mirthless laugh. "No wonder! You're right here on Souk!"

"I'm here to put a stop to the sumi issue once and for all, Ilyssa. If it takes violence to do so, then that's the way it'll go. I'm supposed to meet with the resistance and see to it that they're supplied with arms and whatever else they require. We're aiming to establish a direct link between the underground leaders and the Coalition."

"So Ruel was correct in that regard. I thought diplomacy was your trade, not terrorism, my lord." She lowered her gaze to study her fingernails, but not before he'd glimpsed the disapproving expression on her face.

He grimaced in annoyance. "Call me Rolf. Circumstances require more direct measures in this case. Pashas like Ruel won't listen to peaceful overtures. The only thing he understands is warfare. It's what he practices every day when he sends his pirate ships out to attack innocent victims."

"But the Souk Alliance conference might show good results."

"You know about that, too?" She must pick up a lot of information when she visits Ruel, he thought.

"Some of the pashas are supportive of emancipation. They're in favor of hired labor, feeling it would benefit Souk economically to be able to join the Coalition. They want to avoid the bloodshed the planet is headed for.

That's the reason the conference has been convened."

"The resistance doesn't think it's going to work."

"Ruel thinks the Coalition High Council is supporting the resistance with the goal of toppling the Souk Alliance."

"That's ridiculous. We're only trying to support a movement that's started from within the Souk hierarchy." He paused. "I have to get to that conference in Drobrok."

"What for?"

"As an observer. Someone's going to be there I have to see." He hesitated, feeling uncertain. "Well, Ilyssa? Are you going to help me?"

She leveled her gaze on him. "I don't know yet. I'm not certain I agree with your methods."

"Fine. You tell me another way to go about accomplishing the same goals and I'll take it."

"Perhaps with arbitration—"

"That doesn't work on this planet, damn it. This isn't Circutia. People are dying here."

Thinning her lips, Ilyssa retorted, "Where do I fit into your scheme of things? It must have been convenient for you when I offered to help you escape. Was your crash a planned event, too? Were you hoping to be captured so you could rouse the sumis to action?"

"No," he said quietly. "I fully intend to keep my bargain with you. I will help you rescue your parents."

"When? After you've completed your mission?" She stood, her voice rising in pitch. "Will you turn me over to your friends in the resistance and tell them to hold me captive until you return?"

Alarmed at the evidence of her growing hysteria, Rolf strode over to her. "I gave you my word I'd take care of you," he said, putting his hands on her shoulders.

She jerked away. "Don't touch me! You lied to me and tricked me. Why should I believe you now?"

Looking into her panic-stricken eyes, Rolf swallowed. "Please, Ilyssa. I've confided in you. I thought this would help."

"Oh, it helps all right. Now I see things more clearly. You needed me to get you out of the mining camp and now you're ready to discard me."

"That's not true! I'm a man of honor. I told you I would help you free your parents and I meant it. Blast it, Ilyssa, how can you doubt me?"

His look of pain stabbed at her but she ignored it. The man was a prince in the literal sense of the word. What could she possibly mean to him? He'd been using her, that was all.

"I'm going for a walk to think things over," she snapped. "Don't come after me."

Rolf watched her storm out of the compartment and felt his heart twist in anguish. By the stars, how could he possibly have gone wrong? He'd told her his identity, revealed his purpose in coming to Souk. What more did the woman want? The idea flickered through his mind that she might oppose his goals and become a threat to him, but he just as quickly cast it away. Ilyssa's prime concern was that he wouldn't honor his pledge to rescue her parents. Her own fears and loneliness were sweeping her away in a sea of doubts. He had to make her see she wasn't alone anymore. But how could he go about it?

Maybe by reassuring her that you still desire her as a woman. They had three more days before the final stop in Coroban. He had that much time to gain her trust . . . and hopefully, her affection as well. He suddenly realized he craved them both.

Ilyssa stopped at a dining car and realized she hadn't had anything to eat since the day before. After grabbing a quick meal, she wandered forward, hoping to find a quiet spot in the reading car and think over everything Rolf had said. The stares of the other passengers didn't faze her. Her need to be alone was too great for her to care about what they thought or the possible danger she was placing herself in by meandering about alone. Or maybe her mind was dulled, a lingering result of the drug Rolf had given her. That certainly seemed to be the case when she found a comfortable seat in the reading car and promptly fell asleep.

It was late afternoon when she awoke. Rain was still driving against the casement as the train chugged through a forested incline. A faint chemical odor hung in the air. Ilyssa glanced at her chronometer and frowned. Lord Cam'brii must be wondering where she was, although knowing him, he'd probably come searching for her and left her alone when he spotted her dozing.

She noticed a sanitary at the far end of the car and rose, intending to wash away the dust of travel. Part of her still couldn't believe Sean Breslow was really Lord Rolf Cam'brii. How could the esteemed High Councillor have ended up at the Rocks of Weir? The first time she'd seen the man, she'd thought he was the answer to her dreams. Fate had dropped him from the sky just when she'd needed a pilot and had the means to coerce Bolt into giving her one. Was it also fate that she and Rolf were meant to be together?

Shaking her head in bewilderment, Ilyssa entered the vacant washroom. The issues were too complicated for her to pass judgment so quickly, she thought, splashing her face with cold water. It would be better to find out more about Rolf's plans before giving him her trust. Her primary goal was to save her parents. If he wouldn't help her, she'd have to do it by herself. But now that Ilyssa knew his identity, would he let her go? He'd kidnapped her once already. What would stop him from doing so again?

Exiting, she headed toward the front of the train, still too uncertain of her feelings to confront him. Spotting a lounge car, she winced at the remarkable din that hit her ears when she pushed open the door and entered. Sitting around small tables were clusters of laughing, chatting people.

To her left was a traveling Souk salesman, showing his stock of rugs to a bored client. His thick-lipped mouth moved nonstop as he gave his pitch. Behind him was his harem, ten females at Ilyssa's tally. The veiled ladies were munching on nuts and prattling happily among themselves.

Across the aisle, a fat Souk was arguing with his gima while their children ran screaming up and down the aisle. But what caught Ilyssa's eye with fascination was the group at the other end of the car. A boisterous band of humans, dressed in strange garb, was performing a series of even stranger exhibitions. A bearded man wearing baggy pants and a long jacket over his round torso was standing alone, apparently talking to himself. He made hand gestures that seemed to go along with his words and occasionally bowed. A woman was playing a flutelike instrument, accompanied by a young man clanging a triangular metal piece. Four people were standing stiffly, taking turns speaking, with flat expressions on their faces. And one younger girl was singing, her clear high voice penetrating the din. No one was listening . . . except Ilyssa.

She strode forward, intrigued. "Excuse me," she said, tapping the girl on the shoulder from behind.

The girl, dressed in a miniskirt with a midriff-type top, glanced up in surprise. A contemptuous look came over her face when she saw Ilyssa's green caftan. "Yes, what is it?"

"I just wanted to compliment you on your singing."

"Oh. Thanks."

"Have you been studying long?"

"I haven't studied at all."

"Really? But your notes are so refined. I'm a vocalist myself."

"Are you?" The girl's expression changed to one of interest. "What's your repertoire?"

"I sing ballads."

"Hey, that's prude, man! Are you a performer, too?" She twirled her index finger around a curl on her blond head.

"No, I prefer to pursue my singing for private pleasure." Changing the subject, Ilyssa asked, "Are you and your friends a troupe of players?"

"Yep. Hey, you want to meet the others?"

"I'd love to." Reluctant to return to her private compartment and to Rolf, Ilyssa responded eagerly to the introductions. They were a fun bunch of people and very gregarious. When the lone speaker, an actor named Balthazar and the leader of the group, asked her to sing for them, she declined graciously.

"I'm afraid I don't like to sing in front of a crowd," she said. "What kind of plays do you perform?"

"We keep alive the works of Vernon Balsakk. He was a playwright on our home planet Vilaran many annums ago. Our central library keeps an extensive collection of his artistic works but we prefer to maintain a living trust, so to speak."

He nodded to the other four who'd been rehearsing lines. "I do the soliloquies. That's Mercutio, Nestor, Beatrice, and Luciana. Pinch and Helena are our musicians and Rosalyn is our singer." They all came around, and he added, "We'd be happy to demonstrate some of our lines for you."

Ilyssa took an instant liking to the man. About 20 annums older than herself, he had creases feathering his eyes, giving him a kindly look. His heavy black beard matched his dark eyes and lent him an air of distinction.

Before she could comment, a commotion at the other end of the car drew their attention. A trio of brawny men had pushed their way inside the car and were asking occupants to show their ident cards. All three humans wore identical slate-gray stretch bodysuits and Ilyssa's eyes widened when she saw they were armed.

"On whose authority do you make this inspection?" Balthazar bellowed in his deep baritone voice.

One of the men gave him a cold appraisal. "We're agents of the pasha. Arms smugglers are aboard this train. A reward of five thousand credits is being offered for information leading to their arrest."

Ilyssa gasped. Agents of the pasha? Oh no! And she'd forgotten her veil again! Eyeing a shawl on a seat, she snatched it up and tied it over her head as the intimidating men approached.

Chapter Ten

"Your identification," demanded the tallest customs agent, looming in front of Ilyssa like an ominous shadow. He had shaggy gray hair, cold black eyes, and a snarl twisted his mouth. The other two men circulated among the theater troupe, checking their ident cards. The one who'd responded to Balthazar had dirty blond hair; the other, thinning brown hair and a mustache. All of them looked stern.

"I left it in my compartment," Ilyssa mumbled, her heart thumping in her chest.

"Your name?"

"This lovely lady is one of us," Balthazar said, shoving his own card in his pocket and encircling her waist with a protective arm. "Forsooth, can you not see her great beauty? By her window have I in the moonlight sung verses of unrequited love, and stolen impressions of her fancy with gifts of sweetmeats, bracelets, and bouquets. Fairer than the fairest maiden is our lady, but alas, her heart she is loath to yield. How slowly time passes!" he cried, rubbing a hand over his face. "Like a candle lax to wane, she pretends to be indifferent but melts in my embrace. Knoweth do I that she delights in my presence, but getting her to acknowledge it is like getting a wingless bird to fly."

Tilting his head, he eyed the obviously bored agent. "Shall I continue?"

"Let's go, Gant," the blond said, glancing at them in disgust. "We need to search the private compartments. We'll catch her later."

Gant nodded slowly. "Very well. We have sixteen hauras before our first stop in Vloxvil. No one's going anywhere." His dark gaze fixed on her. "You'd better have your ident card ready when we come around, lady."

He turned away, joining the other two agents. The blond man snickered and made an obscene remark about her as they strode away.

Ilyssa breathed a sigh of relief as they exited through the platform door. Sixteen hauras before the first stopover! How would she elude those men until then? The idea of armament merchants being aboard was enough to send chills down her spine, and now there was the added complication of dodging vigilant agents of the pasha who might stumble onto her identity by accident. And what of Rolf? If he was caught, he'd be executed as a spy.

"You all right?" Balthazar asked, glancing at her with concern. He hadn't taken his arm from around her waist.

"Yes, thank you." She twisted out of his grip and stepped away. Removing the shawl from her head, she dropped it onto a nearby seat.

"I told you we should have hired private compartments," Pinch said, holding his triangle and wand. His tight facial features matched his name, but Ilyssa thought he was rather cute with his unkempt blond hair and lanky frame.

"You know we couldn't afford it," Balthazar grumbled.

Ilyssa's face brightened. "Why don't you come with me? You can rehearse in my compartment, and I understand the paneling is quite soundproof so it should afford some privacy."

"You're traveling alone?" Balthazar asked in astonishment.

"No, I have a companion. I'm sure he won't mind." If those customs agents were about to barge in on Rolf, the theater company might provide a good smoke screen.

For the first time, the troupe leader appeared to notice her caftan with its characteristic yoke. "You're a member of a harem?" he said, his eyes widening.

"No, not really. I just thought it prudent to wear this outfit."

"Oh, I see. You and your friend are not—" He broke off, flushing with embarrassment.

"We're unattached. What do you say?" she asked the others, who'd been curiously listening.

"Let's go!" Rosalyn said eagerly.

They drew numerous odd stares tramping through the train, the players being loaded down with equipment. Chatting noisily, the group was delighted by her offer to practice in the convenience of a private compartment. Ilyssa wondered what Rolf would say but didn't think twice about it. If the customs agents did visit their compartment, he'd be grateful for the diversion.

Anxiously, Rolf dashed his fingers through his hair as he waited in the compartment for Ilyssa to return. She'd been sleeping in the reading car when last he'd checked on her, worried about her long absence. But she'd been gone too long.

Concerned, he headed for the door, intending to reassure her that he still had her best interests at heart. If she'd leave the arrangements regarding her parents up to him, Rolf would offer Ilyssa his protection until she was safely home on Circutia. Would that be so difficult to accept? But Ilyssa was strong-willed and used to making her own decisions. She might not be willing to give up her say in their escape plan. Her independence was a trait he admired even though it contributed to her stubbornness.

He neared the door just as it burst open. Ilyssa glided inside the compartment followed by over a half-dozen people. Rolf cursed. Just when he wanted time alone with her.

Ilyssa made introductions, warning him about the customs agents. "You do still have our ident cards, don't you?" she asked, raising her eyebrows meaningfully.

He'd seen the falsified documents inside her bag. "They're still in the same place."

"We should be all right then," she said optimistically.

The next hauras were taken up with watching the players practice. Ilyssa was charmed by their talent, and she was pleased to note that Rolf appeared entertained as well. The only unpleasant intrusion was when the customs agents arrived. They carefully examined the ident cards she'd obtained. After peering closely at her and Rolf, Gant snorted and signaled for his friends to leave. But his abrupt manner of departure left her with an uneasy feeling.

"Do you really think there are arms smugglers aboard?" she asked Rolf later when they'd returned from evening nourishment.

Feeling full, Rolf loosened his leather belt. "It's possible, but where would they be heading?"

"The resistance meets on the other side of the Koodrash Mounts in the Nurash Desert. They could be bringing a shipment of weapons there. By the way, what's our destination?" Picking up a hairbrush, Ilyssa began smoothing out her long auburn waves.

"I need to get to a village by the Salts of Dorado." His eyes followed her movements.

"What for?"

"To make contact with the resistance."

"Let's hope the arms merchants aren't going to the same place."

"It would be news to me if the freedom fighters have their own supply of weapons. I thought one of my functions was to arrange for armaments."

"You know my feelings on that score, Rolf." She put down her hairbrush and glared at him.

He stepped in front of her, his steady gaze holding hers. "We may have our philosophical differences, Ilyssa, but freedom is still a goal for both of us. Don't you think we can work together?"

With him standing so close that she could smell his masculine scent, she couldn't think of anything but him. Sexual awareness flooded her. Her gaze swept over his handsome face and lowered to his broad chest which stretched taut the fabric of his tunic top.

He saw the look in her eyes and took a deep, shaky breath. "Ilyssa, we can discuss this later. I'd much rather kiss you."

And he grasped her in his arms and pulled her close. As his mouth met hers, Rolf fought the urge to unlock his pent-up passion in a rushed release like the last time. But her lips were so sweet and intoxicating that he began to get lost in the mind-numbing sensations she was creating in him. His sense of logic fumbled for control over the curls of enticement spiraling through him. Vaguely he realized that he should slow down, yet it was difficult to restrain himself despite his awareness that he wanted more from her than she'd be able to give.

Ilyssa felt his mouth moving eagerly over hers and she closed her eyes, remembering the last time in the ore car. Rolf had stopped kissing her then, she recalled, still not understanding why. She'd forgotten to ask him about it, too. Would the same thing happen now? But as his murmurs of passion allayed her doubts, she found herself losing all sense of reason and focusing solely on the pleasant sensations he aroused in her.

By the stars, she hadn't realized how much she'd wanted this. She tilted her head back, encouraging him to trail a line of kisses down her neck. His nibbling movements on her soft skin made her squirm with restless delight.

"Let's lie down," he rasped, urging her to her lounger. He stretched out beside her and ran his hands along her arms, tickling the soft inner surfaces. And when she laughed with pleasure, he kissed her flushed cheeks, her temple, and the bridge of her nose. His lips found hers again, crushing her mouth with the frantic movements of a man lost in lust. When his tongue probed, she parted her lips. Instantly he deepened the kiss, thrusting inside to taste her sweetness.

Ilyssa met his eager probing with her own hesitant explorations. Wrapping her arms around him, she let her hands roam his back, enjoying the feel of strong muscles rippling beneath his tunic. It was a new experience for her, to be with a man like this, and she felt a sudden urge to remove his top, to smooth her fingers along his taut flesh and soak in his masculine essence. Being with him charged her with an energy she didn't comprehend. Squirming, she switched her position so that he lay directly atop her.

He moaned and explored her mouth with renewed vigor. When she thought she'd die from lack of air, he lifted his head and shifted downward to kiss her neck. Ilyssa arched toward him, the tension mounting within her as he flicked his tongue across her tender skin.

"Ilyssa, I want to touch you," he said in a low, husky tone that sent shivers down her spine. His long ebony hair fell across his face as he gazed at her with heatstruck eyes.

Ilyssa's pulse pounded in her throat. Her nipples ached and she remembered the sensation from before. This time, she'd let him touch her there. It could help to relieve the throbbing tingle his physical nearness caused.

"Yes, I'd like that," she agreed, moistening her lips.

He looked at the longing shining so clearly in her green, gold-specked eyes and wanted desperately to make love to her. Take your time, he told himself, sliding his hand across her ribs and brushing it over her breast. He heard her gasp and kissed her, leaving his hand in place until he was sure she wasn't going to protest. Then he began a gentle kneading motion, bringing his other hand into play on the other side. He felt her nipples peak and harden beneath his thumbs and it increased his own need tenfold.

"This would be easier if we didn't have so many clothes on," he whispered, feeling the restriction of his leggings across his swollen groin.

Ilyssa was so lost in the incredible sensations coming from her nipples that she barely heard him. "Yes," she answered, not sure what he was asking. The side fastening on her caftan loosened and gave way, and she realized belatedly he'd opened it. He slipped the sleeves off her arms and lowered the fabric to her waist, exposing the top half of her lingerie. The coolness of the air-conditioning swept over her skin.

"By the corona, you're beautiful," he said, looking at the swell of her breasts. And then he lowered his head and kissed them.

Ilyssa thought she'd go out of her mind as he pushed the remaining material out of the way and maneuvered a nipple into his mouth. She grabbed onto his hair, arching toward him as his tongue stroked the tight tip. Biting her lip in ecstasy, she writhed beneath him.

"Oh, Rolf. I want to touch you," she moaned, pulling at his tunic. Quickly he shed it and then was back, kissing her on the mouth and fondling her breasts. She let her hands slide up the rippling muscles of his arms, across his broad shoulders, and down in front along his pectorals. When her fingers encountered his nipples, she was surprised to discover they were hard as pebbles. Splaying her hands, she reveled in the silken feel of his hairy chest.

Feeling her hands on his skin, Rolf had an unbidden image of Gayla touching him, exploring him with her eager fingers. She had been much more forward than Ilyssa, often making the first move to initiate lovemaking. Yet somehow Ilyssa's shy hesitancy appealed to him more, perhaps because it was such a contrast to her strong personality. Or maybe it was just that as a man, he liked to be the aggressor in the field of love.

Shifting downward, he began removing her caftan from below, exposing her flattened belly. He heard her suck in a breath as he drew the material lower. His breathing grew ragged as he caught sight of her nest of reddish hair.

"Rolf, I don't think—" she began.

"I won't hurt you," he crooned.

But her hand stopped his when he touched her there. "Please stop. I can't go further." Her eyes reflected her fear.

"Am I going too fast? I'm sorry, *larla,* but you're so lovely I can't resist wanting to see all of you."

Ilyssa wished they could continue. What he was doing felt so good, she wanted to find out what it was like to go on. But it was too dangerous. Lost in the embrace of his seductive powers, she might forget her reasons for abstinence.

Pushing him off, she sat up and began getting dressed. "I'm sorry, Rolf, I shouldn't have let things get this far."

"What's wrong?" His eyes showed his puzzlement.

"I never told you what Ruel did to me that day in Haakat, after he'd caught me with the minister and then killed him."

"I know he frightened you and hurt your brother. But he's not here now, Ilyssa, so what's the problem? Are you afraid you'll lose your ability to sing if we . . . if you . . ." Seeing the look on her face, he broke off.

In a trembling voice, Ilyssa spoke. "Ruel took me to the medical clinic and gave orders that I was to be prepared for surgery. Not knowing what he planned, I got so hysterical that I had to be sedated. When I woke up, he said he'd taken steps to ensure he'd never lose the use of my siren song. I was to remain a virgin, and he'd had a safeguard placed inside of me that would sound an alarm if it was ever breached. He'd kill my parents instantly if anyone violated me.

"Then to prove to me that he meant his threats, he led me into a soundproof room where my brother was strapped to a table. Ruel then tortured Devin with an electric prod and his screams followed me as I was led away. I can only believe that my brother died that day," she finished, drained.

Standing, Rolf let loose a string of expletives. What kind of heartless creature could abuse a helpless young man and what kind of evil mind had conceived such a barrier? No wonder Ilyssa feared he was getting too close! Rolf clenched his fists, wishing he could strangle the pasha who'd caused her such suffering.

"You see why I can't, uh, become too intimate?" Ilyssa asked, terribly embarrassed.

"You're afraid that if his safeguard sounds an alarm, he'll assume you've been compromised and he'll kill your parents, right?"

"Yes."

"By the gods, I am sorry," Rolf said, kneeling in front of her and taking her hands. No wonder she was so desperate to rescue her parents. She couldn't have the thing removed until they were safe.

"The safeguard isn't the only reason I stopped you, Rolf." Ilyssa withdrew from his grasp and stepped back from him. "According to the myth of siren song, if I bed a man, I risk losing my singing voice. I need it to become an arbiter."

"Why?" Rolf peered at her, confused. He knew Circutia had arbiters but he had no knowledge of their training.

"On Circutia, we use the arts as a medium of communication to solve disputes. Specially trained artists in different fields are appointed to act as arbiters after annums of study and a formidable selection process. I've been training my voice so I can apply. This has been a goal my whole life. I don't want to lose everything I've been working for merely to sleep with a man."

"I see." Rising, Rolf pulled his tunic top on over his head so she wouldn't see the hurt in his eyes. So she considered her career goals more important than him. All of their time spent together meant nothing. She was ready to cast him off so she could pursue her dream of becoming an arbiter. Normally he'd admire that kind of dedication. But in this case, he was offended.

"I'm going for a walk," he said abruptly. "I would appreciate it if you would stay in the compartment until my return."

Striding down the corridor, he could think only of putting distance between them. He needed time to sort out his feelings. They were confused and contradictory. How could he resent her for being so determined when he was the same way? She'd kept her dreams despite the tremendous odds against her and he should admire that quality as one of her strengths. Instead, he felt angry at her for rejecting him. And because it was a selfish anger, he felt guilty. Damn the woman. Why did she cause him such torment?

His lip curled sardonically as he glanced out a casement in one of the coach cars. Darkness was rapidly descending outside as they climbed higher into the mountains. The air was distinctly cooler as well. The train had slowed, and he wondered how high they were. A panorama of peaks stretched in the distance. Evergreen forests surrounded them, and beyond sharp drop-offs to the side, he caught glimpses of lakes below. They must have already achieved a considerable elevation.

He turned around, having heard a cough behind him. One of the burly customs agents was standing in the aisle staring at him, the man with thinning brown hair and a mustache. Lifting an eyebrow, Rolf continued along his way. The man followed. Rolf began to get nervous, feeling the fellow's eyes on his back. He grew more uneasy when he stepped onto a swaying platform and through the opposite door came the shaggy-haired agent. His snarl deepened when he saw Rolf and he sauntered forward, closing the distance between them.

"Where are you heading?" the agent demanded.

Rolf glanced over his shoulder. The brown-haired deputy was flanking his rear. Both men wore long-sleeved slate-gray bodysuits, their bulging muscles evidence of their strength. "I'm going to the lounge car for a drink."

"No, I mean where are you heading . . . your trip destination?"

"Oh!" Rolf cleared his throat. "I'm getting off at Wheaton," he lied.

"No luggage have you or your gima."

So they'd been checking the baggage cars. "We had to leave in a hurry. A death in the family," he said, putting on a sad face.

The agent didn't appear impressed. His black eyes frosted. "Your business? Point of origin?"

"Pardon me, but I don't have to answer these questions, do I? We'll be crossing the border soon. You can't—oof!" He grunted as the large agent punched him in the stomach.

"Pasha Ruel's laws take precedence here. Answer!"

Rolf looked for a way out, but the only other route was off the edge of the platform on either side where the protective grate ended. "I'm from Kantina where I work as a jeweler."

"Ah!" The two men gazed at him with interest. "Have you any baubles on board?" asked the one with a mustache.

"Sorry, this isn't a business trip."

"Credits, perhaps?"

"You asking for money?" Rolf sneered. That landed him a punch on the jaw. He reeled backward and was caught by the brown-haired man. Trapped in a stranglehold, he contemplated kicking the other agent but decided against it, at least for now. He'd wait and see what they wanted next.

"Where's your ident card?" snarled Mustache at his ear, tightening his hold around Rolf's neck.

"In my compartment."

"With the pretty female?"

"Leave her out of this!"

"Perhaps we should question her," the other man said with a leering grin.

Rolf was getting angrier by the minute but he preferred to negotiate rather than fight. "I'll pay whatever you want," he gritted.

"Now we're talking," Mustache put in.

"I'd rather question the woman." The agent's black eyes never once left Rolf's face. "Loan her to us as part of your payment."

"She's not part of the deal."

"We'll press charges if you don't cooperate."

"What kind of charges?" Rolf asked, his heart sinking. It didn't look like he was going to talk his way out of this one.

"Your ident cards." The man smirked. "They're false."

"False? What do you mean?" He tried to look indignant.

"False, as in stolen."

Rolf stared at him. She didn't, did she? He'd thought Ilyssa had falsified the documents using her computer skills. If these representatives of Ruel's government were correct, they were in deep trouble.

"I thought you were looking for arms smugglers," he said, hoping to distract the customs agents.

"We are. But we caught you instead and could earn ourselves a small bonus for turning you in."

"I'll pay you well for leaving us alone."

"How much?"

Rolf calculated what was left in Ilyssa's purse after paying for the tickets. "Twenty thousand credits."

The agent's eyes widened. "Generous, aren't you? Maybe we should find out what you're hiding. You and the lady might be worth a lot more than that." He pulled a shooter from a holster around his hip. "Talk! Who are you?"

Rolf didn't waste any time. He kicked, catching the man in the groin. The agent doubled over, screaming. Rolf threw Mustache over his shoulder, and pushing past the two, he crashed the door open and charged back to his compartment.

Ilyssa was thinking that she shouldn't rely on Rolf to rescue her parents, not after what she'd just told him. There was no doubt in her mind that she'd offended him. Why should he promise her anything now? He didn't stand to gain a thing by helping her, and he had his own important mission to carry out with a deadline of Lexin thirty-fourth. She couldn't afford any further delays in her purpose either. Her father's condition deteriorated with each passing day. She'd either have to leave Rolf and strike out on her own or take her chances with him and his band of freedom fighters. Further evaluation was needed before she reached a decision.

Frowning at the difficult choices, she went into the sanitary and had just finished washing her hands when the door to the compartment burst open and Rolf rushed inside.

"Come on out of there!" he shouted. "We're in big trouble."

She dried her hands on a towel and hastened over. "What's happened?" she cried in alarm. A darkening bruise was forming on his jaw and he appeared winded.

"Those customs agents discovered our ident cards are false."

She felt the color drain from her face. "How?"

"They must have done background checks on the passengers. They noticed we didn't have any luggage either. At first I thought they'd take a bribe but I offered too much and that made them suspicious. Now they want to know who I am!"

"When did all this happen?"

"Just now, on an empty platform a few cars up. I'm sure they'll be here soon. One of them pulled a shooter and I kicked the *shivas* out of him. Let's move!"

"Where to? They'll find us anywhere we go."

"We'll look for your friends, the players. They'll hide us."

"I have a better way." A cunning expression crossed her face. "Do you still have those earplugs?"

"I think so." Quickly, he rummaged through the knapsack for his robe. With a breath of relief, he found the wax plugs in the pocket where he'd placed them.

"Put them in and stay in the sanitary. I'll deal with this."

"Are you sure?"

"Yes, do as I say."

After he closed the sanitary door, Ilyssa ran to put on her veil. All thoughts of her own safety fled as she prepared to do battle. Heaven help her, she cared for Rolf and couldn't bear the thought of his getting captured. It was up to her to protect him.

She was standing facing the door to the corridor when it crashed open and the two brawny agents charged inside.

"Where is he?" Gant said, hunched over and grimacing as though it hurt him to move.

"What is the meaning of this?" Ilyssa cried. "How dare you invade my privacy!"

"Your man came in here. We want him."

"What for?"

Gant aimed his shooter at her. "I'm sure you know, mistress. Your ident cards are stolen." He approached, slowly closing the distance between them. Behind him, the mustached agent grinned and shut the door.

Glancing anxiously at the direction Rolf had taken, Ilyssa took a deep breath to fill her lungs with oxygen. Then she released the air and melodious notes sprang from her throat. The ballad she sang was rich with passion and ripe with drama.

The customs agents stopped dead in their tracks, staring at her, their eyes glazing over as the song resounded through the confined space, invading their minds with glorious harmony.

When she saw their positions were frozen, she stopped. "You will leave this compartment and not bother me or my friend again," she directed. "We are aboard this train on legitimate business. Our data cards are unquestionably authentic. You have much more important business elsewhere. Forget you ever talked to either of us tonight. As soon as you enter the corridor, you will wake from your trance. Go now."

As though they were robots, the two uniformed men

pivoted and walked out. Ilyssa rushed to close the door behind them, but not before she heard one of them ask, "What are we doing here?"

Smiling, she went to the sanitary and yanked open the door. Rolf stepped out, pointing to his ears. She nodded and he removed the earplugs.

"Did it work?" he asked, his eyes warily glancing about.

"Of course. Why shouldn't it?" she said, grinning.

Seeing that they were alone, Rolf picked her up and spun her around. "You're amazing!" he said jubilantly.

She laughed, sharing his delight. The singing had provided her with a release she hadn't known she'd needed. When Rolf lowered her so that her feet touched the ground, it seemed only natural their lips should come together.

But just as quickly, Rolf released her and stepped away.

Ilyssa looked at him, puzzled. Why was he stopping? She couldn't make love to him, but that didn't mean he couldn't kiss her. After tasting his incredible mouth again, she didn't want him to stop just yet.

Ilyssa felt an inexplicable sense of loss as he strode to his lounger and reclined with his back toward her. She'd brought this upon herself and wasn't happy with the results. She could talk to him about it, but what would she say? He'd accuse her of wanting to start something she couldn't finish.

Crawling onto her bunk, Ilyssa flopped down onto her stomach and spent a miserable time analyzing her confused feelings until she fell asleep.

It was much later when Ilyssa heard strange sounds. She'd been asleep for four hauras already, according to the lit dial of her chronometer. The compartment was dark, illuminated by a dim night-light in the sanitary.

Rolf was making the weird noises that awoke her, she realized with surprise. Groans were coming from his lips as he tossed and turned. Sitting upright, she wondered if he was ill.

His thrashing increased, and her consternation rose when he yelled out in his sleep.

"Gayla!" he shouted, grasping at the empty air above him. "Quick, get to the turret. Use the laser cannon." And later, "No, no, don't die!" His voice broke with anguish. Rolling onto his side, he tumbled over the edge of the lounger and fell on the floor.

"Rolf!" Ilyssa cried, rushing over.

His eyes opened slowly and focused on her. "Ilyssa . . . what happened?"

"You were having a nightmare," she said, her tone cool.

"Not again!"

"You have them often?" she asked, stunned. Sitting back on her heels, she watched him.

"Ever since the crash, I've been getting them every few nights." Putting a hand to the back of his head and moaning, he sat up.

"How did she die, Rolf?"

For a long moment he didn't answer. Then he twisted his head and looked at her. In the dim light, she could see his tormented expression as he stood up.

He began pacing while Ilyssa sat on her lounger to listen.

"We were eloping because Gayla was underage. My friend Artemus helped us get a ship. We took off from Nadira, heading for a planet where we could wed in peace. But along the way, Souk pirate ships intercepted us. Gayla was killed as we battled to get away. I managed to elude them and returned home." He fell silent, shame and sorrow reflected on his face.

"What happened then?"

"Gayla's parents had the right to terminate my life if they so chose. It is the way with Nadiran law. But they recognized the role the Souks played and ordered me to enter the diplomatic corps. I joined with the express purpose of putting an end to the slave trade and the Souks' brand of terrorism."

"So that's why you're here," she concluded.

"It's not the only reason. Coalition outposts and vessels are being attacked by Souk raiders. Innocent victims are being killed or enslaved every day. The only way to stop the Souks is to eliminate the source of the problem, which is the slave trade. The High Council was contacted by the resistance, not the other way around. We decided to establish a regular route of communication and offer assistance to the freedom fighters rather than pursue a direct military attack on Souk, which would be our only other recourse. Believe it or not, we prefer to avoid that type of conflict."

Ilyssa considered what he was saying. It was true that the Souks were responsible for much grief. They were ruthless, trading in human lives and devaluing the worth of even their own females who were kept in harems. But Ilyssa still thought that relief from oppression should be sought in council. The Alliance conference could prove fruitful. The Souks might work out for themselves what others hoped to accomplish through warfare. Perhaps that was the very reason why Rolf came. The High Council sent him to facilitate a peaceful resolution.

"Why were you selected as the Coalition representative, Rolf? Was it because you're a diplomat rather than a soldier?"

"I volunteered." His eyes took on an obsessive light. "I want to find the Souk leader responsible for the attack that killed Gayla."

That wasn't what she'd expected him to say. "And if you do?"

"I'll bring him to justice."

Ilyssa gasped at the murderous look on his face. She wouldn't have thought his nature was a violent one. "Is that the solution to the problems on Souk?"

"No, but it's a solution to a personal torment that's plagued me for annums. It's the only way I can find peace."

Ilyssa stood, her hands on her hips. "Why does Gayla haunt you in your dreams? Are you still in love with her?" Was that why he'd broken off kissing her in the ore car, because he'd been thinking of Gayla?

"No, I'm not," he answered quietly. "She haunts me because I'm the one responsible for her death." Rolf dashed a hand through his dark hair in anguish. "The Souks might have fired the weapons, but if it weren't for me, we wouldn't have been in position for them. Artemus and I planned the elopement down to the last detail. Gayla just agreed and went along."

"But she had to accept your plan!"

"Gayla let me make all the decisions. I can't rest until her death is avenged."

"Do you really think murdering the Souk who attacked you will absolve your feelings of guilt?"

"I don't know, but I want the bastard." Clenching his fists, he glared at her.

She knew the feeling well. That was how she felt about Ruel. How sweet it would be to get revenge for the wrongs he'd done to her and her parents, revenge for torturing and murdering her brother. But violence was not a viable solution as far as she was concerned.

"Discrediting the guilty party might be punishment enough," she suggested. "I don't accept killing as an agreeable alternative."

"It'll make me feel better," Rolf snarled.

Ilyssa glanced at his troubled face and her heart sank. His commitment was to Gayla's parents and his quest for revenge, not to her. Did that mean he wouldn't honor his pledge to save Moireen and Aran? Was he so obsessed about finding Gayla's killer that it was the only thing on his mind? She wondered how he could even accomplish his mission for the Coalition when his personal vendetta was so consuming.

Before she could voice her opinion, the train came to a sudden jolting halt and the lights went out.

Chapter Eleven

"What happened?" Ilyssa cried.

"Stay put. Let me get a lightstick from the knapsack." A moment later, they could see each other's faces in the gloom. "It's a good thing you brought a few of these along," Rolf said, waving the glowing stick in the air.

"They're supposed to last six hauras each."

"I hope we won't need it that long. What time is it?"

"Just past one o'clock."

"Put your shoes on." He donned his boots and hastily stuffed their strewn belongings into the knapsack. Muted shouts and popping noises sounded in the distance. "I'm going to see what's going on," he said, rising.

"Wait! I'm coming with you."

He looked at her panic-stricken expression and shook his head. "You'll be safer here."

"Our door has no lock, remember? I'm coming, Rolf."

A loud crash sounded, accompanied by screams and the rapid-fire staccato of laser weapons being discharged.

Rolf's hand automatically went for his jeweled blade but the space beside his belt was empty. He'd left the blade back on Bimordus Two, he remembered, cursing. Carefully, he approached the door, easing it open, then shut it almost immediately.

"What is it?" Ilyssa's heart thumped wildly in her chest.

"Savages." His voice was grim. "Let's see if we can get out through the casement." He opened it and a blast of cold air hit them.

"It's freezing!" Ilyssa exclaimed.

Leaning out, she shrieked. The scene was like something out of Zor. Primitives, ugly blue-skinned dogfaces wearing loincloths and fur throws, galloped alongside the track on huge, muscular carzen, warbling a warrior chant and waving torches that cast an eerie glow in the darkness. Dozens of them ringed the train. To the far front where the cars curved around a bend, she could see a huge pile of rocks obstructing the track.

Rolf saw it, too. "They must have caused a rock slide. We're trapped here."

"Look, they're taking prisoners," Ilyssa gasped, pointing. Passengers who apparently had been snatched from their loungers in nightclothes were being forced outside into the freezing temperature. The males, mostly Souks, were being strung up on poles so that they hung upside down. Each pole was then lifted and hauled down a path by two stocky savages. The path disappeared around a hilly curve. Female captives of all species were being chained in a line, guarded, and watched.

"Is this a carnivore tribe?" Ilyssa asked fearfully.

"I don't know. Let's hope not." He didn't know which he preferred, being brutally murdered or eaten. Hastily, Rolf shut the casement before they were noticed. "Obviously we can't leave via this route. We could try going toward the freight cars at the rear of the train. Maybe there's a way out in that direction." He was hoping they could escape the train and hide out in the brush. Sooner or later, all the compartments would be searched.

"We can't stay here," she agreed. "The beasts might set fire to the train to force everyone outside."

He gazed at her in horror. "Would they do that?"

"I have heard stories, Rolf." Her voice trembled.

"Great suns."

"I cannot risk being taken. Some of these monsters might like human females. If I were compromised, Ruel would kill my parents even if I am raped. When the safeguard alarm sounds, he won't know the difference."

"By the stars, woman, don't talk like that." She was still thinking of her parents, even now. Ilyssa had better start thinking about self-preservation. More than her virginity was at stake here. He grabbed up the knapsack and Ilyssa's bag and slung them over his shoulder. "Let's go."

Ilyssa put out a hand to stop him, raising her frightened eyes to his face. "I know we have our differences, Rolf, but I want you to know that I . . . I do care for you."

Groaning, he pulled her close and kissed her. He couldn't help it. In the next few moments they might both be killed. The movements of his mouth on hers were hungry and desperate. Through the soft fabric of her caftan, he could feel her slender form and it made him realize how very vulnerable she was. A surge of protectiveness raged through him. He had to keep her safe!

Breaking away from him, she said, "We'd better get out of here."

"I want you, Ilyssa. You know that, don't you?" he said, ignoring the loud commotion on the train.

"Yes."

"We need to talk about this . . . later. All right, let's move out. I'll go first."

His jaw tightening, he approached the door. Just as he neared it, heavy footsteps charged down the corridor outside and the door smashed open, catching him on the forehead. He spun backward, stunned, his head reeling from the unexpected blow.

Ilyssa screamed, "Rolf!"

He recovered his senses and was about to rush to her defense when a half-naked, bluish dogfaced savage fired an electrifier at him. He crashed backward, giving a grunt of agony as the shock wave passed through him. Vaguely he saw Ilyssa being hefted over the war-painted Souk's shoulder and carted out the door, shrieking and calling his name. He started to charge after her, but another painful shock hit him, stronger this time. He crumpled to the floor, his limbs jerking uncontrollably.

"Rolf . . ." he heard her crying before her voice faded.

It was Gayla, summoning him. He was at the controls in the smoky cockpit. Gayla had fired the laser cannon at the attacking Souks, but then she'd fallen silent after a vicious return volley. Something was wrong. He had to get to her.

"Gayla!" he yelled, pushing himself upright.

Staggering toward the open doorway, he squinted. This wasn't right. Where was the turret ladder?

The fog in his mind cleared and, rubbing a hand across his eyes, he swiped at the sudden moisture there. Gayla was dead. Ilyssa was taken. No, they wouldn't kill her, too!

He glanced at the chaos in the corridor and couldn't decide which way to go. Savages, wild-eyed, jagged-toothed drooling beasts, were charging through the private compartments. He saw other passengers, Souk females, carried off, screaming, all being dragged in the same direction. He followed in the hopes that Ilyssa had been taken that way, too. Exiting into the corridor, he turned right.

Emergency lights provided illumination, and it was cold, biting cold. Shivering as he dodged in and out of open doorways, Rolf wondered if the train's generators had been disabled. He and Ilyssa should have put on their robes. Her caftan was thin and she'd be quickly chilled.

Desperate to find her, he wished he could quicken his pace, but the need for caution was paramount. He avoided the compartments where the barbarians were still at work. Souk males, apparently stunned by electrifiers, were being strung up on poles, their captors not even waiting to get them outside. One fat Souk was screaming something that sounded like, "Don't eat me!"

By the corona, did these creatures really intend to devour their victims? The idea was so revolting he could barely contemplate it. Yet it was possible they were taking the females to ravish and the men to barbecue. Now that he thought about it, a peculiar stench was in the air. His stomach heaved at what it might portend and he hurried along. At least the creatures seemed to prefer fellow Souks. That would explain why he hadn't been taken after being stunned.

At one of the platforms, he saw victims being off-loaded. As he quickly stepped across during a quiet interval, he peeked outside. Half-clad savages still rode up and down beside the track on their muscular carzen, waving torches and shrieking warrior cries. Some were females, he realized with a shock. They were inspecting the helpless Souks who were strung upside down on poles. Apparently the males weren't safe from ravishment, either. Rolf's lip curled down. He was lucky none of those female warriors had spotted him. One of them might decide she wanted to sample a human.

The line of chained female captives was getting longer, but apparently not all the Souk ladies were being removed from the train. Some were being dragged past his hiding place behind the sanitary door, kicking and screaming as they were taken toward the rear of the train.

He hadn't caught sight of Ilyssa's bright green caftan or vibrant red hair outside. That meant she must still be on the train. If he was right about the fate of those females being carted past him, there wasn't a moment to lose. But as he stepped out into the corridor, a thickly accented voice speaking standard Soukese stopped him from behind.

"Going somewhere, human?"

Whirling around, Rolf spotted a burly female savage bearing down on him, dagger in hand. She wore a fur throw over her sweaty body, nothing else. Her large breasts bulged at the edges. She looked like a wrestler, he thought grimly, noticing the way her flesh stretched taut over sinewy muscles.

He moistened his lips. "What do you want?"

The female leered at him in response. Shoving her huge bulk forward, she forced him back inside the sanitary. Slamming the door shut, she twisted the lock. An evil grin lit her face as she regarded him, backed to the wall.

Rolf diverted his gaze from her ugly dogface and glanced around the small space. There was nothing he could use as a weapon. She still held the dagger, its tip pointed in his direction. Her body reeked from sweat and as she bared her discolored teeth, he saw the jagged points that indicated a meat eater.

"R-R-Remove your trousers, human," she ordered. "Wish I to see what your frail species offers."

"Get out of my way," he snarled.

Her knife lifted as she stepped closer. "Need I cut you? Do as I say!" And to give emphasis to her words, she grasped his groin and squeezed.

Rolf lashed out with his fist, infuriated, but she was quick. Sidestepping the blow, she jabbed the dagger at him. Rolf caught her wrist and they struggled, their bodies mashed together in a wild tangle of limbs as each one tried to use the knife. The female was strong, her biceps straining as she tried to gain control. Animalistic grunts came from her mouth as she fought him, her snoutlike nose only centimeters from his face.

Rolf's strength prevailed, and her wrist gradually turned inward. The Souk spit in his face, making him squint momentarily, and that was all the distraction she needed to knee him in the groin. As he doubled over, crying out, she punched him in the jaw. As his neck snapped back, he saw her knife flash out and felt his leggings loosen as she slashed at him.

"No!" he roared, kicking, and his foot connected with her midsection. She flew, hitting the back of her head on the door. He hurtled himself at her, rage and hatred fueling him. And then somehow her dagger was in his hand. Rolf wasn't sure how it happened, but as she lunged at him, he brought his hand up, and she impaled herself on the knife.

Their startled gazes locked: hers full of fury and disbelief; his full of loathing mixed with horror. He didn't stop to consider his actions. Even as she slowly slumped to the floor and the blood seeped out of her, he was unlatching the door and jumping over her. Ilyssa was his only concern. He'd lost precious time defending himself. He only hoped it wasn't too late to save her.

Ilyssa screamed until her voice was hoarse. She'd tried singing, but slung over the savage's shoulder with her chest compressed, she couldn't. She couldn't even see because her face was being mashed into the brute's massive back. As he carried her, his hand slid up between her legs and he laughed. An awful feeling came over her about what he intended to do and she thought she'd be sick. They seemed to be heading toward the very end of the train, because she heard the metal clang of the platform grids and felt a blast of freezing air at regular intervals. His hand strayed upward, stroking her inner thigh, and all she could do was whimper as he carted her along.

Suddenly he halted, and she was being tossed onto a pile of rough burlap. Looking around, she realized they'd arrived at a freight car. A faint light came from the door to the platform that they'd just crossed through.

By the Almighty, they weren't alone. Another male was waiting, growling with glee at her arrival. And there was a female warrior.

The three of them encircled her, grinning and making obscene comments, from the looks on their ugly dogfaces. Ilyssa opened her mouth to speak, hoping she could reason with them, but a raspy sound was all she could make. Her voice was too hoarse from yelling so much. With a sense of panic, she scooted back on the rough cloth as her captor finished whatever he was saying and halted, staring down at her.

Giving a loud roar, the Souk leapt upon her, tearing at her caftan, ripping it apart with his bare hands. As Ilyssa cried out at the viciousness of the attack, he mauled her breasts beneath the thin fabric of her lingerie, hurting her with his brutality. The other dogfaces watched and drooled, urging him on. She smelled her assailant's foul breath as he slowly lowered his disgusting face, but when she tried to turn away he grasped her hair and yanked it by the roots, bringing tears to her eyes. His head descended and she stared at him, terrified. His wet nose pressed against hers and he rubbed noses, making snorting noises while he did so. Ilyssa thought she'd vomit as his drool dripped onto her chin. She pummeled at his chest but it was like striking solid rock.

His hands released her hair and he tore away at her thin binder, exposing her breasts. A twisting pain shot through her as he squeezed her nipples. She cried out and he seemed to like that because he drew his head up and laughed, doing it again until she moaned in agony. The female warrior sauntered toward the other savage who was watching and fondled his groin. They muttered a few unintelligible words and the male threw off his piece of fur. Atop her, Ilyssa's assailant glanced at them, and his heavy breathing grew more labored. Shifting downward, he pushed her legs apart.

Ilyssa gave a choked cry. One flimsy piece of lingerie still separated her from him, but it wasn't much of a deterrent. As she watched in terror, the savage cast off his fur wrap and poised above her, naked.

Closing her eyes, she waited for him to rip away the last remaining undergarment and thrust into her. This was it. She was doomed. Her parents would be killed when her safeguard was breached, and she wouldn't last long, from the glimpse she'd gotten of the beast's enormous organ. If she was lucky, she'd be ripped apart by his first plunge and she wouldn't have to suffer an attack by his friend.

A low growl sounded from the direction of the platform but it didn't have the pitch of a Souk. Ilyssa looked up, as did all three of her captors.

"Rolf!" she croaked, seeing the familiar figure framed in the doorway. With his black hair askew, his thick brows furrowed, and his mouth twisted into a snarl, he looked every bit as savage as her assailants. His shoulders appeared broader than she remembered, his body tall and primed for action. In his fist he clutched a long, pointed kather stick.

Her attacker jumped to his feet, grabbed a knife from inside his discarded fur, and began tossing the weapon back and forth between his two hands. An eager light shone in his eye as he straightened up to study the intruder.

"The fun's over. I'm taking the woman," Rolf said to the Souks in their own language. The Souks laughed loudly, slapping each other's palms. Then Ilyssa's assailant quieted, stalking Rolf like a hunter tracking prey.

"Move out of the way," Rolf warned Ilyssa.

Her energy renewed by the sight of him, she snatched her heap of clothes and crawled toward a side wall just as he leapt into the air in a flying kick and knocked the knife out of her attacker's hand. Following with a punch to the stomach, Rolf forced the breath from the Souk's body. Before he could recover, Rolf stabbed the kather stick into his muscular abdomen in a mighty thrust.

The other two savages snarled and bared their teeth as their companion toppled over, the spear stuck in his flesh. Rolf didn't waste any time. He took on both of them at once, the naked savage and the female warrior. In a rapid series of kicks and thrusts, he beat them to the floor.

Looking down at them, he tried to still the fury in his blood. The urge to leap upon them and strangle the breath out of them held him in its grip and he struggled for control. Panting, he tried to slow his respiration in an attempt to calm himself. The vicious, rotten Souks, he'd like to—

"Rolf . . ." Ilyssa saw the murderous expression on his face and was frightened.

He turned to her and cursed. "Are you hurt?" he asked, concern in his tone as he hastened to her.

"No. You got here just in time." Her voice was a raspy croak. Her throat still hurt from screaming.

Rolf knelt beside her. "I would never have forgiven myself if anything happened to you. Come here, let me hold you."

He reached out his arms but she shook her head as she clutched the ragged edges of her caftan to her body. "No. Get rid of them first." Her limbs trembled with a fearful weakness and she felt an intense need to cry, but she hid her reaction. Rolf had unfinished business yet.

Before he could rise, a loud explosion rocked the car. Shouts and screams met the noise of laser fire from outside.

"Now what?" Ilyssa gasped.

"I'll take a look." But when he went to open the platform door, it jammed. "Blast, it must have caught on the other side."

As the door wedged tighter, their meager illumination was lost. He dropped to his knees, searching for their sacks by the entrance where he'd left them earlier. Finding the knapsack, he withdrew a lightstick and ignited it.

"Try the cargo slats," Ilyssa suggested.

Rolf walked toward the outside wall. Spotting a release button, he pushed it and the wide double doors slid open. A blast of frigid air hit them. Ilyssa shivered, drawing her torn caftan tighter around her body.

"Great suns!" Rolf exclaimed, peering outside at the scene of chaos. "Ruel must have sent his troops. Soldiers are fighting off the barbarians. They've got a regular artillery barrage going against the savages."

"Thank the heavens," Ilyssa murmured. Maybe there was hope of surviving this terrible night after all.

As Rolf gaped, bodies fell one after another while bound captives stood by howling in terror. Riderless carzen raced off into the darkness. Savages darted about, hollering as they tried to regroup their tribe. In the mountainous distance, a huge trail of smoke rose into the air. A foul stench pervaded his nostrils, the same odor as before. Rolf thought about the Souk who had been pleading not to be eaten and wondered what that smoke represented. If it came from the savage camp, he didn't want to know.

Returning his attention to the three Souks sharing their space, he handed Ilyssa his lightstick before hauling each of the bodies to the opening. Praying no one would spot him, he rolled the Souks over the edge, grimacing at the thuds that followed. By the time he finished, he was shaking from the exertion and cold. After shutting the door, he rubbed his hands together to warm them. "It's not safe to go outside. We'll have to wait in here until later."

He glanced in Ilyssa's direction. Still huddled in a crouched position, she was shivering. The cold air had set her teeth to chattering and mottled her face. Cursing himself for not tending to her sooner, Rolf scrabbled in the sack for her robe and tossed it to her. "Here, put this on."

She couldn't manage. A delayed reaction to the situation had enveloped her and large sobs were welling up in her throat. Even as Rolf charged over, a tear rolled down her cheek.

He knelt beside her, covering her with the robe. Then he gently pulled her into his arms.

"Let me hold you. There, *larla,* it's all over now."

Tightening his embrace, he patted the back of her hair, speaking soothingly as he would to a child while her body shook with sobs. Her skin was cold and he thought with alarm that with the shock she'd experienced, she wasn't going to warm up too easily.

"You're still too cold. I think the only way for you to get warm is to share my body heat. Open your robe."

"What?" Sniffling, she stared at him with a bewildered expression.

"Undo your robe." Quickly, he took off his belt and tunic top.

"What happened to you?" For the first time, Ilyssa noticed his torn leggings. A long rip extended down the front center, exposing his . . . She raised her questioning eyes to his face.

"I met a female savage in one of the corridors. Ilyssa, open your robe." When she didn't comply, he cursed and loosened it himself. He couldn't help his sharp intake of breath. She'd let her caftan remnants fall so that her breasts were exposed and she wore nothing except for a flimsy undergarment below.

Feeling his bodily response quicken, he wrapped her robe around both of them with undue haste and wondered if this was such a good idea after all. He coaxed her to lie down, and then he put his arms around her, his body stiff. Despite his futile attempts not to notice, he could feel every soft curve of her and it just increased his arousal.

Ilyssa felt the air rush out of her so she could barely breathe. Her breasts were pressed flat against his hairy chest, her groin against his taut belly. And lower, she could feel the bulge between his legs. Her reaction changed from one of shaking relief to one of burning desire. A rush of heat began at her slippered toes and rose until even her scalp felt hot.

He squirmed against her, his face buried in her hair. "Are you getting warmer?"

"I'm getting too warm."

"So am I. What should we do about it?" Lifting his head, he gazed into her eyes.

In response, she tilted her chin and parted her lips. His mouth crushed down on hers, and Ilyssa met his kiss with fervent passion. She was aware that she'd nearly died tonight, and her parents would probably have been killed by Ruel as well. Her escape was so narrow as to make her want to cry with relief. But she'd already used up her store of tears, and now she turned with gratitude to the man who'd risked his life to save her. She entwined her limbs with his so she could relish the rock-hard feel of his body. He could have escaped the train and gone on alone to accomplish his mission. But he had saved her and captured her heart as a result. If he'd done this for her, she must be important to him. And if she meant that much to him, she felt he would keep his word about rescuing her parents.

Her hands roamed his bare back, pressing him closer as she moaned his name. She wanted to give herself to this man, to feel what it was like to make tender love when she had been so close to meeting a horrible end.

A deep yearning rose within her, and she writhed against him. His hardness swelled, pricking her thigh. His kisses became more urgent, frenzied like a man who was about to die of thirst and couldn't get enough to drink. His hands touched her breasts, tentatively at first. When she didn't protest, he rested his hands on them, lightly brushing her nipples with his thumbs.

"By the stars, I want you," he murmured, his hot breath caressing her cheek. His leg wedged between her own. His hand wandered downward, across her flat belly, toward her triangle of curly hairs.

"Rolf," she warned, despite her desire to continue.

"Hush. I won't breach your barrier. I just want to give you pleasure."

And suddenly he was touching her. Her body jerked. "No."

"Trust me, Ilyssa."

He began stroking her, and the most incredible sensations filled her, causing a deep, aching tension she'd never experienced before. And once it began, she didn't want it to stop. Her breathing was uneven and she closed her eyes, feeling his mouth descend upon hers even as his hand caressed her.

Reaching up, she clutched his hair, lost in the sensations spiraling through her. And when she reached her climax, she cried out, shuddering with her release. Never in all her life had she thought it could be like that.

Rolf smiled to himself as he held her. His own throbbing need had not been satisfied, but he was content to rest with her in his arms, to feel the satisfaction of a man who had brought sublime gratification to his woman. He wouldn't risk violating her barrier and endangering her parents. But he could still bring her pleasure in other ways, as he'd just shown her.

"What's going to happen when we free your parents and escape from Souk, Ilyssa?" he asked, stroking the side of her soft cheek.

"Huh?" Her mind was still languorous from abated passion and she couldn't concentrate.

"Can the safeguard be removed?"

She blinked, clearing her thoughts. "Yes, of course! Any competent medic should be able to do it. I don't see that as being a problem."

"Good." He nodded firmly.

Ilyssa sat up, grasping the edges of the robe to cover her near-nakedness. "And what is that supposed to mean?"

"You've seen the pleasure we can bring each other, but this is nothing compared to what it could be like if we went all the way." He leaned on an elbow and watched her.

Her lips compressed. "Why are you bringing this up now? It's not an issue yet. The safeguard is still in place."

He took her hands in his. "It can be good between us. Aren't you curious to experience more?"

"I risk losing my singing voice if I go to bed with you, remember?"

"You don't know that for a fact. Siren song is shrouded in mystery."

"I still intend to go to Athos to learn more about it. And until I do, I won't take the chance of losing my ability to sing. Being an arbiter is what I've wanted to do ever since I was young, and after witnessing the suffering of slaves firsthand on Souk, I want more than ever to work for peace. I'm not willing to sacrifice my dreams for a moment's pleasure."

Rolf fumbled for the appropriate response. "I understand that becoming an arbiter is important to you. It's just that I want you so badly and I'd like you to feel the same way about me. Obviously you don't, or else—"

"Or else what? I'd throw aside my ambitions and jump into bed with you the moment the threat from Ruel was past?" Her voice softened, and she regarded him with a tender expression. "I did enjoy what we just shared, Rolf. I want to be with you, too. But I have my goals and you have yours."

A rumbling vibration began underneath their feet and they stared at each other.

"We're moving!" Ilyssa cried.

"The soldiers must have cleared the track." He felt elated; now they would get back on schedule.

"Can we return to our compartment?"

Picking up the lightstick, he rose and tried the door to the platform, but it was still stuck. "I'm afraid we'll have to stay here for the night. When we get to Vloxvil, we can leave via the cargo slats and then reenter the train further up the line."

Ilyssa eyed the huge crates stacked against the walls. "Someone will be coming for those. What do you suppose is in them?"

He walked over and held the lightstick up. "It says they're carpets." Hearing her teeth chatter, his concern increased. "You're getting chilled again. I'll get one of these rugs out to cover you." His biceps bulged as he maneuvered one of the crates into a position where he could attempt to open it. "I need a lever."

"There's one in the tool kit."

"Right." Rolf fumbled in the sack until his fingers encountered the case. Opening it, he drew out the desired tool and set to work. "Here goes." He cracked the lid and peered inside. Row after row of neatly rolled rugs met his gaze. Reaching in, he tried to lift one out but something solid obstructed him.

"Blast, this is heavy. I can't budge it." He peeled away a corner of the carpet and cursed.

"What is it?"

He glared at her as though it were her fault. "It's a case full of assault rifles. I think we've found our armament smuggler."

Chapter Twelve

"By the heavens, it's the Souk carpet salesman," Ilyssa remarked, astonished.

"Apparently so. Well, these won't do us any good." Rolf contemplated dumping the laser rifles so he could use the carpet but decided against it. He folded the corner of the rug back down, concealing its contents. "I'd rather not disturb this load. I'll look in another container."

Three crates later, he discovered one holding carpets and nothing else. He wondered where and how the weapons were to be off-loaded. There wasn't a shipping address on any of the containers. Wherever these items were going, he and Ilyssa needed to be out of range long before the arms merchant, or worse, the customs agents, showed up.

He unrolled a carpet after sweating to get it out of the crate. "It's too big to wrap around you," he said regretfully, working to seal up the rest of the crates. He'd been hoping there were smaller rugs, but these were floor size, better suited to be used as a bed.

Ilyssa gathered their sacks to use for pillows. Watching Rolf move, she stared at the muscles rippling in his broad back and strong arms. An ache rose deep within her and she suppressed it, determined not to give in to her rising desire. But with the memory of his tender touch so recent in her mind, it was all she could do to stay away from him. She wanted Rolf but couldn't have him and her dreams as well. It was a choice she'd made long ago. Her ambition to become an arbiter was the only thing that had kept her going through the long annums as Ruel's slave. Once his safeguard was removed, she wasn't going to jeopardize her chance to achieve her dream just for a few moments of ecstasy.

Ilyssa tried to focus her attention on their predicament. They'd have to get out of there at the first indication the train was stopping. In the meantime, a peaceful night's rest would be welcome. She felt drained from her ordeal and bewildered by her conflicting emotions for Rolf.

Rolf felt her eyes on him as he finished his task. Avoiding her gaze, he suggested she put on her jumpsuit. "The clothing will provide additional warmth," he said. Knowing she had nothing on beneath her robe was keeping him in a constant state of painful arousal, and he couldn't bear looking at her, knowing how soft she felt and how luscious her curves were under that shapeless garment. If she didn't cover herself better, he'd never get any rest.

Ilyssa agreed. While he pulled on his tunic top, she hastily dressed in her tight-fitting black jumpsuit and short boots. She put the robe back on for additional insulation, then curled up on one end of the carpet.

Rolf stretched out with his back toward her. He lay on the soft surface of the rug, his eyes open, listening to her breathing. If she had been ravished tonight and survived the vicious attack, their situation would be totally different. Her safeguard would have been violated, her parents killed, her singing voice lost. There would have been no barriers left for him to breach. She could have been his by default. But that would have brought him little satisfaction.

Closing his eyes, he let exhaustion overwhelm him. His thoughts drifted, and he fell asleep.

"Wake up!" Ilyssa's voice startled him out of oblivion. "The train is slowing."

Groggily, he sat up. It was dark except for the glowing lightstick Ilyssa held in her hand. "What time is it?"

"Eleven o'clock in the morning. We must be nearing Vloxvil."

He stood abruptly. "I don't think we want to be here when the carpet seller comes."

"This might not be his destination. It's only a small mountain village. He might be headed for the coast."

Hoping he wasn't, because that was where they were going, Rolf stretched. He felt better this morning, more refreshed. "I didn't have any nightmares," he commented, noting the shadows under Ilyssa's eyes. It didn't appear as though she had slept as well as he.

"That's nice."

"You must have chased Gayla from my mind last night."

"Do you think so?" Avoiding his gaze, she took off her robe, neatly folded it, and put it in the knapsack that she'd used as her pillow.

"Damnit, Ilyssa, what's the matter?"

She looked at him then, her eyes as chilly as the weather. "You wake up, and your first thoughts are about her."

"I meant it as a compliment."

"That's not how it sounded." She threw the knapsack at him. He could carry it. Grabbing her bag, she fastened it around her waist. Then she picked up the glowing lightstick from the floor where she'd placed it.

The train came to an abrupt halt. With a loud hissing noise, the hovertrain sank onto the tracks.

"Let's get out of here," Ilyssa snapped.

Rolf grunted as he pried open the cargo slats. "After you," he said.

Ilyssa squinted at the brightness outside. Vloxvil was situated in a small valley surrounded by high, jagged peaks. By the sparse vegetation, she knew they'd reached a considerable elevation. Snow was falling, and a cold wind bit at her nostrils and chilled her skin.

Rolf saw her shiver. "Maybe we should put on our robes."

"No, I'm tired of wearing that thing. We won't be here long." Sometime in the night, she'd decided to stay with Rolf. At least for now, she'd put her trust in him. She did believe he was a man of honor and would keep his word regarding her parents, albeit at his own convenience. She'd just have to impress upon him the need for haste. She also felt she might be a positive influence on him regarding the slavery issue. The Alliance conference was the best chance to resolve the conflict peacefully. She'd urge him toward patience and diplomacy rather than arming the rebels for a fight.

Tossing aside the lightstick in her hand, she jumped down to the track.

Rolf followed, stopping to pull the cargo door shut behind them. Glancing around, he noted the terminal was a short distance ahead. Passengers were already disembarking further up the line. Ilyssa started walking along the gravel roadbed toward the bustling scene of activity.

It was a scraggly group that milled about the terminal. Most of the passengers, mainly Souks, had dazed looks on their faces. The talk centered on the savage attack. Ruel's troops had fought off the beasts and ridden as escort to Vloxvil.

Ilyssa realized some of the soldiers were staring at her, and she looked down. Her tight-fitting jumpsuit and wild auburn hair would make her stand out in any crowd, but among these dogfaces with their veiled harems, she was a noticeable oddity. She hoped the troops hadn't been alerted to watch for her and Rolf.

"You should get another harem outfit," Rolf suggested, his stance watchful, his eyes roving the crowd. He had the knapsack slung across his shoulder. Taking her by the elbow, he urged her forward.

Feeling the heat from his hand, Ilyssa shrugged him off. She didn't care for the idea of donning another caftan but could see the benefit, especially when they were back on the train. She couldn't wear her robe all the time. It would be easier to blend into the crowd if she wore harem garb. Swallowing her distaste, she agreed.

"I need a change of clothes, too," he said, peering down at his torn leggings.

Ilyssa's feet crunched on the snow and she shivered. "Let's hit the main street quickly. I'm freezing."

Needing to touch her again, he put his arm around her with the excuse of keeping her warm. "The air seems thin here. Our elevation must be pretty high. I don't think we should stroll around for too long." Already he felt short of breath. He hadn't noticed it on the train, probably because they'd been confined to the freight car. But now, being outside, the lower oxygen content was affecting him.

They entered the first clothing shop they reached. The Souk owner eyed them greedily. He had keen tawny eyes and long white whiskers that hung down below his chin. "Aye, what can I do for you, humans?"

As Ilyssa stood back, Rolf listed their needs. After a brief exchange, he turned away with a couple of wrapped packages tucked under his arm. He'd been pleased to find a tan jerkin, clean white shirt, and dark brown leggings, while Ilyssa had selected a sapphire blue caftan ensemble. They'd both obtained clean undergarments and toilet necessities.

"I'd like to go ahead and change," Ilyssa said, catching sight of a public facility a short distance away.

"I'll meet you out here. I want to see what other supplies are available in town."

Ilyssa rushed off, eager to have some time alone.

The modern facility was heated, with cleansing chambers and dressing stalls in addition to toilets. She luxuriated in a shower, washing her hair and drying herself off by sonic blower. Afterward, she found a curtained cubicle in which to don her new clothes. As she stood there straightening the bodice, she heard the outside door open. A group of females entered, chattering in Soukese.

"What can we do to get our sister back?" one wailed.

"Kava might be savage soup by now," said another in a bitter tone. "I say we have our friends storm their camp."

"Wise would that not be, sister." This voice was older, calmer. "Other more important goals have we."

"What could be more important than saving one of our own?" a new voice argued.

"Grrr," agreed a chorus.

Ilyssa donned her new blue slippers and exited to examine herself in a reflector. Her bag was slung over her shoulder, her jumpsuit and boots stuffed inside. Immediately the Souk females fell silent, watching her. They were all dressed in identical topaz-colored caftans.

"Who's she? Do you think she was listening?"

"She's a human. They don't all speak Soukese."

"Excuse me," Ilyssa said in her singsong voice, speaking their language fluently. "Aren't you the ladies accompanying the carpet salesman?" She recognized some of the members of his harem from the day before in the lounge car.

They glanced at each other, their expressions alert. One of them nodded slowly. She was the eldest, a refined-looking Souk with an attractively shaped dogface, fine reddish brown hair, and intelligent brown eyes that were focused on Ilyssa.

"I couldn't help overhearing part of your conversation," Ilyssa went on, whirling with a swish of her skirt. She didn't know if these ladies were aware of their master's extra activities or not, but even if they weren't she might gain some useful information. "Did you say you lost one of your sisters in the raid last night?"

"Aye," the eldest replied.

"I'm so sorry. It was horrible, wasn't it? My friend and I were forced to spend the night in a freight car full of crates with nothing but burlap to rest our heads upon. But I suppose we were lucky to escape unharmed."

"Krach, as were the rest of us." The harem leader continued to regard her warily.

Ilyssa rummaged in her sack. She'd had this idea during the night when she was thinking about remaining with Rolf. It wouldn't hurt to be prepared in case she changed her mind about staying with him. These ladies might be able to help.

"I'd like to ask you a favor," she said to them, holding up a ruby bracelet, the only item of jewelry left that Rolf hadn't sold. "This was a gift given to me by a former . . . friend. I don't want my master to see it. I'll pay one of you generously if you can exchange it for credits at the jeweler's shop for me." She'd spotted a place selling carzen tusk items when she was walking down the street with Rolf.

The group exchanged glances; then the eldest nodded. "This will we do. Rheevka, you can go." A solemn-faced sister nodded and took the bracelet from Ilyssa's outstretched hand. She broke off from the group and rushed outside.

"Your name, lady?" the eldest addressed Ilyssa.

"My name is Ilyssa. What is yours?"

"Jarin."

"I'm very grateful, Jarin."

"Arf," she acknowledged. "Go about your business," she told her group, which immediately dispersed. "Mistress Ilyssa, where are you heading?"

"Up the coast. And you?"

"Coroban is our final destination."

Ilyssa knew that from Coroban, one had to switch trains or go by air to reach other parts of the northern continent, most of which consisted of the Nurash Desert. She wondered how Rolf planned for them to get to wherever it was they were going. She'd have to ask him later.

"You're with a human?" Jarin asked.

"Yes, that's right."

"Are you his gima?"

Ilyssa winced. "I suppose you could say that."

Jarin's eyes narrowed. "You do not mind?"

"Mind? What's there to mind?"

"Being subjugated to his orders."

"He doesn't give me orders. We work as a team." Seeing the other's startled look, she amended her words. "I mean, he respects my opinions."

"Lucky are you, then. It is not the way with our Souk masters."

Rheevka returned with the credits and Ilyssa paid her a bonus. Their conversation ended before Ilyssa could probe for more information.

"The deep blue of the caftan turns your hair into the color of fire," Jarin said, on her way to wash her hands. "You should don your veil. Need it will you if you are to please your master. He would not want other men to look upon your beauty."

"Right," Ilyssa said sarcastically. Without heeding the suggestion, she strode toward the door.

Outside, Rolf was nowhere in sight. Ilyssa watched the crowd beginning to stream back in the direction of the terminal. Soon it would be time to depart. Her breath steamed in the cold air and snowflakes drifted onto her nose. She blew them off, wishing she'd bought a new cloak. Stomping her feet to keep them warm, she counted the minutes that ticked by. Panic rose within her as Rolf failed to reappear. Peering up and down the street, she didn't spot his familiar form anywhere.

The harem ladies came out of the sanitary, pushing past her, chattering among themselves.

Ilyssa was about to begin a search for Rolf when a familiar voice called out to her. It was Balthazar, his large shape bearing down on her from across the street. The rest of his troupe trailed behind him. They all wore sad faces and tattered clothes.

"What's happened? Where's Rosalyn?" she asked, noticing the girl's absence.

"Alas," Balthazar said grimly, "she was taken last night."

Ilyssa gasped. "You mean those savages got her?"

"Aye. Pinch was with me and we tried to stop them, but they overpowered us. Mercutio and Nestor were busy saving the other ladies. I asked the soldiers if they could do anything about rescuing her and they said it was probably too late. In any event, their orders didn't extend to attacking the savage camp. Their mission was to get the train up and running again."

"It's abominable. Something should be done to stop those beasts."

The older man shrugged. "This run isn't a particularly important one. Most people take air transport across the Koodrash Mounts. Or those who can afford it take the high-speed express. Only plebeians such as ourselves accept the risk by taking a local."

Helena, the musician with straight blond hair and china-blue eyes, began to weep. "Rosalyn is gone! Oh, I cringe to think what they must have done to her! It makes me sick at heart!"

The other women, Beatrice and Luciana, rushed to comfort her and they all began wailing together. Helena was missing a silver hoop earring, Ilyssa noticed. In her grief, she probably hadn't even realized she'd lost it. The other two women wore identical pairs of earrings.

"A sorry troupe are we now," Balthazar said with a long face. "However, the show must go on. Would you consider becoming a replacement vocalist?"

"Me?" She couldn't have been more astonished. "But you've never even heard me sing."

"I'll take you on faith. Forsooth, we are desperate."

"I'm very sorry." She laid a hand on his arm. "I don't sing in public."

He hooked her hand into his elbow and began walking forward with her, out of earshot of his troupe. "With your beauty, Ilyssa, you would be a wild hit." His dark eyes raked her, his glance warmly appreciative. "You would grace our company. What can I say to convince you to join us?"

She smiled at him. "I'm just not interested, Balthazar."

"No?" His arm snaked around her waist. "Not even if I offered you more freedom than that man you're with? He keeps you in harem garments. If you stayed with me, you could do as you please."

Someone cleared his throat behind them. "Excuse me, am I interrupting something?"

Ilyssa turned her head. Rolf was glaring at them with undisguised fury.

Balthazar's face reddened and he released her. "Think it over," he told her. Nodding at them both, he waved his troupe to follow him down the road toward the shops.

"What was that all about?" Rolf snapped.

"Rosalyn was taken by savages last night. Balthazar was asking me to replace her as a vocalist." She fell into step beside him, eyeing the brown paper bag in his hand.

It smelled like food, and she realized they hadn't eaten since the day before.

"Is that why he was coming on to you?"

She gazed at him, shocked. "He was doing no such thing!"

"It sounded as though he was propositioning you, from what I could hear."

She wondered if he was right but was too angry with him to care. "Who told you to listen in on my private conversations?"

Rolf stopped to face her, his expression stern. "As long as we're traveling together, I expect you to follow certain rules of propriety. You're not available for other men and that must be made clear. You belong to me for now."

"I'm not part of your harem," she retorted.

"No, but I wish you were."

Their eyes locked and held. Stepping closer, Rolf slowly lowered his head, tempting her with his heated gaze and the sensual smile on his mouth. His lips hovered centimeters above hers. He'd showered and changed, and she could smell the scent of soap on his body.

She wanted him to kiss her. With a groan, she gave in to her intense desire for him and moved into his embrace. Closing her eyes, she tilted her head back and parted her lips. But when nothing happened, she looked at him.

"Tell me that you want me," he whispered against her mouth, his eyes glittering just above hers as he held her in his arms. "I need to hear it."

Ilyssa battled within herself. Her raging desire won out over her self-denial. "Yes," she rasped. "I want you, but I can't—"

"You can have this for now." And he crushed his mouth to hers.

Ilyssa relished the feel of his mouth on hers. She loved the taste of him and longed to experience again the sensations he'd aroused in her last night. But wanting him and acting on it were two different things. It wasn't fair to give part of herself to him and not be willing to share the rest.

Reluctantly, she disengaged herself. "I'm not a member of a harem and I never will be, Rolf. Our paths go in different directions. And speaking of harems, I met the ladies belonging to the carpet salesman in the sanitary."

He raised an eyebrow. "Did you now?" He'd seen the uncertainty in her expression and knew she wanted him as badly as he wanted her, but she wasn't able to yield to her desire. They'd just have to find a way around her obstacles, he thought. But then guilty feelings of Gayla's parents surfaced. Here he was being distracted by Ilyssa's charms and drawn away from the purpose of his mission. He was violating his oath. Stepping back, he wrestled with his feelings of guilt.

"Look, there's the carpet seller," Ilyssa hissed, spotting the Souk lounging on a bench. They walked closer for a better look.

He was a stout male with high-set ears fixed close to his head, lazy amber eyes, and a large nose with broad nostrils. His prosperity was evident in the lustrous purple caftan that he wore. It was embellished with silver threads, and several lengths of beaded necklaces hung from his thick neck. Surrounded by his harem ladies, he appeared content. They were plopping grapes into his mouth. Chatting quietly among themselves, their facial expressions were subdued.

"They lost one of their sisters last night," she murmured to Rolf as they moved past.

"I wonder how many others on the train were taken," he said. "Did the ladies say anything about their master's business?"

"Legitimate or otherwise? No, they didn't."

Up ahead, they spotted another familiar face. Gant, the customs agent, was questioning a man with a shaved head wearing an orange robe and rings through his ears, nose, lower lip, and various other body parts. As Rolf and Ilyssa strode past, Gant didn't even look twice in their direction.

"Apparently they're not onto the carpet seller yet," Rolf murmured.

"No, but I wonder where his friends are." The other two customs agents were nowhere in sight. Glancing over her shoulder, Ilyssa frowned when she noticed Beatrice, one of the actresses in Balthazar's group, speaking off to the side with Jarin. She hadn't known the Souk harem leader was acquainted with the women in Balthazar's troupe.

"Let's get back on the train," Rolf said, urging her forward. "I've bought afternoon nourishment. Hopefully by tonight, the dining car will be operational."

They headed for the platform closest to their compartment. An uneasy feeling gripped Ilyssa and she glanced back twice along the way. She felt as if they were being watched. When she saw a quick movement in the shadows, her throat constricted. But then there was nothing. Could she have been imagining someone following them? Unable to shake off her feeling of apprehension, she quickened her pace.

Bolt disconnected the comm link after talking with Kraus and Lork, his two hunters. Straightening his uniform top as he stood before a reflector, he contemplated what he'd just heard.

Kraus and Lork had found out from a ticket vendor at the train station in Kantina that Ilyssa and Sean Breslow had boarded the train crossing the Koodrash Mounts. Taking a jet flyer to Vloxvil, the hunters had picked up their trail. Bolt had told Kraus and Lork that the Dromo had been abducted by Breslow. He wanted them to follow the duo in order to learn their destination.

Bolt's face blanched when he remembered what Lork had observed. If Pasha Ruel found out about the sumi kissing Ilyssa . . . No, that must not happen! He'd think of a way to exit this gracefully. Kraus and Lork would have to be eliminated once they discovered the pair's destination, but he might let them kill Sean Breslow first. So far the gecko still hadn't come up with his damning evidence, so Bolt would say the sumi had been killed trying to escape. Then he could deal with Ilyssa.

Licking his thick lips, he pictured her sinking to her knees in his suite, begging him not to tell Ruel about her liaison with the sumi. In his mind's eye, Bolt ordered her to disrobe. He jolted her with his electrifier until she writhed with agony and agreed to do anything he asked her. And then . . .

The bubble popped as a better idea entered his mind. What if this whole thing was a scheme Ruel had hatched while Ilyssa was in Haakat? The pasha would have had to find out about the sumi's arrival through his own sources, but he might have done so. Then he ordered Ilyssa to stage an escape with the man in order to learn his purpose in coming to Souk. By the suns, it was clever! He should have thought of this himself! It could be why Ruel had kept Ilyssa in Haakat longer than expected, to instruct her.

And did those instructions include using her feminine wiles to seduce the man? No, that would be too dangerous from Ruel's viewpoint. The kiss was still unexplained, and he had a feeling Ruel wouldn't like being told about it. Using this knowledge was a way he could redeem himself, for he was still to blame for letting Ilyssa escape with the slave so easily. Knowing it might have been staged didn't make his guilt any less viable.

Determined to find a way out of his dilemma, he decided to confront the duo himself. As soon as his team reported on their destination, he'd fly out to greet them.

And then he could take credit for the success of this mission himself. He'd claim that he guessed at Ilyssa's purpose and let her escape.

Yes, that was it. He was part of the scheme all along.

Grinning at his own cunning, he marched outside to review his troops.

Chapter Thirteen

"Someone's been in here." Rolf surveyed the disorderly compartment, his mouth grim.

"We didn't exactly leave this place in the neatest condition," Ilyssa announced, glancing at him with a wry expression.

"I dropped the lightstick when we were attacked. How did it get on the lounger?"

"You didn't pick it up?"

"No, I was in a rush to find you."

She looked around, her eyes narrowed. "We didn't leave anything of value here. We'd taken both our sacks. Maybe it was a band of savages searching for loot."

Rolf nodded, but he was thinking that the beasts they'd encountered last night wouldn't have picked up his lightstick and placed it on the bunk. He couldn't brush off the uneasy feeling that their compartment had been deliberately searched.

"Those other two customs agents weren't in town that

I could see. Maybe they were searching the train while Gant was questioning passengers outside. It would have been a good opportunity while the compartments were empty."

Ilyssa's face paled. "I discarded the lightstick in the freight car this morning, and there's also the one that fizzled out last night."

He turned on her, frowning. "What are you saying?"

"Most people aren't going to go around carrying lightsticks. If the person who found this one"—she pointed to the lounger—"also went into the freight car and noticed the two in there, they might connect us with the shipment of arms!"

The idea was so preposterous that Rolf just stared at her. "That's pretty farfetched."

"Nevertheless, I think we should retrieve the used lightsticks from the freight car. Even if they haven't been found yet, they'll be noticed when the cargo is off-loaded. The arms merchant will know someone unauthorized has been inside."

Tightening his mouth, Rolf nodded. It didn't pay to take chances. "Let's go." He kept the knapsack over his shoulder, unwilling to go anywhere without it.

They reached the rear end of the train within a few minutes. Most of the returning passengers were recuperating, having spent a horrible night like themselves. Hardly anyone was moving about. Several of the compartments were empty, the occupants presumably having been killed or taken by the savages.

"The door's unlatched," Rolf remarked from the platform outside the freight car. The metal grid swayed underfoot as the train picked up speed.

Ilyssa clung to a handlebar. "Go on inside."

"It's dark in there. We'll need another lightstick." He maneuvered around so she could grab one out of his knapsack. When she had it lit, he took it and edged forward, pushing open the door against a rush of wind. "Someone's been in here."

"How can you tell?" She lit another lightstick.

Rolf strode to the crates and held his lightstick in the air. "These containers have been moved."

"Just moved? Or opened?" She stood beside him.

"Actually, I think they might have been resealed. I was in a hurry and didn't do such a good job."

Ilyssa spotted a gleaming object on the floor. Stooping to pick it up, she sucked in a sharp breath. It was a silver hoop earring—just like the one Helena had been missing.

"The lightsticks are gone," Rolf remarked, his face grim as he stalked the dark space, examining the floor. "Let's hope whoever picked them up didn't make the connection with us."

Ilyssa pocketed the earring without commenting on it. Her nose wrinkled as she sniffed something foul. "What's that strange odor?"

Rolf grimaced. "It seems to be coming from the crates. I'll check it out. Hand me the toolbox." Knowing they had no business being in there, he nonetheless felt compelled to investigate. He lifted down the nearest crate, his biceps bulging from the strain.

"How do you stay in such good shape?" Ilyssa asked, curious. "For a diplomat, you have an impressive physique." That was an understatement. He had the build of a weight lifter.

He gave her a disarming smile that momentarily took her breath away. "I work out a lot in the physiolab on Bimordus Two."

"But you know how to fight. That can't be part of the training for the diplomatic corps." She was thinking of his actions in fighting off the Souks who had attacked her. Did it just happen last night in this very same car?

Rolf halted in his labor. "I was much more impulsive in my youth. The incident with Gayla subdued my impetuous nature. I try to negotiate rather than fight these days."

"But you've maintained your skills."

"I pursue fencing as a sport. Also, Glotaj enrolled me in a self-defense course before I left on this mission. The hand-to-hand combat techniques did come in handy."

He grunted as he tried to pry open the fasteners around the edges. "Great suns!" He'd lifted off the lid, and just as quickly shut it down and started hammering the fasteners into place.

A putrid odor hit her nostrils. "Whew! What's in there?"

"You don't want to know."

She noticed the pallor on his face. "What is it, Rolf?"

"It's not a what. It's a who."

She gasped. "We were just in here last night. How can—"

"Remember the customs agent with the mustache?" At Ilyssa's nod, he said, "He's in here."

"But how can that be?"

"I'd say he was searching the train earlier and someone surprised him in here."

"The arms smuggler?"

"It would appear so."

Ilyssa thought of Helena's earring. Could the musician in Balthazar's troupe be in league with the carpet seller? She'd seen her talking to Jarin. What was going on?

"We need to get out of here." Rolf finished sealing up the crate. Sweating from his efforts, he placed it back atop the pile.

Ilyssa followed him toward the platform door. She didn't want to be around when the other two customs agents went searching for their friend. Did they even now realize he was missing? Hastening back to their compartment, they agreed to remain inside except for meals. Rolf didn't feel well anyway. He had a headache and thought it was due to the high altitude.

The rest of the journey passed without further incident. Rolf was ill with mountain sickness and Ilyssa felt unwell herself so they didn't do much talking. In a way, Ilyssa was relieved, since her throat was still slightly sore and she wanted to conserve her voice. A couple of times, someone walked by their closed compartment door, stopping momentarily and then moving on. It made Ilyssa uneasy. As the hauras passed, she became more anxious to reach their next destination.

"What do you know of Coroban?" Ilyssa asked Rolf as the train pulled into the station at its final stop. She draped herself in the veil that matched her sapphire-blue caftan, making sure her face was adequately covered.

Rolf peered into the reflector as he straightened his white shirt under the tan jerkin. A wide belt cinched his waist, and the tight dark brown leggings hugged his hips in a comfortable fit. His boots shone from fresh polish he'd bought in Vloxvil. A knife was strapped to his belt, thanks to a survival shop he'd located there.

"I was briefed on this part of the country," he replied. "Coroban is located at the edge of the Nurash Desert. Previously this was Cerrus Bdan's territory, but since his execution at the hands of the Morgots, his cousin Yanuk took control. Proclaiming himself pasha, Yanuk established the dreaded practice of the Koritah, an institution he acquired from another relative across the great Cobalt Wash."

Ilyssa shuddered with horror. "I don't know how familiar you are with the Koritah. It's a doctrine of socially accepted behavior aimed toward females. All members of the feminine gender are to be veiled and accompanied in public by male family members. Makeup is not allowed, nor are trousers or other indecent forms of dress. It is within the rights of the Koritah to examine any suspect females and punish offenders."

Rolf caught the note of fear in her voice. "What kind of punishment?"

Ilyssa studied a spot on the floor. "Violators of the moral code are subjected to imprisonment and up to fifty lashes of a pronged whip. Under Yanuk's fanatical control, the morals police so far have arrested more than two hundred women in the past month alone. Offenses include such things as wearing sunglasses to block out the bright desert sun, permitting more than hands to be exposed in public, and wearing makeup."

"That's absurd." Rolf gazed at her questioningly. "How do you know all this?"

Ilyssa tugged the sleeves of her caftan over her wrists. The fear of the Koritah was so pervasive it had reached her even in Haakat. "It's been reported on the news in Haakat. Ruel is more liberated, thank the stars. He finds it amusing to follow the follies of his less tolerant compatriots. Maybe he's figuring out a way to exploit their weaknesses."

"That seems a likely explanation." Striding over to her, he lifted her veil, studying her face. "Are you worried?"

"Not as long as you're with me," she admitted, giving him a brave smile she didn't feel. Outwitting Bolt was one thing; confronting faceless morals police for breaking a law she didn't understand was another.

"Once we reach the coast, you won't have to be concerned. Landor is pasha there and he's quite modern in his views. In fact, I think he's one of the leaders who supports emancipation."

Gathering their belongings, they exited into the bright, warm sunshine. During the night the train had descended the steep mountain slopes, and this morning found them breathing easier and feeling alert. They'd passed inspection by the border patrol and were free to depart.

Outside, the bustle of the crowd didn't hide the dogfaced Koritah police who patrolled in uniforms bristling with weapons. They cast narrowed glances at the females, including Ilyssa, who wasn't excluded by virtue of her species. All members of the feminine gender were subject to Yanuk's decrees. A couple of Horthas marched with them, making their presence even more formidable.

Luckily Ilyssa was well versed in proper harem decorum. She clung to Rolf's arm and kept her head demurely lowered.

"Hey, friends!" It was Balthazar, lumbering toward them. "Are you leaving without saying good-bye?"

Rolf viewed him warily but the man's attitude toward Ilyssa appeared respectful. He proffered a stiffly polite handshake to the older gentleman.

Ilyssa hugged the ladies in the troupe and wished them well. She watched them walk away, her eyes on Helena's back. The young woman wore another pair of silver hoop earrings, visible through her veil. Even the players had dressed appropriately to avoid the morals police.

Rolf touched her elbow. "Look, there goes the carpet seller."

Jarin caught sight of Ilyssa and waved. Ilyssa waved back, silently wishing her well. And then she saw a couple of familiar faces in the crowd, Gant and the blond-haired customs agent.

Rolf followed the direction of her glance. "Blast, they're still around. I wonder if they're on to the carpet seller."

"If that were so, they would have arrested him for murder by now. I assume they know one of their fellow agents is missing."

"That doesn't mean they know what happened to him. And even if they did, Gant might be waiting to see where the arms shipment is going."

"What if those rifles are headed for the resistance?"

"I don't mind as long as we're not involved." Taking

her arm, he steered her firmly in the direction of the bustling terminal. "We're switching trains. I bought tickets to Saline City further up the coast. We'll double back to Regis, a small fishing village where my emergency contact resides. He'll connect us with the main group of freedom fighters."

They hurried to make the scheduled departure time. While Rolf was at the ticket window confirming their reservation for a private compartment, Ilyssa glanced around. Her attention was drawn to a couple of Souks who slipped around a corner just as she spotted them. One was a lean, wiry individual with a narrow dogface and cropped brown hair. She got a quick glimpse of intelligent yellow eyes staring at her before he dashed out of sight. His shorter companion, dressed similarly in a black belted tunic, had long ears that clung close to the sides of his bald head. Sagging jowls were his memorable facial feature.

Ilyssa wrinkled her brow. They looked familiar, but where could she have seen them before?

Troubled, she followed Rolf into their new accommodations. At any other time, she might have been delighted with the modern conveniences and posh decor of their lodging. But she was disturbed by the feeling of unease that afflicted her. Somehow she felt it was associated with those two Souks.

Rolf tested his bunk. The mattress was firm but plush. "This run takes about twelve hauras. We should arrive in Saline City at twenty-two hundred hauras tonight. We'll have to rent a room in town and resume our journey in the morning."

Dashing a hand through his tousled hair, he complained, "This is already Lexin seventeenth. We can't hope to meet the resistance in the Nurash Desert for a couple more days at the very least. That will give me two weeks before the Alliance conference."

Ilyssa glanced at him anxiously. Would that give him

enough time to rescue her parents? "You'll still have to get over to Drobrok," she stated. "Were you planning on using air transport across the Cobalt Wash?"

He nodded. "My friends in the resistance were supposed to have arranged it, although since I didn't show up at the initial rendezvous, they might have scuttled those plans. They wouldn't have had any idea what happened to me. I suppose they contacted Glotaj to tell him I was missing."

"The Supreme Regent must be concerned about you."

His expression darkened. "It would be very dangerous for the Coalition if I were subject to questioning."

"You seemed to do all right at the mining camp."

"No one knew who I was, remember? If anyone finds out now . . ."

He let the words go unfinished, and Ilyssa's heart caught in her throat. She couldn't bear the thought of him being harmed. Despite her awareness that they had no future together, she still cared for Rolf a great deal. If her brother Devin were alive, he would have admired the noble councillor. Both possessed passionate natures and a determination to pursue their goals. She'd always thought Devin was destined for greatness but his ambitions had been put on hold when Ruel captured them. Any hopes he might have had to find a brighter future ended with his death.

Guilt mixed with sorrow in her heart, and a melancholy sigh escaped her lips. Rolf was at her side in an instant.

"Are you worried that I've forgotten about your parents?" he said, taking her hand.

She looked at him, her eyes saddened. "I was thinking that my brother Devin would have liked you."

"Devin," Rolf repeated absently. The name was familiar, and not because Ilyssa had mentioned him before. A trace of a memory nagged at him but he pushed it aside. "We'll discuss your situation with the resistance leaders.

Perhaps Haakat has been cleared by now and the residents have returned. Your parents could be among them. My friends should be able to find out."

"I hope so." Ilyssa let her hand linger in his. His palm was so large, it dwarfed hers as though it were a child's. His fingers were long and slender, reminding her of an artist's hand, or a musician's. Her father's hand felt like this. Moisture sprang into her eyes and she let go of him. "I'm worried about Papa," she murmured, bending her head. "His condition might have worsened."

"What were you planning to do about his mindwash?"

"I have to find a way to reverse it."

"How?"

She shrugged. "I'll deal with that when the time comes. First we have to free him."

"I'll help you, Ilyssa. I swear I will." He gazed down at her face, and when she tilted her head to stare at him with her wide, vulnerable eyes, he pulled her into his arms. His mouth swooped down to capture hers.

Ilyssa hadn't even known she'd wanted to be kissed. But as she felt the pressure of his mouth on hers, she realized it was what she desired from the bottom of her soul. Wrapping her arms around his neck, she met his hungry kisses with her own. His hands roamed over her body, and even through her caftan she could feel the heat from his touch. It made her restless, wanting more. Her breath quickened, and she melted into him.

"By the stars, Ilyssa, I want you," he murmured against her mouth, his hot breath fanning her face. He claimed her for another kiss and time seemed to dissolve.

Ilyssa let her hands explore his back, relishing the strength of his muscles. Closing her eyes, she lost herself in the heady sensations spiraling through her.

Rolf lifted his head, his eyes glittering as he looked into her face. "I won't be able to stop if we go on. I thought I could just hold you and kiss you, but it drives me wild to feel you in my arms and not be able to make love to you."

"I . . . understand," she mumbled, disappointed.

Their eyes met and for a moment she thought he might kiss her again, but then he dropped his hands and stepped back. "Want to play kather sticks? Now that we've got a fabricator, we can conjure the supplies."

"All right." She'd do anything to get her mind off him. With Ruel's safeguard in place, she had no choice but to guard her virginity. But once the safeguard was removed—

She bit her lip, reminding herself about becoming an arbiter. Was the path to success worth the sacrifices she'd have to make along the way? Assuming she achieved her goals, with whom would she celebrate? Rolf was the first man she'd ever wanted. What if the myth was wrong? What if she didn't risk losing her singing voice when she lost her virginity? How would she know unless she took the chance?

Confused, Ilyssa shook her head. Such speculation was useless until her parents were freed. Only then would the choice be hers, and only then would she make it. She stared at Rolf's handsome face, his long ebony hair, his regal carriage. Inside, she felt as though they were already joined, and she cried out for the day when freedom would allow her to choose her destiny.

The choice came a lot sooner than she'd expected. The identity of those two Souks came back to her during the evening hauras. By the corona, they were Kraus and Lork, Bolt's hunters who specialized in finding escaped slaves! The satrap must have sent them after her.

Ilyssa sat upright on her lounger, peering at Rolf, who was resting on his bunk, his back toward her. Heavens above, what was she to do? They'd tracked her this far but hadn't made a move to take her. That must mean Bolt had given orders to his team to follow her and report back on her activities. What if they kept on her trail? She'd lead them straight to the resistance camp!

Oh God, what if Rolf was captured along with her and his identity was revealed? He'd be sent to Ruel, and the pasha would torment him. She imagined the room in the clinic where her brother had been tortured, only it was Rolf's body that was strapped onto the table in her mind's eye. Ruel had said he wanted Rolf alive, but maybe he'd kill him after extracting information. No, she couldn't be responsible for his getting caught!

A chill swept over her as she considered her options. If she led the hunters away from Rolf, he might be spared their attention. He'd be able to get away on his own and meet the freedom fighters. He meant too much to her, and his mission was too important for him to get captured.

She'd been selfish to ask him to rescue her parents. Her problems were insignificant compared to the scope of his assignment. What he accomplished here could affect the whole Coalition. She'd been forgetting who the man was—Lord Rolf Cam'brii, esteemed member of the High Council, high prince on Nadira, respected statesman and diplomat. It wasn't fair for her to burden him with her personal sorrows. Yes, they'd helped each other up until this point, but now it was time for her to strike out on her own.

Of course Rolf would never agree with her reasoning, so she'd have to sneak away at the earliest opportunity. Even if he caught her then, she'd claim she was returning to Bolt. Hearing that again might make him so enraged with her that he'd cast her off. It was what she had to do, she thought dismally. Tears ran down her cheeks as she contemplated the lonely road ahead, but it was the only way to ensure Rolf's safety. Just as with her parents, Rolf's needs superseded her own.

* * *

The night sky was studded with stars when the train pulled into the station at Saline City, a popular seaside resort. Since the Koritah did not exist in this province, Ilyssa didn't bother to wear her veil. Packing it inside her bag, she slung the sack over her shoulder and glanced at Rolf. Hopefully he had no notion of what she was about to do.

Rolf wondered why Ilyssa seemed so nervous. She'd been unusually quiet as the train had pulled into the station, and even now as they entered the terminal she acted subdued. Long silken lashes veiled her eyes, and her pretty face was pale. Her fingers played at the sapphire-blue fabric of her caftan.

"Is anything wrong?" he asked her, concerned.

"No." She moistened her lips with the tip of her tongue. "I'm just tired, that's all. It's late. Look, there's an information kiosk. Why don't you go ahead and make a room reservation while I run into the sanitary?"

"Sure." He gazed at her, puzzled. Why were his suspicions suddenly aroused? He watched her walk toward the sanitary, her slim figure moving gracefully, and it reminded him of what she'd tried once before in Kantina.

Shrugging off the idea as being ridiculous, probably a result of his own fatigue, he made their room reservation. He was just turning away from the kiosk when he saw the tail end of a blue caftan rounding a corner.

A terrible feeling overcame him. It couldn't be . . . and yet he had the awful idea that it was. Where in Zor would she be going? A couple of Souks dressed in black tunics who'd been leaning against a nearby wall took off after her. To his astonishment and dismay, it appeared as though Ilyssa knew they were on her trail. She glanced over her shoulder with a satisfied smile and continued on. Rolf hurried to close the distance between them.

He watched as she dropped a piece of paper behind her,

and one of the Souks picked it up. A look of surprise came over the fellow's face and he signaled to his companion. They held a quick conference, staring in Ilyssa's direction. She paused to glance back. After noting they held her note, she took off again.

Rolf gaped. Why would she be communicating with those two Souks who just happened to be armed? He couldn't think of any possible reason. She must know them, and yet who were they and where were they from? By the corona, he'd told her his identity and how he planned to make contact with the resistance!

Desperate with fear, he charged after her as soon as the two Souks took a side street in another direction.

"Going somewhere?" he called out when he was close enough for her to hear.

Ilyssa got a glimpse of him and her face paled. Without saying a word, she sprinted forward.

"Stop!" He dashed after her, puzzled and angry. Catching up, he grabbed her arm and brought her to a jerking halt. "Where in Zor are you going?" he demanded. "What was that message you left for those two Souks?"

Ilyssa huffed to catch her breath. Pale and trembling, she shook her head.

"Talk, woman!" He realized people were staring at them, so he steered her toward an alley.

The night was breezy with a salty wind blowing off the ocean. It whipped her caftan around her legs. Ilyssa glanced away, having no excuses to offer him.

"I asked you where you were going." His tone was cold, so cold it brought a shiver to her spine. His hand gripping her arm tightened.

"It's no use, Rolf. I was leaving," she confessed, tilting her chin to gaze at him proudly.

His complexion reddened. "Leaving?"

"Yes, I'm going back to Bolt." Hopefully he'd discard her out of disgust. She'd told the hunters where to meet her. Her message had said she was ready to return to Bolt. They would escort her back to the Rocks of Weir and Rolf could get away.

Despite her determination, her heart sank at the shocked expression on Rolf's face.

"By the corona, do you know what you're saying?" He dug his fingers into her arm. "Do you?"

"Please, you're hurting me."

"That's not all I'm going to do to you! I trusted you. Great suns, the things I told you! And now this!" His eyes glittered like two chunks of ice. "You're coming with me, and I'm not letting you out of my sight again. Either you go peacefully, or I'll have to force you. Which is it to be?" Grappling in his knapsack with one hand while restraining her with the other, he pulled out a length of cord.

"What's that for?" she asked fearfully, knowing if she attempted to run away she'd infuriate him more.

Without answering, Rolf flipped her around so that her back was to him. Snatching her arms, he yanked them behind her, twisting the cord painfully around her wrists.

"How dare you!" she screamed, struggling against him. But his grip was so fierce she accomplished nothing. He bound her wrists so tightly that her skin chafed as she moved.

Rage boiled through his blood as he knotted the cord so she couldn't possibly get free. The witch! She'd betrayed him! All this time, he'd been thinking she cared for him. He'd trusted her! And yet it was all a ruse. She must have been in league with Bolt all along. By the stars, he felt crushed by her treachery.

That's what you get for being distracted from your oath to Gayla's parents, he told himself, giving Ilyssa's binding an extra hard yank. Well, no more. He'd devote his thoughts and actions solely to the mission at hand.

He admitted to being incapable of making rational judgments where Ilyssa was concerned. The woman clouded his senses so he couldn't think straight. He'd deliver her into the hands of the resistance and let them decide what to do with her.

"Rolf, let me go. I was only trying to—"

"Shut up," he snarled, throwing both their sacks over his shoulder. Pushing her from behind, he hid her restraints against his body as he urged her along.

"You rotten snivet-bellied rat scum! Is this what you do to someone who—oof!"

He yanked on her bonds, bringing her up short. He whispered in her ear, "I told you to be quiet, woman. I won't have your smooth words persuading me you're innocent. You will save your talk for my friends in the resistance. They will determine whether or not you speak the truth."

Ilyssa gave a strangled cry, but Rolf ignored it as he shoved her forward. He was so upset he didn't even want to consider any possible explanations on her part. They'd all be lies anyway. Everything she'd ever told him must have been creative inventions. His eyes narrowed. Had the part about Ruel's safeguard been a falsehood, too? Because if it was—

Looking forward to exacting retribution from her, he arrived at the resort and checked in. Steering Ilyssa inside a luxurious suite overlooking the beach, he thrust her onto the wide circular lounger.

Keeping an eye on her, he unfastened his jerkin and threw it onto the carpet along with his belt. "Tell me what you do for Ruel," he demanded, approaching her.

Ilyssa, her hands bound behind her back, pushed against the back of the lounger. She was frightened by the cold look in his eye. "Rolf, I haven't been truthful," she began.

"Don't you think I know that?"

She realized what he meant and swallowed. "About those two Souks just now, I—"

"Shut up. I don't want to hear about them. I asked you about Ruel." His shirt joined his other clothing on the plush carpeting.

Ilyssa's gaze swept from his rigid face to his broad shoulders and muscular chest. With his rage, there was no telling what he would do. She had to calm him.

"I told you the truth about Ruel."

"Liar." He slowly advanced toward the bed, his eyes on her face. His hands went to his waist, where he began unfastening his leggings.

"No!" Ilyssa cried, suddenly becoming aware of his intent.

"You've been after my identity and contacts all along, haven't you? Gods, what a fool I've been. Well, you don't have to worry about tricking me any longer. We'll soon find out if you're telling the truth or not." He stepped out of his pants and stood naked in front of her.

"See what you do to me, even now?" He nodded at the evidence of his arousal. "It's about time I got satisfaction."

"Please, Rolf, you don't understand." As terrified as she was, she stared at his manliness, and an unbidden fire rose within her.

He sat on the bed, sliding a hand up her leg after pushing the fabric of her caftan out of the way. "How I've wanted to do this to you in love, not in anger. But you asked for it, Ilyssa, with your false words and pretense of innocence."

"I am innocent! I was trying to save you. Those two Souks are—"

"Your cohorts." He sidled closer and cupped her chin in his hand, silencing her. "Don't tell me any more lies or it will go the worse for you. Now let's get on with it." He bent his head to kiss her.

Ilyssa tried to slide out of his way but he stopped her.

"Don't resist me. I might hurt you if you do." His voice was deceptively quiet, but she could tell from his furious expression that he spoke the truth.

Closing her eyes, she tried to steel herself against what was coming, but when he mashed his mouth to hers, she was amazed to find her traitorous body responding. Even this way, she craved his touch, burned to feel his hands caressing her skin. And when he drew the caftan off her shoulders and kissed her breast, she stifled a cry of pleasure.

He heard her murmur and raised his head, astonished to find her so responsive. Gods, the woman was still working her spell on him. He should take her quickly, in one hard thrust, to prove the truth once and for all. But when she looked this way, her lips so soft and inviting, her eyes half-lidded, and her breasts rising and falling with desire, he couldn't go on. He wanted to make love to her, not ravish her.

With a grunt of self-disgust, he stood abruptly, grabbed his leggings, and stomped toward the door.

"W-Where are you going?" she stuttered, her eyes flying open.

"Away from temptation!" he snapped.

"My wrists . . . can you unbind them?"

He hesitated. "I suppose there would be no harm in that." And when it was done, he left her.

Ilyssa heard him turn the lock from the other side. Bounding up from the bed, she rushed to the casement. It was too high for an escape route. Disappointed, she rubbed her chafed wrists. Now there was no choice but to go with Rolf to the freedom fighters and cast her fate in their hands. Like the time in Haakat with the minister, she'd made another mistake and would have to pay dearly for it.

Sighing, she turned back to observe her latest prison.

* * *

Early the next morning, Rolf made the arrangements for their trip to Regis, the fishing village to the south where he was to meet his emergency contact. He'd spent a bad night, having had one of the most horrendous night-mares ever. Because of Ilyssa, he'd taken enormous risks that could cost him his mission. He'd never forgive him-self if he didn't fulfill his vow to Gayla's parents and stop the Souk acts of terrorism. His guilt had blossomed, overwhelming him with the possible consequences of his gullibility. No doubt that was the cause of his bad dream last night. Sighing, he realized there was still so much to do and so little time.

First he had to collect Ilyssa and rendezvous with the fisherman who'd agreed to transport them by boat to Regis.

An haura later, he was leading her toward the dock. He'd offered her morning nourishment from the fabricator in the living area where he'd slept on a lounger all night. She'd accepted a meager meal, acting quietly obedient. He couldn't help observing the shadows under her eyes or the pallor of her delicate complexion. Her hair was untidy and he'd offered her a brush, unable to keep his eyes from her lovely face. He wanted her, even after her treachery, and he hated himself for it. God knew why he was being so polite to her. She didn't deserve any kindness after what she'd done to him. Had the woman been reporting his movements all along? Would there be a reception committee waiting to arrest him in Regis? He'd find out soon enough.

The fisherman, an elderly Souk, was waiting for them. Rolf helped Ilyssa into the small boat, assisting her onto a benchlike seat and taking a place directly beside her. The sleeves of Ilyssa's blue caftan hid her bruised wrists. Her body trembled under the soft material but he ignored the impulse to comfort her or otherwise allay her fears. She wasn't going to tempt him again. Steeling his heart against her, he nodded at the whiskered old salt who watched them with amusement in his dark eyes.

The fisherman started up the engine, an old-fashioned combustion contraption that was noisy as a flock of kookaburs. Soon the briny smell of fish mixed with exhaust fumes as they chugged out to sea. A fresh breeze hit their faces, and Rolf drew in a deep breath. He'd rarely been sailing but whenever he had the chance, he enjoyed it. Squinting, he stared at the horizon.

Ilyssa sat stiffly beside him, her shoulders aching from her straight posture. Feeling water sloshing at her heels, she looked down. The floor of the boat was strewn with empty bottles, fishing lines and hooks, bait like tallyrod and tiny frigate fish. She wrinkled her nose, glancing at Rolf's profile to see if the odor bothered him.

His face was stern as he gazed out to sea. Seeing no compassion there, she let loose a small sigh. He shifted, and she knew he'd heard. "Please, Rolf, just listen to what I have to say," she tried again for the umpteenth time.

He turned to her, his expression rigid. "If you try to convince me one more time that you were going to those two Souks to save my skin, I'll throw you over the side of this boat. I'm paying this fellow enough credits so he won't notice."

Ilyssa fell silent. He wasn't going to believe her no matter what she said. Eventually the rocking motion of the boat combined with the exhaust fumes made her feel sick. Compressing her lips, she told herself not to complain. She leaned weakly against Rolf, closing her eyes and concentrating on breathing regularly.

After a seemingly endless period of time, they came to a jolting halt and the engine noise died. Ilyssa stretched, grateful for the journey's end. She couldn't wait to touch solid ground. Glancing toward land, she saw a tranquil fishing village. Pastel-colored buildings covered the sandy hills facing the sea. Souks were bustling about in the midday heat. Without the breeze from the moving boat, she noticed how warm the air had grown.

Tipping the boatman, Rolf led her off the small dock and onto the beach. Her legs were wobbly and she could barely stand on her own. He urged her toward the main street, a short strip of shops and eateries facing the ocean.

A wave of concern washed over him at her sickly complexion but he ignored it, refusing to acknowledge any kind feelings toward her. Besides, she'd feel better after walking around.

"We need to find a music shop," he said. "See one anywhere?"

"Why should I help you? You won't listen to me. I've been trying to tell you the truth."

A warning gleam shot into his eye and he took a step in her direction. Ignoring the fear fluttering in her breast, Ilyssa faced him squarely.

"I guess everything we did together meant nothing," she said, hurt that he wouldn't even consider her explanation.

"You're the one whose actions prove that. At any rate, it's better this way." Rolf's tone was as icy as his eyes. "Even if you have been truthful, you've got your agenda and I've got mine. You told me so yourself. Now let's not waste any more time talking." He gave her a nudge forward.

"Do you have to be so physical?" The man couldn't seem to keep his hands off her. Annoyed, she strode ahead toward the bustling main street.

Rolf's long stride caught up to hers. His hulking presence at her side obliterated all thoughts of anything else from her mind. She wished she didn't care for him so much. His aloofness would be less painful if every nerve in her body weren't screaming for his attention. Her heart ached for his former tenderness. It's your fault, she told herself. You tried going back to Bolt for him. And this is the thanks you get.

Resentment flared inside her. He wouldn't even listen to her rationale. How could he believe she'd betray him after what they'd been through? Were his feelings for her so shallow?

Rolf halted in front of a shop with a hanging sign in Soukese indicating musical instruments for sale.

Jawani was the standard Coalition language, and Bolt as well as the other Souks had spoken it at the mining camp so Rolf and the other sumis could understand. Ilyssa had spoken it to him as well. But in some of these remote areas, only Soukese was understood. Rolf was glad for his knowledge of the language now that he couldn't rely on Ilyssa to help him.

"Inside," he commanded her.

With a rustle of her caftan, Ilyssa entered ahead of him, her shoulders sagging. Rolf saw her depressed posture and wondered about it. Was she upset because he'd foiled her plans with Bolt? Or was it because she cared about him and he was treating her badly?

Shaking his head, he decided the distraction of worrying about what she thought wasn't worth his time or attention. He had to concentrate on his mission, and Ilyssa didn't have any part in that. Her fate would be decided by his friends in the resistance.

Inside the shop, a small-statured Souk with a thatch of gray hair was standing behind a counter serving two customers, human males. A Hortha stood off to the side, its large bulk casting a gloom over that corner of the room. The exchange didn't appear friendly. The shopkeeper had a frightened look on his face as he glanced at Rolf and Ilyssa.

The two buyers twisted around to see who'd entered the shop. At his side, Ilyssa stifled a cry. Rolf gave a hard swallow.

It was the two customs agents from the hovertrain.

Chapter Fourteen

The blond customs agent narrowed his gray eyes at them. "Didn't you two get off the train at Coroban?"

Beside him, Gant snorted in agreement, his hand going to the shooter strapped at his hip.

Rolf glanced at their hostile faces and cursed. "Ilyssa," he muttered out of the corner of his mouth. "What happened to your siren song?"

She threw him a panicked look. "I never told Gant to obey my subsequent commands. He's not mindwashed in that sense, and besides, his friend wasn't with him at the time. If I tried it now, the Hortha would stop me."

"Try giving Gant an order and see what happens," he suggested, a desperate edge to his tone.

Giving him a nod, Ilyssa addressed the agent. "Aren't you part of Ruel's forces? What brings you here?"

The blond man snickered and took a step in her direction.

"Wait, Scard. It can't hurt to tell them." Gant sneered at Ilyssa, demonstrating to her that the mindwash had indeed been of one-time value. "We're tracing an illicit shipment of arms that is headed for the rebels in the desert. This Souk's name was scribbled on a piece of paper we found on board the train, having been dropped by one of the smugglers. We assume he is a contact and we've come here to question him."

The shopkeeper made a choking sound but Ilyssa didn't dare glance in his direction. "You have no jurisdiction here," she remarked.

"No, but we do in Yanuk's land. We'll take him there, and he'll show us where the rebels gather. I think we might bring you along as well." Slowly, his gaze roved over her body so there was no mistake about the meaning behind his words.

Rolf clenched his fists at his side. "We'll just finish our business here and go. Mister shopkeeper," he said, striding forward. "We were hoping to find a three-valved zandozor." It might be his only chance to identify himself to the contact.

The old Souk's eyes lit with understanding. "What designation?"

"I need one circa 2004, Earth chronology."

The Souk shook his head. "No r-r-reeds have I from that time period, but I can r-r-recommend you to someone who does." Glancing surreptitiously at the two agents, he grabbed for a pad of paper on the countertop. The agents listened with bemused expressions on their faces as though thinking they'd humor the Souk before smashing him. In the corner, the Hortha bounced on his heels, restless for action.

The shopkeeper was careful to keep both his hands in full view of the men who were watching while he scribbled instructions and then handed the pad to Rolf. "Be on your way," he told him warningly.

Gant drew his shooter. "Not so fast. Let me see what's on that paper."

"You heard the man," Rolf said. "We're leaving." But as he turned with Ilyssa toward the door, the Hortha gave a snarl and unfurled his stun whip, flinging it in Ilyssa's direction. Rolf pushed her out of the way just as the shopkeeper pulled a weapon from under the counter and shot at the hairy beast. As a howl rang through the store, Gant returned fire.

Rolf tugged at Ilyssa's arm. "Let's get out of here."

They ran, leaving the whine of laser weapons behind. Rolf thought he heard the shopkeeper cry out as they charged through the exit.

"Wait here," he told Ilyssa once they were in the street, ignoring the crowd that was beginning to gather. "I'm going back to help the Souk."

She threw herself in his path. "No! We've got to get out of here. It's not our battle."

His mouth tight, he stared at her and for a moment she thought he was going to cast her aside and enter the fray. But reason seemed to get the better of him, or else he glanced inside and saw the shopkeeper slumped over the counter and the customs agents beginning to toss about the contents of his shop looking for evidence. In either event, the sight of the beastly Hortha clumping toward the door was enough to put wings on his heels.

Grasping her hand, he ran with her down the street. He didn't stop to wonder why she was coming with him so readily. If she'd wanted to elude him or expose him, she'd had the perfect opportunity in the shop. Even now, she could veer in another direction and he'd have to waste precious time charging after her. But she was coming willingly and that caused him to doubt his accusations. Later, he'd ask her to explain. Now there just wasn't time.

Ilyssa needed no further incentive to accompany him. Despite her wish to return to Bolt, she had no desire to be mixed up in an arms-smuggling scheme, and the shopkeeper must be involved if the agents had followed the trail here. The safest route for her and Rolf was out of town, and they might as well go together.

Rolf followed the instructions in the note, and they ended up at a garage in a deserted warehouse district that stank of dead fish. A massive steel corrugated door stood in front of them and it was locked.

"Look in the toolbox in the knapsack. There's a metal file in there that may be helpful," Ilyssa suggested, lifting her hand to shield her eyes from the afternoon sun. "You can use it to pick the lock."

Rolf's training hadn't included such skills so he sought an easier method. "It's strange the shopkeeper didn't give us the means to open the door." Rereading the note, he looked for hints. Finding none, he flipped through the pages in the pad, finally noticing a bulge at the back piece of cardboard. Upon closer examination, he discovered a key taped to the inside. "Here we go!"

The key fit. Excited at what might be inside, Rolf unlocked the heavy door and lifted it. It swung open from below, the hinges being noiseless and well lubricated.

"By the corona!" He caught sight of the object sitting in the center of the garage, its gleaming metal reflecting the light from outside.

"An open-air speeder!" Ilyssa cried. "Look, there's a data card on the seat. Let's see what it says." Fitting it into her data link, Ilyssa read off a complete set of instructions for a route following an ancient riverbed through the desert to a site where the resistance would contact them. "I guess this is our means of transportation."

Rolf gave her a curious glance. "Let's not waste any time. Those customs agents will be breathing down our necks. Get in."

"How are we going to sit? There's room for only one." The sleek oblong vehicle was tapered at the front end and sported a windshield to protect the driver.

"The bags will fit in here." He stuck them in a small storage space behind the seat. "You'll have to sit on my lap. Come on, let's go."

He lowered himself into the narrow space and spread his legs so she would have room to maneuver. She gingerly stepped over the threshold and lowered herself onto his lap.

Rolf felt her weight press against him and he grunted. "I can barely reach the controls with you in my way." She squirmed to get comfortable and he gritted his teeth. "Your hair is in my face," he complained, although that wasn't what was really bothering him. Her buttocks were grinding on top of his—

"Sorry." With a graceful sweep of her hand, she brushed her lush hair forward. Rolf had an insane desire to sweep his fingers through the ocean-scented strands and kiss her long, creamy neck.

Crimson darkened her cheeks as he grunted again. She didn't want to lean back against his muscled chest. If she adjusted her position again, his growing hardness would enlarge more than it already had beneath her derriere. Agitated, she reached forward to punch on the ignition.

Rolf's breath grew short. "By the suns, woman, keep still. I can't concentrate on driving with you gyrating on top of me."

"I am not gyrating! I'm just trying to get comfortable. This space is incredibly tight."

"So am I!" Reaching around her, he flipped the antigrav switch on. All gauges showed the instrumentation in full readiness as the vehicle rose in the air. The hover utilization activated so that when Rolf pushed the throttle forward, they zoomed out of the garage on a cushion of compressed air.

Particles of sand flew against the windshield. They sped past the warehouses, around a corner by the dock, and turned inland, heading east. The rolling dunes at the edge of town rapidly approached. They zipped through the streets until a vast expanse of shifting sand stretched in front of them.

Stories Ilyssa had heard about giant sand slugs and dust storms came to mind and a sudden shiver shook her. She hoped they had enough fuel to get where they were going. Being stranded in the desert without adequate supplies was not a prospect worth contemplating.

Wind whipped about as the speeder carried them across the arid land. At least the sun was to their backs. Sweat trickled down her cleavage from the high temperature. Her lips cracked from dryness. Closing her eyes, she sagged back, resting her head against Rolf's massive chest. He could watch for rising dunes and approaching sandstorms.

They made it to the rendezvous point just as dusk was falling.

"I see why they call these the Copper Dunes," Ilyssa said, stepping out of the parked vehicle to watch the sol descend in a brilliant burst of tangerine and crimson. Particles in the sand glistened a brilliant copper-gold. A high, camel-shaped dune rose off to the left, the signpost of their destination.

Rolf was checking through their provisions. "We've got enough food and water to last a few days, but I wonder how we're supposed to be contacted. We got here a lot sooner than I expected, thanks to the speeder." With his sleeve, he wiped the dust from his face and then squinted at the horizon. Rolling vistas of sand met his gaze. He worried about spending the night here. Unknown creatures might inhabit the dunes, fearsome things that attacked in the dark. The speeder provided little cover for protection.

Glancing at Ilyssa, he noted her flushed face and disheveled appearance. She was cleansing her neck with a wet wipe from their stash of supplies, and he stared at the lovely picture she made. Her auburn hair gleamed with reddish gold highlights in the descending sun. She held it off her face, cooling herself. His gaze rested on her slightly parted pink lips.

Ilyssa felt his eyes on her and her face flushed. Alone with him, she was acutely aware of his appeal. Her breath caught in her throat as he approached.

"Ilyssa, I'm ready to hear your explanation now," he said, his brows drawn together.

Dropping the wipe from her hand, she gazed at him, astonished. And then her eyes lifted to the sand dune beyond and she screamed.

Over the rise galloped six men riding huge muscled torrocks. The visitors were tall, bearded, and menacing in appearance. Each one wore a black sweatband around his head, leather armbands, and black cuffed pants. Long curved blades were fitted at their sides. Fierce expressions creased their faces as they approached.

Rolf turned around and pulled her to his side as the riders neared.

"Who are you?" the head man demanded, reigning in his beast in front of them. His dark eyes were cold as he waited for a response.

Rolf answered him calmly. "I was told we could find a three-valved zandozor circa 2004 in this location."

"Who sent you?"

"I came on my own. I'm looking for someone called Star Gazer." Rolf gave the code name for his contact.

The man's demeanor didn't change but a muscle twitched on the side of his face. "Who asks?"

"I'm the Sun King."

A brief silence met his revelation. Then the man broke into a wide smile. Gesturing to his fellow riders, he shouted Rolf's identity. A series of excited greetings followed.

Left out, Ilyssa wondered what would happen to her. These men must be members of the resistance. Would

Rolf turn her over to them while he left to complete his mission? Would he tell them of her attempted flight back to the Rocks of Weir?

Her limbs trembled. Afraid to draw attention to herself, she kept silent, waiting.

Eventually Rolf introduced her, giving the men her name and saying she was his companion. She threw him a grateful glance but he coolly instructed her to mount one of the snorting beasts in front of its rider. She did so reluctantly, Rolf assisting her. He hoisted himself up on another beast while one of the men took charge of the speeder. Then they rode off over the crest of the dune.

Ilyssa gasped when she caught sight of the ravine on the other side. A panorama of palm trees, a wide stream, and an encampment of tents met her gaze. The oasis was lit by a pattern of lanterns with camouflage netting surrounding it. She noted the strategic location with high dunes all around.

They dismounted by the riverbank, and a swarm of similarly outfitted men encircled them. Ilyssa glanced at Rolf's firm profile and sidled closer to him. Her hands were sweaty and her heart was racing. These dangerous-looking men and the prospects for her own unknown future frightened her.

Standing beside her, Rolf sensed her fear but was hesitant to offer comfort. He couldn't trust his feelings where she was concerned and chose to stick with his original decision to discuss her situation with the freedom fighters.

The man who'd initially greeted Rolf approached, his brow furrowed. "I am Mikeal. Tell me, Sun King, why did you miss your initial rendezvous?" He grinned at Ilyssa, revealing a mouthful of yellowed teeth.

"I'd prefer to talk with Star Gazer." Rolf moved closer to her, stopping just short of draping an arm around her shoulder.

Mikeal grunted. "Very well, I'll get him. Wait here."

The man stalked off, entering a canvas tent a short distance away. Emerging a moment later, he was accompanied by a tall youth with the brightest thatch of carrot-colored hair Rolf had ever seen. The boy was wearing a tan tunic, dark leggings, and boots. Through his belt was stuck a long, curved knife. The hard set of his eyes told Rolf he knew how to use it.

Beside him, Ilyssa gave a strangled cry. Turning to her, Rolf saw with alarm that a sick pallor had come over her face. He was just in time to catch her as her knees folded and she crumpled to the ground.

"By the Almighty!" the youth who went by the code name Star Gazer exclaimed. "Ilyssa! Is that you?" He rushed over, falling to his knees beside her. "Quick, some water," he called to his men.

"Do you know her?" Rolf questioned in surprise.

One of the rebels handed Star Gazer a damp rag. The youth tenderly placed it on her forehead. "Of course I know her. I never thought to see her again." He shook her arm. "Wake up!"

Ilyssa's eyes fluttered open and fixed on the red-haired youth. "Devin," she murmured, her voice filled with disbelief.

"Devin?" Rolf stared at him. The hair color, a shade brighter than hers; the straight but short nose; the hazel eyes . . . they bore a close resemblance. "You're her brother?"

Devin nodded happily as he helped Ilyssa to rise.

"But I thought you were dead!" she exclaimed, her strength returning as an incredible joy filled her soul. No, it was more than joy. It was a release. She hadn't been responsible for his death after all. An incredible weight lifted from her heart and she cried out his name in wonder. "Devin!" She threw herself at him, squeezing him in a tight embrace.

Devin held her, patting her head and murmuring soothingly in her ear. Even though she was three annums his senior, at that moment he was the one in command.

After a moment, she drew away and studied him. His beloved features had matured in the nine months since she'd seen him last. His body was tanned and muscular, his height taller by several inches. But the most noticeable change was the hardened thrust of his jaw, the determined gleam in his eye. A lot must have happened to him in the interval. He'd obviously earned the respect of these men who treated him as their leader, for all his 17 annums.

"Heavens above, I don't believe it," she exclaimed, unable to take her eyes from his face. She felt weak with emotion, but it was a joyous feeling. Wanting to cry and shout with happiness, she did neither and watched him.

"Believe it, sister. We have much to discuss." He gave her another brief hug and then turned to Rolf. "Lord Cam'brii, I presume?"

"I'm a bit late for our appointment." Grinning, he bowed.

Devin returned the courtesy. "I'm sure you have a lot to report, sir." His demeanor becoming serious, he gestured toward his tent. "Come, we can speak privately in there." To the others he shouted, "Let us prepare a proper welcome for our guests."

Shouts rose up from the motley group of men and in a flash, the atmosphere in the camp changed from one of hostility to one of congeniality. Men stood aside, lowering their heads respectfully as Rolf strode past. He was put in the unusual position of trailing behind Devin and Ilyssa, who were already rapt in conversation. Ruefully, he watched the graceful sway of her hips as she moved in the flowing caftan. Had he seriously misjudged her? Did she have a valid reason for her flight? Undoubtedly her brother was going to rule in her favor and it wouldn't put him in a very good light when Ilyssa explained his nasty treatment of her. He'd need his full diplomatic skills to get smoothly out of this one.

Glancing at Ilyssa with renewed appreciation, he saw how her skin glowed and her eyes shone with happiness as she beheld her adored brother. Once she had regarded him in that fashion. Now he'd have to use all his charms to win her affection again. Maybe he could enlist Devin to his aid, once he'd convinced her brother he meant her no real harm.

The inside of the tent was rather spartan, with a small cot, several folding chairs, and a table layered with maps. Devin treated his sister like a princess, finding her a comfortable cushion to sit upon, offering light refreshments and even a change of clothes, albeit men's attire.

Ilyssa laughed, a pleasant musical sound. "I'm fine, Devin," she said as she sank onto a straight-backed chair. "I just want to hear how you escaped from Ruel."

"Same here, big sister." He shifted his gaze to Rolf. "Please, sir, take a seat. Would you like some wine?"

"Yes, thank you," Rolf acknowledged graciously. He waited while the tall youth poured wine into ceramic goblets and handed them around.

"Aren't you the boy who helped Sarina escape from Souk?" Rolf asked, suddenly recalling where he'd heard Devin's name before.

"Aye, that I did." Devin grinned, a wide flash of even, white teeth against a tanned complexion.

"I gather you're in charge here now?" Rolf took a sip of the amber-colored wine. The honeyed liquor slid smoothly down his throat.

"Well, technically Otis is in charge, but the Crigellan doesn't get away very often." He noted Rolf's puzzled glance. "Otis is a lieutenant in Pasha Yanuk's service. He used to be with Cerrus Bdan and he had a hand in helping Captain Reylock and Sarina escape when they were here. But Otis prefers to keep a low profile. He can be more useful that way. His code name is Black Hole, by the way."

"Ah," Rolf said, nodding. He'd been briefed about the code names of the leaders but didn't know their actual identities. "Where shall we start? I know you two have a lot of catching up to do, but I'm concerned about getting to the Alliance conference on time." This was Lexin eighteenth. It had taken him less time than anticipated to rendezvous with the resistance, so he should be able to make it. Sixteen days remained before he had to be in Drobrok.

"I'll make the arrangements. You'll get there in plenty of time," Devin said, smiling broadly. He noticed the way the councillor's glance kept stealing toward his sister. She kept her face purposefully averted, preferring to keep her eyes on him, but Devin could feel the tension emanating from her. It would be interesting to hear how they'd ended up together.

He kept the conversation light so he could covertly study the two. Ilyssa must care about the man, Devin concluded from the way she was acting. He'd never seen her so fidgety. Despite her happiness at seeing him alive and well, something else was obviously on her mind. Her hands kept playing with the fabric of her skirt—a harem outfit, no less—and her eyes skittered, fixing on anything in the tent but the councillor. In his opinion, she couldn't have selected anyone better. Lord Cam'brii was greatly admired for his accomplishments. He cut a handsome, virile figure, and Devin had heard about the ladies who'd been disappointed by his pledge to marry Sarina Bretton. But now he was free and Devin could see that Cam'brii was clearly besotted with his sister from the way he kept eyeing her. Something must have happened to offset their attraction for each other. Maybe he could help to set things right.

Devin's attention kept wandering, and Rolf felt awkward. The rebel leader might want to be alone with his sister. It had been some time since they'd seen each other and their reunion was an emotional one for both of them.

"Look, would you two like some time alone?" he asked, brushing a strand of hair off his face. "I could go for a dip in the stream."

Brother and sister exchanged glances. "That would be appreciated, sir," Devin said, standing. "I'll get one of my men to provide you with a change of clothes." Stalking to the tent flap, he peered out and summoned one of his fellow liberators. "Guido will assist you."

"Thank you." Rolf rose, placing his empty goblet on a small side table before starting for the exit.

Devin's lip curved as he watched Ilyssa. As long as Cam'brii's back was turned to her, her eyes followed him outside. He shifted his chair around so he sat astride it, grinning at her.

Ilyssa gazed with fondness at her brother's freckled face. "Heavens above, it's so good to see you."

"Do you want to tell me about him now? Or maybe you'd rather explain how you escaped from Ruel? And what of our parents?" Thinking of them brought a frown to his face.

Wondering where to start, Ilyssa decided to begin with when they'd last seen each other. Perhaps Devin didn't know the reason why Ruel had tortured him. She proceeded to tell him how she'd offended the pasha by being caught in the minister's arms in Haakat.

"I'm so sorry," Ilyssa sobbed, covering her face with her hands. The scene was still so vivid in her memory: Devin strapped to that examining table in the clinic; his body painfully jolted with an electric prod; Ruel's evil grinning face; her brother's screams echoing in her ears. By the Almighty, she couldn't believe he'd survived.

Devin rushed over and knelt by her side. "Don't blame yourself. It was Ruel's cruelty that caused our suffering." He clenched his fists. "By the stars, I'd like to strangle him with my bare hands."

"We need to rescue our parents first. Rolf said he was going to help me."

"You're on rather familiar terms with the councillor. How did you end up together? Why did he miss his initial rendezvous with us?"

Sighing, Ilyssa stretched out her legs while Devin returned to his seat. "I saw him during a Selection Day at the mining camp." And she went on to explain her banishment to the Rocks of Weir, her duties, and Bolt's treatment of her, then the day when hope had arisen in her breast with Rolf's arrival.

"So he agreed to help you in exchange for his freedom?" Devin asked, astounded by her story. He'd known something dire must have happened to the councillor when Cam'brii hadn't made contact, but to have been captured and thrown into slavery! His respect for the man increased tenfold. Used to a life of luxury, Lord Cam'brii had adapted quickly, keeping his cover intact.

"Haakat had been evacuated by the time we reached Kantina," Ilyssa went on. "I didn't know where Mama and Papa had been taken so we had to abandon our efforts temporarily. Father is ill, Devin." She described his symptoms and her prognosis.

"We must act now, before it's too late. I'll send a message to Otis. Perhaps he can locate them." He glanced at her melancholy expression. "I'd say Lord Cam'brii kept to his end of the bargain. He would have gone to Haakat if the circumstances hadn't changed. By bringing you here, he took the right course of action."

"Did he?" she asked bitterly. "I wanted to go back to Bolt. I figured the satrap wouldn't have told Ruel yet that

I was gone. Bolt's head would be on the stake if he did. But Rolf prevented me from returning."

"I don't blame him!" Devin exclaimed. "I wouldn't have let you go either. How foolish could you be?"

"But my presence is a danger to him. Bolt's sent hunters after me. I spotted them in Saline City. They must have been following us the entire time. I figured if I drew them after me, they'd leave Rolf alone and he could continue his mission. Even now, those Souks might be on their way here. I didn't want to lead them to you, Devin. I tried to run away again. I sent them a note saying I was ready to return to Bolt, but Rolf caught me. He thinks I've betrayed him."

"You mean you were willing to sacrifice yourself for Lord Cam'brii?"

"For our parents," she corrected. "Ruel may not have discovered my absence yet. I might still save Mama and Papa from his punishment if I return to the mining camp before Bolt alerts him."

"And what would Bolt do to you?" Devin shook his head. "I agree with the councillor. You must remain here. I'll deal with our parents. I wasn't able to get near them while they were confined in Haakat, but now that they've been moved . . ."

He eyed her curiously. "I can understand your wanting to turn yourself in for our parents' sake, but why would you wish to take the heat off Cam'brii? Do you care for him that much?"

She lowered her head. "Yes." Her reply was barely audible.

"And have you told him?" He saw from her expression that she hadn't. "I see."

"No, you don't." Determination flared in her expression. "It's better this way. He has to go back to Bimordus Two and I'll be going to Circutia. I still want to be an arbiter, Devin."

"You're both working toward the same goal," he pointed out, annoyed by her obstinacy. "Diplomat or arbiter, you're both promoting peace."

"He doesn't have peace in his heart. He has guilt there." Her brother's puzzled frown prompted her to explain.

"So he blames himself for Gayla's death. Haven't you been blaming yourself for what happened to me? Relieve yourself of the burden, dear sister, and open your heart. Lord Cam'brii needs you. I've seen the way he looks at you."

"He seeks revenge, and I don't condone killing, Devin. I know those are your methods, but I don't like it. I think this conference has a much better chance of settling things peacefully."

"We'll see if the conference achieves anything, but if it doesn't, we're prepared to fight. Our numbers swell every day with escaped slaves and Souks sympathetic to our cause. The push for emancipation is growing. It's only a matter of time before events forge ahead."

She narrowed her gaze. "You were tortured, Devin. That gives you a reason to accept violence. What happened after I left you in the clinic?"

"I was thrown into a dungeon beneath the palace grounds and rescued through a secret tunnel by members of the resistance. Even in Ruel's palace, the liberation movement lives and grows. It is everywhere, Ilyssa."

His eyes lit with enthusiasm. "Now that Lord Cam'brii is here, we'll establish a regular line of communications with the Coalition Defense League. We have a supply of arms, but it's not enough. The League can provide us with the heavier weapons we require for an offensive action. We also need a route to relay escaped slaves such as women and children off planet. Cam'brii's arrival is the final incentive we need to thrust forward!"

"You have a supply of arms, you say?" Ilyssa was thinking of the arms smuggler on board the hovertrain.

"A system of delivery is in place for light weapons such as laser rifles and personal shooters, but we need the Defense League to supply us with more powerful armaments before we can launch our campaign."

"A trio of customs agents boarded the hovertrain crossing the Koodrash Mounts, and two of them showed up again in Regis. They were questioning your contact there."

"Is that so?" Devin's jaw tightened. "Tell me about it." When she'd finished, he mulled over her words. "Hopefully the fellow died without talking," he mumbled, half to himself. But Ilyssa had heard and couldn't believe he would be so callous.

"Who's smuggling weapons to you, Devin? Is it the carpet seller? We found assault rifles hidden in his crates on the train."

"Did you now?" Rising, Devin smoothly changed the subject. "You must be fatigued after such a long and fearsome journey. I'll have you assigned to your own tent." He called for one of his aides standing guard outside, effectively bringing a halt to their discussion.

Ilyssa gazed sadly at him as she rose. He was a striking figure despite his boyish crop of hair, which used to be as dark as hers but must have been bleached by the desert sun. His frame was tall and lean, his muscles well developed. His hazel eyes, hardened by suffering, proclaimed him for the warrior he'd become. Her brother had grown into a man since she'd seen him last. She felt depressed by the gulf widening between them and by the burden Devin's young shoulders had to bear.

"See to it that my sister receives what she needs," Devin ordered the large fellow who'd answered his summons. "And when you've finished showing her to her quarters, bring Lord Cam'brii here. The councillor and I need to have a long talk."

Chapter Fifteen

Wearing a clean white shirt unbuttoned halfway down his chest and a pair of snug-fitting black leather pants tucked into his boots, Rolf entered Devin's tent. The dip in the stream had been refreshing and now he was ready to get down to business.

Devin extended him the courtesy of offering refreshments. When he declined, they both sat facing each other on straight-backed chairs.

"How do you feel about my sister?" were Devin's first words.

Rolf glanced at him in surprise. "I thought we were going to discuss my mission here. What does she have to do with it?"

The rebel leader glared at him. "She has everything to do with it, Lord Cam'brii. We will not proceed in our discussion until you answer my question."

Rolf's mouth tightened. It wasn't enough that he'd had to deal with Souk slavers and customs agents and Hortha beasts wielding stun whips. Facing Ilyssa's brother was the most difficult obstacle yet.

"I admire her," he began.

"Yes?"

"She's strong-willed, brave, and resourceful. She's met tremendous odds head-on and conquered them."

"You have reservations?"

"I'm afraid she's conquered me as well," Rolf admitted.

"Ah. Would you care to elaborate?"

Rolf told the story of their encounter, from the very first time he'd seen her descending the Dromo's residence with Bolt, through their escape and her latest attempt to run back to the mining camp. "I'm afraid I did her an injustice," he said wryly. "I wouldn't listen to her explanation."

"She told me you'd accused her of betrayal, but that's not the case. She planned to return to Bolt for a very good reason, sir. Ilyssa intended to draw his attention away from you so you could continue with your mission."

"Pardon?" He couldn't have heard correctly. Surely she wouldn't sacrifice herself for him? For her parents' sake, he could understand it, but for him?

"Don't you get it?" Devin said gently. "She cares for you. You're the special man she's been waiting for her whole life. She's told you about her, uh, prohibitions, I suppose?" Devin stumbled over his wording but the embarrassing topic had to be addressed.

"Yes, I know about her fear of losing her virginity in relation to her siren song." Rolf stood and began pacing, thrusting his fingers through his hair. Blast, he didn't want to discuss this subject now.

"Frustrated, are you?"

Rolf stared at the younger man. "What difference does it make how I feel? This conversation is irrelevant to my purpose here. I represent the High Council. That should be all that concerns you."

"I'm concerned about Ilyssa. She's suffered enough. You're causing her more torment."

"*I* am? What about the torment she causes me? Every time the woman moves, I—" He stopped, aware of what he'd been about to say.

Devin threw back his head and laughed. "She feels the same way, your lordship. I've seen the signs. She's every bit as frustrated as you are."

"She's got Ruel's safeguard in place." He shot Devin a glance. "Did she tell you about that? Once your parents are free, she said it can be removed by any competent medic. Yet that won't make any difference to Ilyssa. She still won't give herself to me if it means risking the loss of her singing voice. How can you say I'm special to her when becoming an arbiter is more important?"

"Her goals are important to her. Isn't your career . . . this mission . . . important to you?"

"Yes, but—"

"Why shouldn't she feel the same way? What makes you think she should give up her dreams for you? Isn't it enough that she was willing to sacrifice her freedom to give you yours?"

A heavy silence fell between them. Then Rolf said, "If what you say is true, she'll never forgive me for mistreating her."

"She might if you're kind to her, if you respect her goals, and if you reassure her that she's more important than any personal vendetta you're pursuing."

Rolf sucked in a breath. "She told you about Gayla?"

Devin got up to pour them both some wine. "Tell me about this girl who's been dead for over ten annums." He handed Rolf a filled goblet.

Rolf lowered his head. "The Souks killed her. I must avenge her death."

"Which mission is more important to you, Councillor? Aiding the liberation movement on Souk or exacting retribution from Gayla's killer?" the youth demanded.

"Devin, you cut me to the quick." Surely this boy must be older than 17 annums. His perceptions were wise. Sinking back onto his seat, Rolf took a long draft of the wine. "Fulfilling your needs are my priority, of course. But I won't leave until all issues are resolved."

"At what cost, Lord Cam'brii? Are you willing to put your life on the line in the name of justice?"

"I am."

"Ilyssa was correct, then. Guilt consumes you. You hope to assuage it by committing an act of violence."

Rolf's fist tightened on his goblet. "My personal needs will not interfere with my assignment, Devin. Let us discuss what I came here for. What kind of communications network do your people have in place? What do you want to accomplish with a link to the Coalition? What weapons do you need? How are you recruiting members? Who are the leaders of the movement, and what's your distribution of resources among the different cartels?"

Their discussion moved fast after that, lasting for over two hauras as they established the details Rolf was to bring back to the Coalition. Rolf insisted that if any campaign of terror was begun, the slaves at the mining camp would be among the first freed. His strategy was twofold: he wanted to free his friends, including Seth if the man was still alive. And by damaging Ruel's mining operation, he'd cause the pasha to default on his contracts to the Morgots. The furry beastlike creatures were swift to take revenge, as evidenced by his brother Bdan's death.

"I'll arrange for you to meet with other leaders during the next two weeks so you can coordinate your efforts," Devin concluded.

"What about the conference in Drobrok?"

"I am assured the Souks' paid informant will be present. When the time comes, you'll join Pasha Hyrn's party. He's sympathetic to our cause. Disguised as a server, you can move among the guests and search for the mole."

"I have to learn his identity!" Leaning forward, Rolf explained in a hushed tone, "He's doing too much damage to our government. We can never be sure if our communiqués are transmitted in confidence while the informant is working against us. He's been reporting on my movements as well and must be stopped."

Rolf told Devin about the assassination attempts. "Ilyssa thinks Ruel may be behind them. She said he has orders out for me to be captured alive now. I can't conceive of a reason why Ruel would be interested in me other than the First Amendment issue. We've never encountered each other before."

"I don't suggest you confront him now."

Rolf compressed his lips. "I'll deal with Ruel later. First I need to uncover the mole." He heaved a great sigh. "I have too many things to accomplish, Devin. I don't have time for woman troubles now, but I do care about Ilyssa."

"Speak to my sister then, and tell her how you feel. Try to be more understanding of her viewpoint."

A commotion outside brought them to their feet. Mikeal barged inside the tent. "Pardon the intrusion, Devin, but we need you to come immediately."

Their discussion about Ilyssa ended as the men dashed outside.

Inside the tent assigned to her, Ilyssa finished rejuvenating herself. She'd bathed in a tub of warm water brought to her from the stream, then changed into a loose blue shirt and a pair of black trousers loaned to her by one of Devin's men. Both items were sizes too big but she'd fastened them with a sash around her waist. On her feet she wore the low boots that went with her jumpsuit.

The rebel had given her a comb along with a bar of soap, and now she stood straightening her thick waves. There wasn't any reflector available so she couldn't guess at how she looked, but she felt decent, and anything was an improvement over her caftan. She'd packed away her harem outfit, ready to move on with her life.

She wondered what her brother was saying to Rolf. Ilyssa resented the way Devin had summarily dismissed her. The two men were probably discussing important business concerning the Coalition. Hadn't she proven her worth enough to be included in talks of strategy? Was she to be relegated to the unimportant status of a woman even here in her own brother's domain . . . her younger brother, for heaven's sake?

Placing the comb on a small folding table, Ilyssa prepared to confront them both. She was intelligent and clever and could contribute something significant to their discussion. More importantly, she might have a calming influence on Rolf. After accomplishing this part of his mission, he might go rushing off to exact his revenge on Gayla's killer. She'd convince him to wait until after the Alliance conference. That way, he wouldn't foul up the proceedings if his quarry was among the pashas present.

Approaching the tent's entrance, she became aware of loud clanging noises and shouted orders. Pushing open the flap, she gasped at the sight that met her eyes.

Souk females who Ilyssa recognized as being from the carpet seller's harem were supervising the unloading of laser rifles from a number of familiar-looking crates. Their orange caftans swayed at their ankles as they directed operations. Black-clad freedom fighters were transferring the weapons from the containers into a large pit. The glow from lanterns strung up on poles cast a flickering illumination on the busy scene.

"Jarin," Ilyssa called, striding forward.

The harem leader spun around. "Ilyssa, a pleasure it is to see you again," she said in surprise. "What brings you to this oasis?"

"I could ask you the same thing! Where is your master?"

Jarin's pleasant dogface creased into a smile. "The fat lennox lies at Yanuk's palace, drunk and stuffed with sweetmeats. We carry on with our business here."

"What do you mean?"

"We bring arms to our friends so they may fight for our freedom."

Ilyssa was too astounded to reply. The carpet seller was not the arms smuggler. His harem women were the dealers in illicit armaments!

A thin, high musical instrument began to play in the background. Ilyssa turned, recognizing the blond girl dressed in shorts and a binder top. "Helena! What are you doing here?"

"You should know. You found our shipment on the train." She grinned, her eyes twinkling with mischief. "It was you who left the lightsticks in the freight car, wasn't it?"

Ilyssa gasped. "You mean you were the one who searched my compartment?"

Jarin took her arm. "Come, sister. Explain everything will we."

Ilyssa followed her to a soft bed of grass by the stream bank. She noticed Rolf's tall figure moving among the men. Devin was unloading weapons alongside him.

Pursing her lips, she sat cross-legged on the ground. Jarin, two other members of the carpet seller's harem, and Helena joined her.

"So what's this all about?" Ilyssa asked, rolling up the sleeves on her shirt. It was hot, with only the slightest of breezes tickling the hairs on her arms. The smell of dank earth wafted into her nostrils.

"It's about the position of females in this society," Jarin said, her dark eyes glittering in the meager light. Fluffs of clouds obscured Souk's two moons, and the lanterns were too far away to cast much light in their direction.

"For too long have we been the chattel of males of our r-r-race, relegated to a lower caste in society," Jarin stated. "Technology shows us the promise of other worlds, gives us hints of the freedoms that might be ours. Like the captive slaves on this planet, we are enslaved by our masters. The liberation movement is ours, sister. We seek empowerment. We will be free!"

"You started the emancipation movement? Harem females?" She couldn't believe it. She'd always thought a few of the pashas had initiated the push to free the slaves, mainly for economic reasons.

"Yes, it was Souk females such as ourselves," Jarin confirmed, nodding her veiled head. "R-R-Regarded are we as less valuable commodities by our masters, yet we are the ones who run the household, supervise the upbringing of the young, accomplish the day-to-day activities that males have no use for. We're tired of bondage! Like the slaves on Souk, we wish to be free of our shackles. If the Alliance conference fails to achieve our aims, we're prepared to fight."

"Great suns! How widespread are you?"

"R-R-Reach do we across all five continents. We have members in all the major cartels. Many males support us, pashas included. We let them think it was their idea and that's helped swell our numbers. We r-r-refuse to be trampled any longer. The time for progress is now. In freeing the slaves, we free ourselves. Our goal is equality for all."

"Yes, I understand." Ilyssa, too, yearned for the freedom to make her own choices. "But where do you get the weapons? And how are you involved?" she asked Helena.

The musician grinned. "Beatrice, Luciana, and I recruit new members as we travel across the continents doing performances. We have access to all the harems."

"Balthazar doesn't know?"

"No." Her face darkened. "I want to do something to help Rosalyn or at least to prevent other attacks like the one we experienced on the train. I've spoken to Devin, and he said plans have already been made to raid the savages' camp . . . after his force hits a few other hot spots."

"What force?" There couldn't be more than 20 or so men here.

"Who do you think we're supplying weapons for?" Jarin broke in, her expression somber. "A large group of escaped slaves is being trained to fight. Most of them are hiding out in the Thicket of Bayne. Friends and family have they who are still enslaved. If the conference fails, the leaders will give orders to attack. The targets are already selected."

Ilyssa gasped. Was Rolf aware of this? Scenes of bloody civil war came to mind. She had to prevent a carnage! But what could she do, one woman, against an entire rebellion? Lord Cam'brii had the authority to give orders. She must sway him to her viewpoint. Negotiation could work toward achieving peace!

She rose, brushing off her trousers. She'd seek him out at once.

Rolf was straining to lift a crate of rifles, minus the carpets, into a huge vibril-lined pit where they'd be impervious to sensor scans. He'd been amazed at the array of weaponry available, but it was nothing compared to what the Coalition could supply. Seeing the arms, he wondered for the first time about his course of action.

Ilyssa was correct in the sense that he should wait and see how the Alliance conference developed. His assignment wasn't to start a war, and yet by offering heavy weapons to the liberators, wasn't that in effect what he was doing? If the Souks themselves, and not just these displaced slaves, could achieve the same aims through peaceful means, wasn't it worth it to find out?

Doubts assailed him. The claims of former Councillor Daimon came to mind, that the Coalition was wrong to intervene in domestic planetary affairs. Could Daimon have been right? Was Rolf's government's interference in this case unwarranted? Were they promoting a war just to eradicate a practice they didn't condone?

Perhaps he'd been so blinded by his own need for revenge against the Souks that he subconsciously supported an armed conflict. And yet it was innocent civilians like Gayla who were attacked by Souk pirates, killed, or enslaved. It wasn't as though the Souks were warring among themselves. They'd brought their aggression to other peoples, affecting Coalition citizens everywhere. Their reign of terror had to be stopped.

His strength of purpose renewed, Rolf fitted the crate into its narrow space and straightened up, wiping the sweat from his brow. He'd removed his shirt, but it was still stifling hot. All around him, men were scurrying to unload the laser rifles from the skiffs they'd arrived on. Shouted instructions and low male grunts rent the night air.

And then there was another sound, a high warbling noise.

"Invaders!" Devin yelled as he placed a drum of shooters in the pit.

Rolf watched as the men raced to get their arms; Devin ran to his tent; the harem women headed toward the stream bank.

The warbling cry was cut short. Rolf spotted the force of armored hoverscouts bearing Souks in olive uniforms and helmets fly in over opposite rises, flanking the encampment.

"Ilyssa!" Rolf called, spotting her flaming hair down by the stream. He'd seen her walking off with the other females but had wanted to finish his work before seeking her out. Now he started to run in her direction, but was cut off as a volley of laser fire erupted around him.

Surrounding the rebels, the Souks ordered them to throw down their weapons. Anyone who resisted was shot. Rolf froze in place as two Souks jumped out of their hoverscouts and pointed blaster carbines at him. Slowly he raised his hands.

Ilyssa and the other females watched helplessly as the camp was surrounded.

"The Koritah!" Jarin gasped, spotting the special enforcers zooming in on the trail of the troops.

Helena gave a shriek, and Ilyssa glanced down at her trousers. Both of them were in violation of the codes. By the corona, she should have remembered this was Yanuk's territory.

"Come!" Ilyssa called, grasping Helena's hand and starting to run toward the closest tent.

"Halt!" A soldier in an olive uniform with a helmet stepped in front of them, weapon pointed. His eyes regarded them coldly from under his visor.

Over another rise came a speeder bearing a large Souk in long, colorful robes and an elaborate headdress. He hovered a moment, viewing the proceedings; then he veered in their direction. Landing the craft, he stepped out and lumbered toward them. The Koritah enforcers caught up to him and followed at his heels.

Ilyssa glanced around, anxious to find Rolf. With his height, it was easy to spot him. He stood with his arms raised, his jaw thrust defiantly in the air. Two Souks had rifles aimed at his bare chest. Relieved that he was alive, she searched for her brother. Those rebels who hadn't been killed had been disarmed and were standing with their hands on their heads. Devin wasn't among them. Feeling a flash of fear, she wondered if he was among the bodies scattered on the ground.

The colorfully garbed Souk stopped in front of them. An obese male, he had a high, ridged forehead with short, pointed ears and fat cheeks. His eyes were close together, giving him a scowling appearance.

"I am Yanuk, pasha of this territory," he said, his voice a harsh growl. "In violation of the Koritah are you. Enforcers!" The two Souks who'd been following him rushed forward. Dressed in silver armored tunics, they had long leather whips encrusted with sharp metal prongs curved around their belts.

Yanuk turned to Helena, who was visibly quaking, her face white with terror. "You expose yourself, woman. Wish you to be indecent? Help you will I!" And with a snarl, he stepped forward and ripped off her outer clothes. Helena shrieked and tried to cover herself, but at Yanuk's signal, two of his troops grasped her by the arms.

"Punish her," Yanuk commanded his enforcers. "Thirty lashes. Human filth." He spat at her.

"No!" Ilyssa cried as the soldiers dragged Helena away, screaming. An enforcer followed, grinning maliciously as he withdrew his whip.

"You dare to speak?" Yanuk addressed Ilyssa, his dark eyes studying her face.

"She's my friend." Feeling far from brave, Ilyssa lifted her chin defiantly.

"Perhaps, then, you wish to add her punishment to yours. Enforcer! Give this one fifty lashes."

Ilyssa gasped. That would kill her! Yanuk stepped forward, reaching out his hand, ready to rip off her shirt.

"Give me the privilege," a familiar voice drawled in her ear. Ilyssa's mouth dropped open as Gant sidled into view. "I wish to claim this woman as part of my reward."

"Our reward," Scard corrected, directly behind him. The customs officers were both garbed in slate-gray bodysuits, shooters at their hips.

"Grrr," Yanuk growled, considering. "Done well have you to unearth these traitors. Along with my team led by Quail, you traced the shipments of arms to this location. Owe you both do I and my compatriot Ruel." He paused. "The woman is yours, but she must be punished for violating the Koritah."

Gant twisted his mouth in an evil grin. "Don't worry, we'll punish her so much better than your enforcers. She'll never venture out in public again after we're through with her."

He turned to Ilyssa, stepping so close she could smell his sweat. His black eyes swept her face, and his grin widened. Before she could utter a cry, his hand darted out and untied her sash. Without the support, the oversize pants she wore slid to her ankles.

"Take them off," Gant commanded, his eyes glittering. Beside him, Scard leered at her.

From past experience, Ilyssa knew that defiance wouldn't serve her under these circumstances. She stepped out of the trousers, leaving her in her short boots and the man's shirt that covered her to midthigh. Feeling exposed, she lowered her eyes.

"I've wanted to do this ever since I saw you on the train," Gant crooned, moving closer. He reached out to undo the fastening on her shirt.

Ilyssa bit her lip, refusing to meet his taunting gaze. Receiving a beating was one thing, but what if Gant and Scard raped her? From the way his hand kept brushing her breast, it appeared there was a good likelihood of that happening. What of her safeguard?

Sounds of a struggle came from yonder and an angry voice cried out, "Leave her alone!"

Gant whirled. When he saw who'd spoken, an angry frown creased his face. "You!" he said, then to a couple of soldiers, "Bring him here. He's caused me enough trouble."

Ilyssa's face paled as Rolf was escorted by two uniformed Souks. She'd hoped he would keep quiet, but now he'd placed himself unnecessarily at risk because of her.

"Do what you want with me, but don't harm him," she pleaded to Gant.

Rolf stared at her. "Ilyssa, how can you say that? You know the danger of—"

"Yes, I do."

"Use your siren song!"

"It doesn't work out in the open. The notes would be diluted."

"Silence!" Gant yelled. He'd finished undoing her shirt and it hung open, exposing her binder beneath. His eyes lit with a feral gleam as he regarded her breasts.

He was just slipping the shirtsleeves off her shoulders when another voice rang out in the night.

"Get your hands off her!" a gruff voice barked, as a large, impressively uniformed Souk descended upon them on a flyboard. Bolt came to a landing directly in front of her and Gant and she recognized Kraus and Lork close behind on their own vehicles.

"Satrap Bolt!" Ilyssa cried, unsure of whether she wanted to cry with relief or cringe at the sight of him. Hastily she refastened her shirt. Bolt could be her salvation, and Rolf's.

"Who are you?" Yanuk queried. He'd been directing his troops nearby but had stomped over to view the newcomer.

"Satrap Bolt in Pasha Ruel's service, Your Eminence. This female and her sumi are my responsibility."

"Says who?" Gant snarled.

"I run the mining camp at the Rocks of Weir. This woman is our Dromo. That man—" he pointed to Rolf "—stole her away from us."

"Arf," Yanuk commented, peering at Rolf with interest. "Understand do you that I have jurisdiction here."

"I do, Pasha, but I serve directly under Ruel. Ilyssa is his special property. He would be most displeased if she were harmed."

"I thought the man was one of the rebels."

"He's an escaped sumi." Ilyssa became frightened as Bolt bared his teeth in a nasty grin and his eyes roamed over Rolf's virile form. "Have special punishments for r-r-runaways do we."

"Krach, us too. In the desert, we stake them out on the ground on their backs. Their eyelids are cut off and when the glaring sun rises, they are blinded by the brightness. Then when they are sightless, the sand slugs come out to devour them alive." Yanuk smiled, exposing a row of jagged teeth. "We don't have many escaped sumis in our territory."

"You may keep him then, Pasha. Like your sentence do I. Come with me, Ilyssa. We return to the mining camp where you and I are overdue for a long discussion." He looked maliciously pleased by the prospect.

"No, Bolt! You can't just leave Rolf here!"

Bolt stared at her, his expression fierce. "What did you call him?"

"Perhaps your leader would like to determine the man's disposition," Yanuk said. "He's been my houseguest these days past. Here he comes now."

Another hoverscout sped into view.

"Houseguest?" Ilyssa queried. What leader was Yanuk talking about?

The craft landed in a cloud of dust, and a tall, familiar figure emerged.

Ilyssa's mouth dropped open in shock.

"Ruel!" she cried, as she felt the blood drain from her face.

Chapter Sixteen

"What is the meaning of this?" Ruel stepped forward, his large bulk encased in a purple caftan embellished with diamella gemstones. In the glare from the spotlights placed around the desert encampment by Yanuk's troops, his garment sparkled richly. Ilyssa cringed at the sight of his familiar features: the bold thrust of his underjaw, his flaring nostrils, his broad forehead, and his mean, slanted eyes.

Ruel's dark gaze swept over her. "Ilyssa, what are you doing here? And Bolt, you too? Explain!"

"These are your people?" Yanuk demanded.

"Satrap Bolt commands my garrison at the Rocks of Weir. This woman is the Dromo for the slaves. Who is he?" Ruel pointed at Rolf, who stood rigid through Ruel's scrutiny.

"Satrap Bolt claims the man is an escaped sumi who stole away with your Dromo," Yanuk said.

"What?" Ruel thundered.

Ilyssa's knees quaked. "I . . . I can explain, master."

But even as her thoughts raced, she failed to come up with a plausible excuse. Desperate, she glanced at Bolt.

"Pardon, master, for not sharing our scheme with you sooner," Bolt said smoothly. "This man's name is Sean Breslow. When his ship crashed by the Rocks of Weir, he claimed to be a trader from Arcturus. Given the strategic location near your piragen ore deposits, Ilyssa and I didn't believe him. Suspecting the sumi was a spy, we decided she would offer to help him escape. Lead her to his friends would he and then we could arrest them. We succeeded, master. He led us to the r-r-resistance."

"Who is he?" Ruel demanded. "The rebel leader? And what was he doing at the mining camp, scouting it for sabotage?"

"Yes!" Ilyssa replied, her heard pounding wildly in her chest. It was better for the pasha to believe this than for him to know Rolf's true identity. Quickly, she gave a brief rundown of their journey, being sure to include how Rolf had saved her from the Souk savages.

"That is of no importance. A r-r-role model is he for other sumis planning to escape, and a traitor for plotting against us." Turning to his private escort of armed Hazars, he raised his hand. "Execute him."

"No!" Ilyssa cried.

Ruel reacted to the vehemence of her protest. "The man didn't touch you, did he? Because if he did, Ilyssa, you'll—"

"No! He did nothing! But you . . . you can't have him killed."

Ruel's eyes darkened as he looked into her eyes. "This sumi's life should mean nothing to you. Do you contradict Satrap Bolt's story?"

"No," Ilyssa whispered, feeling sick to her stomach.

"Good. Then it won't bother you when he dies."

At his signal, the Hazars lined up in front of Rolf, their weapons aimed.

Ilyssa's eyes widened and she looked at Rolf. His cool blue eyes stared straight ahead. Why didn't he say something? Why didn't he reveal his identity? Ruel wanted Lord Cam'brii alive. He could save himself from being shot!

The pasha stood at attention, facing his Hazars. In the background, Yanuk looked on with a bemused expression. Gant and Scard had wandered off and Bolt was standing by, licking his lips in anticipation of the sumi's demise. Ilyssa glanced around, desperately hoping to spot an ally. But no one was available to help Rolf, not even her brother. She was the only one who could save him now.

Ruel raised his hand. "Ready, aim, f—"

"Stop!" Ilyssa yelled. "He's Lord Rolf Cam'brii!"

Ruel whirled on her, his face livid. "What say you?"

"I . . . I did scheme with Bolt. We realized Sean Breslow was someone important and we determined to learn his identity. I . . . made up a story to get him to escape with me; then I accompanied him here to meet his friends."

She glanced at Kraus and Lork who were hovering behind Bolt. "You can ask those hunters to verify that I gave them a note saying I was ready to return to Bolt. I had enough information." She couldn't look at Rolf, couldn't bear to see the expression of horror on his face.

"Ilyssa, no!" Rolf shouted.

"So," Ruel said, walking in front of him, "is it true? Are you Lord Rolf Cam'brii?"

"Yes, I am Lord Cam'brii, member of the Coalition High Council, second son to the imperator of Nadira. Ilyssa speaks the truth. She tricked me into taking her along on this mission." He turned his hard gaze on her. "I never thought she would betray me."

Ilyssa shuddered at his words. Her heart cried out for him to understand that she was saving him, not condemning him, but all she saw in his eyes was hatred. She bit her lip to squelch a cry of despair.

Ruel didn't say a word. The pasha just stared at Rolf, his expression inscrutable. Suddenly he threw back his head and roared with laughter. "By the grace of Krofen, my enemy has fallen into my hands! Bless this day, shall I! Pasha Yanuk, I'll take Lord Cam'brii with me to Haakat, and Ilyssa as well. The city has been cleared of r-r-radiation and my people r-r-return." He signaled for his Hazars to surround the councillor. "Satrap Bolt, was that your scramjet I saw on the flatbed?"

"Krach, master. Do you wish use of it?"

"I do. Pasha Yanuk can provide transportation for you to go back to the mining camp. A commendation have you earned, and a generous bonus. Although I do not approve of your methods, you and Ilyssa did well."

"My thanks, master Ruel."

Bolt snapped his commander a brisk salute, flashing a glance of triumph at Ilyssa. She looked away, her soul seared with agony, as Ruel gestured for her to move to his side. She obeyed, her steps dragging. She felt empty, lifeless without Rolf's regard. It didn't matter what Ruel did to her now.

Ilyssa had flown aboard a scramjet before, so she was familiar with the supersonic combusting scramjet that she and Rolf were herded into along with Ruel and his troops. The spacecraft took off from the flatbed and then leveled off above the atmosphere at a speed greater than the speed of sound. Using this method of hypersonic transport, it would take them only a half-haura to travel to Haakat in the southern hemisphere.

Rolf was sequestered in the front of the scramjet surrounded by armed guards. Ilyssa sat in the rear section with Ruel. She stared at Rolf's broad back, unable to take her eyes from him. Even now, she yearned for his touch, for his glance of warm appreciation. Sorrow welled up in her throat and threatened to choke her. She glanced out the casement, absently noting the orange glow against the night sky that hadn't been present before. Yanuk's troops must have set fire to the rebel tents. What had happened to Devin? Was he among the dead? She hadn't been afforded the opportunity to search for him. Losing her brother again was just another plunge into the darkness of despair.

As he buckled on his safety restraint, Rolf felt Ilyssa's eyes on his back and wondered what she was thinking. Was she happy to be going back to Haakat and her privileged position? Would she celebrate the occasion of his capture with Ruel? Had she even been banished to the Rocks of Weir in the first place?

He doubted everything she'd told him, unsure of where the truth ended and her lies began. And what of Devin, her brother? Had she betrayed him, too?

Numerous questions plagued him, but he realized he was the one who'd be interrogated. His store of knowledge about Coalition policies was voluminous. He might have to use his memory molecule. The fast-acting drug would protect him against a Morgot mind probe, but he only had one try at it. If Ruel's interrogation was prolonged, he'd have to use the other item Glotaj had reluctantly supplied.

Swallowing apprehensively, Rolf endured the trip in grim silence. They made a smooth landing at Haakat, after which he was marched from the spaceport gateway into a closed vehicle for transport to Ruel's palace. Ilyssa went in a separate vehicle with Ruel. He was glad she wasn't with him. It would have made his situation even more intolerable to be in close quarters with the woman who'd betrayed him. At least he was being accorded the respect his position engendered. There was no talk of slave collars or restraints, although that might change. Pushing aside his fears about what Ruel had in store for him, he concentrated on learning all he could about his surroundings.

* * *

Ilyssa was oblivious to her surroundings as she sat beside Ruel in the rear of a landspeeder. As one of his soldiers drove, Ruel held himself stiffly erect at her side. Through his broad nose, he made snorting noises as he breathed. The edges of his caftan swayed against her exposed calves. Ilyssa was repulsed and cringed at the thought of what he would do to her.

"Are my parents in the palace?" she asked, daring to assert herself.

Ruel cast her a dark look. "We will talk later." He glanced at her attire, his features souring with disapproval, but he said nothing.

Her throat constricted with fear. His stiff silence did not bode well for her.

When both vehicles came to a stop, Rolf was ordered out and immediately surrounded by a bevy of soldiers, their weapons drawn. Past midnight, the air was cool and he shivered as a breeze swept over his exposed skin. Ignoring his discomfort, he displayed an attitude of nonchalance while carefully surveying the wide courtyard surrounded by high concrete walls which provided a protective perimeter. The top of the walls, studded with energy posts, indicated a sensor array. It was an effective barrier, Rolf thought, his heart sinking. In addition, uniformed troops patrolled the palace grounds. The Souks appeared sharp and alert, and any notions of a quick escape evaporated.

"Put him below," Ruel ordered, striding over. The jewels on his purple caftan sparkled as he moved. "After you are settled in, visit you will I. R-R-Right now, I wish time alone with Ilyssa." He crooked a fat finger in her direction.

She cast Rolf a pleading glance but he turned away, unwilling to acknowledge her. She was his enemy even more so than Ruel. He wanted nothing more to do with her.

A soldier shoved him on the shoulder. "Move, Councillor."

He was escorted to an arched steel door in an interior wall. His guard opened it with a press of his hand against a touchpad. A long, dingy flight of steps led downward.

Rolf balked at being confined below ground. When he didn't budge, he heard a harsh whisper in his ear.

"A long way down is this. You might not survive a fall."

He nodded grimly, understanding the message. And so he began his descent into Zor.

Ilyssa accompanied Ruel directly to his suite of rooms in the residential wing of the palace.

"It's late, Master Ruel. Aren't you going to allow me to rest in my own chamber?" Her head ached, and she felt sick with fatigue and fear.

Ruel's response was a barked order for her to enter his quarters. He shut the door behind them, excluding the guards.

"Are my parents in residence?" she asked again.

"No, little bird, I have given them quarters elsewhere. They are no longer in Haakat. If you do as I say, I will allow you to speak to them on the comm unit later. Disrobe," he commanded, his slanted eyes cold.

Ilyssa trembled. She'd feared he'd do this once they were alone, and she made no move to obey him.

"Do it!" Ruel's blue-skinned dogface creased in anger.

"Please, Ruel." She hated herself when she begged. "I assure you—"

"*Now!*" he screamed.

Lowering her head, she unfastened the shirt and dropped it to the ground. She stood in front of him, quaking with fear.

"And the rest," he intoned.

Ilyssa bit her lower lip to keep from crying as she removed her binder and panties. The cool air rushed over her bared skin, chilling her. Naked except for her short boots, she stood at attention while Ruel slowly encircled her, his narrowed eyes scrutinizing every inch of her flesh. Her fists clenched by her side as she tried to hide her shame.

"Stand next to the bed," he ordered.

"W-What?"

"You heard me!"

He strode to the bedside table and removed his mediscan, running it quickly over her body. Satisfied that the safeguard was still intact, he put it away and studied her.

"With Lord Cam'brii a long time alone were you, Ilyssa. Have you developed feelings for the man?"

"No . . . no, of course not! I was just carrying out my duty with Bolt."

"Grrr, so you said, yet you cried out for me to spare the councillor's life."

"I thought you wanted Lord Cam'brii alive. You hadn't been aware of his identity when you ordered him killed."

"Nor did you r-r-reveal it r-r-right away." He gazed at her, but she tried to keep her face expressionless. "I like it not that you may harbor sentiment for the man even though you fulfilled your duty. You are mine, Ilyssa. You belong to me, body and spirit. I will not have it otherwise. If I learn that he touched you, your parents will die and another visit to the clinic will you make."

By the Almighty! Her knees trembled. "You see I am unmarked."

Grinning, he stalked to a fabricator and conjured a silken caftan in turquoise with gleaming silver threads. Holding it out, he ordered her to put it on.

She glanced at him, surprised. But when she went to

reach for her underwear, he stopped her.

"No, you will wear nothing beneath."

An uneasy sensation crept over her. Ilyssa didn't trust him, but she had no other option. She donned the luxurious caftan, wondering at his intent. The diaphanous material clung to her body, making her acutely aware of her nakedness underneath.

"You will accompany me to visit Lord Cam'brii. But first, do you wish to communicate with your parents?"

"You know I do. Where are they?"

"Their location remains confidential. Warn you I must." His eyes took on a mischievous slant. "Moireen tried to send word to you of where she'd been moved. Aran, your father, was kind enough to notify me of her transgression. She had to be punished."

"No!" Ilyssa shuddered as horrifying images came to mind of what he might have done to her mother.

"Call her will I on the comm link now."

Ilyssa held her breath in fear. She hoped to get some clue as to her parents' whereabouts, but when the link was established, all she saw was a dimly lit interior space without any furnishings. A shadowy figure cringed in a corner.

"Mama?" Ilyssa called in a tremulous voice.

"Ilyssa, darling," her mother rasped.

"I can't see you well. Please come into the light."

Moireen straightened but stayed in the shadows, her form outlined against the wall. "I'd rather stay here."

"Why? I want to see your face."

"No, you don't. I was disobedient, daughter. I had to be . . . disciplined."

Ilyssa gasped, turning to Ruel. "What did you do to her?"

"She was punished for her defiance, as you will be if you do not follow my precise orders when we visit Lord Cam'brii."

"Where's Papa?" By the corona, had he already succumbed to senilis disease?

"Your father is ill; his mind wanders. He had to be confined for his own safety. Now listen carefully, little bird. If you fail to do as I wish, your mother will suffer the consequences. Understand?"

Proudly, Moireen lifted her head. "Ilyssa, my darling, do what you must. My life no longer matters."

"Mama!" Ilyssa's heart contracted.

Ruel terminated the comm link. "Enough! We go now to the detention block. You will do precisely as I say."

What evil was he plotting now? Ilyssa wondered. Wetting her lips apprehensively, she followed him out of his suite and down the long mazelike corridors of the palace complex. An elite guard of Hazars flanked them on either side. As she walked silently behind Ruel, her head bowed, she clung to the image of her mother that remained in her mind. What had Ruel done to Mama that she couldn't show her face? Was she blackened with bruises? Or had he done something more hideous to her, such as maiming her face?

Terror washed over her. What did Ruel expect of her this time that he'd threatened to cause further harm to Moireen if Ilyssa disobeyed him?

She was dizzy with fear by the time they exited into the main courtyard and approached an arched steel door in a separate wall. Ruel opened it by placing his hand on a touchpad.

"Lord Cam'brii is down there?" Ilyssa said, horrified. A damp, dank smell met her nostrils. Ruel motioned for her to descend the narrow set of stairs.

Lifting her skirt, she stepped downward, glad she still wore her short boots. Rolf must be chilled, she thought, remembering he was shirtless. Moisture sprang into her eyes as she pictured him imprisoned below. At least he was alive, and that was all that counted for the moment.

Her heart was thudding by the time they reached the bottom. Torches were ensconced on the stone walls, providing a smoky, flickering illumination. The air was bitingly cold. A circular space was directly in front of them, with corridors like spokes on a wheel going off in different directions.

A giant Souk wearing an armored silver tunic sauntered toward them. Horthas stood guard at each of the branches. The Souk saluted; then after a brief verbal exchange with Ruel, who addressed the Souk as the warden, he led them down one of the corridors. Rows of heavy steel doors met her gaze. Faint screams sounded from somewhere distant, chilling her blood.

The warden entered a different area, a small vestibule before the cell door. "It's our special guest chamber," the Souk sneered. On the wall was a keypad. "The councillor is inside."

"Leave us, all of you," Ruel barked.

The guards and warden hastily withdrew as Ruel turned his ugly dogface toward Ilyssa. "You will do exactly as I say when we are inside the cell. You will not speak to the councillor or look at him. Keep your eyes focused on me at all times. If you hesitate to do what I command, punishment will be swift. Not only will your mother suffer, but I shall have the councillor r-r-removed to the clinic. You won't r-r-recognize him when I am finished with him."

"No!" Ilyssa gasped in horror.

Ruel touched the keypad.

"Understand, do you, little bird? You will follow my orders exactly without question?"

"Yes, master." Ilyssa bowed her head.

"Good."

Ruel took her by the elbow and guided her inside, then shut the door behind them. The only light in the cell shone from a glowstone mounted on a wall.

Ilyssa's eyes swept the chamber. There he was! Manacled to the far wall! She took a step forward but remembered Ruel's demands. Slowly, she turned to face the pasha, aware by his sound of surprise that Rolf had seen them.

"Greetings, Councillor. Wish I to show you where Ilyssa's loyalties lie in case you harbor any doubts about her motives. She is totally and unconditionally mine. A demonstration of her devotion will I give you. Undress," he ordered her.

Understanding flooded her. By the heavens, he intended to crush whatever remaining feelings Rolf might have for her. Her heart filled with horror, but she'd heard the note of warning in Ruel's voice and feared the consequences if she hesitated.

Staring numbly at the floor, she shimmied out of the caftan.

"Come closer. Look at me."

Her cheeks hot with shame, she stepped directly in front of Ruel, lifting her face to him as she'd been ordered. She inhaled deeply when he put his thick hands on her breasts. "You said you'd never touch me!" she whispered in shock.

"Circumstances have changed. Pretend as though you are enjoying this." His pudgy fingers kneaded her flesh, rounded the outlines of her breasts, and pinched her nipples. She shuddered uncontrollably with revulsion.

Yanking on his restraints, Rolf cried out as Ilyssa saw the energy manacles cut into his wrists, holding him in place. Expletives flew from his lips. Ruel threw him a sly glance and then let his hands rove across her flat belly, over her triangle of hair.

"See, my lord? She is mine to do with as I please. The woman has always been my gima. Is that not so, Ilyssa?" He stroked her and she cringed. In her ear, he hissed, "Fondle me."

"No!"

"Wish you to see the councillor mangled like your mother? You did not see her face. Blinded is she."

Ilyssa gave a strangled cry.

"Obey!" Ruel commanded.

She reached out with a quaking hand, touching him where a bulge tented his caftan.

"Now rub your body against me."

She did as she was told, sickened with loathing.

Ruel bared his teeth in a malicious grin. "Let us go to my bedchamber to finish this," he said loudly. "You do enjoy pleasing me, do you not?"

"Your every wish is my command, master." Ilyssa stood before him, her head bowed, aware of how the scene must look to Rolf.

"You lying bitch!" Rolf yelled at her. "Go open your legs for your fat Souk. He'll never give you what I could have!"

Ilyssa's blood turned to ice as Ruel's face became purplish with rage. "What means he? What could he have given you? You said he didn't touch you!"

Dizziness rushed over her and she felt like she was going to faint. "No, Ruel! He . . . he tried, but I wouldn't let him." Her legs gave way. She fell to her knees, terrified he'd send her to the clinic, fearful of what he'd do to her mother or to Rolf.

"I am yours, master," she cried, groveling at his feet.

"Get up and cover yourself," the pasha ordered. "You can pleasure me in my bedchamber." He strolled to where Rolf hung by his wrists against the wall.

"Comfortable, are you, Councillor?"

"Go to Zor." Rolf spat in his face.

Slowly, Ruel wiped the spittle away. "You may wish you had gone there before I'm through with you."

"Are you going to torture me like your brother Bdan did to Captain Reylock?" Rolf sneered. He'd read Teir's report when the captain had finally returned to Bimordus Two. Cerrus Bdan had been a barbarian.

"My methods are not so crude. Attend to you later, will I, after I finish with Ilyssa." Seeing that she was dressed, he ordered the door to be opened.

Rolf wanted to ask him about the assassination attempts, but he figured he'd have his chance later, after the pasha had his way with Ilyssa. She must have been weak with desire because Ruel practically had to haul her out. Not once had she glanced back in his direction.

Fired with determination, he vowed somehow he'd get out of this. And then he'd make her pay.

As soon as they were back in Ruel's suite, the pasha turned to Ilyssa. "So, it is true. You have an affection for the man."

Ilyssa gasped. "What makes you say that? I did everything you told me."

"You've been with me a long time, little bird. Your feelings are as transparent to me as that teardrop glistening on your cheek. Are you in love with him?" he crooned. "You can confide in me. I won't punish you as long as he didn't touch you."

Ilyssa had fallen for his kindly technique before, but now she was wiser. "No, I'm not in love with him!" she exclaimed, nervously fingering her skirt. Why had he brought her back here? Wasn't he going to let her retreat to her own chamber?

"Your eyes tell me otherwise. Any feelings he might have had for you are dead. I wish you to feel the same for him. All your thoughts, all your sentiments, must be for me."

"They are, Ruel!" She fell to her knees. "You are my master. I obey none other."

"That is not enough!" he roared. "You must be completely mine!"

Pacing, he appeared an immense, forbidding figure as his purple caftan swished back and forth. Every now and then, he shot her a sharp glance as though trying to decide what to do with her. Ilyssa remained on the floor, her hands clasped in her lap. She was afraid to move.

"Go to your chamber," he commanded, his eyes glittering. "I shall attend to our visitor. Looking forward to this have I been for a long time." Rubbing his hands together, he chuckled nastily, evilly.

"Please don't hurt him!" Ilyssa cried, unable to stop herself. She realized too late that her plea confirmed Ruel's suspicions about her feelings for Rolf. He ordered her confined to her quarters, and she was escorted by a troupe of Hazars accompanied by a female caretaker.

The Souk female assumed a position outside Ilyssa's chamber door, and finally having some privacy, she rushed into the sanitary to wash and scrub away the filth she felt from Ruel's touch. After she was dry and dressed in a nightshirt, she sank onto her lounger and stared at the ceiling. Despite her fatigue, she couldn't sleep. Ruel was going to torture Rolf and she had no doubt she was the reason. The pasha intended to crush any affection she had for Rolf by punishing him and making her feel guilty. It wasn't enough that Rolf hated her. The powerful Souk wanted to terminate Ilyssa's feelings for him as well. Ruel desired her complete devotion, body and soul. But no matter what he did to her, she'd always love Rolf.

Startled, Ilyssa blinked. Love him? Was Ruel's perception correct? By the stars, he'd sensed what she hadn't even realized. All her thoughts, her emotions were directed toward Rolf. She couldn't think of anything or anyone else. She did love him! And because of her love, he was going to be tortured!

She engaged in a bout of tears but then pushed them away. Being weak wouldn't help. She had to think of something useful to get them both out of there.

The harem! she thought excitedly. Some of the ladies might be involved in the liberation movement. If she could get into that section of the palace, she'd ask them for help.

Standing and pacing, she began running through a possible list of reasons to make a visit to the harem a necessity. But her plotting came to an abrupt halt when a chime sounded. It was Ruel's secret summons.

Surprised, she grabbed a shawl before hastening to the north wall to the concealed latch. It clicked open, revealing the hidden passage which led to the Shell Grotto. She'd thought Ruel was with Lord Cam'brii. On whom did he need to use her siren song at three o'clock in the morning?

Puzzled, she hurried down the tunnel path, clutching the shawl about her shoulders.

Rolf was reviewing his options and trying to ignore the throbbing pain in his shoulders when the heavy steel door swung open and Pasha Ruel stomped into the dungeon.

"Release his r-r-restraints," Ruel barked at the guards.

Rolf's knees sagged as the energy manacles were deactivated. He leaned against the cold stone wall, rubbing his wrists while the Souk guards hauled in a couple of chairs, a small folding table, and a carafe of wine with two ceramic goblets.

The guards left, leaving him alone with Ruel.

"Have a seat, Councillor. Would you care for a cup of wine?"

Parched, Rolf sank into a chair and nodded. Despite the coolness of the dungeon, a thin sheen of sweat covered his skin. He hadn't been looking forward to this session. He wondered what questions Ruel would ask and what the pasha would do if he didn't answer them satisfactorily.

"Several attempts had been made on my life on Bimordus Two, Ruel. Would you know anything about them?" He decided to try to get his own answers first.

Ruel handed him a goblet, baring his jagged teeth in a grin. "Aye, r-r-responsible am I. Long have I sought you, Lord Cam'brii."

"Would you mind telling me why?" He shook a strand of grimy hair out of his face and gulped down the wine. The tart liquid hit his empty stomach, causing it to contract painfully.

A distant look came over Ruel's ugly dogface. "There was the First Amendment, of course. I tried to stop you from interfering in Souk affairs. Before that, there was another incident that has made me seek r-r-revenge all these annums."

Rolf stared at him, puzzled. "What incident? We'd never met before this."

Ruel leveled him a piercing glare. "You encountered my son, Jared. He was commanding the Souk vessels that intercepted you when you were on your way to the Hut system."

Rolf stood up so abruptly he knocked his chair over. "What?" That was the attack that had killed Gayla.

"An unexpected r-r-resistance did you put up. Artemus did not think you would fight so strongly when he notified us of your plans."

"Artemus?" He looked at Ruel blankly. "Artemus was my friend and neighbor on Nadira. He encouraged me to elope with Gayla and helped me get a ship!"

Ruel gave a nasty laugh. "A fool were you if you believed he had your best interests at heart. He tipped us off about your trip. We saw it as an easy opportunity to acquire two new slaves and a ship."

"But why? Why would Artemus betray me?"

Ruel shrugged. "Who knows? He got paid well for the information. As second son to the imperator, you were an important person even then. We could have obtained a hefty ransom for you. The girl would have gone to my brother,

Bdan." He frowned at Rolf. "You killed him. Your tricks led to his execution at the hands of the Morgots."

"I had nothing to do with Bdan. He'd been after Sarina and Teir, and they escaped from Souk. It wasn't their fault or mine that Bdan reneged on his contract to the Morgot leader, K'darr." He still couldn't get over the role Artemus had played, setting him up for the attack that had claimed Gayla's life. "Why have you continued to pursue me?"

"Your vessel was surrounded by Jared's ships and was severely damaged. My son thought the battle was over. And then you fired one more time. The blast tore through his ship's hull, penetrating the bridge. He was able to get off one more round before he died."

"Gayla fired that last shot," Rolf whispered. "She used the laser cannon, then the enemy ship fired back. It hit the turret where she was stationed. She died as a result."

They stared at each other, each lost in their own private misery and thirst for revenge.

Rolf realized he'd accomplished two of his mission's goals. He'd successfully contacted the resistance, obtaining the necessary information concerning their cause to bring back to the Coalition. He'd learned who was behind the assassination attempts. But he'd never avenge Gayla's death. Her murderer was already dead.

For so long, his quest for vengeance had been the driving force that kept him going. The gory image of Gayla's final moments had haunted him through constant mental replays and nightmarish dreams. All his goals had been directed toward stopping the Souks from spewing their terror at others and satisfying his own lust for revenge.

And then Ilyssa had invaded his mind. Driving away those fearsome memories, she'd taken over his different levels of consciousness. Only now did he realize how pervasive her influence had become. His horrendous nightmares had ended and he'd even begun to hope for a golden future at a point in time when his and Ilyssa's problems were solved. But then she'd betrayed him, and his aspirations had blown away like the dust in the Nurash Desert. Now even his need for revenge had been absolved. Without it, he felt bereft, a man without a purpose.

As a curious sense of apathy overtook him, he gazed at Ruel. Lines of debauchery creased the Souk leader's ugly dogface.

"R-R-Responsible are you not for killing my son," Ruel said finally. "All these annums, I thought it was you, but the girl fingered the trigger." He laughed loudly, raucously. "Vengeance do I seek in vain! She is already dead."

"Same here, Ruel. Ever since we were attacked, I've vowed to bring Gayla's killer to justice. If what you say is true, Jared is already dead, too." He thought a moment. "But Artemus is still very much alive," he added quietly.

A renewed sense of purpose filled him. His muscles tensed, fired with strength. His childhood friend was still on Nadira, a rich and powerful neighbor whose supporters had grown, according to his elder brother's most recent report. Linnie was concerned about Artemus's growing power base but neither their father nor Rolf had ever given it a second thought.

"I must go to Nadira," he determined, not realizing he was speaking aloud.

"Going nowhere are you, Councillor. Do you forget you are my prisoner?" Ruel gloated.

Rolf sighed. "You don't need to take your revenge out on me any longer, Ruel. We both know the truth now. Why don't you let me go?"

"There is still the issue of the First Amendment. Proof is its passage that your government conspires against the Souk Alliance. Tell me will you of your secret policies and plans."

"We have no secrets, Ruel."

"You lie. Why were you sent to Souk in disguise? This is not your normal appearance. Blond hair have you and a straighter nose. You deliberately altered your features to avoid r-r-recognition. Did you crash by the Rocks of Weir on purpose? What is your mission here, Councillor?"

Rolf compressed his lips. Here comes the rough part, he thought, his stomach churning with anxiety. Had he forgotten his pledge to Gayla's parents? He'd vowed to stop the slave trade. His presence in Souk was the culminating result of that oath. He and Gayla hadn't been the only ones affected. Hundreds of people were being killed or enslaved by the Souks every day, and the Souks had to be crushed by whatever means it took.

"Need I use a Morgot mind probe to loosen your tongue?" Ruel asked when Rolf remained silent. "I'd hoped we could do this in a civilized manner."

"I'm trained to resist mind probes," Rolf lied.

"Find out soon enough, won't we? Guards!"

Two hefty Souks rushed inside the cell, accompanied by the warden.

"Take him to the interrogation room," Ruel ordered, his dark eyes gleaming with eager anticipation.

Chapter Seventeen

Dawn was just breaching the horizon in the Nurash Desert when Devin emerged from his hiding place in the tunnel beneath his tent. An escape route, it ran under a dune and led to a slope on the other side of the camp.

At the first alarm sounding the attack, he'd rushed into his tent, scooped up his critical papers, and fled into the tunnel. It was understood among his fellow liberators that this was a necessary and acceptable action. His role was too important for him to get captured. Unfortunately, he hadn't been able to take anyone with him. He'd been caught unawares and had performed automatically.

Now as he exited his tent, he peered at the smoking ruins in horror. Nothing was left. The tents, the rifles, the storage pits, all had been destroyed. What remained were dead bodies, and sand slugs were already at work on those.

Devin moved quickly, searching for familiar faces, afraid that Ilyssa or Lord Cam'brii might be among them. But he didn't find them. That meant they were captured and might still be alive. The harem ladies were missing, too. At the stream bed, he found Helena's bloodied body. From the look of her wounds, it appeared she'd been beaten and hadn't survived the thrashing.

Devin clenched his fists, filled with rage. If the liberation movement was successful, the Koritah would be disbanded and the pashas supporting it overthrown. But that wouldn't happen if Lord Cam'brii had been compromised by last night's raid. He'd have to find out where the Councillor had been taken and organize a rescue. And what had happened to Otis that the Crigellan hadn't warned him of the impending attack?

Grabbing his sack of emergency supplies that he'd kept in the tunnel, he trudged in the direction of Pasha Yanuk's compound, the hot sun burning at his back. He'd find out what information he could before making any further plans.

Six hauras later, Devin arrived at the outskirts of Yanuk's desert abode. Utilizing a method of entry known to him thanks to Teir and Sarina, who'd escaped from there with Otis's help, he slipped inside a secret maze of tunnels and came out in the Crigellan's chamber. It was risky if Otis's connection with the liberators had been exposed, but Devin couldn't afford to lose time by doing things differently.

"Devin!" the lizard-man exclaimed, rising from his computer console. "Thank the stars you're all right."

Devin stepped out from the secret passageway and pressed the hidden latch for the wall to close. "Why the devil didn't you warn me of the assault?" He described the raid to the Crigellan.

"I wasn't here." Otis's green-skinned features crumbled with regret. "I'd gotten a lead on where your parents were, and I decided to check it out while Yanuk was distracted by Ruel's visit. I got back late last night and by then it was too late. But I've been spying on Yanuk's communiqués, and I've learned that Lord Cam'brii and your sister have been taken by Ruel to Haakat."

"Blast. We'll have a hell of a time getting them out. What about my parents? Did you find them?"

Otis noticed the youth's flushed face and hot, dusty appearance and hurried to the fabricator to conjure him a beverage. "They're imprisoned in the fortress at the Isle of Spears."

Devin's jaw dropped as he took the cruet of cold ale from Otis. "That's in the Scylla Sea!" Dangerous swirling currents affected the western body of water which was off the coast of Ruel's territory. Ships avoided the area because of its deadly whirlpools. "The only way to reach them would be by air. We don't have the equipment for a rescue attempt of that magnitude."

"You were unable to retrieve your parents when they were in Haakat. This is the opportunity you've been waiting for."

Devin took several greedy drafts of ale. The cool, tart liquid slid down his throat, easing his thirst. "I have an idea. Lord Cam'brii gave me the codes to contact the Defense League directly. I'll ask for their assistance when I notify them of the councillor's capture. We've got to break him out. Our campaign can't begin until he establishes the supply line we discussed, and he has to return to Bimordus Two for that. I'll contact our agent in Haakat. He wasn't willing to risk exposure over my parents and Ilyssa, but I'll bet you he'll assist us now that Lord Cam'brii is in danger."

Otis regarded him solemnly. "You're talking about a two-pronged rescue attempt. Whom shall we aim at first?"

"We'll coordinate our efforts with the Defense League. Jarin and her fellow Souk females are missing from the camp, and I'm concerned about them, too."

The Crigellan's face paled to a light shade of green.

"Our liberation movement could be severely compromised if the leadership role of the harems is discovered. All the pashas would order an immediate crackdown and our biggest force would be neutralized. It's possible Jarin's group was brought here. I'll check it out while you go to Haakat." He smiled broadly. "I have just the method to get you there."

Rolf felt the cold, hard metal of a shooter pressing against his back. Pasha Ruel marched in front of him, his posture ramrod straight. Flanking Rolf were Souk guards. This is it, he thought, swallowing hard. He was being taken to the interrogation room. A cold sweat broke out on his forehead and bile rose in his throat. He'd known fear before, but never had it been so intense.

Ruel stopped to hold a whispered conference with the warden. Then they continued on their way, veering to the left. Rolf saw ahead of him, across a broad circular space, the stairway leading to the surface.

"Where are we going?" he croaked, his throat dry. He'd thought the torture chamber would be down here.

"You'll see. I have something special in mind for you," Ruel sneered.

The weapon prodded his back and he climbed the steps.

Outside in the courtyard, the night was still. A squad of marching guards was the only sound other than the drone of nocturnal insects. He followed Ruel across the brightly lit square, through an archway, and into a manicured garden at the north side of the palace structure.

"I wish to show you a unique design," Ruel said, turning to give him a twisted grin. "It's called the Shell Grotto. Interesting will you find it, Councillor."

Rolf frowned, bewildered. Did this have something to do with his interrogation? The surroundings were too pleasant for such a grisly purpose. Shaped bushes and colorful beds of blossoms were interspersed with gravel walkways illuminated by low footlights. A strange structure made entirely of seashells was at the opposite end.

"A man such as yourself can appreciate the intricacy of the design," Ruel commented as they neared the place. Ducking under a low archway, he led Rolf inside, motioning for the guards to remain outdoors. Ruel closed a heavy wooden door and then gestured to the curved walls and ceiling. "Thousands of shells decorate the place, as you can see."

Rolf peered at the inlaid figures of sea creatures and geometric designs. "It's quite amazing." He still didn't see the point of the visit.

"Listen. Hear will you the music of the sea."

Ruel turned to him with a secretive smile. Rolf noted the sly look in the Souk's beady eyes and figured the pasha was up to something. He hadn't been taken here just to admire the view. His eyes followed Ruel as he casually strolled to a wall and leaned on one of the larger shells.

Instantly the room flooded with the most incredible sound. Clear, high notes rose and fell in harmonious melody. Rolf's mouth dropped open as a wave of pleasure washed over him. It was the most beautiful singing he'd ever heard.

Singing?

His eyes widened. Great suns! It was a woman's voice, and Rolf realized its significance. Ilyssa was using her siren song to seduce him into a state of everlasting servitude. And after he was mindwashed, Ruel would be able to extract any information he wanted about the Coalition, the resistance, anything!

His mind yearned to listen to the incredibly mesmerizing music. Feeling his willpower begin to fade, he lifted his finger to his mouth. Desperately, he sucked on his fingertip where the memory molecule was painted onto his nail. The bitter taste was absorbed by his tongue, and then his mind went blessedly and totally blank.

Numbly he stood there, Ruel watching him with a grin on his ugly dogface, as the soprano notes cascaded through his mind and reverberated off the shell-encrusted walls. The music played along his nerves and thrummed through his veins like a haunting symphony, drawing him into its intensity. The controlled power, the range of pitch, the equality in the tones, captured his attention and made his soul soar to the heights of heaven.

But how was he so aware of the effect? How could he think critically about what he was hearing? By the stars, the memory molecule must have failed to work! Yet his mind had emptied for a brief instant. It must have been effective at that point. So what had happened to bring him back to awareness? And why wasn't he mindwashed by Ilyssa's song?

His eyes widened as a possible explanation came to him. Perhaps the drug's chemical action provided a temporary shield against Ilyssa's song. In return, her siren song must have neutralized the memory erasing effect of the drug. They'd counteracted each other!

It was an amazing notion, yet as the music faded, he realized it was the only rationale that made sense. As Ruel chuckled evilly and approached him, Rolf realized he'd better pretend as though the mindwash had worked. The fact that Ilyssa had applied it to him confirmed her allegiance to Ruel. With great difficulty, he forced a blank look to his face and stood silently, waiting to be commanded.

"You will obey Ruel's word," Ilyssa ordered from behind a hidden partition. Rolf heard a creaking noise, and then he sensed that she was gone.

Ruel grinned as he faced his adversary. "You will follow my orders, sumi!" he said, gloating as he gazed at Rolf. He released a barking cackle.

"Return to your cell," he ordered. "Guards!"

Rolf obeyed while wondering what he would do if Ruel questioned him. He had to escape in time to make the Alliance conference. There was still the Souk informer to unmask; then he'd be done on this accursed planet. He needed to get back to Bimordus Two to set up the link to the resistance. Yet how could he do anything under the circumstances? He was being forced to act the role of a mind slave wherein any sign of independent thought would immediately crush his chances for escape.

Back in his dingy, damp cell, Rolf stood silently, wondering what Ruel would order him to do next.

"Leave us," Ruel said to the guards. He lowered his bulk onto one of the chairs remaining in the room.

"Kneel before me," the pasha ordered. When Rolf had complied, Ruel said, "Every time you greet me, you will bend with humility until I tell you to rise. You will not speak unless commanded to do so, and then you will call me master. You will do whatever I r-r-require of you. Now, tell me about the Defense League fortifications in the Quantum sector."

A frisson of alarm shot through Rolf. Still kneeling, he said, "I am not privy to Defense League operations, master."

"Grrrr. Give me the details on the new treaty with Tendraa."

There was no secret about those, so Rolf told him.

The interrogation seemed to last forever. Rolf answered whatever he could truthfully, gave half-lies where acceptable, and outright prevaricated in many instances. He was careful to keep his expression completely impassive while his stomach churned with fear that Ruel might discover his deceit. The questions about the resistance he fielded the best way he could, revealing as little information as possible. He couldn't help the sheen of sweat that covered his body and hoped Ruel would be too absorbed in listening to notice.

At last he was left alone with the furnishings removed, the door shut and locked. Giving vent to his exhaustion, he flopped on the cold stone floor and ate the meager meal he was supplied. Time passed slowly. He counted the drops of moisture on the damp walls and the number of cracks in the floor. He paced back and forth, did situps and other muscle flexing exercises, and considered different options for escape.

His thoughts drifted to Ilyssa, his mind replaying the good times they'd spent together, the caresses, the soft murmurings, the feel of her pliant body against his. Had she been playacting the entire time? How could he have been such a fool to fall for her?

Unable to erase her image from his mind, he tried to focus on his mission. The time for the conference was rapidly approaching. If he didn't break out soon, he'd miss it for sure. He had to learn the identity of the mole!

As the days went by, Rolf was frequently called to Ruel's chambers to perform menial tasks or for more questioning, but no opportunity for escape arose. Ruel's elite guards, the Hazars, accompanied Rolf everywhere. The pasha seemed to take a particular delight in humiliating him, forcing him to kneel at length until his legs cramped and he grew too stiff to move. And not one word of protest or complaint could he utter.

One day Ilyssa was called to Ruel's chamber while he was present.

Despite his ire, his heart soared at the lovely sight she made framed in the archway. Her delicately shaped face, her feathery eyebrows, her clear green eyes, and her perfectly shaped mouth made his heart constrict with pain. Her lithe form was encased in a sparkling ruby caftan. Backlit from the flamelights in the corridor, her long auburn hair cascaded over her shoulders like a fiery sunset. Seeing her aroused in him a yearning he couldn't suppress. He had to remind himself of his status, and after that first quick glimpse, he remained kneeling in front of Ruel, awaiting the pasha's command with a blank expression on his face.

"I thought you might like to see Lord Cam'brii," Ruel's loud voice rang out.

Ilyssa stared at Rolf in shock. For days she'd tried to get information about him but Ruel wouldn't tell her anything. He'd ordered her confined to her quarters and the female caretaker to wait on her. For her transgressions, she was given two scant meals a day and nothing to read or entertain herself with. The isolation, the boredom, the lack of adequate food had weakened her will as she knew Ruel had intended.

"Rolf?" she asked, taking a tentative step toward him. Her walk was wobbly.

"He is mindwashed, Ilyssa," Ruel said, grinning at her. "When you sang in the Shell Grotto the other day, he was the r-r-recipient."

"No!" she cried, horrified. She remembered wondering who the victim had been. By the stars, could it be true? Had Ruel tricked her so grievously, knowing she'd never perform her siren song for the man she loved?

As she approached, she saw how Rolf stared ahead as he knelt before Ruel. The man she'd known would never kneel before anyone.

"By the Almighty, what have I done?" She fell to her knees beside him, touching his arm. When he didn't respond, tears of hatred sprang into her eyes and she leapt up, turning to Ruel.

"How could you?" she cried. "Look at what he's become!"

"You would prefer that I tortured him? This way, he has given me the information that I need. Even now, Pasha Yanuk and I are taking steps to crush the r-r-resistance, thanks to the information Cam'brii supplied and the intelligence our own agents have gathered. As for the councillor, no longer is he the man he once was. Didn't I tell you that you're mine, Ilyssa?"

Ruel sauntered over to her, lifting her chin in his hands. "But what is this I see in your eyes, still a flicker of defiance? Even after my attempts to weaken you, you still r-r-refuse to give up your love for this man?"

"I don't care what you do to me, Ruel. I'll never stop loving him. You've already used your power against me. You made me pretend to be your gima by threatening to harm him and my mother if I didn't obey. I was never so hurt in my life as I was by the hatred shining in Rolf's eyes when he saw me strip before you. You made me do that and I've despised myself ever since. There's nothing else you can do to me now that will harm me."

"You're wrong! I won't have you love this man. You belong to me!" He narrowed his slanted eyes at her. "I'd hoped by breaking your will and showing you the results of his mindwash that you would give up your feelings for him. Need I do something more drastic?"

"What does it matter, Ruel?" She shot Rolf a pitiful glance. "We both obey your commands. What more do you want?"

"I want your soul!" he screamed. "I own you! Need you a demonstration for proof? I own both of you!"

He turned to Rolf. "Show her how you obey me. Strike her with your hand. Beat her until her love for you turns into blazing hatred."

Rolf nearly widened his eyes in shock. All through Ilyssa's recital, he'd knelt there, his feelings tumbling in confusion. She loved him! Ruel was tormenting her because she had feelings for him. She'd acted as the pasha's gima only because his life had been threatened, and her mother's. By the stars, was it true? But what about her scheming with Bolt? Hadn't both of them confessed? Unless . . . unless they were both saying it to avoid Ruel's wrath.

Great suns, he'd been ordered to strike her. How could he hurt her when all he wanted to do was gather her into his arms and beg her forgiveness?

Standing, he mumbled, "I obey, master." Slowly, his steps carried him in her direction. His head lifted, and he gazed into her terror-stricken eyes.

Did Ilyssa see something flicker behind his expression? For an instant, hope surged within her, but then his hand swung back and she cried, "No, Rolf!" just before he slapped her across the cheek. She stumbled back, her face burning where he'd hit her, but it was nothing compared to her heart that tore asunder.

He approached again, swallowing at the look of panic on her face. He couldn't make himself strike her again. Regardless of the consequences, he'd have to make a move against Ruel. Pretending to obey, he raised his hand, wincing inside when Ilyssa cringed. He was an instant away from spinning around and rushing the pasha when Ruel spoke.

"Enough!" the Souk snarled. "You see, little bird? If I ordered him to kill you, he would do so. Leave us now. I wish to command my slave to prepare my bath."

Her hands cupping her face, Ilyssa rushed from the room. She was barely aware of her caretaker's stern look or the Hazars who escorted her to her room. Inside, the caretaker made certain the chamber was secure before leaving her, a wilted heap collapsed upon her lounger. Nothing Ruel had done to her before had crushed her spirit as much as his turning Rolf against her. Ilyssa's face still stung from where he'd struck her. Giving in to her despair, she curled into a ball and cried for all her lost dreams.

Another two days passed before Ruel summoned her again. One of his harem ladies was present, fastening her gilded bra when Ilyssa walked in.

"Can the lady help me comb my hair?" the Souk concubine requested. "It tangles easily even though it is short."

"Krach," Ruel agreed. He walked away while Ilyssa and the Souk female situated themselves in front of a reflector.

Ilyssa pulled the comb through the female's coarse brown hair, thinking she didn't care what she was asked to do because nothing mattered anymore. She drove the comb harder, bending her head against a sudden onslaught of tears.

"Do not give up," the Souk female whispered. Ilyssa glanced up in surprise. "Help is on its way."

"Help? What kind of help?" Ilyssa hissed. Her eyes sought Ruel's image in the reflector. He was at the other side of the chamber, out of earshot.

"We'd expected you to visit us but confined to your chamber have you been. The r-r-resistance intends to free you and Lord Cam'brii."

"You're with the liberators?" Ilyssa had hoped to get into the harem herself but she hadn't been allowed the opportunity. "What's the plan?" she asked eagerly, but Ruel interrupted before the female could respond.

"What is it you two find so interesting to talk about?" he thundered, striding in their direction.

"I was advising the lady to comb her hair at least twice a day in order to avoid snarls," Ilyssa lied, her hope surging. If the harem females could smuggle her and Rolf out of here, she'd try to reverse the effects of his mindwash the same way she'd help Papa. But what of her parents? Where were they being held hostage?

"You may go," Ruel ordered his concubine. Silently she rose and left after giving Ilyssa a sharp, warning glance.

"Ilyssa, allow you will I to r-r-resume attending our evening banquets, but you must behave."

She kept her head lowered, plucking nervously at her

skirt. "When will you let me speak to my mother again, master?"

"When you stop thinking of *him!* I know he is still in your thoughts. What else do I have to do to—" Ruel was cut off by the chime of the comm unit. "Computer, open channel."

"This is Yanuk." The other pasha's face appeared on a viewscreen on the wall. "A progress r-r-report have I for you. Successful have we been in r-r-routing the insurgents in the Thicket of Bayne, but more pockets of r-r-rebellion are cropping up. Spoken with the other pashas have I, and if you agree, we'll move up the date for the conference to four days hence."

"Arf, a good idea that is."

"Jarin and her friends will not loosen their tongues. Not much longer will they last. Their endurance under torture is strong."

Ilyssa pretended to study her fingernails while she listened intently. Jarin and her ladies were being tortured? How horrible! What had happened to the others in the camp, to Devin?

"Why haven't you used a Morgot mind probe?" Ruel asked.

"Like my predecessor, Cerrus Bdan, I prefer cruder methods." Yanuk laughed evilly. "But use it shall I before they die, cousin."

"Keep me informed." Ruel didn't turn off the comm unit after Yanuk signed off. "Computer," he said, "send a message via subspace radio to the Communications Center on Bimordus Two. Direct it to Pimms and instruct him to leave immediately for Souk. Oh, and tell him Lord Cam'brii is my prisoner. He'll appreciate that bit of news." He cut off the comm link, giving a nasty barking laugh.

Rolf wrestled over various plans of action but kept tossing them out as being too risky. Everywhere he went, he was escorted by the Hazars. The pasha had taken to humiliating him in front of others, using him as a lackey at state dinners. For those occasions, he was allowed a fresh change of clothes and a shower, but even then, he was so closely guarded there'd been no opportunity to make a break. He had to free Ilyssa as well as himself, so that made his escape more complicated. Added to his burden was the treatment he received. Despite his supposed mindwash, Ruel had decreed that he was to be fed one meal a day. As the pasha had explained to a cohort within his earshot, he didn't want Rolf to appear in better physical condition than himself. It would lower his image in the eyes of others. He preferred to keep his slaves in a weakened state to show his superiority.

Frustration tore at Rolf, but he curbed his impatience and bided his time. The day would come when he could make his move. Until then, he focused on developing plans for completing his mission.

Ilyssa was invited to banquets when Rolf was the featured entertainment. It grieved her to see him forced into such a lowly position. It was like the Rocks of Weir all over again, only this time instead of being a laborer, the once powerful statesman had been reduced to a mindless minion, jumping at Ruel's word and rushing to obey his commands. Suppressing the tears that sprang into her eyes, she stared at her plate and wondered when the resistance was going to make its move.

Thinking of her family threatened to start another flood of tears. Ruel wouldn't allow her to speak to her mother, so she'd been unable to discern her parents' location or condition. Of Devin, too, she knew nothing. Her world was crumbling and despair filled her heart. Feeling alone, she called upon her reserves of inner strength to get her through the long nights.

Late one evening, she was bedded on her lounger.

Ruel had left for the Alliance conference, so she wasn't worried about being summoned to his chamber. Tossing and turning, Ilyssa's thoughts drifted to Rolf. She recalled their early days together: how they'd fled from Bolt's mining camp, sharing a kiss by the light of Souk's two moons to celebrate their freedom. Then had come the flight on the ore tram car and the journey by hovertrain. She remembered raking her fingers through his long black hair, tracing his determined jaw, splaying her hands across the muscular planes of his broad back. She hungered for him even now. His touch had aroused a responsiveness within her she'd never known existed.

Plagued with an aching need that wouldn't be abated, Ilyssa turned toward the wall. Dear heaven, she could almost feel his hands on her body, his fingers caressing her skin. Regret washed over her that she hadn't been able to fully accept the fruits of passion he'd offered her.

Silently, she proclaimed her love for him. As tears trickled down her cheeks, she yearned for his whispered words of affection, for his arousing touch. Her need was so great she could almost feel his hot breath fanning her ear.

"Ilyssa," his voice whispered.

She jumped as someone touched her on the neck. Instantly, a hand clamped over her mouth.

"Don't make a sound. It's me, Rolf."

Her eyes widened.

"I came in through your secret passage. Come, we're escaping."

He released her and she flipped around. Rolf stood before her, his blue eyes clear and alert. His hair was askew and several days' growth of beard covered his jaw. He held up a finger as he saw the question forming on her lips.

She understood. Wordlessly, she rose and followed him

toward the open archway that led into the secret tunnel. But as soon as the door shut behind them, she fell into his waiting arms. His tight embrace crushed the breath from her. Over and over he murmured her name, smothering kisses on her ear, her cheeks, and her mouth.

After a moment of frenzied kisses, he lifted his face.

"Forgive me for hitting you in Ruel's chamber," he rasped. "I had to pretend to be mindwashed."

"But how is it that you aren't?" She wanted to melt at the expression of tenderness on his face.

"I'll explain later. It's rather simple, although I'm not sure I understand it myself."

"I thought you hated me. Ruel made me act like his gima in front of you. I was repulsed but he said he'd hurt you and my mother if I didn't obey."

"I know." He drew her against his body, burying his face in her hair. "Let's not waste words with explanations. I'm just grateful to be with you again."

"How now, sister? No greeting for me?" a figure said stalking out of the shadows.

"Devin!" she exclaimed, breaking from Rolf's embrace to rush to her brother. "You're alive! But how did you get here?"

"I came disguised as a member of Balthazar's troupe." His face sobered. "They came here under the guise of performing for Ruel, but someone named Gant was in court and identified them as being associated with the resistance. Ruel arrested them. I'd already made contact with our local representative, so I wasn't caught with Balthazar's group, but a warrant has been issued for my arrest as well."

"What about Jarin and her ladies?" Ilyssa asked, worried.

"Yanuk took them prisoner, but his harem females got them out before they were tortured to death. Yanuk is furious but he doesn't know whom to blame." He paused. "I used these tunnels when I escaped from Haakat originally. I believe you know Ivex, the controller for the division of economy. He's the friend who aided me."

Ilyssa's jaw dropped in surprise as the Souk sauntered into view. "We must hurry," he said nervously. "Everyone's on alert since the Alliance conference failed to reach an accord yesterday afternoon. My people wait for Lord Cam'brii to establish a supply run from the Defense League in order to begin our campaign. In the meantime, the opposing pashas are cracking down on any pockets of r-r-resistance they can find."

"Blast, you mean I missed the conference?" Rolf said, cursing. "Now I've lost my one chance to uncover the Souk mole in our government."

"Is that why you needed to attend?" Ilyssa asked.

Rolf nodded and tersely explained the situation.

"If the informant works out of Bimordus Two, I may know how Ruel contacts him." She told Rolf how the pasha sent messages to someone named Pimms at the Coalition capital.

"By the stars, it's even more urgent that I get home!" he exclaimed.

"Rolf, my parents—"

"They're being retrieved," Devin cut in, his tone brusque. "I contacted the Defense League. They have sent a team headed by Captain Teir Reylock. Mama and Papa are being held on the Isle of Spears in the Scylla Sea. Lt. Commander Deitan Sage, a diving expert in the SEARCH Force short for Sea and Aerospace Command Detachment, is leading the rescue. His mission was to drop offshore, swim to the island underwater, and lay out laser markers to guide in the rest of the team. Commander Sage would then neutralize the guards while the others freed our parents. I understand a shuttle from the *Valiant* would be standing by to get them off the island. If they succeeded, they'll be on their way here to pick you up. We've got to hurry!"

Touching her elbow, Rolf urged her along. Devin raced ahead of them. Ilyssa regarded her brother's broad back and carrot-colored hair with a rush of love. Seventeen annums, and already he'd experienced so much. She hoped they'd have a lot of time to spend together now that their rescue was at hand.

They emerged from inside the Shell Grotto, crossed the garden in the darkness of night, and entered another secret passageway by an outside wall. A fork in the tunnels appeared.

"Go ahead with Devin," Rolf said, coming to a halt.

"You're not coming?" Ilyssa's eyes widened in shock.

"I can't leave Balthazar and his troupe to face Ruel's torturers. Ivex will help me free them while the harem ladies stage a diversion. Stay with your brother." He hurried off before she could protest.

"No!" Ilyssa cried, but Devin was already tugging on her arm and urging her to go in a different direction.

They surfaced in the city and ran smack into a contingent of Souk troops patrolling the outside perimeter of the palace. Noting the area was half-enclosed behind a guard station, Ilyssa automatically used her siren song. The soldiers froze when they heard her melodious notes.

Ilyssa whirled to speak to her brother, but he wore a strange expression on his face. "Devin!" she screamed. She'd forgotten he wasn't immune!

His eyes focused and he turned his gaze to her. "What's wrong, sister? I just heard the most wondrous thing: a multitude of voices singing in harmony. It was beautiful." His face was rapt. "I can hear things so clearly now: the wind singing through the leaves of trees, plant stalks pushing through the ground, dew forming on the flower petals in the garden. It's amazing."

She stared at him. No other male had ever exhibited such a reaction to her song before, but then Devin was her brother. Perhaps the quality that gave her the ability to sing was imbued in him as well and was just manifesting itself differently, having been triggered by her song.

"When is Rolf coming?" she asked, shattering his reverie.

"He shouldn't be long. Order those troops to go away."

She did so, and the soldiers marched off, their expressions glazed. The minutes ticked by until a commotion from behind made them turn. Rolf burst out of the secret tunnel, followed by a grimy Balthazar and his five remaining players.

"Ilyssa, lass, never a sight has been kinder!" the bearded gentleman cried. "We'll be forever grateful to your man for getting us out of that horrible wasting pit."

A loud humming vibration sounded overhead.

"Here comes your transportation," Devin said.

Ilyssa looked up at the night sky and shrieked, "A wingboxer!"

Rolf laughed. "No, that's a shuttle made to appear as a flying creature. Utilizing the principles of molecular alteration, it can appear in any desired configuration. We'll have to let them know we've got company. Balthazar, I hope you don't mind coming along. It's not safe for you on Souk any longer." Rolf revealed his identity and mission to the troupe leader.

Devin turned to Ilyssa while the others were busy talking. "Much work needs to be done here, sister. I will stay on Souk and act as liaison to the Coalition."

"No, Devin. You can't!" she protested, horrified.

"I do what I must. Wish our parents well for me. I'll miss them, and you. Take good care of her, Councillor." He extended his hand to Rolf.

Rolf gave him a firm handshake and a clap on the arm. "I'll contact you as soon as I reach Bimordus Two and make the necessary arrangements."

"Remember what we talked about in my tent," her brother said.

"I shall."

"Goodbye, Ilyssa." Briefly, Devin embraced her. "I fear Ruel will be furious once he learns of your escape. I'll keep Lord Cam'brii informed of his actions. While he's in power, he remains a threat to you both."

"Be careful!" Ilyssa cried, distressed to be leaving him behind.

With a cavalier gesture, Devin signaled to the shuttle and it descended.

Chapter Eighteen

"All I want to do is hold you," Rolf said, pulling Ilyssa into his arms as soon as they were alone. Teir had given them his cabin aboard the *Valiant.* The rest of the captain's crew were sharing the remaining quarters, with Balthazar's group assigned space in the cargo hold.

Rolf glanced around the compact area. It was small but luxurious compared to the dungeon in Haakat, and he relished being able to spend four days in close quarters with Ilyssa.

"I finally have you all to myself," he said, burying his face in her hair. Her silken strands, scented with the perfume of keela blossoms from Ruel's garden, tickled his nose. Being with her again made him never want to leave the ship.

Ilyssa closed her eyes, enjoying the feel of his hard body enveloping hers. His strong arms encircled her, making her feel protected and warm. She felt content and more secure than she ever had in her life.

She'd greeted her parents earlier. They were using the cabin vacated by Commander Sage. Papa was gaunt and barely responsive. He wasn't eating much and his frailty of health worried her. Without Ruel to direct him, he ambled about like a lost soul, totally disregarding his personal needs.

Thankfully, her mother was able to assist him. Ruel had lied about Moireen being blinded. She'd been put into isolation as her punishment. Moireen had endured and simply hadn't wanted her daughter to see the dark circles under her eyes or her sunken cheekbones.

Ilyssa had told Moireen all about Rolf. She'd introduced them and her mother had thanked him profusely for bringing her daughter to safety. Later, when they were alone, Moireen had given her blessings to Ilyssa. She'd suggested Ilyssa complete her trip to Athos, their original voyage having been interrupted eight annums ago by Ruel's pirates. Moireen supported her goal of becoming an arbiter but didn't want to see it stand in the way of her daughter's happiness. Ilyssa still needed to learn the truth about siren song. On Athos, too, was the possibility of finding a cure for her father's mindwash.

Ilyssa agreed that the voyage was a necessity but put off approaching Rolf about it. The Coalition capital was their immediate destination. She understood that Rolf had urgent business on Bimordus Two and didn't want to interfere. At the appropriate time, she'd ask for his help in reaching Athos. For now, Ilyssa just wanted to enjoy his company.

"I missed you so much in Haakat," she told him, cherishing the time they had together. "All those nights I spent alone in my bedchamber, I kept thinking of you and dreaming of being held in your arms."

Groaning, he lowered his head and kissed her. It was a wild, passionate kiss full of pent-up longing and desire. As his mouth moved over hers, he crushed her body closer, never wanting to let her go. His hands roamed over her back, but as he felt her nightshirt under his fingers, he yearned to touch her naked flesh.

"Gods, how I want to make love to you," he rasped, pulling back. "I think, deep down in my heart, I felt you would never betray me. Do you forgive me for doubting you?"

"Of course," she said, smiling.

Her radiant expression made him want to kiss her again, but he didn't. "I need to take a shower," he said, stroking his beard for emphasis. "Ruel's dungeon wasn't very conducive to cleanliness. Care to join me?"

His teasing glance tempted her to accept, but she shook her head instead, preferring to sort out her own thoughts while he was occupied.

"Wait for me," he said, giving her a devastating grin.

Ilyssa watched him enter the sanitary, her body still burning from the close contact between them. Already she felt forlorn by his absence. She couldn't wait until he emerged so her gaze could feast upon his handsome face and powerful physique. Rolf had lost weight, but he must have kept up with his exercises because he appeared leaner but trim.

Stepping to the fabricator, she conjured a hairbrush and various other toilet articles along with a change of clothes, a jumpsuit in a flashy metallic blue. No more caftans, she thought exuberantly. Now she could make her own choices. With a wild leap of her heart, she acknowledged that her enslavement on Souk was over. Freedom! The word rang in her ears like a cymbal clanging before the gates of heaven.

At last, she could pursue her ambition to become an arbiter. First she would go to Athos to learn more about her gift and find a cure for her father, and then return to Circutia to put in her application for the coveted position. Ilyssa realized that fulfilling her dream was possible only because of Rolf, and yet didn't she risk losing him by achieving what she most desired? If he asked her to stay on Bimordus Two with him, which choice would she make: to pursue her career or her man?

She was still contemplating the possibilities when Rolf sauntered out of the sanitary, stark naked.

"Your turn," he said, wiggling an eyebrow at her. "Need any help in the shower?"

Her eyes drank their fill of him. His long black hair hung damp to his broad shoulders. Drops of moisture clung to his freshly shaven jaw. His chest hair appeared shiny and soft. At his flat abdomen, a feathering of hair tapered lower.

Her face reddened when she noticed him watching her with a bemused expression. She fled into the sanitary, shutting the door behind her.

After throwing her nightshirt in the disposer, Ilyssa stepped naked into the shower. Pulsating side sprays of warm water pounded her skin. Reaching for a bar of soap, she scrubbed herself and had just finished rinsing when a low, masculine voice interrupted her.

"I thought you might want company." Rolf's head peeked around the partitions.

Ilyssa shrieked, "What are you doing in here?"

"I need you," he said, stepping inside the tight space. He was still naked and very much aroused.

Ilyssa wet her lips. "Rolf, you know I'm not able to—"

He nodded. "There are other things we can do instead." A lazy smile curved his lips. "I'll be happy to show you."

He sidled closer and her nerves leapt into a state of charged awareness. Her tiniest hairs stood on end, the electrical tension between them like a vibrant physical force. Rolf halted with his massive chest directly in front of her face. The warm water sprayed them both, making their bodies glisten with moisture. Rivulets of water ran down his chest and her eyes followed them as they trailed downward.

Aching for him, needing him, she reached out to touch his hair-roughened skin.

With a groan, he swept her into his arms and lowered his head. His mouth sought hers, his lips frenzied as he pressed her to him. The needles of water pouring onto her back only served to heighten her sensitivity.

Every place he touched her, she felt an intense tingling sensation. Needing to be closer, she flattened her breasts against his chest, pressed her belly against his hard stomach, and locked her legs with his sturdy lower limbs. His large organ prodded at her thighs, tantalizing her with its closeness. The fragrance of soap on his body combined with his scent of musky masculinity stirred her blood into a fermenting boil.

He lifted his head, gazing at her with heatstruck eyes. "By the stars, Ilyssa, I can barely control myself when I'm with you. I don't want to go off early like I did the first time we . . . in the ore tram car."

"What do you mean?"

He gazed at her, amused. "You never did understand, did you?" His hand caressed the side of her face. "Your innocence is one of the qualities I adore about you, among others. You're very special to me."

Slowly, his fingers traced her jawline, brushed over her lips, and wandered down her throat. His other hand tangled into her hair, supporting the back of her head. "You're so beautiful. I want to make you mine."

"I am yours, Rolf. I just can't—"

"Hush. I told you there are other ways."

His mouth captured hers, the tenderness of his kiss making her heart melt. By the corona, she wanted to give herself to this man. She wrapped her arms around him, pulling him tightly against her body, gyrating her hips against him as the water from the jet sprays cascaded over them both. Her need for him burned in its intensity, and the droplets from the shower seemed to sizzle from her body heat. The flavor of liquor was on his breath and she thrust her tongue out in order to taste more.

Instantly he met it with his own tongue, exploring her, entering her mouth and probing its far reaches as though trying to devour her. Her legs weakened. Her veins burned with liquid fire. She never wanted this moment to end. If a simple kiss produced such ecstasy, what would joining with him do? She trembled at the thought of it.

His hands roamed her wet body, sliding over her slippery skin, tantalizing her with tiny circular motions and a light tickly touch. When he cupped her breasts, Ilyssa sucked in a breath and clutched at his back. His thumbs teased her nipples into taut, raised peaks.

Ilyssa moaned, arching toward him. Her fingers splayed across his shoulder blades, kneaded the muscles under the skin of his back, traced his bony prominences. She longed to explore all of him. And with that in mind, she moved her hand to the front of his body and tentatively brushed her fingers across his groin. His sudden intake of breath told her she'd excited him. Boldly, she wrapped her fingers around his shaft.

"Show me how to please you," she whispered, her breath coming in short, erratic gasps.

Groaning, he took her hand and Ilyssa stroked him, wondering at the feel of him. He was curiously hard and soft, petal smooth and firm. Deep sounds of pleasure growled from his throat as she caressed him. A sense of power crept over her, bringing an upward curve to her lips as they moved beneath his.

Rolf was oblivious to the water spraying at them, to the hiss of the jets, to anything except the softness of her mouth and the wonderful sensations her hand was arousing in him. His body responded with urgent movements as he became lost in a heady spiral of delight that drove him toward the stars.

Suddenly his body spasmed and his release was complete.

"Ah, *larla,* the things I want to show you," Rolf murmured lovingly, seeing the incredulous look on her face. He enjoyed her sweet innocence so much it amazed him. Ilyssa was all he desired, all he'd searched for during his annums of torment following Gayla's death. She'd healed his soul and made him feel whole again.

Kneeling in front of her, he let the water run over his head. "A slave to Ruel I would never be again . . . but yours, always." And he pushed her thighs apart and his mouth touched her sensitive, throbbing flesh.

"Rolf!" Ilyssa gasped, shocked.

"Let me pleasure you," he murmured. And his lips began kissing and suckling, his tongue flicking, stroking side to side, tormenting her with an exquisite sensuality.

Ilyssa moaned and leaned back, opening her legs wider. She couldn't help herself. His hands reached around to her buttocks, pushing her forward so that his head was buried deep. His tongue seduced her into a mindwash of ecstasy. Dear heaven, what he was doing to her! Her mind became lost in a swirling cloud of numbing arousal. Hot fires stirred within her as she closed her eyes, clutching at his ebony hair. The fires melded into a pool of lava and rushed upward, exploding into a violent cataclysm of pleasure.

When her spasms subsided, she leaned weakly against him.

"That . . . that was incredible," she whispered.

Standing, he kissed her soft, honey-sweet mouth. Already his eyes glittered with renewed desire. "We have four days, Ilyssa. I just want to be with you the whole time."

But even as he pushed the button for the drying stones to activate, he thought regretfully of the work ahead. It couldn't wait forever. No matter how seductive their personal needs, they'd have to be put aside until his business with the Souks was settled.

"How long do you think it will take you to finish your business on Bimordus Two?" Ilyssa asked while they were getting dressed.

"I have to establish a communications link to the resistance, set up a supply run, and do a host of other jobs." Rolf pulled a clean tunic over his head. "More important, I need to identify the mole in our government."

He looked at her, his eyes narrowed as he considered all the tasks ahead of him. "If the informant hasn't yet returned from the conference on Souk, he will soon, and you've given us the means to catch him. I'll ask Teir to send a message to the comm center on Bimordus Two for a fellow by the name of Pimms. We'll put a surveillance team on the place. They should be able to identify him when he retrieves the message. Once that's done, I have to go to Nadira."

Ilyssa gave a cry of disappointment. "I'd hoped to ask you to help me find transport to Athos! There's still so much I need to learn about siren song, and Papa's condition is worsening. I might be able to find a cure for him on Athos."

"I'm sorry," Rolf said gently, looking into her anxious eyes. "I must go to Nadira to see Artemus." He told her what had transpired during his talk with Ruel. His childhood friend posed a threat that could not be ignored. "I'd like you to meet my parents," he said. "Will you come with me?"

Excitement swelled within her. He wouldn't offer to introduce her to his family unless she meant something special to him. "I'd love to," she said, with a mixture of pleasure and doubt. She still needed to get to Athos, and the delay wouldn't bode well for Papa.

As Ilyssa finished getting dressed, Rolf contemplated what he'd learned about himself from his journey to Souk. Because of his own personal tragedy, he'd tended to lump all Souks into one category. But now he'd seen for himself that good people existed on Souk, citizens who would give their lives to help others and to end their race's aggressiveness. He'd learned the meaning of captivity and the joy of freedom. And finally, he'd realized that revenge wasn't as gratifying an emotion as he'd once believed. His hatred had eaten away at his soul, blinding him to the needs of those around him. Love as a motivating force was so much more fulfilling.

Love? His eyes widened, and he stared at Ilyssa. Wearing a metallic blue jumpsuit that molded to her exquisite form, she was just finishing braiding her hair. Of course he was in love with her. How else could he explain the need he had for her, the feeling of wholeness she gave him? Her image filled his days and nights with pleasure. The feel of her in his arms stayed with him constantly, and he yearned for her whenever they were apart. Yes, he loved her!

Seeing the worried expression on her face, he felt a brief flicker of regret. He understood her urgent need to go to Athos, but his business on Bimordus Two took precedence. She knew he had to set up a supply route for the resistance on Souk. Devin was relying on him. And it was imperative for the mole to be exposed. As for Artemus, Rolf had a score to settle. He had to go to Nadira.

Once those tasks were off his mind, he could aid Ilyssa in her quest. No one even knew where Athos was located. It was said to be somewhere in the Spidrex Nebula, but it was also postulated that a black hole existed in that remote region of space. Ships that went into the Nebula didn't come out. Even the existence of Athos was questionable, and he wondered how they'd find a pilot willing to take them there. Of course he'd accompany her. Rolf wouldn't let her go alone. Perhaps he could lease a ship to take her, but not before his own work was complete.

Ilyssa surveyed the determined man in front of her. Garbed in an embroidered claret-colored tunic with gold trim and matching leggings, he appeared more like a prince than the slave laborer she'd known on Souk. His azure eyes regarded her warmly but with a reservation that hadn't been there before. Was this a herald of things to come? Was Rolf turning into a stranger? On Souk, they'd been thrust together in a frantic journey to freedom. Now that he was resuming his role as Lord Cam'brii, high government official and member of the royal House of Raimorrda, would he still want her?

Seeking reassurance, Ilyssa fell into the comfort of his arms. But even as his embrace closed around her, she realized their relationship had already changed.

The gulf between them widened when they reached Bimordus Two. Ilyssa stared out a viewport in the lounge. "That's the Coalition seat of government?" The planet was brown and barren.

Rolf stood beside her as they made their descent into the atmosphere. The *Valiant* was making its approach toward the spaceport.

"This site was chosen for its centrality, not for its hospitality to member species," he explained. "It's very cold on the surface, so an artificial atmosphere had to be created. That huge bubble you see in the distance is a biosphere. Inside the dome is a large-scale ecosystem made up of several biomes. The residential section is called Bimordus Central, but there are also the Nutrition Pod, Rain Forest, Marine Habitat, and Biogenesis Research Center. Each biome is self-sealing, with its own recycling process for water, air, and nutrients.

"I live in Spiral Town, the residence for High Council members. You and your parents can stay with me." He glanced at her excitedly.

His enthusiasm was contagious, and after they got through the ceremonies of their arrival—the entire terminal was filled with dignitaries giving Rolf a hero's welcome—she looked forward to being shown the wonders of the city. Rolf requisitioned a four-seat speeder and they made their first stop at the Wellness Center, where her father was admitted as a patient. His body needed nourishment even while his mind waited for a cure from Athos. Moireen remained with him, asking Rolf to pick her up later. Ilyssa left with Rolf, satisfied her father was in good hands.

As Rolf took her on a tour, she marveled at the modern city bustling with midmorning activity. Flying speeders, slowly cruising airbuses, and snakelike people-movers swept along the wide paved avenues crowded with all known species. Rolf explained that the different types of transport were available at a vehicle exchange center at no cost, and additional terminals were located throughout the city. It was an easy, safe public transportation system.

Ilyssa particularly liked the style of architecture. Spiral towers made of white marbelite and glittering pink stone thrust toward the crystal-domed sky. The look pleased her artistic eye, but it also made her yearn to return to Circutia, her home planet. Moireen would have to notify their relatives that they were alive and well. Perhaps her mother could get a transfer of credits. That way, once Ilyssa returned from Athos, she and her parents could book passage on a commercial vessel to take them home. A pang of anguish struck her as she thought of leaving Rolf. How could she leave him? Yet what would she do if she remained here?

They arrived at Spiral Town and she pushed her thoughts away. Residential units fanned out on different levels from a central round tower, the individuality of design giving each apartment a uniqueness that contributed to the structure as a whole. Rolf told her that due to space limitations, individual dwellings were not permitted in Bimordus Central, with one exception: the Supreme Regent had his own residence. Spiral Town was located near the Great Hall where the government convened.

Rolf showed Ilyssa into his apartment, proudly pointing out the plush ivory carpeting that chimed musically when stepped on, the curved, iridescent furniture, and his colorful collection of paintings. He demonstrated how to use the entertainment center, offered her a drink and refreshments, and showed her where the guest room was located. There were two sleeping chambers and a living area downstairs, and a workstation upstairs beyond a curving staircase.

"You'll share the guest room with your mother," he said, handing her a cool beverage in the living area.

"Your apartment is lovely." She accepted the drink, her fingers brushing his. Instantly, a tingling sensation shot up her arm where he'd touched her. Alone with him in this new environment, she felt a sudden shyness overwhelm her.

"I never imagined returning from Souk with anyone like you." He regarded her flushed expression and his loins stirred. "Ilyssa, we have just enough time to—"

"Yes."

They spent the next haura in his bedchamber, tearing off their clothes, wrapping themselves around each other's bodies in a frenzied expression of passion. Ilyssa yearned to join with him, to unite with this man and hold him so close he'd never let her go. As his gentle hands roamed her pliant body, she wished she could remain here with him forever. But there were other obligations that called to both of them. The chime of his comm unit alerted her that it was already beginning.

He rolled off the lounger, groaning as he pulled on his leggings. "You'll see there's never a moment's peace around here."

It was Glotaj, summoning him for a report. Rolf left to visit the Supreme Regent, after which he began making arrangements to support the freedom fighters on Souk. He checked to see that his orders regarding the mole had been carried out. Eventually, he sent someone else to pick up Moireen because he'd become too engrossed in his work to take a break.

"I hardly see Rolf anymore," Ilyssa complained to Sarina several days later. The Great Healer had been among those in the terminal to greet them on their arrival, and she'd come for a personal visit the following day. Ilyssa and she exchanged stories and were becoming quite friendly. Sarina had taken her on a detailed tour of the capital city and introduced her to her friends. Ilyssa had met Glotaj, the Supreme Regent, and was proud when the Coalition leader praised Rolf for his courage and accomplishments.

"You must be patient," Sarina said. She was an attractive blonde with silvery gray eyes and a figure rounding more each day. Her pregnancy had been announced as soon as her husband had returned from his rescue mission. They'd taken an apartment on Bimordus Two so they'd have a home when they weren't aboard the *Valiant.* She and Rolf had been invited there often, and vice versa. Sarina and Teir were elated for her and Rolf, proclaiming that Ilyssa had given him a new lease on life. Before leaving for Souk, they'd told her, Rolf had been tormented by guilt and by his hatred against the Souks. Now there was a gentler, more tender emotion that shone in his eyes whenever he looked at Ilyssa.

But she wondered how Rolf really felt about her. He hadn't asked her to remain with him on Bimordus Two. Maybe he was waiting until their trips to Nadira and

Athos were over. Impatience consumed her. It didn't matter what her decision would be. She yearned to hear if he wanted her to stay.

"He's always in meetings," Ilyssa complained to Sarina. Rolf and Teir had gone off somewhere together that afternoon and Moireen was at the Wellness Center visiting Aran. "I know he's busy setting up the supply line to Souk, but how long does it take?" Each day that passed, her father's condition worsened despite the palliative treatments he received.

But two bright points had illuminated her days. One was a brief visit to the Wellness Center, where Ilyssa had her safeguard removed. She and Rolf had celebrated that night by dining in one of the city's natural eateries, but it hadn't made any difference in their level of intimacy. Ilyssa still needed to retain her virginity to become an arbiter. Despite her wish to be with Rolf, she clung to her ambition. Once it had been her lifeline. Now it was her prime goal. Away from Souk, her memories of the suffering there were fresh in her mind. If she could aid in achieving peace, she owed it to herself to try.

The other was her visit to the study center to learn more about Athos. The sources she had found confirmed the rumors that the planet was located in the Spidrex Nebula. A search of the central data banks from Rolf's workstation at home however had revealed nothing more.

Balthazar and his troupe had been booked for a series of performances in the Pleasure Palace, the city's arts and entertainment complex. Though thrilled for them, her own anxiety hadn't abated as time passed and she accomplished nothing.

Seated across from her in Rolf's living area, Sarina gave her a sympathetic smile. "At least the Souk's informant was caught. No one ever suspected Ruzbee of being the mole. It makes sense when you think about it, though. Ruzbee was the elected representative from Arcturus. Many Arcturians support the Souks because of the scarcity of minerals on their world. They need the trade agreements with the mineral-rich Souk colonies."

Ilyssa still wasn't appeased. "Why can't Rolf leave the rest of the work to others? He's given his report and set up the initial links. The resistance has already begun its campaign. I need to go to Athos to help my father, and Rolf insists we stop off at Nadira on the way!"

Sarina leaned forward, her golden hair cascading over her shoulders. "I'm sure Rolf understands the urgency."

Ilyssa's feelings took a turn for the worse when a stranger walked in, accompanied by Teir. The man was tall, with short curly blond hair and features disturbingly similar to Rolf's. His blue eyes twinkled as he caught her staring at him.

"It's me, Ilyssa. I'm back to my normal self."

She couldn't believe her eyes. *This* was Rolf? Of course, he'd told her he had assumed a disguise to go to Souk, but where was the man she'd fallen in love with? This Rolf not only looked different but dressed and acted differently, too.

He quickly walked to her, taking her hands in his. "I'm still the same person inside, *larla,*" he told her. "I'm sorry I haven't been able to spend much time with you. There's just been so many things to do. I've finally received clearance to leave Bimordus Two."

"At last!" she said, jubilant.

The corners of his mouth turned down. "I have some bad news. Ivex sent us a warning from Haakat. Ruel is after us, and he's coming personally this time. He's vowed to make us his slaves for life."

She gasped. "I thought we were safe!"

He shook his head. "The pasha has left Souk, and no one knows his destination. He took a number of his troops with him. We're in danger as long as he remains at large. It's possible Artemus might know Ruel's plans if they're in contact with each other. We'll find out when we get to Nadira. I've got a ship ready and have already filed a flight plan."

"Any word from Devin?"

Rolf smiled broadly. "Your brother's a brave young man. He led a strike force against the mining camp at the Rocks of Weir. Bolt is dead, and the slaves have been freed. Many are being readied to transport home via the new route we established. Others are staying to join Devin's force and fight. Several of the friendlier pashas are cooperating. They've renounced slavery and agree to comply with the Equality Edict." He'd been pleased to learn Seth and his family were among those liberated from the camp.

"What about the pashas who support the Koritah?" Ilyssa remembered Jarin and the other harem females who sought their own brand of emancipation.

"Heavy pockets of fighting are still going on in Yanuk's territory and elsewhere. Ruel's stronghold remains firm with another cousin, Niak, in charge during his absence. Despite the liberation movement's initial victories, it still looks as though this will be a long, drawn-out campaign."

Ilyssa sighed, grateful that Devin was all right. Her main concern now focused on saving her father. "How long before we reach Nadira?"

He grimaced. "Three days. From Nadira, we have a voyage of at least eight days to reach the Spidrex Nebula. If we knew exactly where Athos was located, I could give you a more precise estimate of our arrival."

"Perhaps we should bring Papa along," she said, her voice anxiety-ridden.

"That's not a good idea. We could encounter a variety of problems." Rolf lifted her chin in his hand. "Don't worry. The ship I requisitioned is fully armed."

He kissed her, then turned to show Sarina and Teir out the door. They'd been engrossed in their own private conversation.

The way things were going, Ilyssa thought dismally, it appeared that she and Rolf would never surmount their obstacles to be together the way Sarina and Teir were. Now Ruel was searching for her and Rolf. The pasha could show up anywhere, at any time. Neither one of them would be safe until he was destroyed.

Chapter Nineteen

The ship Rolf requisitioned for the trip to Nadira was the *Destiny.* It was a small, swift Stinger equipped with powerful warp-drive engines and two stabilizer fins attached to the main cylindrical-shaped body. The fins rotated horizontally for landings and locked vertically for combat and flight. Weapons systems included two fire-linked laser cannon turrets, a proton torpedo launcher, and a concussion missile docket. Since Rolf had refused an armed escort, he wanted to be certain he had the firepower to defend himself if necessary. He wasn't a fighter pilot, but he was skilled and capable in defensive maneuvers.

Having left orbit around Bimordus Two with their course locked into the computer, Rolf turned his attention to the beautiful woman sitting in the copilot's seat beside him. Ilyssa peered intently out the viewscreen, a look of awe on her face.

"I don't think I'll ever get used to spaceflight," she commented, moistening her lips. Rolf's eyes followed her movement, then roamed to her hair, gleaming like a river of burnished copper where it flowed down her back and over the vibrant lime stretch bodysuit. She wore bright hues now that she could choose her own clothing, and the material fitted her body like a second skin.

"I travel often on diplomatic missions," he replied. "You'll have to get used to it if you come along with me."

She glanced at him, surprised. "What do you mean?"

He leaned over, putting his hand on hers. He'd been doing a lot of thinking on Bimordus Two. Even though he'd been busy, Ilyssa had remained constantly in his thoughts. Each day, he couldn't wait to come home and find her in his apartment. Her being there brightened his world and gave his life meaning. He'd confided in Teir and the starship captain had advised him to tell Ilyssa how he felt.

"I want you to stay with me, Ilyssa. According to the customs of my people, when a couple is betrothed, they must spend sixty days together in order to become intimately acquainted. During that time, they are considered as one even though they are not yet wed. I believe we already have a head start on those sixty days. We just need the ritual words pronounced to make it official, and we can have that done on Nadira."

"Is this a proposal?" she asked, stunned.

He gave her a devastating grin. She'd thought he was attractive before with his muscular build and long black hair, but now with his curly blond head, twinkling blue eyes, and powerful aura of authority, he was magnificent.

"Yes. Let's retire to the stateroom while you consider your response. I'd rather talk to you without this damn console in the way."

He checked the readings once more before unfastening his harness and helping her to rise. Silently, she preceded him out the hatchway, down a short corridor, and into the one and only sleeping cabin with double berths.

Whirling, she faced him. "Rolf, how can you want me when . . . when . . ." Embarrassed, she let her voice trail off uncertainly.

"When we can't consummate our relationship? We'll find a way around that problem. All I know is I can't live without you." He swept her into his arms. "Say yes, *larla*."

Ilyssa gazed up into his intense sapphire eyes. Being in such close physical contact with him, his mouth hovering centimeters above hers, she felt weak with desire. Yet to mate with him, she'd have to relinquish everything that gave her life meaning: her singing voice, her home on Circutia, the dream that had sustained her through annums of suffering on Souk. With all her heart, she wanted to stay with Rolf but couldn't commit herself to a marriage in name only. To be truly his, she'd have to discard everything she'd worked toward for most of her adult life. Now that the decision was upon her, Ilyssa knew what she had to do.

She pushed herself away to tighten her resolve. "I'd like to say yes, but I can't. I've waited too long for the chance to become an arbiter. Ruel made me use my siren song for evil. This is my chance to turn its use to good. I have to end the suffering, Rolf. I have to work for peace."

"I'm not asking you to give up your ambition. If you say you'll be mine, we'll work things out. There's got to be a way. Please don't make a final decision yet," he added. "Wait until we go to Athos. We're bound to learn more about your siren song on the planet of its origin."

"Very well."

She didn't want to say no. As she moved back into his arms and raised her head for him to kiss her, Ilyssa wanted more than anything to accept his proposal. But her intent to use her voice as a tool for good had only strengthened from her personal experiences. Music was a powerful mediator. It had the ability to heal, to comfort, to make the spirit soar. Music came from the spiritual realm, touching the innermost essence in everyone who heard it. It transcended bodily existence, thrusting the listener into a state of heightened awareness and increased receptiveness. She was blessed in being able to use her song to promote peace.

Tears moistened her eyes as she was fired with passion to realize her dream.

Rolf kissed the salty drops on her half-shut lids, murmuring her name. When he deftly began to unfasten her bodysuit, she didn't protest. Devotion to her cause had suddenly turned into the fiery passion of desire. And so commenced three days of blissful intimacy, the only restriction being that they were not able to join in body what they already felt in spirit.

"Tell me about Nadira," Ilyssa said 72 hauras later as they were entering orbit around Rolf's home planet. Down below, a greenish-blue globe spun against the velvety backdrop of space.

"The climate is tropical, vegetation is lush, and we have an abundance of water. With its beautiful scenery, Nadira is a popular vacation site for Coalition citizens." Rolf sat in the pilot's chair, monitoring the systems as the computer prepared for their descent through the atmosphere. "Exotic fruits and wines are popular exports along with rare plants."

"It sounds delightful. Where does your family live?"

"The imperator's palace is in the province of Najor. That's a hilly region to the north. We'll be landing at the spaceport closest to home."

"Your father is actually the leader of the planet?"

Rolf nodded. "Our heritage goes back many generations through the ruling House of Raimorrda. My elder brother, Erlin, is next in line for the throne." He flashed her a grin. "We call him Linnie."

When Rolf entered his family's home with Ilyssa, Linnie greeted them with enthusiasm. Rolf was grateful for his warm reception, especially when his father refused to acknowledge him. Rolf was hurt that even after all these annums, his father still hadn't forgiven him for his disgrace. He hadn't expected otherwise but hoped he was wrong.

Stifling his pain, he greeted his mother, who rushed out to meet them in the royal palace garden. Tall and dignified, her silver hair coiffed high on her head, Dorra appeared not an annum past 50 although she was nine annums beyond. The imperatrice was delighted to meet Ilyssa. She ushered her off on a tour, their gowns swishing along the gravel path. When Rolf had mentioned his father was a stickler for formality, Ilyssa had chosen to wear a long emerald dress for the visit.

"Why have you come?" Linnie asked when they were alone.

Rolf gazed fondly at his elder brother's fine features. Linnie was a blond like himself but there the resemblance ended. Although he did possess the Raimorrdan blue eyes, he was thinner, with a more angular face and lanky frame. What he lacked in weight, however, he made up for in agility and endurance. Linnie loved fencing as much as Rolf and was good at hunting, archery, and quippet, a competitive sport involving an obstacle course and hurdle jumping. For all his interest in sports, Linnie took his family obligations seriously. He kept abreast of political developments and worked as his father's aide on many difficult issues.

Rolf wanted to ask him about the family but his business took precedence. "I'm here to see Artemus," he stated, squinting. The sol was high at midday and the brightness was reflected by the brilliance of his brother's attire. Linnie looked elegant in an oyster-white ensemble with gold braided trim. At his belt was a jeweled blade similar to the one Rolf wore with the family crest on its hilt. Rolf's outfit was no less splendid. He wore a burgundy-colored tunic embroidered with silver threads and matching leggings.

"Why do you need to see Artemus?" Linnie asked.

"I have reason to believe he betrayed me." Rolf paused, taking a deep breath. Then he told his brother of his mission to Souk.

Linnie's expression ranged from disbelief to shock to dismay. "If Pasha Ruel was being truthful, Artemus is a traitor!" he declared when Rolf had finished.

"Indeed. I shall seek him out now. Will you see to Ilyssa, brother? I think it best if she remains here."

"She's a charming woman. Are you going to apply for the rites of betrothal?"

Rolf averted his gaze. "Not yet."

"I wish I could find someone like her." He gave a rueful smile, crinkles nestling in the corners of his eyes. "Father keeps introducing me to princesses and daughters of heads of state, but none of them appeals to me."

"Love will come when you least expect it." Rolf grinned. "I take it you are being pressured to find a mate."

Linnie inclined his head in a royal gesture of acknowledgment. "I bow to no one, brother. I shall find the lady of my heart in my own good time."

Rolf clapped him on the shoulder. "No doubt you will." And he left, taking a speeder from the family garage.

Artemus's reception was cool and wary. His boyhood friend had grown stout and his brown hair was receding on his wide forehead. The annums hadn't been kind to his features. His nose had grown broader and his tawny eyes limpid. He greeted Rolf within the bastions of his family mansion.

"What brings you to Nadira, my lord?" he asked after offering Rolf a goblet of local wine.

Rolf refused the beverage, preferring to get straight to the point. "I heard some news that disturbed me," Rolf said, facing him in the elegantly decorated salon. "Remember when I was young and smitten with love for Gayla? You urged me to elope with her."

Artemus's eyes narrowed. He stood by a stone fireplace, his arm resting on the mantel. "I beg to differ with you, Lord Cam'brii. You were the one who was too impatient to wait until Gayla became of age."

"I was impatient, but the idea of eloping never entered my head until you brought it up. And then conveniently you had a way for me to obtain a ship. Once you mentioned how easy it would be, it was as if I had no other choice." Running his fingers through his curls, he said: "You set me up, Artemus."

Artemus snorted. "You were so eager to be alone with Gayla that you took any carrot dangled in front of your face."

Rolf felt heat rise in his face and he clenched his fists. "Why did you tip off the Souks about our flight plan? They knew just where to intercept us. Were you hoping for a cut of my ransom payment?"

Artemus glared at him. "What is the point of this conversation?"

"I accuse you of betrayal. Do you deny it?"

For an instant, anger and hatred flared in Artemus's eyes, but then it was quickly covered by a deceptively calm expression. "No, I don't," he said, giving a small, tight smile. "But you have no proof, do you?"

Rolf stared at him, wounded by his confession. "Why, Artemus? I'd thought we were friends. We did everything together when we were younger: hunting, fishing, camping out in the Forest of Mirages. How could you go against me?"

Snickering, Artemus sauntered up to him. "Very simple. You had been bequeathed the piece of land adjacent to my father's property. I knew one day I would inherit everything, but if I could get hold of your property, too, I'd be rich beyond my dreams. According to the law, if you died, your personal real estate possessions would be put up for sale if you didn't have a will. I knew you had made one out, but you'd left everything to Gayla. You were both supposed to die."

For an instant, Rolf felt an irresistible urge to throttle him. But he held in his rage in an effort to gain information.

"That's not what Ruel told me when I encountered him on Souk." With gratification, he saw Artemus's expression crease with surprise. "He said I was to be ransomed and Gayla was to be sent to his brother Bdan as a slave."

Artemus shrugged. "Knowing the Souks, they'd have killed you after your father paid the ransom, and Gayla wouldn't have lasted long in a Souk harem. Either way, the result would have been the same."

"You've been monitoring my activities, reporting on me to the Souks. Why?"

"You always did have more than me." Artemus's eyes went cold. "It isn't fair. The best of everything always fell your way even when we were boys. It sickened me. And I still want that piece of property. It sits beside my land like a thorn in my side. You're not even here to administer it."

"I can have you arrested for your actions. Plotting against a member of the royal family is treason." Rolf straightened his shoulders. "Where is Pasha Ruel? He's left Souk and I want to find him."

"I wouldn't know. Let me warn you about taking any action against me, Rolf. I have friends in high places.

Don't think I'm the only one who considers the royal family to be an outmoded, expensive vehicle for power. You'd best beware."

Rolf was alarmed by his words. Was there a conspiracy here of which even his father was unaware?

Resting his hand on the hilt of his blade, he wrestled for a moment with the surging rage that charged through his veins. He should exact the penalty on Artemus himself for his grievous insult. But that would accomplish nothing. He needed to learn more about Artemus's activities and traitorous friends.

Facing his neighbor, he gave a small bow. "This isn't finished," he warned.

"Neither your family's power nor your position with the High Council can protect you from the winds of change. I suggest you return to Bimordus Two and remain there." Artemus bared his teeth in a thin-lipped smile. "You wouldn't want any evil to befall your lady friend while she's here, would you?"

"You wouldn't dare!" Rolf sucked in a breath at his impudence.

"Such an honor for you to visit. Until the next time." Artemus moved meaningfully to the door.

In his younger days, Rolf would have challenged the man to a duel and fought him. But now that he was older and more circumspect, he settled for stalking off, his head held high. For his own safety he feared not, but for his family he was concerned. He had to learn more about this ominous threat.

Upon his return home, Rolf sought an audience with his father at once, insisting on remaining outside the Receiving Hall until he was announced.

At last his father agreed to see him when told the matter was one of urgent concern to the throne. He looked well for his 60 annums. His hair had grayed and was slicked back over his shiny wide forehead. His blue eyes were piercingly alert. His sturdy form was still trim from what Rolf could see of it in his crimson royal robes. The refined features, reflected in Linnie's face, wrinkled into a frown when Rolf approached the dais.

Rolf made his expected obeisance, thudding his fist to his heart and bowing. Then he raised his face to look his father squarely in the eye.

"It's been a long time," he said.

"The first announcer told me your news was urgent." The imperator's expression remained impassive as he regarded Rolf.

Quickly, he related his suspicions about Artemus.

"Where did you learn of this treachery?" his father thundered. They were alone in the room. The imperator had dismissed all attendants when Rolf entered.

Rolf told him about his sojourn to Souk, describing the details of his mission, his spacecraft crash, and his internment in the slave labor camp. He told him about Ilyssa and their escape. And lastly, he told his father about Ruel and the pasha's final vow of vengeance.

He'd been standing the whole time while the imperator listened with a steady eye. Restless now, he shifted back and forth on the balls of his feet.

"Keep still," his father snapped, lost in thought. "If there's any truth to this, I must discover it. You will tell the council about Artemus." Then he called for the first announcer to summon his advisers.

When the six men and women arrived, they all retired to a conference chamber and sat around a long rectangular table with their leader at the head. An extra seat was brought in for Rolf, and Erlin was summoned to join them. The meeting lasted less than an haura: then the advisory council disbanded, appointing Linnie in charge of pursuing an investigation.

"If we uncover a plot against us, we will be grateful to you," the imperator said, rising from his seat. He strolled toward Rolf, stopping behind his chair and putting a hand on his shoulder. "I'm glad you have come home, son." The words were said hesitantly, embarrassedly.

Rolf twisted, peering up into his father's face. It was lined with sorrow and regret. Rising, he squared his shoulders. "I have paid for my mistakes, Father. Will you forgive me?"

"It is you who must forgive me, Rolf. I'm a foolish old man. I should never have punished you, knowing how much you were suffering already." He stepped forward, holding out his arms as though they were weighted with lead.

Rolf stepped into his embrace and hugged him tightly, his heart constricting with feelings of redemption and love. From his mind a heavy load was lifted, but he had one more place to go before it would be entirely dissipated.

Rolf went to see Gayla's parents. Kneeling before them, he offered his homage and his story. When he'd finished, they told him to rise. "You were tricked and betrayed," Gayla's father said, his tone sad. His amber eyes reminded Rolf of Gayla and for a moment he felt a twinge of pain. But it was only a feeling of loss for a girl's gentle life lost out of the impetuousness of youth and the treachery of a childhood friend.

"You have paid your dues," Gayla's mother said, her soft chestnut hair framing a face unlined by the annums. "We no longer hold you responsible for Gayla's death. You have discharged your obligations regarding the Souks. Go now, Lord Cam'brii, and find happiness for yourself."

Elated, Rolf left to seek out Ilyssa, to tell her he was free, to express his joy and love to her.

He took her to the Rainbow Glen, his favorite hideaway on Nadira. "I love this place," he said, leading her to the banks of an aquamarine lake nestled in a lush valley with a waterfall cascading in the distance. The spray from the waterfall misted the humid air and coated the fronds of palms and giant ferns with sparkling droplets of moisture. Fields of bright orange and red tubella blooms swayed in the breeze amid the lush tropical greenery, their musical tinkle riding on the warm current of air.

Rolf knelt before Ilyssa, taking her hand in his. Lovingly, he drank in the sweet picture she made with her red hair falling over her shoulders, the golden highlights gleaming in the sun. Her gold-specked green eyes were warmly fixed on his face. She sat on a flat-topped rock. Rolf had come here many times with Gayla. They'd frolicked in the water, naked. As his eyes roamed over Ilyssa, he thought he'd like nothing better than to slowly undress her and make love to her here among the perfumed flowers with bird songs twittering in the air.

"I've fulfilled my duty," he began, giving her an account of his meetings with Artemus, his father, and Gayla's parents.

As Ilyssa listened, she was filled with a strange sense of peace. Being here in this tranquil setting, with the man of her dreams about to pledge his devotion, she felt like bursting into song. And yet the fact that she couldn't became like a painful vise around her heart. It made their trip to Athos all the more imperative so she could discover the truth about her siren song.

"I'm glad you've reconciled with your father," she said kindly, smiling at him.

"Do you realize what this means, Ilyssa?" His earnest azure eyes stared into hers. "I'm free now. I can live my own life for the first time in over ten annums. Please say you'll be part of it. We can hear the rites of betrothal spoken before we leave. I want you to be mine. I love you, Ilyssa."

Her eyes filled with moisture as she bid him to rise. She stood and faced him. "I wish I could accept your offer, Rolf, but I have my own course to follow. Having lived firsthand as a slave, having suffered the horrors of bondage and seen the stirrings of war, I must do my part to promote peace. I shall use my gift to that end."

"So you'll keep your virginity. You've seen there are other ways we can satisfy each other." Desperately, he clung to her hands.

"No, it wouldn't work. You need a woman who can devote herself to you, who can support you in your illustrious career. I heard hints on Bimordus Two that Glotaj was getting ready to name you as his choice for his successor. After Athos, I go to Circutia. I have to remain there to train as an arbiter."

"You can't leave me!" He pulled her into his arms, burying his face in her hair.

Ilyssa shared his pain and yearned to accept his love. But although his soul had been cleansed and he was free of his bonds, she wasn't released from her obligations. She had only this short time with him before she'd have to go her separate way. Her arms snaked around his neck, then she lifted her head. She wanted to make every minute count.

His mouth was on hers in an instant with a crushing kiss. How could she leave him? he asked himself, tormented. What would he do without her? His hands roamed her back as though by his frantic movements he could convince her to become his mate. She'd refused to give up her goals for him, but he'd find another way to keep her at his side. Clutching her closer, he decided to enjoy this time alone with her.

"Ilyssa, we'll talk more of this later. I want to make love to you now, to feel your body close to mine." Already his breathing was rough and ragged. Stepping away from her, he cast off his clothes, standing before her naked.

Heat rose to her face as her gaze traveled downward. By the stars, she longed to join with him, to know what it was like—

Eagerly, she began stripping off her long gown. They could at least enjoy each other, even if they couldn't consummate their love. As he'd said, there were other ways, she thought as she followed him into the lake.

Standing hip-deep in the water, naked, and kissing Ilyssa with wild passion, Rolf remembered another time, another place, when he'd been with Sarina in a replica of the Rainbow Glen on Bimordus Two. Intent on impressing her, he'd been totally oblivious to his surroundings and the threat of assassination. Then, as now, he'd been defenseless. If it hadn't been for Teir's vigilance when the Twyggs attacked, he and Sarina would both have been killed.

As his mouth moved over Ilyssa's, his eyes roamed the peaceful jungle. Before long, his mind became caught up in a rising tide of sensual pleasure and he spiraled out of control. But despite his burning flame of passion, in the back of his consciousness remained a reminder that somewhere, somehow, Ruel was going to make his next move against them.

Chapter Twenty

Rolf glanced at Ilyssa seated beside him on the bridge of the *Destiny.* She was scanning the data banks aboard the ship, searching for reading material. Feathery wisps of auburn hair swept across her brow as she leaned forward, peering intently at the readouts on the monitor screen.

They were en route to Athos, several days away even at a speed of warp eight. Little of interest existed on the main viewscreen. Drifting molecules undetectable to the naked eye were the only phenomenon present in this region of interstellar space, and boredom was setting in. Glancing at Ilyssa's shapely legs beneath her short-skirted outfit, Rolf fancied an easy diversion.

"Want to retire to the cabin?" he asked, smiling. He wouldn't accept her refusal to wed him. Somehow he'd convince her things could work out to their mutual satisfaction. Like her, he was hoping to find a solution to their problems on Athos.

Ilyssa's eyes sparkled as she glanced at him, but before she could utter a response, a familiar voice broke in on the subspace radio frequency relegated to the Defense League. "This is the *Valiant* calling *Destiny.* Is everything all right?" Teir Reylock's voice rang out loud and clear.

"We're fine. What are you doing here?" Rolf asked, surprised.

"We're on patrol in the Theta sector. I just thought I'd check in."

"Our long-range sensors aren't picking up anything, but we're keeping a sharp lookout," Rolf said, his eyes automatically sweeping the instrumentation.

"If Ruel is anything like his late brother Bdan, he won't give up on you." Tier's voice was gruff. "Are you sure you don't require an escort?"

Rolf smiled grimly. "We're fine."

"Are you carrying a personal shooter these days, or still that favored blade of yours?"

"My blade is sufficient."

"You might reconsider going to Athos. You don't know what kind of a reception you'll get, assuming you locate the place."

Rolf looked at Ilyssa and rolled his eyes. "Your concern is duly noted and appreciated. Have you anything to report?"

"The Admiral heard from Star Gazer. The mines at the Rocks of Weir have been out of operation for a couple of weeks. Rumor has it that the Morgots have sent an emissary to learn why their trade agreement has been violated. Their orders for piragen ore have not been filled and someone's going to take the heat."

"Ruel's in trouble," Ilyssa said, grinning. "What else did Devin . . . Star Gazer . . . say?" She was relieved her brother was doing well.

"He said something about experiencing strange sensory effects after hearing you sing. What's that about?"

Ilyssa exchanged glances with Rolf. "He heard my siren song. I'm not sure what happened to him. Did he elaborate?"

"No. He said he might want to go to Athos himself."

"We'll check it out first," Rolf said. "If we don't cut communications now, Ruel or his spies might find us before we get there."

"Right." Regret sounded in Teir's voice. "Reylock out." The link terminated.

Rolf scratched his itchy leg. He was casually dressed in a loose blue shirt and navy trousers. "What happened to Devin when he heard you sing?" he asked Ilyssa.

She shrugged, her long braid swaying with the movement. "He said he was able to hear things he'd never heard before, like sounds of nature. I'm not sure I understand. But speaking of siren song, the females on Athos might possess the same talent as I do. We need to get you another set of earplugs."

As she rose to head for the fabricator, her thoughts turned to the mystical planet of her song's origin. Did Athos really exist? Who lived there? How had she obtained the ability to seduce men into a trance with her song? Would she find a cure for her father and learn the truth about the myth?

Several days later, they broke through the Spidrex Nebula and discovered the planet on the other side. The world was hidden by the brightness of the emission cloud but the coordinates matched the supposed location for Athos. A plasma-charged atmosphere made sensor readings of the surface impossible.

"We're going to have to go in blind," Rolf said as he maneuvered the ship into orbit. "If the environment appears inhospitable, we'll reverse course." Foremost in his mind were the stories of ships that had been lost in the area. Rumors of a black hole near the Nebula kept most travelers away. Rolf was curious to learn what had happened to those missing ships but not if it proved too dangerous.

To their shocked surprise, once they descended to a low altitude, a dazzling landscape met their eyes.

"By the heavens!" Ilyssa exclaimed, leaning forward as she peered out the viewscreen. "Everything's made of crystal." Glittering cities with multihued crystal spires ringed the globe. Forests, fields, mountains, and oceans filled their eyes. The land masses were entirely carved from transparent colored rock. "Where will we touch down?"

Sensor readings popped onto the command display. "Here's a signal coming in," Rolf said, excited. "It leads over there." He pointed to a large city in the distance. "Looks like they have a spaceport. Computer, lock onto nav beacon and begin automatic landing sequence."

"How can the crystal grow in this fashion?" Ilyssa said, amazed. A myriad of colors splashed everywhere. As they approached the spaceport, she caught sight of the terminal, a huge complex shaped like a transparent ruby prism in a diamond shape. She gripped her armrests, preparing for the landing.

Emerging from their spacecraft, they were greeted by a reception committee. The women were tall and powerfully built but dressed very erotically with their full-figured bodies sheathed in colorful drapes. The combination of strength with feminine allure didn't go unnoticed by Rolf. Warily, he fingered the earplugs in his pocket. He'd dressed in his full diplomatic regalia: a royal blue tunic with elaborate gold trim, matching trousers, and shiny black boots. His jeweled blade was fastened at his side.

Ilyssa had dressed for the occasion by clipping back her hair with two diamella gemstone clasps Rolf had given her on Nadira. She wore a jade-green gown, its tightly fitted bodice complimenting her figure. A flared skirt came to her ankles, and she wore soft-soled shoes to match. She wanted to make a good impression since this could be considered a diplomatic mission. Rolf represented the Coalition, and it wouldn't do for her to violate a dress code. Some cultures, like the Souks, did not appreciate women in breeches.

"Welcome to Athos," said a young woman with long black hair whose lush form was sheathed in a lavender drape. Her violet eyes regarded them in keen appraisal. "I am called Alita. These are Hanna, Althea, and Raman. We will take you to the Liani."

"That's your leader?" Rolf asked, falling into step behind her along with Ilyssa. He walked with his hand on the hilt of his blade. It paid to be cautious, no matter how innocuous a setting appeared. He'd learned that through experience. None of these women were armed and their planet seemed defenseless, but they could have other ways to dispose of unwanted visitors.

The *Destiny* was the only ship in the dock, which made him wonder why there was a spaceport at all. If these people lived in isolation from the rest of the galaxy and most travelers steered clear of the area, why would they need a facility of this size?

His suspicions deepened and he kept a sharp lookout, noting the route they were taking in case he and Ilyssa had to make a quick exit.

After being led through a maintenance area, they came to a tunnel system where a huge transparent plasticine bubble rested on an open platform. Inside the bubble Rolf could see four rows of seats. As indicated by their hostess, he entered the open hatchway and settled on one of the clear crystalline seats. He was taken aback when it shifted to accommodate his size. Ilyssa sat beside him, close enough that their shoulders touched. He inched his hand to cover hers.

"This is our public conveyor system," Alita said in her singsong voice, a smile playing upon her lips. She took a seat in front of them, and the other three females took up a position behind them. Rolf's feeling of unease increased. This reminded him of the time when he'd sat in Ruel's scramjet, only then it had been armed Souk guards flanking him, not beautiful women. These females could be just as dangerous if they possessed the gift of siren song.

"Assembly Hall," Alita intoned, and a whirring sound filled his ears. The hatch swung shut and they were enclosed inside the bubble. With a sudden lurch, the vehicle whizzed off through the tunnel, through an area of blackness, then zoomed out into a city of such dazzling brightness that Rolf couldn't see until his eyes adjusted. A whole network of transparent tubes crisscrossed the city. Bubbles like theirs streaked past on other byways. They were whisked around so fast his stomach lurched.

"You get used to it," Alita grinned, as though sensing his discomfort.

A few minutes later, their journey ended. Their bubble stopped in front of a huge pyramid-shaped structure made entirely out of topaz crystal. The late afternoon sun struck the building at such an angle that the steep sides glowed like fire.

"What is this crystal rock?" Ilyssa asked, stepping out onto a moving walkway that led into the building.

The Liani answered her question after greeting them inside a small reception chamber. She offered them refreshments while they sat and explained the purpose of their visit.

The Liani was a kindly faced, older woman with gray hair twisted around her body like a coverup over her diaphanous peach drape. Her body was still firm even though her lined face suggested she was in her sixties.

"The crystal is *vacchus,*" the Liani explained. "It is alive."

"Alive!" Ilyssa exclaimed. Glancing around, she observed with keen interest the smooth, ivory walls and the ledges that extended out to serve as shelves; the crimson table that rose from a pedestal fixed in the floor; the lighting that came from hidden recesses around the room. Small mementos and objects of art lined the shelves. Electronic gizmos were noticeably absent. Ilyssa wondered about their level of advancement in communications and technology.

"Where do you get your food?" she asked. Athos was isolated from the trade routes. Everything had to be grown here and recycled.

"We use hydroponic farming techniques, and the seas have an abundance of fish. The *vacchus* supplies most everything else we need."

"It's like my aramus," Rolf said in astonishment. "The ivory carpet in my apartment is a live creature who loves to be trampled. It shows its pleasure by the musical chimes it plays when you step upon it." He spoke to the Liani. "Do you have a symbiotic relationship with your *vacchus?*"

She nodded. "The *vacchus* lives and grows with music. We sing to it; it forms into any shape we desire. I'd give you a demonstration but you would hear my siren song."

"I have earplugs." Rolf stuffed them into his ears, signaling for the Liani to continue.

The older woman opened her mouth and Ilyssa heard the clearest notes ever emerging from her throat. The walls rippled for an instant like a mirage.

"Give us an armchair if it pleases you, Rock of our Ages!" the Liani commanded.

The marblelike floor at their feet distorted and a blob of gelatinous liquid emerged in an upward thrust where it shaped itself into a chair and solidified into a beautiful piece of furniture, albeit colorless.

"Make it coral," the Liani said, and the chair infused with color.

"This entire world is constructed from living crystal," the Liani continued when Rolf returned the earplugs to his pocket. "The only exceptions are the oceans and the Forbidden Mountains to the west. None of our kind has been there in recent times. It is said the trees on the verdant slopes are living beings and they twist apart any trespassers to their territory. The only creatures known to roam the fertile forests are unicorns, animals of such astounding beauty that images of them were carved onto the walls of ancient crystal caverns by our earliest inhabitants."

"You say the *vacchus* thrives on music?" Ilyssa asked, leaning forward to help herself to a sweetcake from a dish on the table in front of them. "Does this mean you can all sing, or do you play instruments?" She took a bite of the cake, careful not to make crumbs. Rolf sat rigidly at her side on the double lounger, his stance tense. Ilyssa wondered why he didn't relax. If the Liani had intended to beguile him, she wouldn't have warned him about hearing her song.

The Liani smiled. "We all sing, sister. Our song and the beauty of our land is why travelers who stray here never leave. Either way, they're entranced by the place."

"I didn't see any men," Rolf stated.

"We haven't many, but they are here. Although ours is a matriarchal society, we honor our men. They give us children, our future."

"What about boy children? Do they remain here, too?" Rolf asked.

"Certain peculiarities in our environment predispose us to bear mainly girls. When a boy child is born, he usually leaves with his father. Of course, the father is sworn to secrecy about his sojourn here."

"So the occasional visitor does leave," Rolf said.

"Indeed. Occasionally a sister decides to leave us also. We do not restrict our populace from departing; we just don't encourage it. I suspect this is how you inherited your gift, Ilyssa." The woman's green eyes turned on her. "One of your ancestors must have been from Athos. Siren song is a sex-dominant trait for females but men can be carriers."

"My brother Devin was affected by my song but not by becoming mindwashed. It seems to have enhanced his listening ability. He's able to perceive sounds he never heard before."

The Liani's eyes crinkled appreciatively. "Invite him to visit us. I should like to study this unusual reaction."

"My mother says it's possible that the trait came from her family, even though my father is the one with musical talent. He's a composer of popular music and now he is ill. He's been mindwashed for eight annums and suffers from senilis disease. I want to know what I can do to help him."

"A mindwash can only be reversed by listening to a shell from the Sea of Serenity."

"What's that?" Hope surged in her breast. At last, here was a possible cure!

"It's a special mollusk that must be obtained at dawn as the tide recedes. Should you wish to go to the Sea of Serenity, I shall have to make arrangements at once." She smiled at Rolf. "You may remain here and enjoy our hospitality."

"No, thanks," he replied. "I'd rather accompany Ilyssa."

A shadow crossed the Liani's face. "We have many wonders we could show you. I'll assign an escort to show you around. You can meet the men of our city and see how happy they are to share our lives."

Rolf weighed her words. Did she hope to add him to the collection of males entrapped here? Would the Liani sing to him once Ilyssa was gone?

"I'll go with Ilyssa," he insisted stubbornly. Besides, he didn't like the idea of her going anywhere alone.

"Hers is a personal quest to aid her father. Perhaps Ilyssa wishes to complete her task alone. You would do best to remain here."

The words almost sounded like an order. Rolf gave her a suspicious glance but her impassive expression told him nothing. Suddenly the tranquillity of the place and its beauty struck him as a fragile bubble that might burst at any moment. Something wasn't right here. His sense of impending danger strengthened.

"Another time," he said in his gracious, diplomatic voice. Rising, he held out his hand to Ilyssa. "We'll both head for the Sea of Serenity, Liani, if you would be so good as to direct us."

The Liani bowed, but not before he saw the hasty flush of anger on her face. "You make things more difficult," she muttered. "So be it. Follow me."

Behind the building was a launchpad for a solar sailer. Rolf had seen this method of transportation used on Altara Four. It consisted of a passenger basket, currently tethered to the ground by ropes. Sturdy wires attached the basket to a main rig of billowing sails.

"The course is already laid in," the Liani said, ushering them into the basket which on Athos was made out of woven crystal strips.

"How did you know where we'd be going?" Rolf asked, narrowing his eyes.

The Liani appeared at a loss for words. "I . . . I guessed you might have come here on an errand of mercy," she said at last, looking flustered.

Rolf's conviction increased that something was dreadfully wrong but he didn't want to worry Ilyssa. He'd bide his time until she got the seashell.

"What does the shell look like?" Ilyssa asked, wondering what they would do if the beach was strewn with different types of mollusks.

"There is only one at the Sea of Serenity." The Liani smiled enigmatically.

"We have to wait for dawn? What then? How do we get back here?"

It was too late for answers. A couple of female workers had unleashed the ropes and they were rising.

Up, up they drifted and then the whir of a motor kicked in and the apparatus veered left. Ilyssa cried out, alarmed. It was difficult to keep her balance in the swaying basket. The crystalline city receded below and she clutched at Rolf, frightened.

"It's just like a flyboard," he reassured her.

"This goes higher." Her breathing was shallow. What if they got caught in a fierce downdraft?

"Rest easy. I don't think they would have sent us up here if it wasn't safe." He plopped down on the pebbled surface of the basket's interior and peered out through the ruby tinted crystal strips. The view below was strangely beautiful with the late afternoon sun casting a surreal glow over the crystalline earth.

Ilyssa sank into a position beside him, curling her body against his to protect herself from the wind. The air was cool and dry.

"You'll get that shell for your father and then we'll leave," he told her, putting an arm around her slim shoulders.

"I can't." She looked at him. "I have to ask them about the siren song and . . . and what would happen if I . . . if you . . ." Embarrassed, she faltered for the right words.

He clamped his lips together. "Of course." How could he have forgotten? During the voyage, they'd shared a cabin on the *Destiny,* falling into each other's arms at every opportunity. But he was becoming restless and dissatisfied, unable to resist his growing need for her, and he knew she also felt the urge to join with him, to unite their bodies in the ecstasy of love. But she'd rather deny her desire than give up her lifelong dream. They couldn't leave Athos without learning if there was a solution.

The sun was beginning to descend by the time they reached their destination. Having spent a couple of pleasant hauras kissing Ilyssa and caressing her, he rose from his cramped position and stretched. She got up, her face flushed, her hair in disarray, and her lips reddened from his touch.

Straightening the skirt of her gown, she grabbed at him when the whirring noise from above suddenly quieted, leaving a noticeable silence amid the rush of wind. The basket dipped and swayed.

Before they realized what was happening, a cobalt-blue sand beach was rushing up at them, and they caught a glimpse of waves crashing to shore. The water reflected the pink glow of the sky. Their touchdown onto the soft bed of sand was bumpy but rapid. Dazed, they stepped out of the basket and peered around.

"What are those dots on the water?" Rolf asked, squinting. He could have used a set of viewfinder glasses.

Shading her eyes with her hand, Ilyssa studied the horizon. "I don't see anything. According to the Liani, we have to wait for dawn. I'm thirsty. I wonder why she didn't give us any provisions."

Glancing around, she noticed tall sand dunes rising behind them. The setting sun gleamed off the tiny particles as though they were shards of blue glass. The sand seemed to be composed entirely of minuscule blue rock crystals.

Her gaze slid back to the water and her eyes widened. "You're right, I do see something out there!" As she watched the dots grow larger, her ears picked up the sudden whir of the solar sailer motor coming from behind.

"The craft is lifting!" Giving a cry of dismay, she ran over to grab at one of the dangling ropes. Jumping high, Ilyssa couldn't reach it and gave up.

Rolf watched their sole means of transportation sail away. Compressing his lips, he turned to stare out to sea. The objects on the water were heading in their direction.

"Great suns! Those are combat hovercraft." They were similar to the ones driven by Yanuk's troops in the Nurash Desert. Helmeted figures became distinguishable and Rolf saw they were Souks dressed in gray military uniforms. As the lead vessel sped into view, the shock spreading through him exploded.

"It's Ruel!" he hollered.

Beside him, Ilyssa screamed.

In unison, they turned to run toward the dunes, but more hovercraft flew into view from over the rise.

Ilyssa screamed again and threw herself into his arms. "Don't let him capture me!" she cried, hysterical. "I won't be his slave again!"

"Neither will I," Rolf vowed, thrusting her to one side. With the speed of lightning, he unsheathed his short sword. But even as he took a fighting stance, he knew their situation was hopeless. They were incredibly outnumbered. Ruel had brought scores of troops with him, all with the aim of capturing him and Ilyssa. They'd been set up, he realized grimly. He wondered if the seashell they sought even existed. The Liani had sent them into a trap.

Ilyssa took a position back-to-back with him. She was determined to fight. Cursing her soft-soled shoes for not having any heels, she dug into the sand to gain a steady foothold.

The soldiers unloaded from their vehicles in a crouching run, their weapons aimed. Ilyssa's heart sank as she understood they wouldn't even have the chance to fight with those laser rifles pointed at them. Ruel would demand their immediate surrender. The pasha was nearing and as soon as he reached shore, it would be over.

Her gaze fell upon the blue sand beneath her feet. What a beautiful beach. She hated to soil it with her blood but she refused to be taken alive. She opened her mouth to tell Rolf she'd rather die than be Ruel's prisoner again, when an idea suddenly struck her and the words died on her tongue. She kept silent, thinking fast.

The soldiers formed concentric circles around them, leaving space for their leader. When Ruel landed directly in front of them, the Souk commandant barked out an order and the safety mechanisms on their weapons were released.

Ruel lumbered up to them. "A pleasure it is to see you again. Lord Cam'brii, cast aside your sword."

"You'll have to kill us to take us," Rolf gritted, glaring at the pasha.

"Wish you to make things difficult?" Ruel's hand went to his utility belt where a number of weapons dangled. He'd worn a uniform for this excursion rather than one of his usually cumbersome caftans.

"It is you who must surrender," Ilyssa said, moistening her lips. She tilted her chin upward at the amused glance the pasha gave her. "I will use my voice against your troops."

Ruel guffawed. "Your siren song doesn't work out in the open, and even if it did, we've altered our implanted linguist patches so as not to hear changes in human female pitch. How else do you think we coerced the women of this planet to obey us? Defenseless are they without the power of their song. I told the Liani you would probably show up in an effort to save your father, and r-r-revealed the cure did she. The trap was easily laid. Already my ship had entered orbit around a small moon on the other side of the planet so it wouldn't be detected by your sensors. Came down by shuttle did I. When the Liani told me about the shell, I decided to wait here for you."

"I'll give you one more chance," Ilyssa said coldly. "Give up now or lose."

The pasha threw back his head and laughed. Rolf glanced at her, hoping she wasn't bluffing.

"Rolf, put your earplugs in."

Hastily, he complied with his free hand, uncertain what she hoped to accomplish but trusting her.

Ilyssa's lips curled into a smile. "Watch and learn," she told Ruel. Taking a deep breath, she filled her lungs with oxygen. Then from her throat came a single high, sustained note that pierced the air.

The sand shifted beneath their feet.

Ilyssa rapidly alternated two notes in a trill.

The blue sand spurted.

Ilyssa stared at Ruel. "Give us protection if it pleases you, Rock of our Ages!" she commanded, using the same sequence of words as the Liani had.

And the sand rose up, swirling at the feet of each soldier, spiraling in a column around them, until their astonished features were obscured in a cloud of blue particles.

"Not him!" Rolf cried, pointing to Ruel, and Ilyssa stopped the blue sand from enclosing him. "I want him for myself," Rolf said, yanking the earplugs out of his ears so he could hear.

A look of astonishment on his ugly dogface, Ruel whipped an electrifier from his belt and aimed it at Ilyssa. Rolf kicked it out of Ruel's hand before he could fire.

The blue mist surrounding each of Ruel's troops congealed, freezing them inside a case of transparent blue crystal.

Ruel faced Rolf, baring his teeth in a feral grin. "Very clever. Now it is just you against me." He snatched a shooter from his belt, but Rolf deflected it with his sword.

"Ilyssa, get him a blade. We'll do this my way."

A few words from her, and Ruel found a sword in his hand. "You think to defeat me, puny human? Stronger than you am I."

"We'll see." Rolf appraised his opponent. The pasha had the advantage of size but he had agility in his favor, and he was skilled from annums of fencing practice on Bimordus Two. The twilight was a fitting send-off for Pasha Ruel, he thought, bending his knees and tensing.

Raising his arm, he lunged.

After a quick exchange, Rolf forced the Souk into retreat. Having the advantage, he pressed furiously forward, dealing blows which the pasha vigorously parried. Ruel shifted his weapon with great dexterity so as to protect himself, and in some instances, ducked beneath Rolf's attacking sword to deliver a thrust of his own. Still on the defensive, he easily deflected Rolf's blows with his hands and feet and showed no signs of weakening.

Rolf brought his blade crashing down upon Ruel's. Effortlessly, his opponent deflected the blow with a defensive turn of his own weapon. Again Rolf attacked. Once again their blades clashed. They stood, staring at one another for an endless moment through their crossed swords.

"You will not win," Ruel growled, drool on his lower lip.

Rolf didn't waste time with words. He disengaged his weapon and lunged again. With every thrust of his sword, he drove the Souk back. The sand beneath his booted feet shifted with every blow and parry and thrust of his weapon. Ruel used his blade to ward off his aggressive lunges. Rolf tried a feint, stomping his foot to distract his opponent, but Ruel didn't fall for it. Instead, the pasha used a circular movement to lift Rolf's blade and change the line of engagement.

Ilyssa remained off to the side, listening as the clashing of blades clanged through the air. Her eyes were glued on her stalwart champion sweating from his exertions. He was an accomplished swordsman but so was Ruel, and the pasha wasn't even short of breath. The Souk's bulk was pure muscle, and it showed in his athletic prowess. But determination glinted in Rolf's eyes, giving him added strength.

Rolf threatened the pasha with another thrust. His legs shook with the continued exhaustion of battling his fierce opponent. He made a short, forward jump followed by a lunge, his arm aching. He tried to throw off Ruel's timing but the pause didn't work. Ruel's cadence continued to match his own.

Ruel sidestepped a blow, and as Rolf advanced, the pasha slowly moved backward in retreat. Rolf lunged at him with another powerful swing. But when Ruel blocked his straight thrust with a forceful parry, Rolf lost his balance, stumbling. Ruel immediately jumped forward. As Rolf endeavored to parry his thrust, Ruel swung his weapon around, intending to deliver a final, vicious blow. His gleaming blade sliced through the air and would have crashed down on Rolf's head had he not pivoted. The blow ended as a hit to his left arm.

Feeling the lancing pain, Rolf gripped the hilt of his sword tighter in his right hand, but Ruel had already gained the advantage. Now their positions were reversed. Ruel was on the offensive, Rolf on the defensive. The whites of Ruel's eyes shone as he delivered a series of crashing blows, but Rolf successfully fought him off. Dancing back and forth on the balls of his feet, he found it hard to remain steady on the shifting sand. His blade swished through the air, clanging against Ruel's time and again until his body shook with exhaustion.

Determined to finish the fight, he broke out of their latest engagement with a bind, taking his opponent's blade from a high line diagonally to a low line. Using the inner portion of his sword, he forced Ruel's arm down, then hooked the weapon out of his hand and sent it flying.

Ruel stumbled backward, losing his balance, and ended up sprawled on the ground.

Rolf thrust the point of his sword at Ruel's throat. "So," he sneered, "you'll win, will you? Who's the victor now?"

"Go ahead, kill me. My brethren will take their revenge on you." Ruel's breath came in loud snorts.

Rolf pushed the point of his blade forward so it pierced the pasha's bluish skin. "Before I went to Souk, I would have gladly run you through. Indeed, my intent was to take my revenge on Gayla's murderer, but it turned out to be your son who was already dead. Then I learned that you were the one who'd ordered assassins to kill me."

"Is that what you plan to do with me, then? Take me back to stand trial before the High Council for attempting to assassinate you?"

"You're a criminal," Rolf responded. "You've violated the First Amendment, attacked our citizens, killed and enslaved thousands of innocent people. The winds of change have swept your land, Ruel, and a new age of freedom is dawning. Your tyranny has ended. I hear the Morgots want to talk to you about a breach of contract. You know what they did to your brother, Cerrus Bdan. It is only fitting that you should meet the same fate. By my hand, you will not die, nor will you stand trial before the High Council. The Morgots will act as your judges."

Ruel's face paled. "What do you mean?"

"Summon your ship."

"Communications are impeded by the plasma-charged atmosphere. Have to r-r-return directly by shuttle do I."

A faint whirring noise sounded in the air, and all three looked up. Billowing in on the wind was the solar sailer. It landed and the Liani emerged from the woven crystal basket. With her were several of her aides.

"I see you have rid our land of these invaders, sister," the older woman said to Ilyssa, smiling.

Ilyssa was relieved to see her. She'd wondered how they would get off the beach. Night was falling rapidly and the salty air was growing cool. She hadn't relished spending the dark hauras here with Ruel and his ghostly comrades who stood frozen like crystallized ice formations needing only the sun to melt them. Their twisted blue shapes made an eerie landscape.

"You knew I'd think of some way to use my song, didn't you?" Ilyssa asked the Liani.

The planetary leader's drape fluttered in the breeze despite the long tendrils of gray hair she'd wrapped around it. Her green eyes twinkled as she replied. "Our *vacchus* takes care of us. Had you not commanded it, it would have seen you had come to no harm. You are one of us, Ilyssa."

The Liani turned to her assistants. "I'll ask the *vacchus* to partially lower the shield around each Souk soldier. Use your adjustors to alter their implanted translators so they can hear our song."

"I thought you couldn't use it out in the open to mindwash people," Rolf commented, a puzzled frown on his face. Singing to command the crystal rock was one thing; singing to mindwash someone was different. "Ilyssa told me the notes would be too diluted."

"On Athos, our song works everywhere. What do you wish to do with Pasha Ruel?"

"Alter his translator and mindwash him," Rolf said grimly.

"No!" Ruel screamed, scrabbling to get up. Rolf's sword point pricked at his throat, forcing him back.

"Ilyssa, order him to return to his ship and set course for Morgot space. His fate will meet up with him there," Rolf commanded.

Ilyssa noticed the dark blotch on the sand and her eyes widened. "You're bleeding!"

"It's just a superficial cut on my arm. I'll take care of it later. Let's get Ruel out of here." He stuck his earplugs in his ears and waited.

"You can't mindwash me!" Ruel bellowed, his ugly dogface distorted with rage and fear.

But the sisters entranced his soldiers and a couple of Souk troopers held him while his implanted translator was adjusted. They continued to hold him while Ilyssa sang.

Ruel screamed his protest until he heard Ilyssa's clear, high notes carrying on the breeze, and then his eyes glazed and his cries died on his lips.

After she gave her orders, he rose and commanded his soldiers to head for the hovercraft. They'd rendezvous with their shuttle and lift off, docking with his ship in orbit around the moon. Then he'd set course for Morgot space. At the instant he met defeat, he would become fully alert so he could realize what was happening. Ilyssa considered it to be a gratifying send-off.

She watched him depart, thinking at last she was free of him. Turning to Rolf with joy, she was about to throw herself into his arms to celebrate but stopped herself when she saw he was otherwise engaged. Rolf was tending to his wound with a tissue regenerator the Liani must have produced after he'd removed his earplugs. Watching his bent blond head, she thought of the other reasons she'd come to Athos.

"The seashell . . . does it really exist?" she asked the Liani.

The leader of Athos had been gazing at the ocean but now turned her attention to Ilyssa. "It does, sister. You must remain here until dawn."

"Until dawn? What are we going to do until then?" One way to pleasurably pass the time came to mind. "Liani, is it true that if I love a man my singing voice will be lost?"

The Liani raised an eyebrow. "To learn the answer to that question, you must abstain from touching your man until the sol sets again. When you have obtained your seashell, return to our capital city of Melos. The solar sailer will come for you in the morning."

"I can't touch him at all?" Glancing at him watching her with a crooked grin, she yearned to run her fingers through his thick curly hair, to taste his lips and merge her body with his. Their recent danger had heightened her desire.

"Remember, you must abstain," the Liani said, smiling enigmatically as she made her departure.

As the moon rose and cast its silvery glow on the water, Rolf gazed longingly into her eyes. "I guess we'll have to wait, won't we?" he whispered huskily.

Twenty-six hauras passed before Ilyssa and Rolf were ushered into the Liani's presence again. Exhausted, they'd fallen asleep on the beach and had awakened to a glorious dawn. Glancing at the shoreline, Ilyssa had panicked when she didn't see any seashells. The cobalt sand was as smooth as powder. It wasn't until she had waded into the water that she discovered the large mollusk half-buried in the sandy bottom. The shell had a thick pointed spiral shape with a wide outer lip and a smooth pink concave surface.

The solar sailer had arrived for them as promised, and they'd landed back in the city. Already it was late morning. They'd been taken directly to the reception salon, where the Liani greeted them. Offering refreshments, the leader insisted on hearing Ilyssa's full story. Ilyssa found herself telling the Liani about her life on Souk, how she and Rolf had met, and her ambition to become an arbiter. But before she could think selfishly of herself, she had to help her father.

"How does this work?" she asked finally, holding up the hefty seashell.

"Hold it to your ear," the leader of Athos said.

Ilyssa did so, her eyes widening in astonishment. "I hear . . . voices."

"All of our sisters who came before us deposited their song with the Rock of our Ages. Their singing is what you hear echoing in that shell. It's a powerful force, and listening to it can reverse the effects of a mindwash."

"Papa just has to hold this to his ear and he'll be cured?" A sense of wonder lit her features. "I must get this to him at once!"

"You forget the other matter you inquired about," the Liani said, glancing significantly at Rolf, who stood waiting expectantly off to the side.

Ilyssa's face flushed. "Oh, yes."

"This is a decision you must make, sister. To love your man, you risk losing everything you've worked toward your entire life: your singing voice, your dream of becoming an arbiter. It is your choice."

"B-but I thought you were going to tell me the truth of the myth."

"This is something you must discover for yourself."

"I don't understand."

"Come, our ladies will show you to chambers where you may prepare yourselves. You will meet each other later in the Devotion Garden after the sol has set."

The Liani smiled, crinkle lines framing the corners of her eyes. "Go now, and follow your hearts. Enlightenment will come from within."

Ilyssa entered the Devotion Garden with trepidation. It was nighttime, and a full moon shone overhead, casting its silvery light upon the crystal rock formations in the garden. Glowstones lit the way along gravel paths. A scent of perfume was in the air even though the colorful blooms that sprouted everywhere were made from crystals. Jewel-tone colors sparkled in the moonlight: ruby, sapphire, emerald, amethyst, and topaz. In the light from the moon, the garden shone like a glittering fairyland. A faint breeze ruffled her loosely bound hair as she strode toward the illuminated domed pavilion at the far end.

Rolf would be waiting for her inside, she'd been told. One of the Liani's aides had taken her to the baths, a communal affair where she'd bathed and then entered a soothingly warm pool. Afterward, she'd received refreshments and a shimmering turquoise and silver drape to wear. She'd used the diamella gemstone clips to pin back her hair from her face, but the rest of her thick wavy locks tumbled down her back.

While she'd been soaking in the bath, Ilyssa thought about her decision. Should she risk everything to mate with Rolf? Or should they just carry on as they'd been doing, satisfying each other through alternate means?

It wasn't very gratifying to taste the fruits of passion and not be able to consume them. All it did was make her hunger for more. She yearned to join with him, to become as one, to blend with him in the flesh what she already felt in spirit. She'd been willing to relinquish her freedom for him on Souk. Why not take the chance and give him her love? If she lost her singing voice as a result, it would be worth it to be able to express the depth of her feelings for him.

Excited, Ilyssa readied herself to make the ultimate sacrifice.

Her bare feet padded quickly along the crunchy gravel path. Ahead, the domed pavilion glowed with light. It was made of a translucent alabaster material and she could see a figure moving inside. The large form approached the entry.

Ilyssa sucked in her breath. Tall, handsome, his blond hair dipping onto his forehead, Rolf stood in the archway dressed in what she could only describe as a short wraparound rust-colored skirt that hugged his hips. His chest and legs were bare. Her own body, naked under the diaphanous turquoise drape, began tingling in response.

He grinned as she approached. "The native style of dress suits you," he said, his warmly appreciate glance raking her body.

"I like your outfit, too." She moistened her lips as she neared the pavilion.

"The facilities are comfortable." He stood aside so she could pass. Her thigh brushed his leg and her heart struck a rapid tempo. Just being near him, knowing what she was about to do, was enough to drive her wild.

Curbing her rising passion, she glanced around. The inside furnishings were simple: colorful silk cushions, a carpeted floor, a low stone table on which sat a decanter filled with an amber liquid and two crystal goblets.

"They say this nectar comes from a wildflower at the foothills of the Forbidden Mountains. It's very precious and used just for this occasion," Rolf said, his low voice thrumming along her nerve endings like a symphony.

He poured them both a drink and handed her a crystal glass. "Apparently whenever a sister takes a man for the first time, they must come here for the . . . deflowering. It's a ceremonial rite, I understand." He smiled at her, his eyes warm and loving. "We're in the Devotion Temple."

"I see." Ilyssa took a sip of the liquid. A sweet, spicy flavor burned its way down her throat.

Rolf took the goblet from her and put it down with his own on the table. "What decision have you reached, Ilyssa?"

She looked into his steady gaze and swallowed. "This one," she said huskily, loosening her drape so that it slid to the floor. Naked, she held out her arms.

She was his, Rolf thought, a cry of joy escaping his lips. How many nights he'd dreamed of seeing her open and ready for him like this. His glance drank in her ripe womanly figure and rested on her sweet mouth. He'd longed for this moment and wanted to savor it forever.

"Are you certain this is what you want?" he asked quietly, his heart swelling with love. He knew the sacrifice she was making and it made him appreciate her all the more.

When she nodded, he slipped off his wrap and approached. Gently pulling her into his embrace, he lowered his head, brushing his lips across hers in a tender kiss. But he couldn't rein in his passion for long. He wanted her too much. Groaning, he tightened his arms around her and deepened the kiss until the movements of his mouth on hers were feverish in intensity.

She clutched at his back, feeling that she was drowning in sensations of ecstasy. Being in his arms, feeling his muscled body against her naked flesh was heavenly. Closing her eyes, she gave herself in to the frenzy of his hot kisses, relishing his liquored breath and the exquisite rapture of his hands roaming her skin. This time there would be no holding back. She yearned to experience all of him and knew it wouldn't be enough.

Feeling her sway in his arms, his passion flamed. She was all he'd ever wanted and more. Without moving his mouth from hers, he lowered her beside him to the carpeted floor. His hands explored her softness and traced the outlines of her curves.

Ilyssa touched him, wanting to feel every inch of his taut body. His hard length writhed against her pliant one, causing heat to rise within her from her toes all the way to the roots of her hair. Rolf shifted his position downward, taking her nipple into his mouth, and the tingling sensations he aroused shot through her. She squirmed restlessly, wishing he'd address the ache between her legs, but he was busy fondling the sides of her breasts. Her own hands clutched his hair as she arched under him.

He ministered to her other nipple and then traced scores of kisses along her flat belly and down into her triangle of reddish hair. "You're so beautiful," he murmured. She let her head roll back as he moved lower to stroke her acutely sensitive flesh with his tongue.

"By the Almighty, Rolf, enter me now!" She opened her thighs, feeling a rapturous spiraling sensation spread like fire throughout her body.

He shifted, and with one smooth thrust drove inside her. "You're tight, *larla,* but it feels wonderful. Are you all right?" He poised there, watching her expression. Her eyes were closed and a half-smile graced her lips.

Her eyelids fluttered open. "Yes," she said in a breathless whisper. "I never knew it could feel like this."

"There's more." And he began moving, keeping his rhythm slow so as not to hurt her.

Ilyssa filled with joy at being one with him. It was incredible. There was no pain, only a feeling of warm fullness. Her hands splayed across his broad back, feeling his muscles rippling with each urgent movement he made. His thrusts came faster as he grunted with primal passion. She wrapped her legs around him, wishing to increase his pleasure, but she became lost in her own twirling delight. Her release exploded at the same time as his. Her body shuddered along with his. Then he collapsed, the weight of his body heavy atop hers.

"By the stars, Ilyssa," he said finally, his voice a husky croak, "I've never felt so content." He rolled off, leaning on his elbow to gaze at her. Her hair was askew, her lips swollen, her expression dreamy as she regarded him with a smile.

"I'm glad I never knew what I was missing before or we would never have left Souk. We'd have been spending all our time doing this."

"Don't talk about Souk. We have our future to discuss now. Come home with me, Ilyssa. Be my wife and live with me on Bimordus Two. I need you and love you."

She sat up and traced her finger along his jaw, warmed by the love shining in his eyes. "I love you, too. Yes, I will wed you. I don't ever want to be apart from you again."

At her words, he pulled her into his arms and kissed her, his tears of happiness mingling with her own. But then Ilyssa drew back.

"I must try my voice, Rolf. Now that I've been . . . that I'm not . . . I have to see if I lost it. Do you have your earplugs?"

"The sisters told me I wouldn't need them."

She gave him a sly smile. "If I can sing and you're mindwashed, I'll make you pledge your everlasting devotion to me."

"Maybe that's why this is called the Devotion Garden."

But when Ilyssa took a deep breath and tried to expel the notes from her throat, nothing came out but the off-tune sounds any ordinary person might make.

"I've lost my singing ability!" An overwhelming sense of loss struck her. What would she do with her life if she couldn't sing? She'd become Lord Cam'brii's wife, she told herself. It had been her choice, her decision.

"Regrets?" he asked hesitantly, tickling her inner arm.

His masculine scent drifted into her nostrils, arousing her again. "None." Her eyes met his anxious blue ones. "All I ever want is your love. We belong to each other, Rolf, and that's what matters."

A murmur of voices drifted their way, accompanied by shouts and laughter. Panicking, she snatched her drape. She'd just covered herself and so had Rolf when a procession of women led by the Liani entered the pavilion.

"You have honored our temple with your devotion," the Liani said, smiling indulgently at them. "Ilyssa, stand in the archway with your man and sing to him of your love. The Rock of our Ages yearns to hear your song."

"But I can't sing anymore!" she cried. Surely the Liani realized she'd sacrificed her gift to join with Rolf.

"Do as I advise, sister."

Seeing the firm expression on her face, Ilyssa shrugged. She took Rolf's hand and walked with him to the archway facing the garden. Outside in the cool of the night, the crystal rock formations were bathed in brilliant moonlight. The flowers and trees glittered like living jewels. Her nostrils filled with a fragrant perfumed scent and she breathed it in, glad to be alive, grateful she'd been given the chance to love and be loved.

Turning to Rolf, she couldn't help the swell of rapture that engulfed her. Before, she'd always expressed her emotions in song and now was no exception. She opened her mouth and the beauteous notes sprang from her throat. Amazed, she ran through her scales to determine the full range of her ability and then sang one of her favorite ballads about a woman searching for true love. When she finished, the final notes faded away on the breeze.

"That was amazing," Rolf said, unable to put into words his supreme feeling of peace and happiness. Hearing her sing was a fantastic experience. Her voice was like nothing he'd ever heard before. It had touched him deep in his heart and transported him beyond the realm of humanity to the heights of heaven. "But how is it possible? I'd thought you couldn't sing anymore. And I wasn't mindwashed either!"

The Liani, waiting in the pavilion with the other women, responded.

"You've retained your ability to sing but have lost your siren song. Now may you share your music with others. It is your destiny, Ilyssa Serah Barr."

She hadn't heard her full name pronounced since she'd left Circutia. Soon she would be Ilyssa Cam'brii.

Turning to Rolf, Ilyssa said, "What about the rites of betrothal? Do we need to go back to Nadira?"

"To Zor with the rites. As far as I'm concerned, we've passed the allotted time. We'll be wed as soon as possible after our return to Bimordus Two. I can't wait until you're mine." And he gathered her into his arms, kissing her in front of the entire assemblage.

As a collective sigh from the happy onlookers rose in the perfumed air, the crystal Rock of the Ages trembled with contentment.

Epilogue

"I'm so glad our parents were able to come," Ilyssa confided to Sarina at her wedding reception on Bimordus Two several weeks later. She adjusted her ivory gown. Sarina had helped her and Moireen plan the ceremony, knowing a huge crush of people would be attending to celebrate with Lord Cam'brii and his bride, especially after Glotaj had announced Rolf was his choice as his successor. Ilyssa was thrilled for her husband and proud of his accomplishments. For his part, he said he fully intended to make their marriage a partnership in the true sense of the word.

"Your father looks much better," Sarina commented, glancing to where Ilyssa's parents stood conversing with Rolf's.

Ilyssa smiled. Papa still needed to gain weight, but his brain was alert, and that was the most important step in his recovery. He'd listened to the shell from the Sea of Serenity and it was like a veil lifted from his mind. Clarity had flooded his features and he saw her and Moireen in a true light for the first time in annums.

Moireen had perked up with all the wedding plans and with her husband's attentions being showered upon her. Using a stash of funds transferred to her from home, she'd found a temporary apartment for her and Aran. Moireen had confided in Ilyssa that she looked forward to a period of leisure wherein she and her husband could become reacquainted. Once Ilyssa was settled, they'd think about traveling to Circutia.

Ilyssa had so many reasons to celebrate, she thought joyously. Ruel was no longer a threat. Intelligence reported that his vessel had been destroyed as it entered Morgot space.

She also understood Devin's decision to remain on Souk. Fierce fighting was still going on in many areas and his services were critically needed, both as liaison to the Coalition Defense League and as rebel commander. Admiral-in-Chief Daras Gog, head of the Defense League, had been impressed by his leadership and had offered him a commission. But Devin declined, vowing to stay on Souk until the people were free and slavery was abolished. She was proud of her brother.

Raised voices sounded in the reception hall, terminating her reflection. Ilyssa frowned at Sarina. "Look, those Quatorians are arguing again," she murmured. "I don't know why they were sent as the delegation from their planet when they can't get along."

"I'll suggest they save their discussion for later," Sarina said, setting her mouth in a firm line. But before she could march off, Rolf approached them.

"Ilyssa, my parents want to hear you sing, and so does Glotaj." Now that her siren song wasn't a problem, he enjoyed listening to her music. "Sing one of your ballads for us. We have a guest who will be happy to accompany you on his string instrument." Stepping aside, he gestured toward Pinch, who was approaching with Balthazar and his troupe.

"Congratulations!" the bearded player boomed, giving her a smacking wet kiss on her mouth while Rolf glared jealously from the sidelines.

"How good to see you!" She exchanged greetings with all of them and then allowed Rolf to lead her toward a central dais.

A short time later, the final notes of the music faded as she finished her song. The room was silent. Then applause broke out, loud and prolonged. Ilyssa smiled, tears in her eyes. It felt so good to be able to sing in public. Losing her siren song might have been a loss in one way, but the gains were much more rewarding.

Glancing in the corner where the Quatorians had been arguing, she was stunned to notice them grinning. Ignoring the congratulations of the well-wishers around her, she stepped down from the dais and approached them.

"Your song was beautiful," one of the diplomats said, bowing.

"Aye, it was lovely," the other added. "I am left with a feeling of . . . tranquillity."

"You know, I cannot conceive of what we were arguing about, my friend."

"Nor I. Come, let us attend the refreshment table."

They walked off arm in arm, Ilyssa staring after them.

By the corona! Could her song have done this? She might not be able to beguile men, but it appeared she could calm them.

"Rolf," she said, hurrying to him. He was involved in a discussion with Teir and both men looked up at her approach. "I can still use my song!"

Rolf's brow wrinkled. "What do you mean?"

"Those Quatorians. They were arguing before I began to sing. Listening to me made them calm down."

"Your singing gives me a sense of contentment. Perhaps it's a residual effect of your siren song."

"Do you know what this means? I can be an arbiter after all."

"I was going to suggest you apply for the position. Since you've retained your vocal talent, there's no reason for you to deny yourself what you've always desired. We'll work out an arrangement for your training period."

She'd barely heard what he said. "Now I'll be able to mediate between two hostile sides more effectively. Think what I can accomplish!"

Rolf looked at her eyes shining with excitement and drew her into his arms. "Think what *we* can accomplish, my sweet. There's no limit to what we can achieve. Together, we'll work toward peace, and the galaxy will be ours."

His head lowered, and he kissed her in front of the cheering crowd.

Nancy Cane would love to hear from her readers. Write to her at: P.O. Box 17756, Plantation, Florida 33318. A self-addressed stamped envelope would be appreciated for a reply.